# NORTH DAKOTA WEDDINGS

## THREE-IN-ONE COLLECTION

Elizabeth Goddard

BARBOUR
PUBLISHING

Dear Reader,

I'm so glad you could join me in this three-book journey through the state of North Dakota. The state is not only one of the biggest crop producers in the country, it has also been home to most of the country's nuclear missile sites built during the Cold War. With nothing but stars for miles and miles on a dark night—the wide, lone North Dakota prairie is a stargazer's dream, as you'll read in *Disarming Andi*.

The Badlands are rich in history and attract scientists—geologists and paleontologists, to name a few—from around the world. If that's not enough, Fargo is home to numerous high-tech companies, including a Microsoft Campus, and is in line to possibly become the next Silicon Valley.

With the backdrop of an incredibly diverse state, there's no end to story possibilities, and as you'll see, I've tried to include a little bit of everything you might find on a drive through this state that's rich in history and a culture all its own. On the journey, I hope you'll find yourself in a deeper place with God just as the characters work their way through the challenges life presents only to find God was there with them all along.

I pray many blessings on you.

Elizabeth Goddard
www.elizabethgoddard.com

# DISARMING ANDI

# Dedication

Dedicated to my husband, who always encourages me, and my children who understand when Mom has to write. A special dedication goes to the missileers—America's "Underground Air Force" who guarded our country during the Cold War—and those who continue protecting us today. Thanks to Ed Peden of Twentieth Century Castles and Gina Shipman of Shipman Construction, who shared their expertise and advice. And to Julie Neidlinger whose family owns the Echo-0 launch control facility, thanks for allowing me to draw from your experiences.

# Prologue

## Fargo, North Dakota

*S*"*how your face here and you're dead.*"

The words, though said in jest, came rushing back to Vance Young as he returned to work late that night, plodding through the revolving doors.

Vance ran a hand down his face. He should have left for vacation earlier in the day. He'd been delayed, but it worked in his favor because in the middle of the night, no one would see him at the office, hence he was in total compliance with CEO Peter Lundgren's wishes. No one would see his face.

Well, except for Tom, who stood tall and intimidating at the granite-topped security counter. Behind him, chrome letters formed the words ANND SYSTEMS. *Artificial Neural Network Defense.* Everyone pronounced it Andee.

The name seemed to leap at Vance from the backdrop of azure marble. He inserted his laminated ID card through the thin slot, then pressed his thumb into the fingerprint reader, hating the jump through security hoops every day. Wouldn't it be nice if Scotty could just beam him up?

Accustomed to seeing Vance working all hours of the night, Tom nodded and offered his usual friendly smile. "Evening, Mr. Young."

Vance made his way to the elevators, his steps across the marble floors echoing, and stared at his reflection while he waited for the metallic doors to open. He'd be long gone now if he hadn't forgotten his telescope. Somewhere on the North Dakota prairie was a house his great-uncle had bequeathed him. On a beautiful night in the middle of July, the stars would be easy to see in the country away from light pollution. Vance was looking forward to some quiet time.

"Mr. Young?" Tom blurted from the foyer.

What now?

Tom stood behind him, staring at him in the reflection.

"Mr. Young."

Vance turned to face the security guard, who'd never followed him before now. "Hey Tom, what's up?"

"Thought you were leaving for your vacation today."

"I forgot my telescope." The elevator doors swooshed open. "Hope it doesn't take too long. I'm ready to be outta here."

"I hear you." Tom nodded.

Vance stepped into the elevator, grateful for the speedy precision with which the doors closed. On most mornings, he cursed their slowness as he struggled to gain access with a score of others shuffling to their jobs in the morning rush.

Alone in the elevator, he allowed himself to lean against the flimsy wall for support as the undersized box rushed to the top floor. The small bead of sweat that usually formed on his temple spread across his forehead.

Finally, the doors slid open and he stepped into the software development department. He took another step forward and began to relax as he strolled past a score of gray, empty cubicles on his way to his office.

Vance passed the dinosaur pen—the glassed-in halo-protected processing room—where the data-crunching mainframe he called Cindy resided. Oddly, the humming sound created by the processing of massive amounts of data soothed him.

Peter preferred using mainframe computers because of the sheer volume of data, approaching petabytes, or one quadrillion bytes. Eh. All they needed was what amounted to a bunch of PlayStation 3s clustered together.

Once in his office, Vance didn't bother switching on the lights. He took a deep, peaceful breath. Late at night he had a stellar view of the stars.

Over on his desk, Vance noticed something out of place, so he flipped on the lights. A woman stared back at him from a picture frame. It should have been face down, exactly where he thought he'd put it several days ago when Peter had said the only thing better than a computer was a girlfriend. Yeah, well, Vance had a girlfriend once. But then Janice only wanted him for his brains. What a joke. She'd used him to help her through some of her more difficult college classes this past school year. Though he'd graduated five years ago, he knew computer science.

Vance had pulled her picture out of the frame, only to see the photo of a gorgeous blond model that had come with it. With hair cascading a bit past her shoulders and soft, delicate features, she held her chin just so, giving her a feisty air of defiance. Big blue eyes and oh. . .that smile. Well, no wonder he'd left her photograph in the frame. Over time she'd become his dream girl. She was out there. Somewhere. . .

Vance began packing up his telescope.

"Mr. Young." Tom's voice boomed from behind, startling Vance.

He turned to face the security guard, stifling his irritation. "What's up?"

"Sorry to bother you again. Just got off the phone with Mr. Lundgren. He said I was to escort you out of the building since, well, you're *supposed* to be on vacation."

"What is he? The keymaster?" He clamped his lips tight to keep from spewing what Tom could take back to Peter. It wasn't Tom's fault. That was some way for Peter to treat him though. He had no right. "Well, did you tell him I forgot my telescope?"

"He said you need a vacation and he would kick you out if he had to."

Tom's grin was teasing. "If you ask me, you do look kind of pale, could use some sun."

"It's hard to get ultraviolet radiation when you're hidden away like a Morlock." Vance grinned, hoping to disarm Tom.

The security guard smiled back. "Morlock, sir?"

"You know, from H. G. Wells's *The Time Machine*."

Tom gave him a funny look.

"You see there's this guy who invents. . ." What was he doing besides wasting time? "Oh forget it."

Tom laughed.

"Let me finish packing. There's no need for you to wait."

Tom stiffened. "Just doing my job, Mr. Young. You don't want me to get fired, do you?"

"Not at all." Peter wanted Vance to be at his best when he returned, but in order to do that, he had to actually leave. If only he could shake the sense that Peter *needed* him gone.

Peter had enticed him from his job in Texas with talk of a classified government contract and the promise of promotion to vice president of. . . something. Vance knew data mining and thought it would be stellarific to have a shot at stopping the bad guys. Like a simple Boolean equation, the answer was obvious and he hadn't thought twice about saying yes. Working for Peter, he'd labored for months on the software to find specific patterns in data to identify terrorist activities.

It had been like a dream come true, except Vance was miserable and should write the entire experience off as a loss. At twenty-seven, he thought he knew what he wanted. But North Dakota winters weren't to his liking. Dad had warned him, telling him that sometimes a person thought he knew what he wanted and when he got it, discovered how wrong he was.

Telescope packed, Vance walked with Tom to the elevators. They discussed the weather on the way down. Once in the foyer, Vance left Tom and strode to the revolving door.

"You dropped something."

Vance turned to see Tom standing there, holding out a small disk.

Vance searched his memory. "I didn't—"

"Must have fallen out of your pocket."

Vance mechanically reached for the small storage media. "Thanks."

Tom held on to the memory card for a second longer than necessary while he stared at Vance. Then the security guard nodded and returned to his station.

Vance examined the disk. It wasn't his. But then again, at two in the morning maybe it was.

*✐*

He should have waited until morning to leave, but he was packed and ready to go, anxious to get away. Later, after three and a half hours of driving through the early morning along lonely dark highways and county roads, Vance was all the more bleary-eyed. The sooner he found his uncle's house the faster he could sleep for a few days.

An unpleasant thought occurred to him. What if his uncle's house was completely vacant of furniture and amenities? How could he have overlooked that possibility? In that case he'd have to stay in a hotel and make a quick decision on the house. Then he could go to Cancun ahead of schedule.

He came to a small town named Herndon. His uncle's house was somewhere nearby. According to Vance's GPS all he had to do was drive through the town and go another five miles, take a left on a side road for another two. As the sky lightened, his spirits rose and so did his hopes of finding the place.

Vance pulled on to a paved road in the middle of a wheat field that seemed to go nowhere, and then turned onto a gravel road, which ended up at a tall chain-link gate. He climbed out of his car. The fence surrounded a large area that included a metal building and. . . Was that a helicopter pad? Even though he was sleep-deprived, the sun brought a dawning with it that hit him like a bomb.

He was standing at an old missile site—a product of the Cold War.

"You've got to be kidding." His words spoken to no one seemed to magnify the seclusion.

What was going on? There had to be some mistake.

A padlock secured the gate. There was one way to find out if he was at the right place. He found the keys he'd been given to his uncle's property. To his disappointment, one of them looked like it belonged to a padlock. Warily, he inserted it.

The lock opened.

*Stellarific.*

# Chapter 1

Andi Nielsen hit the brakes of her old rusty Dodge pickup. The vehicle ground to a standstill a mere inch from the gated entrance to Vance Erickson's property.

"Um, sis, when are you going to get those fixed?" Her teenage sister, Elisa, gripped the door handle with white knuckles.

"Good gravy. You know we can't afford that right now." Andi jumped out of Dad's old truck. If there was one thing she hated it was squealing old brakes.

Could things get any worse? She'd secured a contract with Vance Erickson months ago to renovate an old decommissioned launch control facility into a lavish home. But he'd died just before they were to begin work on the next section. The major portion of her fee wasn't due until she'd completed the entire project, and there was no chance of that now. This job should have kept her busy for a long time.

She'd been outbid on everything else. Either that or people were listening to talk from subcontractors who wouldn't work for a woman, and in this small town in North Dakota, there were plenty of men who thought taking orders from a woman was demeaning.

From those who didn't care, she had other problems like quality work for the right price. She refused to use subs that cut corners with cheap materials.

Finishing the missile site would go a long way toward giving her construction company respect in the community. With respect would come the referrals she desperately needed. Sure, people remembered her contractor father, but he died a few years ago. His daughter had to prove she had the nails for the business—and at only twenty-one, she had some large shoes to fill.

*Oh Daddy...*

She kicked the tire, then pulled the keys to the missile launch control facility from her bag. She'd never returned them. No one had shown up to claim them either. She grabbed a flashlight from behind the seat.

"Um, Andi. I don't know about this." Elisa clipped at a nail, then stuck the clippers she always carried into her back pocket. "Mr. Erickson is dead now. You can't just waltz in there. You got no right."

Andi glowered at Elisa, wanting to ask what she knew about it, if anything. Elisa had gone out of her way to cause Andi more than her share of trouble. "Look, this is all I have left."

She might not ever finish renovations or see the money, but at least she could look for what her grandfather had stashed inside years before when he'd worked at the missile site. Stomping over to the gate, she jangled the keys, searching for the right one.

Before Andi found the key, Elisa shoved the gate open. "You still think that letter you found means something, like it's a treasure map?"

Andi stared at the chain-link fence. "Hey, I could swear I locked—"

"You're not listening. But what's new?"

"I heard you. Yes, I think it's worth a look." In fact, Andi believed it could be the very reason Mr. E had hired her.

Elisa stepped through the gate. "I should have stayed in bed."

"Wait a minute. I need to make sure it's safe."

"From what?"

Andi swallowed her frustration with her sister, wishing it were a school day and not a Saturday so she could have peace from the constant arguing. After pushing through the gate, she walked up the short drive and cautiously to the right side of the only building Mr. E had left standing on the site. Most of it had burned last year, but they'd managed to salvage part of it.

"You mean who."

Elisa followed Andi and stood next to her. "Huh?"

"Someone's here. I don't recognize the vehicle," Andi said.

"Nice. A brand-spanking-new red Jetta." Sarcasm dripped from Elisa. "It's probably someone who'll want those keys back."

"Whoever it is, I need to look around."

If only one last time.

*⌀❧*

*This is crazy.* Vance had taken the access stairs rather than risk the elevator, but now that he'd gone down several flights, descending a good fifty feet underground, he wasn't sure he'd made the right decision. Did the stairs go anywhere? He'd assumed they did considering there wasn't much left of the building above ground. Most of that had been destroyed except a small section that appeared to house the entrance to the underground. . .what. . .dwelling? Had his uncle actually lived here?

Difficult to believe, that's what he'd been told, though he'd missed the part where someone had referred to nuclear bombs and launch facilities, either that or he'd had a random access memory leak. Or had that information been purposefully left out? Either way, he'd committed to getting this off his smartphone reminders list.

What must Uncle Vance—his namesake—have been thinking to give this to him? Had he known of his nephew's aversion to closed places? No way. Vance wasn't sure his mother even knew. In his estimate, by the time he stepped in front of what looked like a blast door, he'd descended another twenty feet for a total of seventy. The door appeared to be part of the elevator shaft.

To his right was a tunnel. He strolled through the long cylinder and stopped at a convex blast door, shaped like the exterior of a sphere. Another one? He chuckled to calm himself. That and to let the bears know someone was coming. It was best to alert rather than startle. Boy Scouts 101. This would have been a great field trip when he was a kid. As it was, he felt like he was in a science fiction movie.

The door read STAND CLEAR OF BLAST DOOR. CAUTION. DO NOT SPIN WHEEL. TURN WHEEL APPROXIMATELY THREE TURNS TO OPEN OR CLOSE.

He touched the wheel, then paused, feeling the sweat trickle down his back. The surroundings were getting to him. He tugged his shirt collar, even though it was loose to begin with. The site had been decommissioned years ago, he reassured himself, or else he would never have been allowed into the facility. Air Force guards would have been everywhere. Vance took a couple of deep breaths, surprised the air wasn't stale, but rather smelled like vanilla air freshener.

Would he be able to open the door? Shoving aside his growing anxiety, he turned the wheel three times and pulled. The door swung open. Vance fully expected to be required to offer his identity at this juncture. But to whom, he didn't know. He held his breath and stepped into a room. Lights automatically flickered on.

*Sweet fractured motherboards!* He stood in what looked like the decadent inside of a mansion, rather than the sterile drabness he'd expected.

He stepped down into a large open room that housed, among other things, a beautiful modern kitchen with granite counters and stainless steel appliances.

Suddenly, his stomach grumbled. He hoped the fridge was loaded, but that was probably asking too much. Opposite the kitchen was a living area, sufficient for a gathering of at least twenty people, along with comfortable furniture and a large screen television.

Jazzy, but no windows. He wouldn't be able to look at the stars. Sure it was spacious, but he didn't know if he could tolerate the sense of confinement.

"Why couldn't this have been above ground?"

"Because it was used to house the launch control center of a nuclear missile site," a woman's voice answered for him. "It's called Ground Zero."

Startled, Vance swung around to see...

...the gorgeous blond from the picture in his office. She stood there, one hand behind her back. Her blond hair was pulled back into a tight ponytail, but it was her.

Vance rubbed his eyes. The light must be doing something to him. Or his anxiety from being boxed in was giving him hallucinations. Thank goodness it wasn't a complete phobia, or maybe he'd see her standing next to a red Lamborghini, too. He was already tired before he'd started the trip, now he was dreaming.

He took a few steps closer, peering at her.

"What are you doing here? This is private property belonging to Vance Erickson." She placed her free hand on her hip.

"I. . .uh. . ." Vance took a step toward where she stood in the kitchen. "Have you ever done any modeling?"

# Chapter 2

As the stranger approached, Andi stood her ground, gripping the mallet she'd brought with her. A girl couldn't be too careful. Besides, he didn't look local. Most folks around here were farmers and ranchers. He was dressed in a suit, well, white shirt and suit pants, but she bet he'd been wearing a tie and coat earlier. The last person she'd seen dressed like that around here was—a knot suddenly rose in her throat—Jorgen.

The man moved closer and she gripped even tighter, lifting the mallet so he could see she had it.

He adjusted his glasses and squinted at her.

What did he think? She was an apparition? "Whoa. I'm packing here. No need to come any closer. I'll ask you again—"

"You all right, sis?" Elisa spoke from behind.

"I told you to stay up top." Andi brushed off her sister and waited for his answer.

The man stepped forward. "I'm being rude. Let me introduce myself." He grinned and offered his hand.

"That would be nice." Andi didn't budge. This guy wasn't going to charm his way out of trouble. She doubted he could if he tried. If she had to size him up, she'd say geek, though she did like his dimples. But she and smart guys—well, they never got along too well.

"I'm Vance Young. My uncle left this place to me."

Andi stepped back, feeling like he'd thrown her a box of bricks and she'd caught it. Resentment crashed down on her. She'd had to work hard for every morsel. If there was one thing she hated it was people like this man who received things without earning them. If anything, Mr. E should have given the place to her. He owed her, didn't he? This character didn't care one scrap about this home or the surrounding community. He'd inherit the place and would probably never realize its value.

Composing her emotions, she finally shook his hand. "It's nice to meet you."

"Now it's my turn. This is private property. What are you doing here?"

Andi had prepared to be challenged at some point. But not like this. "I'm Andi Nielsen of Nielsen Construction and Remodeling, and this is my sister, Elisa."

"Andi?" The man frowned, releasing an odd laugh. "Is this some sort of joke?"

"Excuse me?"

"Uh. . .it's just that. . .nothing. So *you're* in construction?"

Andi bristled at what sounded like skepticism but kept her composure. She'd learned to deal with that sort of chauvinistic reaction. She motioned to the setting around them. "Yes, my company is responsible for this room. Do you like what you see?"

The man's eyes subtly glanced over her, then to the room. "Yes, very much so."

Unwelcome warmth flitted through her. Had he referred to her or the room?

"So, you remodeled this place. What are you doing here now? Did you forget something?"

Andi moved around the large granite-laden island to the refrigerator and set the mallet down. She opened the fridge and retrieved a bottle of water. "Actually, it's complicated."

The young Vance crossed his arms, waiting.

She took a swig, giving herself time to think. This was her chance. She had to convince him. Elisa moseyed to the sofa and plopped down, announcing her impatience.

"You say your uncle gave this to you. Probably put it in the will, expecting it to be of value. But it's worth nothing until it's complete."

He cocked a brow. She could see he wouldn't be so easily convinced. Definitely not bad looking, but with his black-framed glasses and thick brown hair shagging well past time for a haircut, he had the look of what?—an astrophysics professor? She was beginning to feel intimidated. Not good. She reminded herself she had a year of college toward her business degree.

She raised her chin. "I'm not finished with the remodel. You'll never be able to sell it until the renovations are complete."

"And after the renovations? How much would it be worth?"

"In the hundreds of thousands. Maybe millions. Your uncle had big plans."

She'd grown a soft spot for the old man, and at the thought of him, pain filled her. As she stared back at Mr. Young, she noticed he was really a younger version of his uncle.

"It looks pretty good already. I'm not sure it needs anything else."

"Why don't you let me show you around before you decide."

"It hardly matters. I don't plan to stay."

Andi hoped her smile would hide her sinking hopes. "You can't expect to make an informed decision until you've seen what needs work."

Vance looked thoughtful. "All right, on one condition."

"What's that?"

"There's another bottle of water in the fridge, though I'd prefer something that's sugary and fizzes."

Andi laughed and peered inside the appliance. "You're in luck. There are two sodas my sister left from when we were remodeling. And if your luck holds, you should find the food storage room stocked. I'll be happy to show you around."

"That would be cool." He took the soda from her. "And I like that the place comes with its own tour guide."

Andi hoped she could be more than a tour guide by the time they finished the tour. "Do you know anything about its history, Mr. Young?"

"Nothing at all, I'm afraid. And call me Vance."

"All right, then. Vance." Andi held Vance's gaze. Remove the glasses and put some meat on his bones and he'd definitely look like his uncle might have looked thirty or more years ago.

"I came here expecting to see a mansion. Not this missile silo. Talk about random."

"This is not a silo. It's a launch control facility that's been decommissioned. The room you're standing in now, is the LCC, or launch control center. Of course, everything the Air Force used here, especially what they used to launch missiles, was removed during the decommissioning. Of the missile sites that were decommissioned in North Dakota, all the silos were filled in, completely destroyed."

Vance cleared his throat. "And the blast doors?"

"Oh, those. Mr. Erickson wanted to keep them for nostalgic reasons."

"Nostalgia, huh. So, can you tell me why he chose a missile launch facility? He must have been eccentric."

So the young Vance didn't know his uncle very well, and yet, he'd inherited all this. A knot of resentment grew in her throat.

While Andi agreed with him on the eccentric point, she had her suspicions of why his uncle had purchased this particular site. But she couldn't share those with his nephew. Not yet, if ever.

"Don't kid yourself. Plenty of people have purchased decommissioned missile sites like the Atlas, Titan, and Nike all over the country for conversion into homes or other uses. By the way, this is an old Minuteman facility."

"I know that much. It was part of Grand Forks Air Force Base. I heard a joke about North Dakota being the world's third strongest nuclear power."

Andi sighed. "Yeah, I'm sure after a few missiles were deployed, nobody would be counting anymore."

She had to steer the conversation back to remodeling. This morbid talk was likely to scare him off, and she intended to find out what her grandfather hid here. But to do that, she had to convince Vance to let her finish the work, which would also be money in her pocket—something she desperately needed if she were going to pay the bills. Eating would be good, too.

✍

"Well, enough on the history." He grinned. "Give me the tour."

He tugged his glasses off and bit the end of the earpiece so they hung from his mouth. Everything there was to know about missile sites and the people who lived in them was available for perusal on the Internet later. Right now he needed to know what to do with this one.

"Oh, an important question for you. Is this place wired?" Vance could connect through his mobile networking system from anywhere, except maybe seventy feet underground. To think there was something he hadn't explored. He'd have to seriously reconsider his goals in life.

"You mean for Internet and other communications? Sure. The military already had communications in place, of course, but your uncle made sure everything was up-to-date with satellite communications, the works. I hired an independent contractor if you'd like to talk to him. It's not my expertise."

*Thank you, Uncle Vance.* "Not necessary. As long as it works, I'm good."

"Let's step out of the living quarters through the blast doors." Andi went first.

After a glance back at her sister reclining on the sofa, he stepped through the blast door while shoving his glasses back on.

"We'd planned to begin work on what was once the equipment building. Much of the unusable materials have already been cleared out. We put in new environmental control systems that are much quieter than what the military had in place."

Vance followed Andi through the cylindrical tunnel into the area where the elevator waited. "Does that work?"

"The elevator? Yes." She tilted her head, looking at him. "You took the stairs?"

The way she said it made him feel like he should be embarrassed. He snorted. "Look, I had no way of knowing if it was safe, okay?"

She nodded. "I guess you're right about that. But still, those stairs. . ."

"Yeah, they're brutal."

"Your uncle had us put those in. They didn't come with the original site. He just had a quirky fear of elevators. Was afraid he wouldn't be able to get out, say if the electricity were to go off. But then he was afraid he couldn't make it up the stairs so he suffered through the elevator." She smiled softly, a distant look in her eyes.

Ah. So his uncle had an almost-phobia as well, not too dissimilar from his own. "Makes you wonder why he wanted to live underground, then, doesn't it?"

She laughed. He could get used to that laugh.

Then she looked thoughtful for a moment. "I don't think being underground bothered him as much as smaller spaces."

They continued on to see another blast door. "Allow me."

She stepped back. "Be my guest."

Vance stared at the door, which was different from the other one. He scratched his head.

"You have to pump open the steel lock pins just there."

He nodded. Maybe it was some macho thing that had inspired him to show off his amazing talent to open blast doors—though he was sorely lacking in experience—but after three minutes of pumping, he glanced her way.

She smirked. "Give it two more minutes."

"Shutting and opening these things every time is taking the nostalgia a little too far, don't you think?"

"You're the new owner. You get to decide." Her smile radiated warmth.

*Stellar.* Vance was in some sort of competition. What was it? More importantly, what were the winnings?

*Click.* Finally, he unlatched the lever and pushed. The door didn't budge.

"This is where you really have to show some muscle."

Ah. She knew how to work the men. Challenging their manhood would produce results. Something she probably learned in construction.

He shoved his shoulder against the door.

"No, like this." She put her back to the door. "Help me."

He joined her and together they slowly pushed the monster door open. Breathing too hard for the cool composure he liked to portray, Vance hissed at the door, "Fiend."

Andi threw her hands up. "See, no one wants to open that all the time. Imagine trying to sell this place with that door."

Vance tried to envision living in a place where reminders of imminent nuclear conflict were everywhere.

Stepping into the room, darkness greeted them. That—and the sound of water dripping in the distance, echoing off empty walls—made the room seem like a large cavern. "Now that you've piqued my curiosity, I'm expecting to see stalactites and stalagmites."

Her laugh resonated through the room. "No, nothing so exotic."

Vance shuffled forward into the darkness, brushing her shoulder. She had nice shoulders.

Andi flipped on her flashlight. "You can see this entire section needs to be remodeled. Your uncle died before we began working in here. We'd need to strip it down first, leaving only the superstructure in place, then build on top of that."

Vance noticed the sadness in her eyes. Was she sad because she wasn't able to finish the job? Or had she cared about his uncle?

"If you're not going to stay, I'm assuming you're going to sell."

Vance took a deep breath. He hated admitting it, but he didn't have the brain circuitry available to process all of it at the moment. He stepped back through the blast door and waited on Andi.

Once safely beyond the grip of the ogre door, she took up a get-down-to-business stance. The way she morphed from a mallet-holding property protector to businesswoman-closing-a-deal intrigued him.

"Mr. Young, allow me to finish what I started here, and we can both walk away with a lot of money."

"It's Vance, remember?" He rubbed his chin and the back of his neck, then caught her staring at him with a funny look on her face.

"You look exhausted."

"That bad, huh?"

"I'm sorry, I didn't mean it that way."

"I'm wounded nonetheless." He grinned to ease her concern. "I'm sure I look like something that crawled out of a grave. I haven't slept in too long."

Maybe that's why he had the crazy urge to touch the lone strand of hair that loosened from her tight do.

As if hearing his thoughts, she pushed the hair from her face. "You've got a comfortable place to rest. And even though there's a lot of renovation to be done, you can stay here while we work. Your uncle did. There is part of your living space that needs to be finished, but I can show that to you later. You just look. . ."

"Like I'm about to collapse."

"Yeah."

"He must have been some paranoid old fool to buy this place."

Andi smiled. "Okay, I wasn't going to say it, but I'll agree with you, after all."

"Let me sleep on it. I'd be crazy to make any decisions just now."

"Here's my card." She held it out between two fingers.

Taking it, Vance studied her reaction. Her wide, beautiful smile didn't hide the disappointment behind her intense blue eyes. Somehow, he felt disappointed, too, and wished he could give her an answer. The one that she wanted. But he already carried the burden of bad decisions made in haste.

He wouldn't make another one.

# *Chapter 3*

Back in the bodacious remodeled section, Vance watched Andi and her sister exit through the blast doors, leaving him alone in the space pod floating through the universe. Considering his love of astronomy, that was probably the best way for him to think about it—a sort of virtual reality of the mind. How else was a guy who hated close quarters to tolerate living in a small underground capsule?

With some serious mind control.

Plopping on the still-warm sofa where Elisa had lounged, he chuckled, thinking of the great impression he must have made looking like a sleep-deprived zombie. No wonder Andi'd brandished the mallet.

He flipped his cell open but, of course, got no signal. *The landline it is.*

He dialed his parents' number and absorbed his surroundings while waiting for an answer.

"Hello?"

"Dad, hey."

"Son, we've been wondering about you."

"I'm at Uncle Vance's house, if you can call it that. Did you know about this?"

Dad chuckled. "You mean you didn't know that it's a refurbished missile site? What planet are you on?"

Dad knew him too well. "I'll admit, the construction company has done some amazing stuff."

He pictured Andi showing off her work. Even though she'd put on a good show as a professional, her veneer of confidence was a little too thick in his opinion. He'd seen a crack and, underneath, she seemed desperate to finish the rest. Maybe business wasn't too good in Herndon, North Dakota. Or, maybe she wanted to focus on a niche market.

"Son? You seem distracted."

Too late Vance realized his thoughts weren't on the conversation. What had Dad been saying? "Sorry. This whole thing threw me, that's all."

"Well, what do you think you'll do?"

"I'm not sure. I think the woman who owns the construction company wants to finish the work she started for Uncle Vance. I think she needs this job."

"You know you can't make a decision based on her need for a job."

Couldn't he? "Right."

"The quicker you decide, the better. But we can talk about it when you get here."

*Great hacking malware.* He'd forgotten to tell them he wasn't coming to Texas until *after* Cancun. God created procrastination for a reason, and Vance was willing to give it a chance. But Mom would be. . .well, he didn't have a good euphemism for her at the moment.

"I'm not sure when that will be, but I'll let you know when I know."

"Good enough."

Vance ended the conversation. His father wasn't one for long talks anyway, preferring to get to the point.

Except for the humming of the refrigerator, complete silence surrounded Vance. Once the lights were off, total darkness would envelop him as well. What was he supposed to do with a missile site—all underground? Although all evidence of a nuclear arsenal poised for war had long been removed, the place unsettled him. Thankfully, he would be leaving in a few days, heading to Cancun.

He'd done what he said he'd do. His parents had urged him to look at it, stay a few days, see if he could figure out why Uncle Vance had given it to him. Decide if he wanted to keep it. But after seeing it, he knew there was no way he could live here, so he'd definitely sell.

Could Andi be right when she said finishing the remodel could mean a lot more money when he sold? Made sense. But could it be enough for him to start his own company? Forget about working for Peter?

The thought wormed its way deeper, but even that couldn't combat the heavy fatigue that crashed over him. He needed sleep. A fluffy blue pillow, compliments of Uncle Vance, rested next to him on the sofa, so he grabbed it and, after reclining, pressed it over his eyes.

The pillow was a partial lunar eclipse, leaving just enough light to prevent sleep. He found the light switch, hoping the lights that came on automatically when the blast door opened could be shut off again when inside. He flipped the switch. Complete and utter darkness engulfed him, magnified by the fact he was in a box. Underground.

He grappled for the switch and flipped it on like a little kid afraid of the dark. Except this darkness would alarm even the biggest tough guys. Without infrared or night vision goggles, he couldn't see his hand in front of his face. If he woke up in the middle of the night and stumbled for the bathroom, he could end up falling down a dark shaft somewhere.

What he needed for comfortable sleep was soft dark. If he hired Andi the builder, he'd make that his first request—a dimmer that would create soft dark. Eh, he'd buy a few nightlights next time he was in town.

A large window in the ceiling so he could gaze at the stars would be good, too. Not only was that impossible, it was unnecessary. He wasn't staying.

Then why did he have to keep reminding himself?

With the lights remaining on for now, Vance lay on the sofa and once again tugged the pillow over his head, willing himself to rest. This time, images of the missile site remodeler kept sleep at bay. If only she didn't so closely resemble the photograph in the frame at his office, which he'd dubbed his dream girl. Though Andi had pulled her hair into a tight ponytail, he imagined the gorgeous blond strands lying across her shoulders or blowing in the breeze like in an overdramatized shampoo commercial. Her blue eyes soft and receptive, rather than guarded and secretive.

He smashed the pillow against his face. If he pressed long and hard enough, he'd pass out before he suffocated, getting some sleep.

Hours later, Vance woke up to a growling stomach and the feeling he'd been run over by a military tank. He rose from the couch and walked to the fridge. In addition to food, he could use an energy drink to take the edge off his fatigue. Once his brain got going, it'd forget that the rest of him was still tired.

What were the chances the fridge was stocked with anything he would want to eat? Nope. Nothing there except one last soda and a few bottles of water. Andi hadn't shown him the food storage room before she left, so he made his way through the rest of the refurbished area, noting the bedroom, then a small bathroom, which he quickly took advantage of.

Though he would have appreciated seeing food in the fridge, he wouldn't want to see anything left over from his uncle's time at the house either. He couldn't call it a house, or his home. He settled on what Andi had called it.

Ground Zero.

What sort of person wanted his home underground in a place protected from everything but a direct hit from a nuclear bomb? He'd have to call Mom to find out more about his great-uncle. She'd known him much better because he was really *her* uncle.

A set of double doors beckoned him at the end of the narrow corridor. Vance opened the right door and came face to face with the food storage room. One glance and his hopes sank. He wondered if food set aside for long-term storage was really fit to eat. A seemingly limitless supply of freeze-dried meals stared back at him, featuring everything from chicken teriyaki, spaghetti with sauce, lasagna, and beef stew to more chicken and beef and noodles. It was all the same stuff, just prepared differently.

Yum.

A voracious hunger tearing at his gut, Vance made the trip to Herndon, only a few miles away, and stocked up on real food—stuff a normal person could survive on like Ding Dongs, chips and burritos, pizza, limeade and energy drinks, and a bag of broccoli crowns with ranch dip for good measure. Every guy needed his vitamin A.

While at Gary's Grocery Store, Vance noticed Andi's business card, along with those of other area businesses, pinned up on a small bulletin board, proclaiming her skills. She looked professional. He'd hire her if he were hiring.

For some reason, Cancun didn't sound as interesting as staying in town and watching Andi transform the rest of Ground Zero. If he hired her to finish the site after all, he'd cancel his plans. Cancun had been Peter's idea to begin with. Not his. The more he thought about it, the more jazzed he became about Andi's completing the work, then his selling for a huge profit. Afterward, if God directed, he could start his own company.

While he stared at the bulletin board, an elderly woman approached him. "You looking for a church?" She touched her finger to a brochure pinned to the board.

"Well, that depends on how long I stay." Vance explained the reason for his visit to town.

She nodded her understanding, welcomed him to town, and continued into the store to shop.

Back at Ground Zero he explored Uncle Vance's office just off the living area. Vance opened his laptop and while it booted he assembled his telescope. As evening neared, he grew antsy, feeling like a caged animal. Now would be a great time to contact Andi and offer her the work. She hadn't left his mind all day. Maybe that was God's nudging him to give her the job. Finding her card, he opened his cell but there was no signal. Instead, he used the landline.

"Hello?"

"Andi, this is—"

"This is Elisa, I'm on the other line. Can I take a message?"

Vance paused, surprised at the girl's rude tone. "Sure. This is Vance Young. Please let her know that I called and—"

"Okay." *Click.*

Vance stared at the phone, disappointed he couldn't talk to Andi. He'd been looking forward to hearing her voice. Or was it simply human contact he needed? At least in an apartment or house the normal sounds of life surrounded a person. He usually tuned it all out, but now that he was holed up underground, he noticed the quiet. He put in a call to Dad and let him know of his decision to hire the contractor after all, and that his plans didn't include Texas at the moment.

After placing a pizza in the oven, he popped the top of an energy drink, then took a sip. He positioned himself on the sofa with his laptop and, after chugging the drink, crushed the can and tossed it at the garbage, missing. He'd have to change that habit if Andi would be stopping by, though she never said how involved she would be in the remodel. For all Vance knew, she might work from her office, allowing her subs to do all the grunt work.

In the meantime—the sugar had done its job. An image of Tom handing him a small disk came to mind. He'd completely forgotten and found it in his pocket. He loaded it. No password was required, allowing him instant access.

Incredulous, he stared.

"What. . .is this?"

Who had dropped it, and why had Tom given it to him?

Regardless, only one thing ran through Vance's mind as he stared at the data spilling onto his computer screen.

*This is just. . .stellar.*

⚜

The smell of bacon lingered in the air, and if there was one thing Andi hated, it was walking into a house that smelled like stale bacon. That or fish. She grabbed the air freshener and started to spray, then eyed the last piece of bacon on the plate. Elisa wouldn't appreciate tasting Cool Caribbean Breeze on her bacon.

"Come on, Elisa!" She'd have to eat her breakfast running out the door.

Andi scraped the stack of bills and late notices into a box, then grabbed her large leather bag of a purse, cell phone, and organizer from the kitchen table. "You're going to be late for school and you're going to make me late, too."

If Elisa had even heard her, it wasn't likely she cared about Andi's schedule. Even though there wasn't much business to speak of right now, Andi never quit trying. Plus, she planned to stop by Freya Emerson's this morning. Take her some cookies. Freya had been one of her grandmother's long-time friends, and since Grandma's death, Andi had neglected to have Freya over. Though Andi missed the visits, life seemed to get in the way anymore.

Thank goodness only a few more weeks of summer school remained. Andi wasn't about to allow Elisa to take the bus today. In the fall Elisa would enter her sophomore year. Andi intended to make sure her sister made it to the high school even if it took until Elisa graduated. Despair overshadowed the aggravation she felt that she couldn't trust her sister to walk into the school, sit in her seat, and do her work.

And she hated starting every day with the yelling, but she couldn't get a response any other way. "Eli—"

"Okay, okay." Elisa rounded the corner from the hall. "You don't have to yell." "Don't I?"

Elisa downed her orange juice, then tugged on her backpack before heading out the door without another word.

"Guess you don't want your bacon." Andi grabbed the crispy piece and stuck it in her mouth, then rushed through the door, spraying the air freshener behind her. She set it on the counter just before closing the door.

Juggling everything, she locked up. She climbed into the driver's side of the truck and slid in next to Elisa, who had already tuned her out with an MP3 player and ear buds. She nudged her sister, who responded with the look. "Turn it down. I shouldn't be able to hear it."

"What?" Utter disrespect dripped from her lips.

Andi fought to stifle her anger. Oh, how she hated starting her day like this. *Lord, if You're there, please help me.* But then, she knew He wasn't. She sighed long and hard. "Look, those things can damage your ears. I shouldn't be able to hear the music."

"Whatever." Elisa tucked them back into her ears and stared out the passenger side window.

Andi deserved Elisa. Especially after all the trouble she'd given their father when she was a teen and then their grandmother who raised them. She'd died a year ago. It made Andi wonder what her grandmother or father had done to deserve *her*? Where did the cycle begin? Regardless, she was sorry for every time she'd given people a hard time when she was growing up.

She started the truck and backed from the drive, taking solace in the fact that Elisa had turned the music down. Even so, Andi didn't think God had answered the silent prayer she'd sent up. He stopped caring a long time ago. Out of nowhere, tears formed.

*Gut it up, this is life.* One long sniff through her nose and she was good to go. She wouldn't give up. Not now. Not ever. Never mind that Mom left Dad when Andi was a girl and Elisa a baby. That Dad had died four years ago. That Grandma had left them with scarce funds when she'd died last year. That Andi had had to leave college to take care of Elisa.

The house Dad had left them still had a mortgage on it. She'd had to think fast to keep it, so she ended up following in his footsteps, starting her own business. She'd obtained her license to become a contractor. It was all she knew to do. College could have changed that, but it was out of the question now. Still, she'd had a tough time winning any bids.

Then Vance Erickson had come to the rescue, hiring her to remodel the missile site. She couldn't have asked for a better job. Now he was gone, she had no new jobs, and what little money was left wouldn't hold up long against the mounting bills.

His namesake had shown up two days ago—a little strange like his uncle and cute in a nerdy sort of way. A whisper inside her said God had sent him. That He was listening after all. But she shoveled and buried the thought. Life had been too hard on her, and Vance Young didn't deserve to inherit a property like that—he hadn't even known his uncle. She had.

Mr. E had loved her grandmother, wanted to marry her when they were younger, before Grandpa. Andi liked to think if they had both lived, they would have married.

Waiting at a red light, she glanced at her cell phone resting on the seat. Still no call from Vance Young. She shook her head. Why hadn't the guy called? Surely he could see that work on the missile site had to be finished.

Plain and simple, she was desperate.

She pulled up to the curb at the school.

Elisa went frantic. "No! Park *away* from the school. I can't be seen in this." She slunk down into the seat.

Andi drove past the school and stopped. "Okay. I'm going to sit here and watch. If I don't see you walk into that building, I'll park in front and walk you in myself next time. You hear me?"

Elisa stepped from the truck, then stuck her head back in, smiling. "Thanks, sis. Oh, I forgot. That missile base guy called." She slammed the door, then took off toward the school.

"What? Wait. When?" Andi stuck her head out the window. "What did he say? Elisa?" But she'd been talking to the street. Elisa hadn't heard.

Andi ground her teeth. *That girl.* She watched until she saw her sister meet up with friends and walk into the building. What more could Andi do than that? The truancy had to stop. She shifted the truck into gear. Maybe she needed to get her sister counseling or therapy. Or maybe Elisa needed to get a grip like Andi had.

She looked at her cell phone but found no messages there. Why hadn't he called her on her cell? Likely Elisa told him she'd pass on the message.

Andi growled. "Teenagers!"

Without his number she couldn't call him back. She'd have to remember that little trick in the future—ask for a cell phone number!

If his answer wasn't positive, she sure didn't want to drive all the way out. She wasn't in the state of mind to persuade him otherwise. If she found a number on caller ID, it might be Vance Junior's. Except if he'd called her on his cell and now he was down under, he'd never get her return call. How could such a simple thing be so complicated? What was the matter with her?

*Elisa is the matter.* While Andi was trying to keep both their heads above water, Elisa was determined to drown them both.

Andi placed her palm against her forehead. *Get a grip.* Was the phone that rang directly into the base still working? She dialed Vance Erickson's old number to the missile base and allowed it to ring twenty-five times without an answer. Her spirits sagging, she hung up.

A visit to Freya would do her good at the moment, then she'd try Vance Young again. After she swung by the local grocery store to grab the cookies—white chocolate and macadamia nuts—Andi headed to Freya's, wishing she had baked them fresh. Didn't Freya deserve that much? Andi turned off a street onto a bumpy dirt road. The older woman lived a few miles outside of town near the railroad tracks in the same house where she grew up. Freya's Oldsmobile of twenty years was parked in the driveway. Good. Andi hadn't made the drive out for nothing.

Before Andi climbed from her truck, Freya stood on the porch, holding the screen door open for her. "Well, aren't you a sight for sore eyes?" she called out to Andi.

Andi smiled, grabbed the cookies, and shut the truck door. Once on the porch, she said, "I brought you something."

Freya patted her back as she entered the house. "Thank you. You rest on the davenport over there, I'll get us some tea. Chamomile?"

"Sounds good." Andi breathed in the smell of the old home. Memories flooded in on her. Because Freya and Andi's grandmother had been close friends, Andi and Elisa had spent time here, eating pot roast on Sundays, playing cards in the evenings, and running around in the fenced-in backyard.

Freya approached, offering a teacup on a saucer. "What's bothering you?"

Gently taking the cup and saucer, Andi sighed. She didn't want a trip down memory lane right now. A big smile would throw the woman off. "Nothing at all. So how've you been?"

Freya proceeded to share long-drawn-out tales of her two dogs—they had taken to barking incessantly. There must be a wild animal nearby. Then on to the local gossip.

"I hear there's a new tenant at the old missile site." Sipping her tea, Freya lifted a questioning brow.

Andi almost spewed her tea. "What? How did you hear that?"

"Someone talked to a fellow at the grocery store. Said he was staying there."

"Mr. Erickson's great-nephew. His name is Vance Young."

Freya winked. "Thought you might know of him. Have you met him yet? Is he anything of a looker like his uncle?"

"I guess you could say that." She glanced at her watch.

"More tea?"

As much as she adored Freya, Andi felt sure the woman wanted her to stay so she could pry more news from her. But Andi really had nothing to share. At least not yet. "No thank you. That reminds me. I'm working on a bid, so I have to go now."

"That's my Andi. Your business is going to take off. Just you wait and see."

After a quick peck on Freya's cheek, Andi wished her well and left. Back in her truck, she tried to call Vance again.

"Hello?"

*Sweet potatoes.* He'd answered. Relief was quickly replaced with panic. What if he turned her down? "Mr. Young. . .uh, Vance, this is—"

"Hi, Andi."

Andi liked the sound of his voice. "My sister informed me this morning that you called."

"I told you I'd get back to you."

"Yeah, you did. Have you made a decision, then?"

"I have."

Andi's breath hitched. "And?"

"Let's do this."

Trembling, she almost dropped the phone. Maybe, just maybe, God was listening after all.

There was only one problem—by now the subs she had used were probably working on other jobs.

# Chapter 4

The next day, Andi drove on the stretch of highway that passed through the North Dakota prairie and farmland to her revived worksite—the old missile launch control center. A coyote darted across the highway, causing Andi to slow up. Clear blue skies promised a beautiful day, though that wouldn't matter since the bulk of their work was done underground. Still, some of the messier jobs—like cutting tile or granite with a wet saw—were best done outside.

She'd spent yesterday lining up subs, relieved that she'd have her old standbys, brothers Lars and Karl Handley. They'd both known her dad years before and had been more than happy to give her a chance when she started the business.

They'd worked at Ground Zero and knew how to do almost everything in construction. They worked well together, which was good because she didn't want to give the new owner any reason to doubt her ability to finish the job. He'd sounded doubtful when she informed him she was a contractor. Still, he'd seemed impressed with the work.

How could he not be impressed? It was beautiful.

Only one problem tried to dampen her mood. Elisa moaned from the passenger seat as though she could read Andi's thoughts.

Andi pounded the steering wheel. "What am I going to do with you?"

"Just leave me alone," Elisa mumbled, leaning her head against the window.

Andi pursed her lips. She wanted nothing more than to give Elisa a good tongue-lashing, but she figured Elisa had had her fill of lectures. Andi knew from experience there came a point when a person wouldn't listen anymore. What Andi had to figure out was how to reach her younger sister.

Teenage years were never easy, but Elisa had pushed Andi to the edge. She'd stayed out all night last night—a school night, no less—and come dragging in during the early morning hours. Andi had thought she'd been asleep in her bed all night.

Not only did Andi have to watch the girl walk into the school building— "Do I have to check up on you every five minutes now?"

Only a grunt came in response. Any response at all was a surprise.

Andi pressed her lips together again, wanting to say more, oh so much more. She pulled up to a stop sign and slumped against the seat. After the lone car passed, Andi drove across the intersection.

"What am I going to do?" she asked, for her own benefit. She didn't expect a coherent answer from her hung-over sister. She couldn't send her to school because she was too sick to function. Nor would Andi dare leave Elisa at home alone.

If there was one thing she hated, it was feeling like she had no control over a situation, and the situation with Elisa had definitely spiraled out of control.

"If you're bent on skipping school, then you can just work with me." Andi still had a job to do and a secret to discover within the walls of Ground Zero.

"Could you stop talking?" Elisa leaned forward and put her head in her lap.

Andi shook her head, giving up for the moment, and focused on the drive ahead. Dealing with Elisa had put her behind this morning. Again. Though the missile site wasn't too far now, she'd be lucky if she made it there before Lars and Karl. She drove into the parking area where the brothers were unloading their trucks.

She stepped from the cab of hers. "Hey boys. Thanks for coming to my rescue."

Between the three of them, they should be able to handle the bulk of the remodel. Andi and Vance had agreed that the quickest path to completion would be for him to foot the costs of materials and subs—he had a decent savings—but she'd have to wait on a good portion of her contractor's fee, again, until Ground Zero sold. Selling a lavish underground home could take awhile. Until another job opportunity came through, it was the best prospect she had.

Remodeling would also mean she'd get to see more of the younger Vance. Why had that thought dropped from the sky? *Get a grip.* She pressed the intercom to announce their arrival to Vance below ground and waited for his response, which, if nothing else, should prompt the elevator door to open—all designed for the older Vance. When Vance Junior didn't respond, Andi used her key to unlock the elevator lock-down button, figuring he hadn't heard the intercom for some reason. It occurred to her that she hadn't shown him how to use the system. At the time, he'd seemed eager to get some rest, and she wasn't sure he'd be staying for even one night.

The men followed her into the elevator, loaded down with ladders and tools. It was a tight fit. Today they'd trim out the portion of the launch control center that served as an extra bedroom. She'd have to get the electrician in before they could do anything on the equipment building. That, and pump any excess water out.

She didn't bother to rouse Elisa. When it grew warm enough, she'd come inside. Andi glanced at her watch, glad they were getting started bright and early. Though she'd called to remind Vance to expect her crew today, since he'd not answered, she hoped they wouldn't be stumbling into anything. . . embarrassing.

The elevator doors swooshed open and they hiked through the tunnel. Lars opened the blast door for them, then Andi cautiously stepped through into the well-lit living room.

"Hello?" She crept slowly, hoping not to startle Vance, Lars and Karl behind her. Even if he were the type of person to sleep in, their clanking gear would have woken him by now.

They'd have to agree on a plan for her entry every day. Most mornings, his uncle would greet her crew with bacon and eggs. Not a requirement, but it made a great start to the day. Oh, how she missed that. Missed him. Why had Grandma not fallen for him back in her day?

Another step and Andi froze. Vance slept on the couch in his sweats, one arm over his eyes. No wonder he hadn't answered the intercom. He was sound asleep.

Andi stared for longer than necessary, but she couldn't pull her eyes away from his sleeping form, his physique like that of a tennis player rather than some muscular brute who played defense on a high school football team. Completely unlike. . .Jorgen.

*Good-night pajamas.* When would she stop thinking about Jorgen? What was she doing comparing Vance to him? Or Vance to anyone for that matter? Besides, a guy like him—good-looking, smart, and with a bank account—had to have a girlfriend.

A laptop along with electronic equipment she didn't recognize lay scattered around the room, as well as an expensive-looking telescope.

Make that a *smart* girlfriend.

"Uh, Andi." Lars snickered. "We should just get moving and let *you* take care of *him.*"

Her cheeks were over-heated pipes, full of steam and ready to explode. How long had she been standing there lost in her ridiculous thoughts? *Get a grip.* She couldn't think of a client as anything other than just that. Lars and Karl shuffled past her to the room they'd left incomplete a couple of months ago. They made plenty of noise passing Vance.

He moved his arm and opened one eye, looking right into hers.

If she thought she couldn't be any more embarrassed, she was wrong. Her face felt like a rocket had just blasted off, using it for a launch pad. Why had she let her guard down, allowing herself to admire him?

She sucked in a deep breath. "Hi. . uh. . .Mr. Young. I mean, Vance." She shrugged with a smile. "Sorry, I didn't mean to surprise you. I hoped you'd be expecting us."

"No problem." Vance sat up and rubbed his eyes, then wiped a hand down his unshaven face. "What am I saying? I did expect you. I obviously overslept. The apology should be all mine."

"Yeah, looks like you were up and waiting but fell back asleep."

He glanced around the room and laughed. "Looks that way, doesn't it?"

Vance stood and stretched, appearing like he hadn't gotten much sleep. Unfortunately, to Andi, he still looked good. Especially when he grinned. She loved his accent. Was he a Texan?

She walked over to where he'd set up his telescope. "So, you like to look at the stars, then?"

"Yeah, I'm a stargazer."

"It's amazing." She moved to touch it.

"Don't—"

In a flash he was next to her, gently taking her hand into his, sending a surge of heat up her arm.

"What was that?" she asked, and snatched her hand back. Oh no, had she spoken that out loud?

"Sorry. I'm way too obsessive about my stuff, especially when it's new and expensive."

She'd meant the electrical current he'd sent up her arm, but she could hardly tell him that.

"Just ignore me. I'm a complete idiot on most days." He found his glasses and put them on, transforming him from ruggedly handsome to seriously smart.

"And on days when you're not?" She smiled and put some distance between them. He might be cute but he'd nailed it when he called himself obsessive.

"Afraid there's not too many of those."

"It's too bad you won't see stars down here."

Vance stared at her and cracked the grin she liked. She *liked*? How had he managed to chip away at her defenses in no time at all? She straightened her back, resolving to be impervious to his charm. She had a job to do, and he was her client. Nothing more. She'd never liked women who fell too easily for men who eventually trampled over them, leaving them behind.

Hurting them.

"I like wide-open spaces. That's why it didn't take me long to decide to sell the place. I was expecting something much different."

"I see. You wanted a big view of the night sky." Now, there was a *big* difference between Vance and his uncle. Mr. E seemed to enjoy his underground dwelling.

"Something like that." Vance tugged his glasses off and stuck the end of the earpiece in his mouth, studying her.

"Listen, let me say I'm sorry again. I shouldn't have panicked when you touched the telescope. I guess you could say it's a little quirk of mine."

"Okay, I'll say it. It's a little quirk of yours."

When he laughed unexpectedly, it warmed her insides—a clear warning that she had better get to work and keep her mind off Vance Young.

He moved around the kitchen island, then leaned against it. "Would you like a cup of coffee?"

Without waiting for an answer he reached into the cabinet and grabbed the same two cups from the cupboard that Mr. E would grab when he shared with her.

"Thanks, but no. I'd better get busy." She'd already downed a large mug at home, which was probably the equivalent of three cups. "We can't make our money until we complete this job."

"You mean until I sell it."

"Right." She smiled, despite the discouragement seeping in. At least she had the job and the opportunity to find the secret that lay within.

After pouring himself a cup, Vance took a long gulp of black coffee and squeezed his eyes as though he hated the stuff—the mannerism reminding her of his uncle. She looked down at the granite counter, a smile creeping onto her lips.

So, they had some similarities after all.

Vance's uncle had often said to her he wished he were a lot younger, then he would have tried to win her heart. She'd laughed with him at the sweet comment, not knowing at the time of his affection for her grandmother when he was young. But with a much younger version of him standing on the other side of the counter right now, she wondered how far the similarities went.

And the differences.

☙

Andi the builder glanced at the junk he'd strewn around the living area. "We're going to work on the extra room today and maybe the rest of this week. I don't plan to start on the equipment building until we get the power on there. I hope we don't disturb you."

"You won't bother me at all." Vance watched her walk away. Nothing unfamiliar about watching a gorgeous woman walking away.

He hung his head over the counter. A laugh escaped. Vance dumped the rest of his coffee. She'd taken an interest in his telescope and what did he do? *Idiot.*

He'd practically yelled at her. He could still see the look of shock on her face. When would he ever learn?

In his few encounters with her, she always acted wary, untrusting, but like she wanted to open up, like she needed a friend. It was weird, but not in a science fiction sort of way. Stomach growling again, he grabbed a muffin and stuffed his face. A hot shower would clear his mind.

When he'd arrived at Ground Zero, his trip to Cancun was just a few days away. Now he'd dug himself in deep—deciding to finish what Uncle Vance had started. But whether his uncle's intentions were to finish the missile site or help Andi or both, Vance wasn't sure. Honestly, he wasn't even sure of his own intentions. But the arrangement could benefit them both.

Add to that, something was out of place at ANND Systems. After seeing the anomalies on the disk, call it a gut feeling or a sixth sense, he had a strong niggling feeling he was involved—that it would all somehow come back to him. In that case, he could be in big trouble. Unless what he'd seen was nothing more than the product of a sleep-deprived brain drawing the last of the juice from an alternate power source.

But what exactly had he seen? He'd have to figure it out, turning this into a working vacation. Fun and rest seemed about as accessible as the moon right now. After looking at the disk Saturday night, he'd tried to focus, even drank several of his usual energy drinks, but going for weeks without sleep in order to make the project deadline had worked against him. When he crashed, he typically crashed for days, but now he didn't have the luxury of that much time even on a vacation. Until he figured out how to get a real snooze in this temporary underground home, he couldn't be at his best.

He was heading for the shower when Andi stepped out of a room to the left and walked right into him.

He grabbed her arm to steady her. "Sorry about that."

"I should watch where I'm going." Appearing flustered, she continued about her business.

"No problem." Vance waved, then scowled. Why had he just waved at her?

He blew out a breath. The remodeling would be a distraction for him, especially with Andi here. How much of the work did she actually do herself? It seemed odd—her in construction. She appeared dainty compared to his idea of someone in that line of work. He wondered how she got into the business. Had she dreamed about managing a construction site or remodeling homes all her life? Or was it more about surviving? She was attractive and interesting and. . .

*What are you doing?* Any interest in her would lead him to the same place it always did—nowhere. It didn't help that he felt like he'd been looking at her every day for months now. Maybe if he'd not grown attached to the face in the picture frame he could more easily shrug off any ideas about Andi.

How many times would he need to learn his lesson? Women weren't interested in him. Sure he could get dates, but once they got to know him, that's when the relationships ended. He couldn't keep their interest.

Vance took a long, hot shower, reflecting that there weren't too many things in life that felt as good when a person was stressed. Afterward, feeling refreshed, he dressed and set up an office in the living room instead of going to Uncle Vance's small office. He wanted to be available in case one of the workmen—who was he kidding?—in case Andi needed him. Of course, she could always find him. But staying visible gave him more opportunity to interact with her. He squeezed his eyes. He really was a desperate geek.

Nestled comfortably on the sofa with his laptop open on his lap, Vance focused on the data from the small disk Tom had given him. Peter had landed a big government contract for data mining of the specialized sort—to identify and track possible terrorist suspects and activities. It was all about predicting what might happen. Vance had spent a year writing and testing the algorithm—a real breakthrough for the project and for the company.

Then why was he staring at a tweaked version of his algorithm—a program that shouldn't be floating around on a disk or especially ending up on the floor of the company foyer? Vance scratched a nonexistent itch on his jaw. What was going on here? Had Peter given the go-ahead for others on their team of programmers to work on it, and if so, why hadn't he told Vance, or why weren't they working together on it? He should be part of that decision.

If he asked Peter what was going on, the guy would block him from the system to make sure Vance got his vacation time, and he'd have to listen to a lecture.

Vance weaved his fingers through his still-damp hair. An errant thought wrestled to get in and finally won. Peter hadn't been upfront with him on a few other occasions. Disturbing. There was the slight possibility he wouldn't get the truth if he asked.

Working on secret projects cast shadows in all directions. What if there was something underhanded going on? The algorithm belonged to Vance, or at least the company, and not just anyone should have hands on it. He needed to know if it was being used for some other purpose and why and by whom.

Was he paranoid? Maybe. But he didn't need Boolean logic to know he shouldn't see his algorithm on a disk lying on the floor. Vance would find out what was going on, *then* he would ask Peter.

He'd do a data run, a small test sampling, the kind his laptop—a microprocessing computer—could handle in comparison to the supercomputers in the dinosaur pen at work. For that, he needed test data—something he might not have access to except at ANND.

"First things first."

"Excuse me?"

The words startled him. He looked up to find Andi's sister standing over him. Too caught up in his thoughts, he'd not noticed her. He quickly averted the screen.

"You were talking to yourself." Her smile was like Andi's.

"Elisa, leave Mr. Young alone. Can't you see he's working?" Andi strode over and looked down at him. "I'm sorry. She wasn't feeling well, and I didn't want to leave her at home alone."

"No problem." Vance snickered. "Make yourself at home, Elisa."

"What's so funny?"

"The thought occurred to me that this place might protect us from a nuclear blast, but not from a cold virus."

Andi gave him an odd look. "She's not sick like that."

"Well, even if she is, she's welcome to make herself at home, raid the refrigerator or pantry for junk food."

"Really?" Elisa perked up.

Andi cocked her brow. "That's all right. I had intended for her to work with me."

"But I thought she wasn't feeling well."

Andi frowned. "I—"

"She's punishing me." Elisa slipped past her sister and meandered toward the exit.

Andi looked at him apologetically. "I'm sorry about this. She won't interfere with your work, or mine for that matter."

"There's nothing to apologize for." What was going on with Andi and her sister? "Is there anything I can do to help?"

"It's that obvious?"

Vance set the laptop on the coffee table and stood up to look directly into Andi's soft blue eyes. "Nah. Just the usual family drama when adult and teenage worlds collide."

"I guess you're right."

Women liked men who were sensitive, understanding. "It helps to talk about your problems. I'm a good listener."

"Thanks for your offer, but it's not your problem." She sighed, her guard up again. "You have work to do. So do I." She gave him a flat smile and followed Elisa out.

Vance plopped against the sofa back. She put on a tough veneer but he'd seen a glimpse of the softness inside. Why did he have to be curious about this woman?

# Chapter 5

At the end of the day, Andi stood with Lars in the tunnel junction outside of the equipment room. "The electrician should be here on Thursday. Hopefully he'll get the power on in there so we can begin work."

"Karl will be back in the morning, but I've got another job," Lars said.

"I understand. There's not enough work left in the other room for all of us at this point. Just the trim. Can you ask Karl to bring the pump so we can get that water out tomorrow? Then we can seal the leaks."

Lars tilted his head. "You betcha."

"In the meantime, I'm going to explore." Andi rattled her flashlight for Lars's benefit.

"Be careful." He nodded and left.

With Lars and Karl gone for the day, she was free to conduct her search, even though it was mostly in the dark. Nothing could pull Vance away from his computer so she needn't worry about him. She'd put Elisa to work with the Shop-Vac in the room that was near completion.

After opening the blast door, Andi switched on the flashlight, shining it around the large equipment room. Every time she read the letter, she became more convinced that Vance Erickson had hired her to renovate the place so she could find what her grandfather had hidden decades before. Why anyone would go to so much trouble she didn't know.

Hidden in the underground launch center was something of value meant for her grandmother, and Andi intended to discover it. Like everything else in her life, she had to work hard for it, earn it.

She took a step down into an inch of water. A slow drip joined the echo of her footsteps as she explored. Why hadn't Mr. E just told her what to look for? Good grief. What if one of the other workers had found it and said nothing?

Yet another thing she'd never know. All she had to go on was the letter she'd discovered in her grandmother's things, written by Mr. E. At least Andi could have asked him about it if she'd found it before he'd died.

She wasn't sure how the new owner would take to the news that she was searching for something that belonged to her family but was hidden on his property, and until she knew him well enough, she probably wouldn't tell him. For that matter, would she want to know him that well? He might be cute with his charming grin and searching gaze, but he was a geek in anybody's world—consumed by things like computers and telescopes. She'd already been discarded by his type—no sense in setting herself up for that again.

For the time being, she'd keep things to herself. She sure hoped Mr. E knew what he was doing when he'd given this place to his nephew. At the moment, it didn't appear that he did. Vance Young wasn't keen on living underground.

Though she was excited at the challenge—at the opportunity she'd been given to complete the missile site, after all—the thought of renovating this room suddenly overwhelmed her. What if something went wrong? What if the younger Vance changed his mind? She knew from experience things could change overnight.

*Get a grip.* She drew in a deep breath and plodded through the water, shining the flashlight around and wishing she'd taken a look at the specs again. Where would her grandfather, then a young deputy flight commander, have hidden something?

The missileers who'd worked there had a lot of time on their hands even while they stayed in a state of alertness. The first time she'd been inside, she'd seen artwork painted on the blast door by what Grandma had called America's Underground Air Force. Andi couldn't imagine the pressure of being part of a missile crew, waiting for the call. One turn of the launch key could end millions of lives.

Nor could she imagine the boredom that must have accompanied the hours of waiting for a call they hoped never to get. Her grandfather had plenty of time to hide something. The fact that he'd concealed it in the nerve center of a missile launch control center told Andi he'd meant for it to stay buried, which piqued her curiosity even more.

If only she knew what she was looking for. Chances were the item was long gone. Her grandfather hadn't worked here in decades, and the place had sat decommissioned for at least ten years.

A sense of failure slammed her. She hated admitting it, but her search could very well be a lost cause. Hope started to slip through her fingers. She sucked in a breath. Nothing she hated more than watching people give up. While she had this opportunity, she would do her best. For her grandparents and Mr. E's sake, she'd search the base, and she'd wait to tell the younger Vance when the time was right.

Andi climbed to the top of a ladder and shined the light, studying the walls, looking for any sort of variance. She ran her right hand over the smooth surface while holding the flashlight with her left hand, leaning as far as possible before she'd have to move the ladder. Without more light this could take forever, and once the power was on, Lars and Karl would be working. How could she conduct a search without telling them? She hated secrets.

"What are you doing?"

*Caught.* Her heart pounded. The flashlight fell from her hand.

"Watch out!"

Her foot slipped on the rung but she gripped the ladder, halting her fall. Having regained her balance, Andi pressed her head against the ladder and took a deep, calming breath. She looked over at the figure standing in the doorway, light pouring in.

"Are you all right?" Vance made his way to the ladder.

"Why'd you have to scare me like that?"

He lifted his palms in surrender. "That wasn't my intention." He picked up the flashlight and shined it around. "But your reaction does make a person wonder what you were doing."

Andi began the climb down. His vague accusation made her bristle. "You startled me, how was I supposed to react?"

Vance handed her the flashlight as she stepped into the water. "I'm going up for some fresh air, thought you might like to join me."

"You did?" Andi was relieved he didn't pursue his line of questioning. But why would he think she'd want to join him? "Can't you see I'm working?"

"In the dark?"

"What else would I be doing in here?"

"I don't know. That's why I asked."

Andi paused, flustered. Vance didn't know what was hidden, did he? For the first time, she considered the possibility. Mr. E could have told him all about it—could even have asked him to look for the treasure.

"Yeah, I think fresh air would be good after all."

"So, what were you doing in here?"

Andi shined the flashlight in his face and watched him squint, but he didn't back down. "You hired me to finish Ground Zero. I'm checking things out to make sure I know what to do. The electrician will be here in a couple of days. What's with all the questions?"

Vance grinned. He was entirely too attractive. Andi stiffened, deflecting the effect he had on her.

"It wasn't a challenge, just a simple question. I'm curious about your work. That's all." He shrugged, then walked away.

Andi felt ridiculous. Her reaction would put him on alert. Still, even if she hadn't been on a search, she would have bristled at his question. It was like asking if she knew what she was doing at her own business.

Almost at the exit, he turned to look at her. "You coming?"

"Sure."

Andi followed, already regretting she'd agreed to go up with him. She was attracted to him, and she shouldn't be. What was it about this guy? He stood at the door like he needed to hold it open for her, waiting. She avoided his gaze as she moved passed. He smelled good.

Andi tightened her ponytail, nice and snug—one painful way to snatch her thoughts from the young Vance's charms. An uneducated girl like her would never fit into his world.

She'd been through that before and didn't need a second lesson.
At least she was that smart.

⚮

Wearing dirty jeans and a smudged T-shirt, Andi finally looked the part of a contractor. Well, except for her curvaceous yet slim figure, which Vance attempted to ignore—he experienced a total malfunction there. Still, her lack of enthusiasm caused him to second-guess inviting her up with him. Feeling the effects of being closed in like an animal, he'd needed the break. Pleasant and distracting conversation was more in keeping with his plan, not her peculiar brand of hostility.

Her crew was gone already, yet she remained behind. Andi the enigma was a Rubik's Cube personified, which made her all the more appealing to Vance, as long as he could get her to dump the brick wall act. Rocking from heel to toe as he waited for her to step into the elevator first, he grinned as she swept past, ponytail swinging.

As soon as Vance stepped onto the elevator, his pulse increased, and to think he'd managed to control his panic inside the Ground Zero capsule. Admittedly, Ground Zero wasn't nearly as small as the elevator. A distraction from that fact would be good about now. But if he hoped for conversation, he was out of luck. Except for his heavier than normal breathing, an uncomfortable silence swallowed them.

Rubbing his neck to ease his anxiety, he decided he'd definitely made a mistake. He wasn't a great conversationalist, and if she wasn't going to meet him halfway, what was the point?

Finally, she sighed. It was something at least.

"You know, if the elevator bothers you that much, we could have taken the stairs."

The elevator door opened. Vance held it for her. "What gave me away?"

Andi shrugged and stepped through. "Your uncle, remember? He had a fear of small spaces. Acted just like you're acting now. All nervous and breathless. Opened and closed his fists a lot."

Vance looked at his hands, not realizing he'd done that. "Yeah, makes me feel cagey and nervous, especially when they're in motion. It's not quite a phobia, but still, it helps to focus on something else."

Once they stepped into the fresh air the sunshine hurt his eyes. He shaded them with his hand. "I need to get out more."

Andi laughed, making Vance think of the soothing tones of a wind chime.

She stood next to him, scanning the lone prairie that stretched for miles. "Haven't you brought your telescope outside yet?"

They strolled away from the complex, held back from the endless grasslands by the chain-link fence surrounding the missile site. "I haven't had a chance."

"Oh, come on. What's so important it takes up all your time?"

Vance leaned his head to one side and eyed her. "You serious?"

"That's right. You're a computer whiz. You spend all your time in cyberspace, while you miss what's going on around you."

*Ouch.* Vance covered his heart, acting mortally wounded. "You've exposed my virtual identity as a cyber spy."

Andi's mouth dropped open, then she closed it and laughed.

"How have you figured me out in such a short time?" Before they'd even had a proper dinner date, too.

She hung her head and kicked at the ground, then peered up at him. "I'm sorry. That wasn't nice of me. I'm sure what you do is very important. And I hope you're not really a cyber spy."

Vance grinned, soaking up her attention. "Is that because you're afraid I'd have to kill you?" Or because she actually cared?

She nodded.

"I don't spend all my time on the computer, you know? I do have that one hobby."

"The stars, yeah. Just another kind of space, if you ask me."

How he'd love the chance to change her mind about that. "Listen, I do have a reason for bringing you out into the daylight."

"Go ahead."

"I was thinking of adding on some sort of an aboveground building."

"So you can look at the stars? I thought you weren't staying."

He cocked his head. He wasn't sure why he was exploring this, but he surveyed the area. "Have you noticed it gets cold at night around here?"

"Where'd you say you were from?"

"Texas."

Eyes teasing, she smirked. "To North Dakotans, it doesn't get that cold at night in the summer. Are you saying it doesn't get cold in Texas?"

"Not like this, no. In the summer it can be ninety degrees at ten o'clock at night."

"Can't imagine that. How long have you lived here?"

"A year."

"And you're not accustomed to our climate yet?" She cocked her head with a questioning gaze.

"Are *you?*"

"I grew up here." She laughed, then flashed him a hundred-watt smile.

Her smile sent a jolt through Vance. "So, tell me what you know about this missile site. Do you know why my uncle would want this place for his home? It boggled my mind when I saw this instead of the mansion I expected."

"Well, considering it's farmland, maybe you should have at least expected a farmhouse."

"True, but then I didn't get that either."

Andi jabbed her hands into her jeans, a thoughtful expression in her eyes as she looked at something beyond him. A gust of wind lifted a few strands of hair from her ponytail.

What would she look like with her mass of tresses hanging down across her shoulders?

"My sister and I lived on a nearby farm when we were kids. We'd ride our bikes a few miles up the road to watch the airmen play football. But this site and I. . .we go back much further."

They strolled on for a few more moments until the fence prevented them from going farther. Still, Andi said nothing.

Vance broke the silence. "Do I get to know the rest?"

She glanced at the ground and grinned, tucking her stray hair behind an ear. "I don't know where to begin. Besides, to a guy like you, this stuff is probably boring."

"Hey, I asked, didn't I? I want to know." He started walking along the fence line.

"It's the decommissioned missile sites. This all meant something to my parents, to the folks who lived here. It's like they were a part of something bigger than themselves."

"I understand."

"My grandfather was in the air force and worked at this very site."

Vance stopped. Was it mere coincidence that she was renovating this site? He'd never been a believer in coincidence, not with the Creator of the universe running things. Andi the builder now posed an even bigger puzzle.

She looked at him with warm eyes, drawing him in. "And when Dad was still alive, we explored the base after its decommissioning. Funny, we found a carpeted concrete door in the building that was standing at the time. I always wondered what was hidden behind it." A soft sigh escaped. "I've said too much. I need to get back to Ground Zero now."

What had he said to shut her down? "The workday is over, isn't it?"

"Yeah, it is. I've got to find Elisa, then head home."

Vance couldn't stand the thought of going underground again. At least not yet. "I'm going to town to get some more groceries."

She walked backward as she spoke. "Didn't I show you the food storage room? Your uncle stocked it just in case."

"In case of what? A nuclear meltdown?"

"Yeah, something like that. He was funny that way."

"I gather." Vance thought of the freeze-dried food. "I discovered the survival food. All those meals ready to eat. Not interested, thank you very much."

Andi snickered. "You're more interested in muscle drinks and candy bars." She turned her back to him, then entered the stairwell.

"They're energy drinks," he said, but she'd already disappeared into the abyss of his eccentric uncle's missile site.

He could have enough trouble on his hands at ANND Systems. Why was he borrowing more by attempting to get involved with a woman by the same name?

Vance headed for his car, then to the grocery store to get some more salsa for his chips—another procrastination technique he'd developed called restocking the condiments.

# Chapter 6

With a couple of hours of daylight remaining, Vance pulled through the gate and drove up the road to the old missile base. Gravel crunched as he neared the building housing the elevator entrance. He shut off the ignition. A garage might be nice, especially in the winter.

Would the lack of one scare away a potential buyer? He hadn't exactly had time to do research on missile sites converted to homes and how well they sell. On that, he'd given Andi his complete trust, hoping he wasn't just another poor sap for a pretty face. But wasn't every guy?

Vance dragged himself from the car and grabbed the two grocery sacks from the back seat, a box of Ding Dongs sticking from the top of one, and headed down under. He entered the living room, his eyes adjusting to the fluorescents. He set the bags on the counter just as his stomach growled, and grabbed a frozen burrito. Microwaves were a product of God's mercy.

After eating dinner, he opened a bag of chips and plopped onto the sofa, the scent of Andi's perfume in the air, a reminder of what he was missing. What he'd always missed, and what he would always miss—a girlfriend. A woman's attention. Companionship. This place was the epitome of his life. Dark. Lonely. Boring.

Was this the plight of all computer geeks? His brother Matt was happily married, his wife expecting a child.

Vance blew out a breath. Hope yet remained.

The laptop sat on the coffee table where he'd left it open, applications running, and looked back expectantly. For once, he was tired of staring at his computer, but he had work to do, and procrastinating wasn't getting him anywhere. Hard to imagine.

It was just that. . .he was fried. Having to use his so-called vacation, which should have been for rest and recuperation, to work on this. . . Well, he counted it as severe loss.

After running test data all day, he'd needed fresh air. Now it was time to get down to real business. What exactly was that second algorithm producing?

Though he wasn't a data analyst, he could easily compare sample data output from both programs. The second data set produced by his government-contracted algorithm gone rogue appeared to produce a dissimilar data set. The records he'd flagged as the "bad guys" in his original algorithm weren't being flagged as often in the second.

Serious bogosity was happening here—a sham he might even call mission creep: his proprietary algorithm was being used for an entirely different purpose.

It reminded him of when he'd watched two of his colleagues fired from the Texas-based company. They'd agreed to write the company's proprietary software for someone else, in essence, selling company secrets.

But what happened when it was government secrets?

The sensation of being boxed into a small place came over him. An adrenaline rush sent sweat to his palms. His pulse raced.

Only one thought coursed through his burned-out circuits—someone wanted to produce output that was a less-than-accurate prediction of terrorists and their activities.

Could Peter be in on this? And if so, who had lined his pockets? The only reason Vance knew about it was due to a lost disk. Nothing was a coincidence.

"Okay, Lord, You wanted me to see this. I get it. Now what?"

What should he do about it?

Both hands on his head, he squeezed. Despite today's adept computer forensics, Vance could potentially go down with the mission creepers, if they were caught. How could he prove he wasn't involved? Especially since Peter was a long-time friend—even though he'd changed a lot. And if Peter—assuming he was involved—was willing to go this far, might he actually try to set Vance up?

The last thing Vance should do was touch this—but his fingerprints were already all over it. His impulse was to do something now. But that's what he'd done when he'd joined ANND Systems. He'd listened to Peter's persuasion, rather than praying first. No. This time he'd pray for direction.

☙

Construction noise stirred Vance awake the next morning. He'd lain awake most of the night, his thoughts in turmoil, then finally fallen asleep in the early morning hours. Rubbing his eyes, he sat up, sure Andi had a meager opinion of him for sleeping late and forgetting to let her in as per the agreed upon protocol. She'd shown him the intercom, but he never heard her calling. He should tell her to dispense with the protocol since it wasn't working anyway.

After pulling on jeans, he headed to the kitchen where he poured a cup of coffee, compliments of the auto brew. He squeezed his eyes as the dark liquid slid down his throat. It would give him the kick he needed. After the first cup, he added fillers. Sugar, vanilla syrup, milk. That was more like it.

He hadn't exactly gotten an earful from God last night, but he'd come up with a plan. He'd write a viral worm or some other slow-to-discover interference for their project until he could gather enough information to make a rational statement to the authorities.

Trading his algorithm out for the imposter was the only difficulty.

Cup of sweet coffee in hand, he propped his back against the kitchen side of the island in an obvious leave-me-alone-I'm-thinking manner.

"You really should take better care of yourself," Andi suggested, her voice sounding lighthearted.

Couldn't she read his mind? Didn't she know he had to concentrate on his own problems?

Conceding the error of his thought, he turned around. "What are you talking about?"

Though his question had sounded much too brusque, Andi didn't appear to notice. Leaning over the island on her elbows, she indicated the junk food he'd left out last night. "Let's see, Ding Dongs, Ho Hos, potato chips of every variety. What sort of diet is that?"

Vance watched her, confused by her unusually friendly demeanor. "Well, it gets me through. I need those sudden bursts of energy." He couldn't seem to inject any warmth into his tone this morning.

"That's what you call brain food, yeah?"

Andi playful and teasing? Why couldn't she act like this when he was in the mood to enjoy it? He frowned, studying the woman who looked similar to the photo on his desk. Andi Nielsen was nothing like he'd imagined the woman in the photo would be. Andi might bait him with her momentary charm, then an instant later her defenses would go back up, secreting her away behind guarded walls.

Was she a Christian? He didn't see a cross hanging from her neck, or any action to indicate one way or the other. With what he was about to do, he had to wonder if he was a Christian himself. Trusting God had been easy enough while things were going smoothly at his job. While life was good. But when life became volatile, that's where the true test of faith came in—how much muscle did he really have when it came to his faith?

He had a feeling he was about to find out.

Andi cleared her throat, causing him to realize he hadn't responded to her question about his brain food.

"Well, I can see you're one of those people who needs coffee before they become human."

"I've got a lot on my mind today." Guilt threaded his conscience. What was the matter with him? The woman was actually paying attention. "Like your favorite mantra, I've got work to do."

"Then you'll need one of these for that brain of yours." She pulled out a Hostess cupcake, unwrapped it, and stuck it out to him. Her hundred-watt smile burned away his irritation.

A grin broke through his frown, spreading until he laughed. How could he not? "Give me that."

He grabbed the chocolate gooey-goodness and stuffed part of it into his mouth.

"There, that's better. I've done my job." She smiled again, then flipped her ponytail as she snapped around and waltzed away.

Enchanted by her spell, Vance was unable to do anything except gape.

Andi the builder had somehow wiped away his tension, using her strange magic. She was unpredictable. He weighed the trait, deciding he liked that about her, and finished off the cupcake and coffee. As he began work on his blindsiding tactic, he hoped he could be unpredictable as well.

He hoped he hadn't made the discovery too late.

After picking Elisa up from school, Andi headed back to Ground Zero. Best not only to drop her troubled sister off, but to pick her up as well. That way she could stave off concern over Elisa getting into trouble. At least while she was working.

They'd spent the morning pumping out the water in the equipment building. Guy Landers had stopped in to do a quick electrical check afterward. He'd told her he'd discovered the problem right off, when she was leaving to get Elisa. Arriving at Ground Zero, she noticed Guy's truck was gone now. She and Elisa rode the elevator down.

This morning she'd learned she'd won a bid on a job for Nielsen Remodeling. Things were finally looking up, putting her in a good mood, and for some reason, she found herself wanting to share the news with Vance. Since he'd not been in the greatest of moods, she kept the news to herself. Instead, she'd tried to encourage him, lighten things up, surprising herself. As she exited the elevator, she wondered how he was feeling now. Andi marched straight to the equipment room, the blast door propped open, and peered inside. The lights were on, lifting her spirits even higher.

She stepped through the door and looked around the large room—almost as big as a two-story house. The diesel generator as well as other equipment had been removed. All that remained were the four shock absorbers in case of a bomb blast. Though she grew up hearing stories about the Cold War era, it was difficult to imagine living with that fear, even though there were still plenty of armed missile sites around the country, especially in North Dakota.

"So this was why you were anxious to get back." Elisa stepped into the room behind her.

"Yeah, I wanted to see if the electrician got the power working. We pumped the water out so he could work." Andi motioned for Elisa to come all the way in.

"The place is a mess."

"You think?" Andi teased, happy Elisa took an interest, no matter how small. "It feels good when you transform a mess into something beautiful."

"So, why did I have to come? Why can't you just drop me off at the Rhubarb Festival? It started today, you know."

Andi kept her focus on the room so she wouldn't react. Did Elisa honestly think with her attitude that Andi would drop her off for a little fun? She'd been having a little too much fun for months now. Hence, summer school.

"I wanted to check the power. But starting tomorrow, I'm going to put you to work so you can learn responsibility."

"I've got homework, you know."

This coming from a person who was hard-pressed to even attend school? Andi eyed her sister, soon to become a woman. She wanted Elisa to have every opportunity and planned to try a different tactic. Scolding her would only drive her further away.

"We'll figure out how to make this work."

"I doubt it." Elisa turned on her heel and trotted out.

Andi sighed. She saw great potential in Elisa. If only her sister would see the same. Though Andi might listen to her own advice. Ever since Jorgen dumped her because she wasn't as educated—would no longer fit into the life he wanted—she'd looked at the world differently, feeling anything but adequate. No one could ever accuse Andi of not trying, but now Elisa was the one with opportunities ahead of her, and Andi wouldn't let her throw them away.

Elisa was right about one thing though. This room was a mess. Once Ground Zero sold, Vance would pay her the balance of her fee plus some, and that was enough motivation to wash away her fears.

She closed her eyes and imagined discovering what her grandfather had hidden. Was it a slice of history? Or was it something valuable in terms of cold, hard cash?

Guilt began dropping on her like splotches of paint. She'd almost told Vance about her search the other day when she'd shared about her grandfather working at the military base, but she'd been afraid of how he might react. She didn't know him well enough. Would she ever?

Then he'd acted differently toward her this morning. She'd had to coax out of him the grin she liked. Did it have anything to do with the remodeling? She hoped not.

"Hey there." Vance leaned through the open doorway and smiled.

Seeing Vance, Andi straightened. "Hi."

He strolled the rest of the way into the room. "I wanted to apologize for my behavior this morning."

"Oh, you're fine. We all have our good days and bad days." And lately, she'd had her share of the latter.

"It's just that there's a problem at my company. I need to be there to work on it, but I can't exactly work on it there." He laughed and shoved a hand through his hair. "I'm not making any sense, am I?"

Andi laughed. "For a smart guy, no, you're not. But I'm sure it has more to do with my ability to understand than it does with you." Why had she said that?

A pained expression crossed his face. "You're wrong, actually. You're a beautiful and intelligent woman. On the other hand, I'm not so good at communicating."

Andi felt herself blush at his compliment. She wished she could believe him, and averted her gaze. He was being so. . .honest, and she was being so. . . not. More guilt splotches.

"I'd like to know more about my uncle. You worked with him, knew him for a while. What can you tell me about him?"

What was he playing at? Did he know about her search? She studied him. The need to tell the truth chiseled at her. "Since you asked, there is something I have to tell—"

"Can we go already?" Elisa stood in the doorway, arms crossed. "I'm tired and hungry. You didn't even let me get a snack."

*What are you, five?* Andi didn't want to argue in front of Vance. Her shoulders fell. "I'm sorry, I have to go. We can talk later."

She stomped after Elisa into the elevator, swathed in guilt paint splotches because she'd just used her sister as an excuse to avoid telling Vance the truth, and was ready to throw out her earlier resolve not to lecture or scold Elisa. "Did you have to be so rude? I was in the middle of a conversation."

When she received no response she glanced at her sister. That explained it. She was plugged into music.

Just as well. Drained, Andi didn't have the energy to talk to the teenager at the moment. Once outside, they headed for the truck.

"Hey, wait up," Vance called.

Andi turned to see him walking toward her, out of breath. He must have taken the stairs. She admired his lithe form, wondering how he kept in shape with the way he ate.

"Yeah? What's up?"

"I don't feel like eating dinner alone tonight, especially in the dungeon. How about I take you and Elisa somewhere? Where's a good place to eat?"

Andi stood speechless.

Elisa leaned out of the truck. "The Rhubarb Festival. They have food there."

Talk about selective hearing. "Elisa," Andi hissed. She hadn't even accepted the invitation yet.

"Come on, Andi. We can make it a business meeting, discuss the work you're doing." He pulled his glasses off and hung them from the corner of his lip—a mannerism that was beginning to grow on her.

Why did she always have to like smart guys?

# Chapter 7

Vance held his breath. Would she agree? He wanted a replay of the Andi he'd seen this morning—lively and flirtatious, especially after the day he'd had. He wanted to see a flash of her hundred-watt smile.

Instead, she cocked her head. "You're the boss," she said, then climbed into her old pickup.

"Stellarific." Vance grinned, though her words didn't hold much encouragement. Still, it was hard to keep a guy down amid the prospect of having dinner—even at a rhubarb festival—in the company of a beautiful woman. Add to that, coming above ground into the real world for a change was almost like watching a meteor impact on Jupiter—a rare, celebratory event even for astronomy geeks.

Truck started and rumbling, Andi rolled down the window and leaned out. "The festival should have a lot of your kind of food, though mostly rhubarb-related, including pies, a carnival, and competitions between the longest stalk and the largest leaf. What more could you want?"

"Rhubarb, huh?" He'd eaten strawberry-rhubarb pie once. Made him sick.

"I don't suppose you know where the Rhubarb Festival is, do you?"

"I've been out of the dungeon and around the block a few times, but can't say that I do."

"Follow me."

"I'm right behind you." Vance pulled his keys out of his pocket and locked the entrance to Ground Zero.

He climbed into his car as Andi turned onto the main road and sped away like she was running from the law. One thing about this part of North Dakota—it was so flat you could see someone coming for miles. He chuckled as he climbed into his car and followed Andi from a distance for several miles and then into town.

He teased her, pulling next to her when the road allowed, and waved. Only Elisa responded. Waiting behind Andi's truck at a red light, he noticed Andi watching him through her rearview mirror.

He'd told her it could be a business dinner—a small twist of the truth. During his day of writing slightly malicious code to slow the misuse of his algorithm, Andi had permeated his thoughts. When he needed to concentrate most, he couldn't shake her smile or her earlier playfulness, though it had lasted all of fifteen seconds. As far as talk of remodeling the missile site, whatever it took to keep her company. Maybe he was only focused on her because she was his primary human contact throughout the day.

Nah. There was more to it than that.

Vance followed her into a parking lot filled with cars. People headed toward what looked like a pavilion-enclosed farmer's market and a small carnival. He waited as Andi and Elisa got out of their truck. Andi gave a tight smile, giving him the impression she'd rather be anywhere else. Or had she and Elisa been at it again?

"How long does this festival last?" he asked.

"Through the weekend. Today's the first day," Elisa said, as they headed toward the pavilion.

There was a small entrance fee of three dollars a person. Vance paid for all three of them despite Andi's protests. They visited several booths featuring various rhubarb recipes, jams and jellies, bread and cookies, and surprisingly, pork roast, stir-fries, and potpies.

Andi bought two slices of pie, one each for her and Elisa, and offered Vance a bite of hers.

The memory of the last time he'd eaten anything rhubarb prickled. "Shouldn't we eat dinner first?"

Andi worked to swallow her mouthful of pie. "I thought you were the king of junk food?"

Vance enjoyed watching Andi stuff her face with pie. "Once in a while, I get hungry for real food."

Music boomed from the nearby carnival. Elisa handed Vance her unfinished pie. "Here, you can have this."

Vance tossed it in the garbage can next to him.

"Hey sis, I see some friends. I'm going to hang out."

Irritation flashed in Andi's eyes. "Oh no you don't."

Elisa glared, then looked at Vance and softened. "But I want to go on the rides."

"We're here because Vance wanted dinner, remember? Some of the restaurants offer sample meals made from rhubarb. Let's walk across the street to the corner of Main and Houser. Otto's has steaks."

Vance grinned, his mouth watering at the thought of prime rib. "Can I get that without rhubarb?"

Andi laughed and the smile Vance liked almost peeked through. Oh yeah, she was definitely loosening up. Once inside Otto's, a hostess showed them to a booth where Andi and Elisa took their seats opposite each other. There was an awkward moment when he needed to decide where to sit.

Finally, he slid next to Elisa, facing Andi. "This way I can see your pretty face."

"Go, Andi. Vance thinks you're pretty," Elisa said.

Rather than killing her sister with a glare, as Vance would have expected, Andi kept her eyes on the menu, though a light shade of pink rose in her cheeks.

Andi shy and embarrassed because of him? Was he delusional that a girl like her could like a guy like him? Or could he relish the twist of heat in his stomach?

The waiter brought their drinks and they ordered. Andi took a sip of her water with lemon. Taking her time, she shared about growing up in the area. In her voice, he heard a sense of pride mingled with past hurts.

"Tell me, how did you end up in North Dakota all the way from Texas?" she asked.

He would have loved to hear more about her, but apparently she was ready to turn the topic to him.

Funny, he couldn't run from thoughts of ANND or Peter even at a Rhubarb Festival. "My college roommate and I had a competition to see who would start his own company first. Four years later, I got a call to work for him in Fargo—that was last year. I think maybe he just wanted to rub my face in it, but I was tired of working as one of hundreds of droids in a large Texas company. Plus, he offered me the opportunity of a lifetime."

Peter had plenty of talented programmers but had wanted Vance to join him. Better to be a big fish in a small pond, Vance's dad always said.

"So what do you do exactly?" Andi asked.

"Let me guess. It has to be something related to computers." Elisa had her back to the wall, sitting sideways in the booth.

Vance laughed. "Why do you say that?"

Their waiter brought their food and set plates before each of them.

Elisa tore a chicken strip in half and dipped it into rhubarb and horseradish sauce. "You just have that look about you."

Vance glanced at Andi, trying to read her. Andi chewed her food while bearing a friendly smirk.

"So, you, too, huh?"

Vance thought he'd seen a subtle nod, but Andi just smiled.

Elisa laughed. "Andi's last boyfriend was a geek."

Andi scoured her sister with her gaze, then she looked at Vance. Fortunately her expression softened. "You never did answer my question. What do you do?"

Vance savored a bite of his medium-rare prime rib. "You know, they really do have some of the best steak in North Dakota. I'll give you that."

"Yeah, I agree. What do you do?" Andi wasn't going to let it go.

He couldn't exactly tell them all the secret stuff. "I work for a data mining company. You were right, too." He glanced at Elisa. "I'm a programmer. I like to call it software engineer—sounds better."

Elisa leaned closer. "What's data mining?"

"Leave the man alone, would you? Let him tell us what he will."

Now she takes that stance. Well this was it. Once he told her everything, she'd write him off. But then again he was leaving, wasn't he?

"In Texas, I worked for one of the largest database computing software firms in the world. We developed software to manage large amounts of data, which required supercomputers. If you think about it, everything we do in this technological age generates data. Data mining, in the simplest of terms, is looking for hidden patterns in the data."

"But why would you want to do that? What do you do with the information?"

"Predict the future," he said, then took another bite of steak, ignoring the baked potato, and chewed.

Elisa laughed. "You're kidding, right?"

"Not entirely. Patterns in the data can reveal future trends. Behavior."

Andi's eyes grew wide and she lowered her fork slowly to her plate. "Like when I receive a catalogue in the mail that I didn't ask for, it's because they decided I'm a potential customer."

Vance nodded his head in a vague motion. "Yes and no. It's more likely you answered a questionnaire somewhere or bought a product that's related to that catalogue—transaction-based data. Still, it's all about the data."

Vance took a sip of his tea.

Andi played with her chicken Caesar salad. "So, in the company you work for now, what kind of data mining do you do? What are you looking for?"

Vance nearly spewed his tea. That wasn't exactly the sort of question he wanted to answer at the moment. He wiped his mouth with a napkin and composed himself, feeling trapped. "Mostly manufacturing applications. Some government applications as well." There. He'd answered without giving too much away.

Elisa leaned closer. "I want to hear about the government stuff. That sounds so exciting. What do they want to know? Who will be the next president?"

*Stellar.* If he kept talking, they'd have him telling them about the confidential contract and the algorithm he'd written. He'd never thought of himself in a cloak-and-dagger situation, but maybe that's exactly what he was in.

"Who would have thought Fargo would be a place for something like that." Andi laid her napkin on her plate.

"As a matter of fact, Fargo-Moorehead is home to several high-tech companies."

Andi's eyes took on that glazed look so familiar to Vance. Disappointment invaded like a virus. Though he'd expected it eventually, it still hurt. He'd be better off with a protective wall like Andi's.

"Let's talk about something else," he said.

⁂

When Vance's eyes took on a distant look, she could tell he was bored with the conversation, even though it was about him. She didn't know enough to ask intelligent questions.

"I'll be right back." She excused herself and headed to the restroom.

In front of the mirror she tried to compose herself, push away the emotions. Listening to Vance talk about his job and his life in Fargo brought images of Jorgen to mind. Vance was no different than Jorgen. Educated. Brilliant. Lived in the city.

When would she get over how much he'd hurt her?

They'd dated through high school, then Jorgen had gone to college ahead of her and she was able to join him for a short period of time until her grandmother died. She'd had to return to take care of Elisa. He no longer had room for her in his life after that. Once he landed a job with a high-tech firm in Fargo he had big plans that didn't include an uneducated wife. She wasn't good enough. Never would be. Who was she kidding? She'd started the business to pay the bills and care for her sister, but she'd also wanted to make something of herself.

No matter how hard she worked, life worked against her. God seemed to bless others, while Andi stood on the sidelines. She finally had a glimmer of hope, at least for her business. But was it enough? Though Vance had brought her the hope, she resented people like him—people who were handed things on a silver platter. People who were able to fulfill their dreams without working hard for them.

Andi released a breath of pent-up jealousy, sagging as she washed her hands. No matter how hard she tried, she was beaten down at every turn, and Jorgen's breakup had almost done her in. But her attitude was wrong. She couldn't blame Vance Young.

She stared at the mirror again, making certain her face appeared free of the turmoil she felt inside. Vance was her client and to let her mind think of him as anything else went beyond professional. It was ridiculous. Still, she couldn't fight the sense that there was something more between them—somehow she had to annihilate the idea.

When she returned to the table, Elisa was trying to talk Vance into tasting the sampling of rhubarb jam. Andi slid into her seat as she watched, wanting to forget about the pain she felt over Jorgen and simply enjoy the faces Vance made.

"You're like a little kid who won't try something new," she teased.

"Who said I haven't tried it? I have, and I remember what it did to my stomach."

Andi peered at him. "It could have been bad rhubarb or bad eggs."

Before Vance could answer, the waiter returned and asked if they wanted dessert. Both Andi and Vance said no, but Elisa piped up. "I do."

Andi shook her head. "You don't need dessert. We had pie, remember?"

"Look, I ordered a small plate so I could save room."

Andi sighed. "Oh, all right. I'll have coffee since I've got to wait for you anyway."

Vance ordered coffee as well. "So, it's my turn to ask a question."

Andi laughed. "I can't imagine what you could possibly ask me that would be of any interest."

That encouraged a snort from Elisa. "And that's the truth."

Hurt but not surprised, Andi stared at her sister. Elisa smiled and looked down. "I'm only teasing, sis." Then to Vance, "She's very interesting. You'll see."

Embarrassed again, Andi said, "All right, that's enough."

"I know you were my uncle's contractor for Ground Zero, but I get the sense that you knew him as much more."

"What makes you say that?"

Andi looked into Vance's sharp eyes. She saw kindness there. Part of her wanted to know him better, much better. Again, she reminded herself it was out of the question.

"You've said a few things here and there. But when you say his name, you speak it with a warm familiarity."

He noticed that? The sensitive way he said the words squeezed her chest. Her heart warmed, sending a soft smile across her lips as she wrapped her hand around her coffee cup.

"I'll prove it to you. Come on, say his name."

"What?" Andi laughed. "You're not kidding, are you?" She cleared her throat. "Mr. Erickson."

"See? You feel something when you say his name."

She felt it all right. A blush up her neck and cheeks at the way Vance could tell how she felt. Her pulse raced under his intense stare. "He was a good man, though a little strange. I think you would have liked him a lot. If you'd had the chance to spend time with him."

"Like you did." Vance worked to fold his napkin into some sort of origami creature.

This guy was astute, able to read people. She had to squash her growing schoolgirl crush on him—yeah, might as well admit it—before he read that, too. He'd figure out her secret hidden at the missile base.

Sooner or later.

"Your uncle knew my grandparents. He bought the farmland and missile site when it became available several years ago after my grandfather died. Seemed like he was around a lot, spending time with my grandmother. After she died and I had to quit school. . ." Andi hadn't meant to reveal that information. A knot formed in her throat.

"Andi." His voice low, he reached over to place his hand over hers. "You had to quit school? I'm so sorry."

Electricity surged up her arm. Andi stared at his hand, then slowly lifted her gaze to his. Tenderness, understanding, and longing were all wrapped together in one searching look.

It scared her. He scared her. She was in no way ready to be vulnerable again.

*Gut it up.* If she didn't harden herself now, it might be too late. "Thanks, but it's okay." She pulled her hand from his and continued her story. "He approached me to do the work and over time I got to know him better. It surprised me to learn he was wealthy. Made me wonder why he stuck around here."

"So you're not against getting to know the people you work with." He appeared to contemplate his words as though thinking out loud.

She couldn't go there. Not now. Not with him. "Your uncle Vance had the inside story on my grandparents. Had been friends with both of them when they were younger. You betcha, I wanted to hear about them."

Vance smiled. "Really?"

"Yeah." Andi nodded. "You see, he'd had a thing for my grandmother. But she was married to my grandfather, of course." *The letter. Tell him about the letter.* Like Vance, she, too, fidgeted with her napkin but nothing so elaborate as an origami space ship.

Vance pushed against his seat back, appearing surprised. "That is completely stellar and shocking news. It explains a lot, really. You're working on the missile site where your grandfather was an airman. I had a feeling you were more than a contractor to my uncle—more like a granddaughter."

Elisa snickered from her corner. "Andi thinks he only hired her because—"

Andi kicked her under the table. "We'd better go. Elisa has school in the morning." She looked for the check but saw nothing.

Vance held it up and grinned. "You're not getting this. Now go. I've got it. You can get it next time."

Andi frowned, though a warmth spread through her. He was getting under her skin way too fast. He was exactly the kind of man she didn't want to allow in. She resolved there wouldn't be a next time.

Deep inside—*sigh*—she really wanted there to be.

# Chapter 8

For the next week, Andi worked with her crew in the equipment building, preparing load-bearing walls for additional floor space in the form of a loft. One of Andi's friends agreed to give Elisa a ride from school each day so Andi wouldn't need to stop work. And when she did, she made sure to avoid Vance, though he seemed to be caught up in a project, albeit computer-related, of his own.

Once, she caught a glimpse of his somber expression and it worried her more than she had a right to be. She'd itched to drop next to him on the sofa to see what bothered him and imagined listening to him explain his work in what would sound like a foreign language to her. Then, all her insecurities would come crashing down. Why couldn't she just get over what Jorgen had done to her? Why did she believe he was right about her?

Again, she reminded herself, Vance was her client, nothing more, and she intended to keep her distance.

Quitting for the day, Lars and Karl said their good-byes, then took the elevator up. Andi should stop, too, but she wanted to spend a few minutes searching for the elusive item her grandfather hid decades before. The closer she came to finishing this job, the more her hopes sank that she'd ever recover it or that it had even remained undisturbed.

Tired all the way to her bones, her muscles ached and so did her head. As she pondered what to do next, Elisa's laughter drifted through the tunnel.

That was it, then. After gathering her tools into her tool bag, she headed down the tunnel to get Elisa. Soft voices replaced the laughter. Andi peered through the door to see her sister mesmerized, hanging on every word Vance uttered.

Andi's breath caught in her throat. She lowered her tool bag to the floor.

Arms folded, she straddled the blast door frame and leaned against it, watching, listening. Her sister was actually interested in the conversation. Did Elisa only act the rebellious teenager while with her? The truth hurt. But then again, that would mean there was more than enough hope for her sister. For them.

Vance pointed out various parts of his telescope, explaining them. His eyes shone with love for the hobby. Funny thing was, so did her sister's. He'd extracted Elisa from her self-inflicted shell of a bad attitude. Amazing. Another crack in Andi's defenses. It was one thing to harden herself when his tactics were aimed at her, but getting her sister excited about astronomy—why would she put a stop to that?

She observed them, unnoticed from her perch.

"Oh yeah, star clusters, swirling galaxies, nebulae are all there to show us how big God is..."

Andi became lost in her own thoughts while listening to his soothing voice and watching Elisa's vivid expression and shining eyes. She'd not done a good job of raising her sister these last couple of years. Regret clung to her.

Still, Vance...he'd changed things, stirring life into her sister in only a few days. Stirring something else into Andi. If only she could bury her heart much deeper, like the launch control center was buried in the ground with shock absorbers to protect against attacks. She almost laughed at the image.

As though she'd laughed out loud and given herself away, Vance looked up from the telescope, directly into her eyes, pinning her with the intensity of his gaze. Without moving, he stared for what seemed far too long. She could live in the warmth of his hazel-eyed gaze forever. Wanting to shake free, she stepped all the way into the room. That did the trick.

Elisa's demeanor returned to her normal flippancy, hammering the nail of disappointment into Andi. By stepping into the room, she'd destroyed the magic.

"Don't mind me. I still have work to do," she lied.

*ℒ♥*

Vance witnessed Elisa's wall go up the instant she realized her sister had caught her interest in astronomy. And Andi was quick to recover from what looked like disappointment by sliding a hard protective shell over her face before she left.

*What is it with these women?* He wasn't a therapist, but if he were to salvage the light he'd seen in both of them, he'd have to work fast. "I'll show you the stars tonight, if you'd like."

Elisa's eyes brightened again. "You will?"

"Sure." Vance looked at his watch. "It's almost six now. Would nine thirty work?"

Andi peeked through the doorway again, this time a smile cracking open the armor. Vance would have winked but didn't want to risk losing Elisa's enthusiasm again.

Suddenly, Elisa frowned. "I doubt Andi will let me."

"Since when has that ever stopped you?" Andi came to stand next to them. "Vance wants to show me the stars."

*Uh-oh.* The way she said it...

Vance realized that Elisa might have misinterpreted his intentions. "And you, too, Andi, if you're interested."

He held his breath, waiting for her answer.

She looked thoughtful, took her time—he'd bet to torture him—then, "Yeah, I'd like that very much." She pulled Elisa to her in a hug. "We'd like it very much. Thanks."

The look in her eyes sent radiant heat rushing through him—a stellar eruption on his star chart. Well, at least he'd discovered one way to breach her walls. But with the discovery came a disturbing uncertainty. Just what did he think he was doing?

He squashed it. No point in disrupting the joy fest.

Elisa relaxed in Andi's embrace. At least he'd been wrong that Elisa's fascination was more with him than the stars. He almost chuckled at the momentary delusion.

"I'll see you back here at dark?"

Smile beaming, Andi released Elisa. "That sounds fine. We'd better grab some dinner."

"Listen, I'd invite you to eat—"

Andi held up her hand and laughed. "We need something of real sustenance. Not the junk food you manage to survive on. Thanks, but no."

Elisa snapped her fingers. "Hey, I know. Why don't you let my sister cook for you?"

A subtle frown crossed Andi's face.

Vance shook his head, hoping to spare her. "I have a few things to do. But thanks for the invitation."

"Maybe some other time." Tool bag slung over her shoulder, Andi waved and tugged Elisa behind her.

He watched them head out the blast door—a sight he dreaded every night. Andi had a way of livening up the place. Granted, it was mostly the construction noise that kept him company, but since they'd moved into the equipment building, he couldn't hear as much of it.

Smiling, he rummaged through the freezer in search of a microwave meal. Strange he preferred them instead of the survival food in the storage closet. Was there really much difference?

*Who cares?* In a few hours he'd be staring at the stars with Andi Nielsen. It was every geek's dream, or at least this geek's. And he fairly glowed inside at the idea of sparking an interest in a troubled teen, and even better that it helped Andi.

Maybe she'd come to appreciate him. Hating to get his hopes up, he sighed.

He placed a Mexican dinner in the microwave. What was he thinking, allowing any attachment to the woman? His time here would end soon enough, and then he'd be like every other jerk and leave. But he couldn't help himself. He'd seen something—no matter how small—in her eyes that encouraged him to try. Something he'd never seen before, not even in Janice.

An hour before Andi and Elisa were to arrive, Vance was nervous as a schoolboy. He couldn't remember the last time he'd been able to share his love for the stars with someone. Nor could he imagine anyone he'd rather share it with. A seed of doubt pricked at him. Did Andi really want to look at the stars? Or had she agreed only to encourage her sister's interest? He'd been so caught up in the idea of stargazing that he hadn't considered the possibility.

But he refused to let it dampen his spirits. He slathered himself with mosquito repellent. If there was one thing he'd learned, you needed armor against the onslaught of mosquitoes in North Dakota. The cold of summer nights bothered him more than it seemed to affect the mosquitoes. After repellent, he pulled a fleece sweatshirt over long sleeves, then donned a ball cap and a vest with plenty of pockets. As he prepared for the night sky, he prayed he could open up a world of wonder for both Andi and her sister.

Once he found the perfect spot for stargazing he set up his telescope, then rolled out a blanket on the ground and waited. Vance glanced at his watch. Nine forty-five. He frowned. What if something came up and they couldn't make it? He reclined on the blanket and stared up into the sky like he used to do when he was a kid, imagining himself soaring through outer space, through the stars, wishing he could be a Jedi knight. North Dakota was certainly flat enough that a person could block all other images out. No light pollution whatsoever out here. Perfect.

"You look comfy." Andi's face appeared in his line of vision.

He jumped up.

"Sorry we're late." She glanced back at Elisa, who jogged toward them.

"No problem. Everything's ready."

With a strange grin, Andi scanned him from head to toe with her flashlight. "What *are* you wearing?" She burst out laughing.

Vance spread out his arms and looked to see what she found so funny.

"You're swathed in designer outerwear." Andi circled him, looking him over.

Embarrassed, Vance tugged off the vest, allowing himself a laugh as well. "When you shop in a Dallas sports store, gearing up for the North Dakota climate, this is what they tell you to wear."

Andi laughed heartily at that.

"Let's just say I wanted to be prepared."

"I've learned something about you." She cuffed his cap. "You like to shop."

Feeling defensive, Vance added, "There's not much else to do in a city that has more square footage of shopping than Manhattan."

"Uh-huh." Andi collapsed on the blanket. "So show us the stars, city boy."

Elisa giggled.

And there it was, the playful Andi that Vance had hoped to see again for over a week now. "There's a lot you can see without my telescope. As long as you have dark skies. That's key."

Elisa stood near the telescope. "What about a mountaintop? Wouldn't that be best?"

"Well, I don't see many of those around here." He pointed at the sky. "Can you identify any constellations?"

"Um, no."

"Look. There's Libra."

"Well, what about something more exciting? Everyone knows about constellations."

"Coming right up. Let me explain a few things first. I don't want you to be disappointed at what you see. This won't be like those pictures from the Hubble."

"What's the Hubble?"

Vance stifled the sigh. What did they teach these kids in school? "It's a giant telescope that orbits earth, which allows it to view the universe without interference from earth's atmosphere. But you can't see those types of images from a small telescope like mine." No matter how expensive it was.

"Hey, don't apologize," Andi offered.

"Still there's an advantage. The stars are like diamonds and, well. . .you'll have to see for yourself."

Vance looked through the eyepiece and adjusted it. "I'm looking at Jupiter right now. Actually, you can see it with the naked eye. But with a telescope, you can see the moons. Or at least a couple of them tonight." Vance stepped aside, allowing Elisa access to the telescope.

Elisa peered through the eyepiece. "That's cool. It doesn't look like it does in those science book pictures. It looks more like. . .a whole world!" Excitement emanated from her voice.

"I've always wanted to know how stars get their names." From the blanket, Andi gazed upward, looking thoughtful. . .and beautiful as. . .*a glimmering star. . .*

The small light that flickered inside of him when she was around began glowing brighter. But it wouldn't do to appear like some goggle-eyed schoolboy. "IAU. International Astronomical Union. They use the Greek letters, naming stars according to their brightness and constellations where they reside. For instance, Alpha Centauri."

"Let me guess. The first star in the Centaurus constellation?" Andi asked.

Vance cut a glance her way, surprised at her quick response. "Yep, it's the brightest. You're a smart one, but then I never doubted that."

Andi rose from the blanket and moved next to Elisa, nudging her. "Okay, it's my turn to look now."

"Wait." Vance adjusted the telescope and peered through the eyepiece, tapping it gently. "This is a globular cluster."

"A what?" both women asked.

For the next few minutes, Vance enjoyed answering their questions, sharing his love of the stars.

Eventually, all three of them reclined on the blanket and stared at the night sky—diamond-laden black velvet. Vance couldn't remember when he'd been happier. Why did he have to have the trouble with his job?

"Since you enjoy the wide-open sky, no wonder you don't like living underground." Andi sounded relaxed, though sadness remained in her voice. "Tell me, when did you first become interested in the stars?"

Vance had hoped she would ask. "For as long as I can remember, I've loved to look at the night sky. It makes me realize how small I am compared to the universe. And to think that the Creator of this universe cares about us, cares about me even though I'm tiny in comparison. He cares about the smallest sparrow."

An uncomfortable quiet filled the air, contrasting the previous relaxed atmosphere. Vance pushed past the growing anxiety that he'd ruined the mood by simply bringing God into it. But how could he not? "There's a star that's 650 times the diameter of our sun. In other words, if it was our sun, its mass would encompass all the planets out to the orbit of Mars. Imagine that!"

"What's it called?"

"Betelgeuse."

"Beetlejuice? Like the movie?" Andi rolled on her side and propped on her elbow.

"Yeah, it's hard to comprehend. Like standing deep in a large cavern. You can't see how large it is," Elisa said, almost reverently.

"Back to God. I'm not so sure that the Creator of the universe really cares about us like that, I mean every little detail of our life. How could He?" Andi asked.

"That's just it. The universe shows how awesome and big He is. And yet, He's able to care for even the smallest in His creation. It's mind-bending."

Andi sat up and began picking up their things. "I can't buy that."

"You're leaving already?" To Vance, they'd only just started. He enjoyed the deep thoughts about God that always seemed to result from staring at the stars. He stood. How could he be sorry for talking about God?

Andi nodded, sadness in her eyes. "Remember, it's a school night. We should get going."

Vance folded the blanket, attempting to shove aside the pain that seeped too deep for him to say a word in response.

# Chapter 9

As they drove down the dark highway, Andi could feel her sister's tension.

"What was that about?" Elisa sounded close to tears.

"What?"

"It was just getting good and you jumped up to leave. It was...weird."

"It's a school night. You knew we couldn't stay long."

"Who cares about school? I learned a lot more tonight than I ever have in school."

Andi sighed. "I don't want to get into an argument."

Bright headlights beamed toward them as a lone car passed. Andi focused on the road since the other driver hadn't dimmed his lights. She wasn't sure why she'd had the urge to leave. Maybe the conversation was getting too serious.

Once back at home, Andi listened to her phone messages. "Elisa, you have a message from Todd. Who is he?"

Elisa came out of the bathroom, brushing her teeth, eyes wide. She ran back in and returned, having rinsed out her mouth. "Todd called? What did he say?"

"Something about going out tonight." Andi wished she hadn't told Elisa.

"Are you serious?" Elisa grabbed the phone from Andi.

"What do you think you're doing? You're not going anywhere, and you're not calling boys." Grandma had drilled that rule into Andi, but Andi hadn't often obeyed. She could see Elisa wasn't much different. "Besides, it's after ten. It's rude to call people so late."

"Just because you can't keep a boyfriend, doesn't mean you have to keep me from having one."

Andi's planted her hands on her hips. "Excuse me?"

"You heard me. Just because Jorgen dumped you, you don't think you're good enough for anyone. You're jealous of me. You don't want me to be good enough either."

Andi was almost too incensed for words, as fury and hurt stabbed her insides. "What happened with him has nothing to do with this. Or with you."

"Doesn't it? I see that Vance has eyes for you, but you won't let him get close. You don't want anyone to get close to me either. That's why you won't let me have fun anymore. You watch me like I'm your prisoner. I wish I didn't live here with you." Tears filled Elisa's eyes and she rushed away from Andi, slamming the bedroom door.

Andi dragged herself to the kitchen table and slid into a chair. Numb with pain, she put her head in her hands. How dare her sister speak to her that way. She'd lost Jorgen because she'd left school, and she'd left school for Elisa.

But. . .

Part of Elisa's accusation was true. Jorgen had hurt Andi more than by simply breaking off their relationship—he'd made her feel like she wasn't good enough, nor would she ever be. For some reason, she'd taken Jorgen's proclamation over her life to heart, and she wouldn't give someone else the chance to hurt her like that. Ever again.

Elisa had seen right to the heart of the matter. A cold draft wafted over Andi, and she rubbed her arms. It was one thing to carry that burden, but to make Elisa carry it, too?

For Elisa's sake, Andi had given up her own dreams. Why couldn't Elisa see that part of the equation? Elisa had the chance to make something of herself, and she wouldn't have to quit school for anyone or any reason.

Guilt throbbed inside. Could Andi be forcing her own dreams on Elisa? Or was she punishing her? Lost in thought, Andi rose from the kitchen chair, then prepared for bed, though she knew she wouldn't sleep. Instead, she laid her head on her pillow, wide awake.

Vance had spoken of the Creator of the universe, caring for people and all the details of their lives. But she didn't feel like He cared. At least not about her. Without any help from God, she took care of herself and Elisa. She protected them from people who had the ability to destroy their lives.

People like Jorgen who'd given her up for superficial reasons. People like Vance. Elisa's words filtered through her thoughts. *"Vance has eyes for you."*

She thought she'd kept the door to her heart—a blast door—tightly sealed. But somehow Vance Young had shaken it loose. She'd have to slam it shut again—the thought bringing an ache to her heart.

How did Vance feel? Was he lonely, too, shut up in the darkness of the underground capsule? If she closed the door on possibilities, all she'd have would be the chilling prospect of a lonely future.

But Vance wasn't lonely—he had God. She sensed that for Vance, looking at the stars brought him closer to God.

"God of the universe, if You really do care about the little things in my life, show me. Help me get over this pain."

*And please help me find the treasure my grandfather hid.*

᪾

Vance spent the next week amid the distant sounds of construction and renovation, hammering on his keyboard and testing a program to render the rogue algorithm he'd discovered ineffective. It would take them—whoever they were—time to discover what had happened, then even more time to fix things. In turn, Vance would have time to learn what exactly was going on, and hopefully he'd have concrete evidence to present to the authorities—evidence that didn't lead to him as the principal architect and instigator.

The quandary he'd yet to resolve was how and where to install the new algorithm.

Thankfully, his concentration on the problem took his mind off Andi. She'd come and gone every day without much interaction with him—a simple hello if he saw her in the morning and, if he were lucky, a good-bye at the end of the day.

She'd distanced herself even further from him the night they'd looked at the stars. Any hopes she'd have an interest in him beyond their business relationship had disappeared like a Mars space probe. Should he give up altogether? A more important question loomed. Their paths had crossed, but their lives were largely perpendicular—why would he allow himself feelings for her when he planned to sell Ground Zero? Planned to leave? It was part of their agreement. Not like he could back out of that.

He had to admit—he had second thoughts about leaving. He credited Andi with that. A somber realization struck him. Could he stop his growing feelings for her even if he tried?

His thoughts went back to the contentment he'd felt the night they'd looked at the stars together. The night sky sans light pollution on the lonesome prairie had given way to an extraordinary stargazing experience like nothing he'd known before. He'd been able to share that with Andi and Elisa. Though they seemed as enamored with the stars as Vance, neither of them had spoken to him about that night.

Probably for the best.

He forced his attention back to his computer screen. The landline phone rang, the interruption annoying him as he glanced at the clock. Four o'clock already? No one ever called on the thing.

"Vance here."

"Can you please give my sister a message?" Elisa's voice sounded shaky.

"What, no 'hello, Vance'?"

"She forgot to pick me up from school. She insisted on doing that today so she can keep me in her own private prison. Just tell her not to worry about me, I got a ride." She hung up.

Vance whistled. Where did Elisa find the energy to be so livid? He scratched his chin, then headed for the fridge, grabbing a soda to fuel his thoughts as he considered Andi. She'd find out soon enough, of course, that Elisa had found a ride home. Still, that wasn't like Andi. She tried way too hard to prove herself a responsible guardian for Elisa. Too bad Elisa couldn't see how much Andi loved her.

Vance blew out a long breath. The sound of construction stopped awhile ago. Why hadn't he noticed? He decided to go above ground to see if she was there along with the crew who usually quit for the day about now. Just to be sure.

Taking the stairs like he'd done every day that week, he noticed a great improvement in his stamina. He wasn't nearly as breathless as he stepped into the sunlight. He shielded his eyes, though the sun had long passed its blinding zenith by this time of day. Karl, Lars, and a new man Vance hadn't noticed before were loading items into the back of their trucks.

"Hey, why do you bother taking that stuff home every night only to bring it back the next day?" Vance asked.

Chuckling, Lars exchanged a look with his brother. "There's plenty that remains underground, in case you haven't noticed."

"Yeah, besides that, my wife's got me reworking the kitchen cabinets," Karl said.

"So, you finish up here only to have to work at home."

"If it makes the missus happy, it's worth it." Karl winked.

The new sub backed up and drove away onto the main road.

Vance noticed Andi's truck was still there. "Say, have you seen the boss today?"

Karl raised an eyebrow. "Haven't seen her in a couple of hours. Frankly, I thought she was talking to you."

Lars laughed and stared at Vance, with one of those knowing smiles—a subtle insinuation. Apparently the brothers thought Vance and Andi had something romantic in the works. Maybe they knew something he didn't, though not likely.

"I haven't seen her all day," Vance said.

The brothers grew serious and shared a glance.

"We'd better go check on her," Lars said.

"So, are you really worried about her?" Vance hurried after them. "You don't think something could have happened, do you? Her sister called. She was supposed to pick her up."

Vance joined them on the elevator.

"There are a couple of places that a person wouldn't want to fall into."

"What?" Vance's gut tightened as he looked from one brother to the other. "What places?"

"No point in borrowing trouble." Karl shrugged.

"Yeah, she's probably looking around by herself like she always does after we leave."

"Looking around? For what?" How did they know she looked around after they left if they were gone? Odd.

Neither brother answered, but Vance didn't miss their shared glance.

While they waited for the doors to open, the thought that Andi could be hurt somewhere on the missile launch center crept over Vance. He shoved it away. Like Karl said, no point in borrowing trouble. But if something had happened to her...

His concerns over his job and the tricky game he played with the algorithm meant nothing to him. He had to find Andi, make sure she was all right. She already meant way too much to him. Never mind that she'd built a barrier he couldn't seem to scale and that it was obvious she and God weren't on good terms.

At the moment, he cared about nothing except finding her.

# Chapter 10

Andi wanted to say a few distasteful words she'd heard from construction crews but bit her lip instead. After the guys had gone up, she'd climbed into an air plenum, looking for her grandfather's hidden prize. The air plenum had been secured with screws, which she'd heartily dismantled to allow herself entry. Then she'd heard a slow scraping followed by a heavy thud. At the time, intent on her search, she'd thought nothing of it. But later, when she'd tried to back out of the space, it suddenly dawned on her. Something had fallen—probably sheetrock—blocking her escape.

After several unsuccessful attempts at pushing away the object that held her captive, she gave up. If they found her—no, *when* they found her—she'd never live this down.

Though embarrassment crashed against her, there was no way around it—she'd have to call for help.

Andi yelled, feeling as though her cries didn't go much beyond the walls imprisoning her. Unfortunately, the only chance she had of being heard would be if someone were in the equipment building capsule.

"Oh no." Andi pressed her forehead against the wall. She'd missed picking up Elisa. Hope lay in that disruption—that is, if Elisa cared that Andi hadn't shown up to get her.

Andi wished she could at least sit or lie down. Even though it was an air plenum, the space was too small for her to do much but stand. The air became stuffy, her body sticky with sweat. She didn't want to stay here all night.

After minutes ticked into an hour, her humiliation gave way to panic.

A nervous laugh escaped, precluding a whimper. She thought of Vance's reaction if he were stuck in this small space. But she couldn't imagine him wedging himself into such a precarious position.

"Andi. . .Andi?" Vance's voice echoed from somewhere nearby.

"In here! Vance, I'm in here!"

A few seconds later, she heard Vance groan, then heave. Again, then several times more she heard his efforts accompanied with panting. Andi pushed the wall plate she'd dismantled as relief flowed through her. The plate gave way. Vance's face appeared in her line of vision, as he tugged the wall out of her path.

She smiled, defying the torrent of embarrassment and relief entwining her, and stepped out of the compartment. "Oh, thank—" Shaky legs gave way as her knees buckled under her.

"Andi!" Vance swept her against him, steadying her. "Are you all right?"

His words were breathy, laced with concern.

She allowed herself a moment, relishing his embrace. All comfort and strength, his heart beat rapidly. He felt so good.

Breathing a sigh, she became aware she'd stayed too long and stepped free.

"Yes, I think so." She stood as tall as she could and faced her humiliation. She'd shown herself weak, practically collapsing into his arms. What sort of ninny was she?

"Looks like all that sheetrock fell over and wedged you into that space." Vance peered into where she'd been trapped. "What on earth were you doing in there?"

This was the part where Andi should tell him she was searching for something her grandfather supposedly hid. But sharing that information on the heels of what just happened might give Vance all the reason he needed to shut her down, keeping her from searching.

"Well, what do you think? I need to know what is behind every cavity, every nook and cranny, every hidden space in order to make this an efficient living area." There. Her answer had been confident because it was true. Under most circumstances. She stared back, looking into his searching gaze, glad he knew nothing about construction.

Or did he?

He smiled, but wariness lurked in his eyes. "I'm just glad you're all right. But let your crew do that sort of thing for you next time, will you?"

Funny. He hadn't made her feel like an idiot for getting stuck. On the contrary, he appeared concerned. Very concerned. And she'd worked hard this past week to avoid him and his God talk. Now she wondered why. Being with him made her feel good inside. Though he was brilliant, he never made her feel ignorant, or less than him. Never spoke to her in a condescending way.

Holding out his hand, he said, "If you're ready, I'll escort you up top."

She laughed as she took it. "Is that to make sure I leave?"

His gaze lingered before he replied. "I never like to see you leave."

What did he mean?

"Well, if you don't mind, I want to use your restroom and wash my hands. I feel grimy. Oh, and I need to call Elisa."

"You can thank her. She called to say she'd found a way home, but she wasn't happy that you weren't there to pick her up."

"And that's when you became concerned?"

Vance nodded.

Andi's heart warmed. She realized they were still holding hands.

"So you found her!" Karl and Lars stepped into the room, beaming with relieved smiles. Their gaze flitted to Andi and Vance, holding hands. She quickly released his, but not fast enough.

Lars chuckled. "Well, looks like everything is under control down here.

We'd better head home."

After Andi refreshed herself she headed up top, leaving Vance to his computer. From there, she called Elisa.

She got no answer and huffed. Climbing into her truck, she noticed Vance standing there, watching. "Are you checking on me again?"

"I thought I might."

How she loved his Texas accent and wished she had an excuse to stay longer. But Elisa was waiting.

Once at home, Andi walked into the house. "Elisa?"

A quiet and empty house greeted her.

*⌇*

How had Andi gotten herself into that predicament? Though relieved, Vance remained concerned for her well-being as she continued work on the missile site. But then, was there any line of work that was safe? As his thoughts returned to his own problems, he recognized that he was putting himself into a precarious position, too.

Vance munched on a bag of sour cream potato chips, then washed them down with a cola. He'd remotely searched the ANND Systems computers for all versions of his algorithm, finding nothing out of the ordinary. The one thing he had going for him was that he'd known Peter a very long time. That was to his partner's disadvantage. No wonder he'd wanted Vance away. Vance guessed that Peter was running a parallel system, within the mainframe—a system that Vance wouldn't know to look for unless, of course, he had a reason.

Should he do it, or should he not? The moral dilemma of the day.

He crumpled the empty bag of potato chips and shot for the garbage can across the room. Missed. His aim was lousy these days, in more ways than one. He'd created the new program, now what did he do with it?

*Stellar.*

Vance had always prided himself on seeing things as either black or white. Something was either right or it was wrong. But he'd entered a situation—partly of his own making—in which things were blurred, morphing into a dull gray. If a parallel system were running a rogue version of Vance's algorithm, then he had to know about it, he had to stop it. There was only one way to find out and that was by logging on to Peter's account. If said system existed, then Peter was certainly in on it. Vance should have done this to begin with. But he'd put it off, not wanting to face reality.

But D-day was upon him. With a heavy heart Vance released a long, slow breath.

Several weeks ago while in Peter's office, Vance had noticed Peter's last password. It had been written on a Post-it note and stuck on the inside edge of the desk. Vance hadn't intended to see it, but he couldn't miss it, and once he'd seen, it was forever written in his memory. The guy had changed it by now—but it told Vance everything he needed to know. If he'd learned anything about his former college roommate, he knew how he selected passwords. The sticky pad told Vance he hadn't changed his method.

Peter used acronyms based on activities he enjoyed. That, plus four numbers tacked on the end. They were always the same four numbers—5624. That was the problem with passwords. They had to be something a person could remember, so switching the numbers around made no sense. But add them to a new word and you had a strong password. At least against cyber attacks.

Vance made a list of Peter's activities and from those created acronyms, then tagged Peter's four numbers at the end. Like any fail-safe system, ANND allowed three attempts. Satisfied that he'd included as many acronyms as possible, Vance sat back and closed his eyes, relaxing. He wanted to pray for God's help, but he didn't feel right about asking God in on his somewhat uncouth activity. That thought alone should tell him to stop.

Vance pulled up the login for ANND Systems and with nervous fingers entered in his first attempt.

*Unsuccessful.*

A rush of moisture slammed his palms.
He entered the second password.

*Unsuccessful.*

Heart pounding, he slumped against the sofa back. He wasn't wired for covert activities.

Closing his eyes, he remembered his last conversation with Peter in the boardroom, with Carolyn hanging close to Peter, practically clinging to him. Peter had dated several women in the office—ANND had no policy against interoffice romance, resulting in at least two married couples. Carolyn was his latest. No one seemed concerned about harassment. Natasha, Sybil, Angela, Vespa, and Carolyn. NSAVC. Vance sat up. Could that be it?

He wondered, though, if Carolyn's initial should be included or not. The guess was as good as any. He typed in NSAVC5624. Almost too many letters. He swallowed and, despite his hesitation, sent up a silent prayer, then pressed the login button.

*Welcome, Peter Lundgren.*

"Yes." Vance pumped his arm.

Because he was after only one thing, he avoided looking at anything else on Peter's account. He scrolled through files to systems manager and opened it. Two systems appeared. Vance opened the one he'd been unaware of, searching for his algorithm.

There. A sick feeling hit the middle of his stomach. He ignored it, putting his mind to quickly creating a new username and password that would give him access to the parallel system. He then logged out of Peter's account. The less time he spent on Peter's account the less likely someone would notice the unauthorized access.

Using his newly created account, Vance logged in again. What he was about to do would eventually be discovered. He hoped his plan worked.

The phone rang. Vance kept his eyes on the screen while the program loaded, watching for any glitches. "Vance here."

"It's Andi."

The nervous edge in her voice put Vance on alert. "What is it?"

"Elisa's gone."

# Chapter 11

W hat do you mean?" Vance asked.

This was awkward. It wasn't any of his concern. Really. But Andi had already called Shawna next door. She hadn't seen her sister. But Elisa *had* called and spoken to Vance. Maybe she'd told Vance something.

Andi tried to calm her voice. "She wasn't at home when I got here. I can't locate her at any of the usual places. What exactly did she say when she called?"

"Give me a sec."

Andi paced her kitchen, waiting for his answer. She sprayed air freshener around the stale-smelling room, then knocked over a cup, spilling coffee.

"Just that she was getting a ride home and not to worry about her."

"That's all?"

"Yeah, but she was pretty incensed. . .oh wait, she did say something about your keeping her in prison."

Andi huffed. "Leave it to her to put a spin on everything."

"Listen, Andi. What can I do to help?"

"I. . .uh. . ."What could he do? "I just needed to know if she'd told you she was going somewhere. I'm sure she's fine."

"I'm coming over. I can help you look."

She cleared her throat. "That's not necessary. I didn't want to bother you but had hoped you might know something."

"I probably have your address written down somewhere, but what is it again?"

"Vance. . ." She hesitated, realizing she'd carried a small twinge of hope. Just being with him lifted her spirit. And that's exactly why she had to avoid him. "You don't have to do that."

"I need to get out for some air. Besides, I care about your sister."

*What about me?* The unwelcome thought irked her.

Still, bringing Vance into the equation would defuse an explosive situation, that is, once she found Elisa. Her sister liked him, opened up to him. Ready to detonate, Andi steadied her voice. "Four fifty-five Glenwood."

"See you in a few."

Andi cleaned up the spilled coffee, cleared the counters, and loaded the dishwasher, but her mind was far from these tasks. She and her sister hadn't spoken much to each other since their argument a few days before—the night they'd gone stargazing with Vance.

*"You watch me like I'm your prisoner. I wish I didn't live here with you."*

Elisa's words bombarded her. At the time, Andi had taken them for an idle threat. But what if it wasn't?

Gazing out the kitchen window, Andi thought about the possibility. Had Elisa run away? It was clear that Elisa was completely miserable, but wasn't that the way of things? Andi wasn't all that happy either, but at Elisa's age, kids were pretty self-absorbed.

Shaking her head, she sighed. She wouldn't put it past Elisa to pull a stunt like this, considering everything else she'd done. Andi hung her head over the sink, fighting back tears. Once again, God wasn't there for her, for them.

Wouldn't it be nice if she could simply wish upon a star—one of the brightest shimmering in the sky like she'd seen the other night—and have her wish answered? Why couldn't God work like a wishing star?

She had to be strong and fix this problem—as usual, on her own. Having a talent for fixing things, she'd started her business for that very reason. Unfortunately, that talent didn't extend to family problems or she'd have resolved hers long ago. But she had to try.

Now she wished she'd not allowed Vance to come. Rather than wait for him, she could be driving around town, looking for Elisa. She listened to the messages on the house phone and cell phone voice mail one more time while she glanced around for a note Elisa might have left.

Her room! If Elisa had run away, she'd have taken a bag of clothes. Things remaining in place would go a long way to drive the worry from Andi's mind. She opened Elisa's door and flipped on the light. The bed was askew, nothing new there. Clothes spilled from the too full closet. Andi relaxed a little.

A sudden pang of regret for their bad fortune in losing family and being on their own pummeled her. Elisa was probably safe somewhere, but the remote thought that she wasn't unsettled Andi. She began picking up the clutter. A surge of love ran through her. She wanted to do better. Had to.

*Lord, please bring her home safely, and help me to be a better sister and guardian. I'm asking for Elisa, not for myself.*

She'd added the last part to be sure God heard her. He had a soft spot for children, didn't He? Grandma had made sure she got to Sunday school at least some of the time. Though Elisa was probably closer to an adult now than a child, Andi remembered something about Jesus wanting the little children near Him.

A knock on the door jolted her. Elisa? Andi fairly ran from the room. Elisa would have come through the door without knocking though.

Unless she'd forgotten her key.

Hands in pockets, Vance stood on the porch with a muted grin.

"Hi there." At seeing him, Andi tugged her hair back into her usual ponytail.

He sent her an odd look, resulting in flutters to her insides. "Hey. Any luck finding her?"

Andi frowned. "Nope. Come on in."

Vance meandered through the small foyer, following Andi into the living room. "What's the plan then?"

Andi rubbed her forehead. "You know, I feel ridiculous having you come all this way. I should have just driven around town. She could be anywhere that kids hang out."

"She doesn't have a cell phone?"

Andi swallowed and looked at her hands. "It seems such a small thing now. But no. . . I didn't want to spend the money, and we live in such a small town, it didn't seem necessary." Number one on her list to do better.

"Who've you called?"

"The parents of her friends and even the few friends whose cell numbers I have before calling you. No one has seen her." Now that she'd said the words out loud. . . Andi sank to the couch.

Vance sat next to her. "Don't panic. You stay here to answer the phone and wait for Elisa. I'll drive around town."

She eyed him, wary yet hopeful. "You'd. . .do that?"

"Of course."

"But I can't just sit here."

"Of course you can. And I'll do more. I'll pray."

Andi hoped his prayers would do more good than hers. "Thanks."

Though she appreciated his words, she shook her head and looked away. Why was she letting herself get worked up? If they hadn't had that stupid argument. . .

*

Vance walked to the door. "Stay calm. She's all right."

*At least until Andi gets her hands on her.* Then Andi would explode, of that Vance had no doubt. He closed the door, leaving Andi sitting on the sofa, looking forlorn. He jumped in his car and backed from the drive of the small ranch house.

"Lord, You have Elisa in the palm of Your hands, so just keep her safe. Let me find her. Please."

As Vance drove down Main Street, it occurred to him that maybe God had sent him all the way to North Dakota to help this family. An arrogant thought, at that. But he cared about them both—Elisa and Andi. . .well, Andi made his insides feel too strange for comfort, but in a good way. And if there weren't any coincidences, then what else could he think? Still, he had to tread carefully. He had every intention of leaving once his long vacation was up. And go where? He didn't know that yet, but one problem at a time. One thing he knew as a software engineer—structure was everything. First things first.

Tonight's problem apparently had to do with a lost teenager. First he'd tackled the local fast food joints. Dairy Queen, Burger King, McDonald's, and the local taco place. He smiled. Dairy Queen was a Texas-born company, but apparently Taco Bell execs—out of San Antonio—hadn't gotten their claws into this small town in North Dakota yet.

Vance drove into the shopping center parking lot, looking at the young people coming in and out of the store, some loitering, then to the nearby coffee kiosk. On a hunch, he drove through the kiosk window and ordered an iced caramel macchiato with an extra shot.

"Say, do you know Elisa Nielsen?"

The kid shook his head. "Sorry."

Vance frowned. The town was bigger than he thought. "Where do kids go in this town to hang out?"

"You got me. I'm here all the time."

Vance tipped the guy. "Keep up the good work, then."

He chugged the sugary, caffeine-loaded drink, hoping to fire his neurons. The last thing he wanted was to go home empty-handed to Andi.

*Home?* He blew out a breath. What was he thinking?

Elisa had talked about some guy from school that she liked, saying he was smart. Vance leaned his head against the seat and squeezed his eyes. What was his name again? Todd. Todd something. Had Andi called his house? He wasn't sure she even knew about the boy. Elisa always clammed up about him when Andi walked through the room. The guy had a name similar to an actor's. That's all Vance could remember. Using his smartphone, he scanned the Internet for actors.

*Tom Cruise!* That's it. He dialed information and called all three Crews families, asking for Todd. Once he found the correct residence he asked for Elisa. She answered, cautious rebellion in her voice. Vance wanted to put her at ease—a big brother, on her side. On his way there he phoned Andi to let her know he'd found Elisa and that she'd been studying. He hoped it was enough to defuse the bomb.

When Vance pulled up to the curb next to the Crews home, Elisa, carrying a couple of textbooks, came out of the house but turned to speak to a boy in the doorway. Vance waited patiently, thinking about how vulnerable Andi was where her sister was concerned. What could he say to Elisa without causing more strain between the two?

Elisa finally opened the door to his car. Her smile, as she stepped in, was tight. "So, Andi sent *you....*" She looked out the passenger window. "Too busy to pick me up herself," she mumbled.

Vance heard the hurt she carried. Never finding himself in this position before, he was surprised at how quickly a lecture formed in his mind. *Careful now.* He would try to handle this differently than Andi because lectures weren't getting her anywhere with Elisa. He turned onto Main Street, heading back to Andi and Elisa's home.

"Actually, your sister had no idea where you were."

"Figures."

Vance needed to find something else to talk about. He peered at the books on her lap. "Geometry and biology. Two of my favorites. You mentioned Todd made good grades. Is he tutoring you?"

Elisa relaxed. "Something like that. I want to do better. We only have a couple more weeks of summer school."

Vance turned left onto Glenwood. "Good girl."

"I have tests coming up. It'd be nice to surprise Andi with good grades for a change."

After pulling into the driveway, Vance shifted into PARK and with a wide grin tilted his head at Elisa. "That's the best news I've heard all day."

She smiled in return and pulled on the door handle. The door clicked but didn't open.

"Wait."

Elisa looked at him, curiosity in her expression.

"I need to prepare you. Andi had an accident today."

Elisa's eyes widened. "What? Is she all right?"

He hadn't meant to word it that way, but her reaction told him she loved her sister. *Good.* "She's fine. But she got stuck behind a wall. Nobody knew where she was." For the first time since looking for Andi, Vance recalled the brothers' comment about her searching for something, and Vance's initial suspicion when he asked her why she'd climbed into the small space.

He scratched his chin. Something to consider, but later. Much later.

For a moment, Elisa's eyes appeared to tear up. "Don't tell me. She was trapped and that's why she couldn't pick me up."

Nodding, Vance put his hand on her shoulder and squeezed. "That's right, but it was your phone call that alerted me to a possible problem. We found her, thankfully. Then she came home and couldn't find you."

Vance was certain that's why Andi's nerves were on edge, contributing to her overreaction at not finding Elisa at home.

Elisa stared out the windshield, where drops of rain began to play on the glass. With a thick voice, she said, "I'm in trouble now."

Vance almost chuckled. She would have been in trouble anyway, but knowing that her sister had been trapped had opened a part of Elisa's heart to see.

"Look, I'm no psychoanalyst, but I'm thinking she'll just be glad to see you."

Hands on hips, Andi stood in the doorway, looking anything but patient as she watched them sit in the car. Vance and Elisa stepped from the car. Elisa hurried to Andi and hugged her.

Andi wrapped her arms around her sister in return, her gaze finding Vance's, gratitude shining in her beautiful blue eyes.

She said, "Thank you," without putting voice to the words.

His heart skipped a beat, Elisa's words echoing in his mind.

*"I'm in trouble now."*

# Chapter 12

Releasing her bear hug on Elisa, Andi waved to Vance, disappointed to see him go as he backed from the drive. He reminded her of a handsome prince who'd stepped from a fairy-tale book, though he couldn't be real. Nor was she a beautiful princess.

But more than a prince, he seemed to be an answer to her prayers—prayers she had no faith to pray. Joy and happiness swirled inside, emotions she hadn't felt in years. It was as if he'd uncovered a hidden treasure inside her she'd not known was there.

"Um, shouldn't we have invited him in or something?" Elisa swiped her eyes.

Elisa crying? Andi had feared she'd fall into lecturing again, which would then digress into the usual argument. But with Elisa's apparent change in attitude, how could she be angry?

"I suspect he's giving us some time to ourselves." She wished he'd stayed but wasn't about to chase him down.

Elisa followed Andi into the house. "Vance told me what happened today." Elisa hugged her again. "You need to be careful."

Andi couldn't believe what she was seeing and hearing. "Who are you and what have you done with my sister?"

The question elicited a laugh from Elisa. "Stop it. You know I love you. You're my sister." After setting her textbooks on the coffee table, Elisa meandered into the kitchen and lifted the lid on the saucepan, sniffing the Hamburger Helper Andi had thrown together earlier. "Glad I ate at Todd's."

Andi sighed. "I thought you'd run away." There, she'd said it, the words laced with regret rather than fear and anger.

"What? Why would you think that?"

"Our argument. Don't you remember the words you said to me?"

Elisa peered into the refrigerator, blowing a loose curl from her face. "I know what I said. I didn't mean it."

Andi pulled a box of French vanilla cake mix from the cabinet, intending to make Elisa's favorite. "I'm sorry for everything that's happened between us, and I want you to know that I'm going to try to do better. I hope you know that I love you."

After pulling out a soda and popping the top, Elisa slurped from the opening. "I'm as much to blame as you. I know that now."

Pouring the mix into the blender along with eggs, oil, and water, Andi focused on the task, afraid she'd say the wrong thing like she always did. Still, she couldn't help herself. "Can I ask what's changed?"

Elisa stiffened, knitting her brows. Thankfully though, she soon relaxed, the hint of a grin at the left corner of her mouth. "Todd." Her eyes fairly shone when she said his name. "He's changed things."

Oh no. "Aha." Boys would come and go, Andi knew from her own painful experience. This wasn't good, but what could she say that wouldn't further alienate Elisa?

"And Vance, too. He knows so much and he loves learning."

Until that moment, Andi hadn't realized how much Vance had influenced her sister. With cake batter blending in the mixer, Andi chewed her lip, wishing she'd had more of a hand in Elisa's much-improved attitude.

"That's where I was tonight, studying. Todd talked to me about my attitude."

Andi cocked a brow, disbelieving. "How old is this guy?"

Elisa giggled. "He's a senior, but I think you'd like him, sis. He. . . uh. . .invited me to church. Invited us."

"He what?" Might Todd actually be a good thing for Elisa?

Andi poured the batter into a pan and stuck it into the oven. She and Elisa chatted for a while longer until she'd pulled the cake from the oven to cool. This had been a long and rough day. She'd spread strawberry icing over the cake in the morning. After Elisa headed to bed, Andi did the same, thankful the day had ended better than she thought.

As Andi readied for bed that night, brushing her hair from the tight ponytail she wore every day, she considered the changes in her life. When she'd had to quit school after their grandmother's death to care for Elisa, Jorgen had ended their relationship. Mr. E had been the only person to help her out of the pit, and she'd been on a downward spiral ever since his death. Until Vance showed up. The younger version of the elder—wavy hair and glasses and a brain the size of the North Dakota Badlands—had set off warning sirens in her head.

Despite her best efforts to guard against his charms, he was making inroads into her heart. But was that intentional on his part, considering he would be leaving soon?

Elisa had not been immune to him either. Still, Andi was happy with the changes she'd seen in her sister, and if that were to Vance's credit, she was all for it.

Andi had been fighting for so long to hang on to what little she had left, she was afraid to trust what appeared to be good things happening in her life.

A simple thing like trust—why was it so hard?

*

The lights automatically flipped on as soon as Vance walked through the blast door to the Ground Zero living room. He didn't even remember the drive home, his mind on continuous replay of Andi's face as she thanked him, her eyes glowing with gratitude. He was practically floating. Janice had never made him float.

The emotional high was lost as soon as he plopped on the sofa and looked at his laptop. The problem with ANND rushed toward him like a meteoric fireball. He pressed his head into the sofa back and groaned. Hadn't he done enough for one day? Saving a damsel in distress, loading an interference program, and finding the whereabouts of a lost teenager? He couldn't solve all the problems of the world in one day.

Exhausted, he went to bed, leaving the lights on. The only time he thought about buying night lights was when he wanted to sleep, never when he was in town.

The next morning he woke with a start, feeling as though someone had nudged him awake. He sat up on his elbows and squinted. No sounds of construction awaited him. What time was it anyway? He looked at the small clock next to the bed. Eight o'clock.

Great. He'd overslept. Still. . .this was supposed to be his vacation. He scratched his head. He wouldn't hear Andi and crew because they were at the far end of the underground complex in a completely different capsule on the other side of the blast door.

Dread kept him in bed for fifteen more minutes. Did he really have to face this day? Or could he ignore the fact that he'd hacked into Peter's parallel system and replaced the rogue program with another? He jerked upright. What if it was all on the up-and-up? Government-approved and contracted? Who was he to say it wasn't? Did he have oatmeal for brains?

After a good night's sleep he suddenly had a new perspective? Hadn't he slept on it before making the decision? *God in heaven, help me.*

Growling his displeasure, Vance jumped from bed and sprinted into the living room in his sweats, eager to put a stop to his crazy and irrational nonsense about somehow being able to save his reputation, and save ANND from running the wrong program.

An e-mail from Peter awaited him.

*Sweet streaming malware!* Had the guy discovered his intrusion already? The program he'd loaded shouldn't have been caught yet—in only a matter of hours. Pulse raging in his ears, Vance opened the e-mail and read.

They'd hit a snag and needed his help. What snag? Everything was working perfectly when he'd left, though the fact that they were still in beta testing had disturbed him. In the e-mail, Peter suggested that there wasn't any need for Vance to come all the way back from Cancun—he could make the fix remotely. The adrenaline rush subsided, relief washing it away, then. . .Vance saw Peter's sign off.

*Show your face here and you're dead.*

*Oh man.* What did that mean? Peter was kidding of course. Under normal circumstances. But this was anything but normal. Was there a hidden threat within the e-mail? What had he gotten himself into?

Peter had spent the better part of a year courting Bob Sitze, one of his government contacts, which made Vance more than a little nervous about calling Bob regarding his discovery. Considering most everyone at ANND resented Vance because Peter brought him on as his star programmer, Vance was hesitant to trust anyone else.

*Oh man.* The situation was anything but stellar. *Just calm down.* Vance logged into the system and took a look at the data Peter called to his attention. Nothing to do with Vance's hacking last night. But. . .

*This just gets better every minute.*

Specific systems were off-line for security purposes. Peter should know Vance could only make a full diagnostic sweep with in-office-only access.

*Great solar masses.*

Peter had just told him he was dead if he showed his face. How in the world did Peter expect him to resolve this otherwise, especially from Cancun? Except if Vance had kept his plans to go there, he would have been back by now. He'd just have go to the office after hours and hope—no, pray—that no one else was there.

Vance stood and stretched, taking several long and much-needed breaths. Oxygen would go a long way to get his mind going. If he didn't have this mess to clean up, how he'd enjoy seeing Andi this morning. At least he had one thing to look forward to.

He closed his eyes as he finished up a long stretch and imagined her sweet face, still wary. . .but sweet.

"Good morning."

He opened his eyes to a vision. Andi stood in the doorway, her dazzling smile nearly bowling him over. Fumbling for words, he could only smile in return. His day had just soared to five stars from the negative end on the how's-your-day rating system.

She meandered into the kitchen and looked at him across the island. "I see you haven't had your morning coffee."

Vance laughed. "You offering to pour me a cup?"

Two mugs in her hands, she grinned. "I was hoping to steal a cup for myself, too. That all right with you?"

"As long as you're pouring, I see no problem with that."

Pressing her lips into a playful grin, she filled both cups. "You'd better watch out if you don't want this coffee in your face."

Vance threw his hands up in surrender and moved to the island. "Okay, I give. I don't want to start my day out on the wrong side of you."

She giggled and handed him the coffee-filled mug. "Got a late start this morning."

As Vance took it from her, his fingers brushed hers, sending a charge through him. Spooning into his coffee the usual fillers, he couldn't help the smile playing on his lips as he considered how she made him feel all gooey inside, like the space-time continuum had folded and he was in the crease.

"Listen, I wanted to thank you for what you did."

"It was nothing. Elisa is a good kid. She's got a great head on her shoulders." Vance took a sip of his coffee. "Just like her sister."

She stared into her cup. Was that a blush creeping over her face? Hmm. Pretty. He liked this side of her.

"Elisa's out of school today. I almost played hooky from work, but then that wouldn't be a good example for her, would it?"

Vance opened his mouth to reply that she should have spent the time with her sister but then. . .an idea slammed him.

# Chapter 13

"Are we there yet?" Sitting in the back, Elisa pulled on the front passenger seat.

Andi giggled. "You sound like a little kid." She enjoyed watching the landscape go by. "This was a great idea, Vance."

Staring ahead at the road, he flashed her a quick grin—a look she was becoming insanely attached to.

"It's been awhile since I've been to Fargo," she said. Unwanted memories of being together with Jorgen at North Dakota State University drifted through her mind.

"Unfortunately, I don't think it's been long enough for me."

Andi gave him a side glance. "Really. Are you saying you're growing attached to Ground Zero?"

Vance didn't answer at first. "You know, it has kind of grown on me. But I think that might have more to do with the company I'm keeping while there."

Andi's pulse jumped. Before she could react she felt the familiar pressure on the seatback.

"Thanks, Vance, we like you, too." Elisa laughed, then plopped back.

"This trip will be great for Elisa," Andi said. Elisa would be able to see there's a world of opportunity waiting for her—a world beyond the small town of Herndon.

"So what do you want to be when you grow up, Elisa?" Vance asked.

For the next couple of hours, they talked about every topic they could think of, and sometimes drove in comfortable silence. Andi couldn't remember when she'd been so happy, so relaxed.

But that was the problem. She feared getting too close, and yet here she was like a meteor drawn by the gravitational pull of a planet called Vance—he even had her thinking in astronomical terms. If she didn't watch out, she'd end up crashing. And this time, she suspected she wouldn't be the only one hurt. Elisa looked to Vance like he was a big brother.

She'd been more than surprised when he'd invited her and Elisa to go with him to Fargo. Stunned had been more like it, and then one quick, impulsive decision and she'd found herself agreeing to go. And still, she felt good about it.

Besides, she'd told herself, it was for Elisa. She and Elisa needed some time together to have fun. What better place than the largest city in North Dakota?

As Andi watched the North Dakota wheat and sunflower fields go by, she almost dozed. Finally, the traffic on the highway increased as a mass of buildings and houses took shape in the distance. Anticipation filled the car.

They drove down Broadway, then past Main, the heart of Fargo.

"That's the second tallest building in Fargo." Vance pointed as he drove through a green light. "That's where I work."

"*Uff da.* Can we go there?" Elisa asked.

Vance grinned. "It's a bit complicated. My partner warned me not to come in while I'm on vacation. I'm not going in until after hours."

Andi detected a subtle unease in his tone. "We won't get to see where you work then?"

"You just saw it." Vance laughed. "That building is where I work."

"I understand." She hoped she hadn't sounded as disappointed as she felt. It's not like she expected the grand tour.

"Look, I'd love to take you inside so you can see the big computers. But maybe next time, all right?" He glanced at her and winked.

She responded with a nod.

"And here we are." Vance pulled into the Radisson Hotel parking. "This is the tallest building in Fargo."

Vance had arranged for their stay in Fargo, but she doubted she could afford this. "Isn't there another hotel? Maybe even a motel?"

"Don't worry, I'm getting this. I invited you, remember?"

"But—"

"Don't. Now, let's get you checked in and while you're unpacking, I need to run by my apartment. I'll be back to pick you up in an hour and take you to a late lunch."

She stood tall and smiled. "Sounds good." They'd just have to eat cheap. Maybe this wasn't such a great idea.

Panic swelled. Andi had imagined them walking around town, exploring sights, but because it wasn't something they did often, she hadn't considered that it might cost more than she had in her bank account at the moment, especially with what Vance had in mind. They could have a conflict of interest. She so did not want to ruin the day.

Vance grabbed their bags while Elisa skipped into the lobby, sending a tender pang through Andi. No, this was the right thing. They both needed to get away, even if only for a couple of days.

Once Andi and Elisa settled into their hotel room, Elisa was all smiles, then suddenly frowned. "I still wish we could have invited Todd."

"You know why we couldn't." This was Vance's idea and he didn't invite Todd. Nor was this a romantic getaway weekend.

"Can I call Todd?"

Andi wasn't sure why Elisa bothered to ask. "You know the answer to that as well."

"Where are we going? What are we going to do?" Elisa plopped on the bed. "I'm hungry."

Andi stared at herself in the mirror. "If I didn't know better, I'd say you were eight years old."

For that, she received a pillow in the back of the head, messing up her ponytail. "Now look what you did." She tugged the elastic band free. "I'll have to redo it."

"Ah, come on, sis. Don't you think it's time for you to let your hair down?" Elisa smiled into the mirror from behind Andi.

Andi gave her the look as she brushed her hair out. It fell across her shoulders with a golden sheen, and for the first time in a long time, she thought she might actually be pretty. But only a little.

She'd not taken the time to look at herself like this in much too long. She ran her hand over her cheek. Maybe she should have worn makeup like some girls did.

"Well, you don't have to listen to me, but I think you look beautiful with your hair down. Why not just leave it like that?"

Andi looked in the mirror at her sister, unconvinced. "You think?"

"I think."

Someone knocked on the door and before Andi could do a thing about her hair, Elisa opened it, revealing a dashing man who leaned against the frame with his hands in his pockets. He was much too handsome for this plain-looking small-town girl.

He whistled. "I like the new do."

Heat rose up her body and neck, then spread into her cheeks. Andi tried to focus, a difficult task, her head swimming as it was. "Thanks, but it's nothing special."

Vance remained in the doorway.

"You coming in?" Elisa asked.

"Nah. I'm hungry." Vance stared at Andi, something akin to longing in his eyes. "Let's go eat."

Andi grabbed her purse, fumbling and feeling strangely like her friendship with Vance had just climbed another rung on the ladder, all because she'd let her hair down. She hadn't intended to send him a signal, had she?

As she strolled past him through the door, the scent of his cologne made her dizzy. She hadn't noticed his wearing it in the car.

*≈♥*

Vance felt like he was floating in a no-gravity zone. Andi's hair. . .wowser. He'd known she was beautiful, but this. . . He cleared his throat as he turned into the restaurant parking lot, then parked. "Emilio's is my favorite Italian restaurant."

Racing around the car, Vance made sure to open the door for the ladies before they got out. Andi smiled as she stepped from the car and pulled her hair back like she was about to imprison it again.

Vance touched her hand, stopping her. "Please, don't."

Andi stared into his eyes, searching. "I'm not accustomed to wearing it down. I feel. . .funny."

"But you look. . ." *Scrumptious.* "Drop-dead gorgeous. You wouldn't want to deny a guy, would you?" Though Vance enjoyed teasing her, he wondered if he were going too far. Andi might feel compelled to be nice to him simply because she wanted—no, he knew she needed—the contract to finish Ground Zero. On that thought the anticipation of an enjoyable couple of days with her deflated.

Andi frowned, stepping out of the way as he shut the car door.

But maybe deflating was exactly what he needed. Besides, he had a purpose in coming to Fargo and needed to remain focused on that. Why had he invited her again?

As if he were in a trance, Vance remained next to the car, unmoving, as he watched her stroll toward the restaurant.

She flipped her hair off her shoulder and turned back to look at him, smiling. "You coming?"

Throat suddenly dry, Vance swallowed. He knew exactly why he'd invited her along. And at the moment, thinking about the work he'd come for was the last thing on his mind—the beautiful woman before him a huge distraction.

They enjoyed lunch together; the pleasant banter between the three of them couldn't have been more fun. Andi and Elisa were getting along better than he'd ever seen them.

"The last time I was in Fargo was to visit my boyfriend. Well, he's my ex-boyfriend now." Andi sipped her tea.

"What happened?"

"Long-distance relationships don't work. That and I had to quit school, so he didn't think I was his equal since I don't have a college degree."

"I'm sorry to hear that, Andi. The guy must be an idiot, so I don't think his degree did anything for him."

His words brought the smile back to her face.

"Why'd you go and bring that up, sis? Jorgen is a dope for letting you go. Right, Vance?"

He nodded his agreement but a frown crept into his smile, his mood. He wondered the same—why had she brought it up? The topic shone a searchlight on his heart and on their situation. Why was he entertaining the idea of a relationship with her if he had no plans to stay in Herndon? It wasn't fair to her. To either of them.

Elisa stared into her soda and played with the straw.

Vance resolved to enjoy the weekend. They were here. "Come on. We've got lots more to see."

"Really? This isn't Dallas," Andi said.

"Maybe not, but I know where there's good shopping."

Andi giggled as they left the restaurant and smacked him with her bag. "Ouch. What's in that thing?"

"You *are* a strange one, Vance Young. I always pictured people in Texas wearing cowboy hats and Wranglers. But you...you're anything but a cowboy."

"Why, thank ya', ma'am." He tipped his imaginary hat. "You experience a lot more of that in Houston than in Dallas. But in Houston, a city with millions of people, you have to run in the right crowds to see anyone dressed in Wranglers and a cowboy hat."

Vance opened the car door for the two women. Andi thanked him. He climbed into the driver's side, noticing Andi digging through her purse. Just like he didn't fit her idea of a Texan, he never imagined this side of her. At Ground Zero, she was all business and tried to put on that tough construction contractor appearance. But today, in her peach and lace knit shirt and pastel slacks, she was...soft.

All woman.

Vance sighed as he put the key into the ignition.

"What next?"

"Well, there's the zoo or a museum or"—Vance glanced back at Elisa—"the mall."

"The mall!" Elisa screamed.

He shared a knowing smile with Andi. She held his gaze, then her eyes drifted over his face as though looking at him for the first time. A pleasant sensation filled his chest.

"You didn't think we came all this way for you, did you?" Andi laughed.

Vance chuckled, too, as he drove out of the parking lot. He let her words put him in his place. Of course, they hadn't come with him to simply be in his company.

If he had any brains he would keep his distance.

# Chapter 14

Sitting at the restaurant during dinner that evening, Andi felt slaphappy. "I never knew a person could cram so much into one day." She yawned and quickly covered her mouth.

Vance watched her and chuckled but seemed distracted. "You're tired. We'll call it a night."

"Ah, I thought we were going to see that movie." Elisa chewed on a straw.

"No, Vance is right. He still has to work. Besides, hours at the mall and then the zoo. . .what more could you want?"

"A movie?"

Vance grinned at Elisa. "There's always tomorrow. But your sister is right. I've got to do the work I came here to do."

"But it's late."

He grinned, toying with his glass of water. "I planned to go in after hours."

"Why?"

How Vance could frown and grin at the same time, Andi didn't know. "Enough with the questions." Still, she wondered what he was up to.

The dinner bill already paid, she stood. Vance drove them back to the hotel, quiet and distracted. She knew he must have been thinking about the work ahead of him.

He pulled into the hotel parking lot rather than under the passenger drop-off.

"What are you doing? You don't have to escort us inside."

"I know."

Andi was glad when he came around to open her door. She could get accustomed to this, but that was the problem. They walked into the foyer where the registration desk was lined with people checking in.

"Must be hosting a conference," Vance mumbled as he strode toward the elevator and punched the button.

Was he going to escort them all the way to their room?

The elevator door opened, and Elisa stepped in. Unsure if Vance would follow them, Andi paused and looked up into his eyes. "Thanks for today. It was a great time for Elisa. She needed that."

"And what about you?" In his eyes, she saw. . .what? Yearning?

Vance brushed his fingers down her cheek—she closed her eyes, melting at his touch. A quick gentle stroke, it was over too soon. And with it, she'd revealed far too much to him.

Others flowed onto the elevator, pressing her to say good-bye.

"I'll pick you up in the morning." Vance's eyes flashed, now seemingly filled with regret.

She nodded and stepped into the elevator just as the door whooshed closed, shutting her in and leaving him on the other side. Wariness crept back into her heart.

That night, Andi and Elisa each lay in their separate full-sized beds, giggling and talking like schoolgirls. Of course, Elisa still *was* a schoolgirl, albeit a freshman. It felt good to have some time for girl talk. They'd both enjoyed Vance's company today, but sometimes it seemed as if they were competing for his attention. Still, Elisa apparently missed Todd.

The girl sounded like she was in love. Andi knew the feeling well, but she also knew it was just that—only a feeling. And much of the time, at Elisa's age, it didn't last, leaving at least one, or both, people with a broken heart. Elisa wasn't inclined to listen to Andi on the topic. What teenager would be? When you had the feeling, it was like a drug and you couldn't get enough. No one could tell you that you weren't in love.

Andi sighed, listening to Elisa talk about Todd, wishing she could feel the same about love and be free to chatter on about it without fear. Andi huffed and rolled on her side.

"What's with all the sighing over there, sis?"

"Was I sighing? I'm sorry. I'm listening."

"So, is that how you feel about Vance?"

"Elisa!" Andi had probably revealed more about her emotions with that outburst than anything. She calmed herself. "Vance isn't my boyfriend. He's a client and has now become a friend. That's all."

She felt she owed him for all he'd done to bring Elisa around. That was it, wasn't it?

"I've been telling you all my secrets. Don't you think you should be as honest with me?"

How did she feel about Vance? Didn't he make her stomach flutter and her heart pound? She couldn't wait to see him again and missed him when he wasn't around. "Okay, I'll admit that he's sort of cute."

Elisa giggled in reply. There. Andi'd shared a secret. The last thing she wanted was to have Elisa close off to her again. Maybe if Dad or even Grandma had lived, this would be a normal interaction. But with Andi playing the parent, a barrier had been thrown up between them.

"Why don't you admit more than that? Maybe you should be honest with yourself, Andi." Elisa turned on her side and propped up on her elbow, facing Andi. "You know, he's not like Jorgen."

"I know." Andi's voice fairly croaked.

"But, since we're being honest, I'm worried for you. I hadn't thought about it before, but with Vance bringing us here and showing us where he works. . ."

"He lives and works here. From the sounds of it, that's not going to change."

"So, in that way, maybe he is like Jorgen."

Andi rolled away from her sister and squeezed her eyes to stop the sudden pain behind them, knowing tears might follow. How did the conversation end with Elisa lecturing Andi about love?

"Today was a good day, Elisa. I don't want to ruin it with talk of Jorgen again."

❧

The alarm clock sounded, waking Vance. He sat up in bed, disoriented at first. After dropping Andi and Elisa off at their hotel, he'd taken a short nap, wanting his mind to be clear for the work he had to do during the night hours. As he shuffled around his apartment, getting dressed and grabbing an energy drink from the fridge, he thought about Ground Zero—the last place he'd ever want to live. But. . .

He actually missed the dungeon.

A chuckle escaped. *Who'da thunk?* The underground launch facility and bomb shelter—because that's what it was, a bomb shelter, too. In a word, the place was zany. He stood tall and put his hands on his hips, looking around his living room.

In a word. Boring.

Vance grabbed his keys and headed to ANND Systems. Sitting in the garage-enclosed parking lot, he decided to wait until after midnight when Tom's shift would begin. Vance wanted to probe Tom about the disk he'd found and given to Vance, believing he'd dropped it.

Someone else must have been in that night. Would Tom be willing to share that information?

At 11:45, Vance only had fifteen more minutes to wait. In fact, he'd give it another thirty to be sure the other guy was gone, though Vance had come on legitimate business—Peter had requested his help, after all.

He leaned his head against the seat, thinking of the day spent with Andi. All day watching her smile. All day listening to her musical laughter.

Oh, how he loved her response when he touched her cheek. And he wanted to do so much more than touch her cheek—he wanted to kiss her. But the place, the moment wasn't right.

He pounded the steering wheel. *Idiot.* What did people do when they found themselves falling for someone in an impossible situation? He'd already put in a call to his old boss in Texas. They wanted him back. His family wanted him back.

In Texas.

More than anything, he'd wanted to be part of running a company, and Peter's offer had seemed the answer. He shook his head. His vacation was meant to clear his mind, help him to know what he needed to do next. Where he needed to go.

Instead, all he could think about was Andi Nielsen, and she didn't fit into any of his plans. Feet planted firmly in North Dakota soil, she'd left college to care for her younger sister. She wasn't likely to pull up her roots, leaving North Dakota or the small town where they lived any time soon. Nor would Elisa want to leave. She had a boyfriend.

Vance rubbed his eyes and sent up a silent prayer. Somehow, he had to focus on ANND, and the work he needed to accomplish once inside. It could take hours to look at the data. Could he finish this task tonight?

Working on the legitimate program was the least of his worries. He'd panicked earlier today, and rightly so. Tonight he would attempt to discover if he'd overreacted about the rogue program that had practically fallen into his lap—the whole thing made no sense, especially considering there was no such thing as a coincidence. On the other hand, if Peter were involved in something illegal, working on what Vance had termed the mission creep project, then Vance needed to find something concrete with which to contact the authorities.

Finally, the digital clock in the car read 12:45. Adrenaline surged through him. He wasn't cut out for this. But. . .

It was time.

*Lord, I think You've led me down this road. . . . Help me to find what You need for me to see.*

Carrying his soft briefcase into the lobby, with phony confidence Vance looked up and smiled at. . .who was this? It wasn't Tom. Heart hammering, Vance went through the security measures, then signed his name at the desk under the scrutinizing eyes of the new guy who looked young and—thankfully—inexperienced.

Vance averted his eyes, certain they were bloodshot. No point encouraging the man in trivial conversation. Vance's athletic shoes squeaked as he crept across the cream-colored marble tiles and wiped his sweaty palms against his jeans. The sound echoed through the huge, silent foyer. Another fifteen feet to the elevator corridors and he'd be out from under the security guard's scrutiny.

His jaw itched. After punching the button to retrieve the elevator, he scratched his chin and tried to inspect his appearance in the reflective doors. With the way he looked, it was a wonder Andi paid him any attention. The weight of his job had pressed against him heavily and it showed.

"Mr. Young?" the security guy blurted from the foyer.

Vance couldn't exactly pretend he didn't hear, considering they were the only two in the foyer, maybe even the building, at nearly one a.m. Maybe the elevator would accommodate his need to get away.

The guy stood directly behind him, staring at him in the reflection.

*No such luck.*

"Mr. Young."

*Déjà vu.* Vance turned to face him. "Hey, where's Tom tonight?"

"Tom? Oh, you mean the other night security guard. I don't think he works here anymore."

"Oh, sorry to hear that." *Stellar.* Vance turned to face the elevator again. He needed to talk to Tom about the disk.

"It says you're on vacation."

*It* as in the computer. Vance fought the urge to run his hand down his face, revealing his anxiety. "Uh, yeah. I am, but Mr. Lundgren called me in to work out a problem." The elevator doors swooshed open, and Vance stepped in. "Hope it doesn't take too long. I'm ready to get back to my time off."

The security guard looked confused and unsure about pressing his authority. "I hear you." He nodded, and the doors shut in his face.

Again, that eerie feeling crept over him that this was all a replay. Minutes later, Vance sat at the four-faced plasma screen in the dinosaur pen. Once he was logged in he began scanning the results of Peter's last data test—the one he'd cited had problems that weren't there when Vance left. They'd made sure of that before Vance walked out the doors. So why problems now?

Though ANND Systems would crunch large amounts of data and spit out the results as defined by the government contract, the government had its own people to analyze the results. Apparently the data was jumbled and unreadable. Vance folded his arms across his chest and leaned back in the chair.

A simple operator error stared back at him.

Anyone could have corrected this. Peter had wanted Vance to do it. Why? Vance made the correction, stood, and took a deep breath, unsure about what to do next. How could he find out what was truly going on without reading Peter's e-mails?—a serious breach of ethical convention, something he'd already done to a point when he'd planted the program in the parallel system.

Should Vance leave the disk he'd discovered for the proper authorities? Would they know he'd not played a role in it if it were in fact part of a criminal act? That was his greatest fear—Peter's government contacts knew him much better than they knew Vance.

Wishing the whole thing would go away on its own, he left the computer processing room for his office. There, on his desk, stood the photograph. He lifted it, peering at the woman in the picture who reminded him so much of Andi. Or was it the other way around?

If he didn't believe in coincidence. . .

He stared at the picture, his heart torn. "Lord, show me what to do about Andi."

*Both of them.*

# Chapter 15

The next day, Andi and Elisa waited in the lobby for Vance.

"I don't understand why we can't stay one more day." Elisa slouched in a plush chair.

"I have no ide—"

"Ready for breakfast?"

How did Vance come in without them seeing? Andi stood to greet him. He looked as if he hadn't slept at all. "Good morning."

Nor had he shaved, looking a little scruffy. Andi liked his rough appearance.

"Let me take your bags." Vance grabbed them, ignoring the bellhop, and strolled through the revolving doors.

As Andi sat down in the car, she noticed for the first time this weekend that Vance hadn't opened her door. She looked out the passenger window, releasing a slow sigh. The romance she'd imagined with Vance was ending before it even started. Just as well.

As they headed out of town, they made small talk. Passing all the pancake houses only heightened the rumble Andi was beginning to feel in her stomach. She thought he'd said something about breakfast. They hadn't eaten the continental breakfast. She wanted to mention it to Vance but he was clearly distracted. Something obviously bothered him. Andi hoped it wasn't her.

"So, what's wrong with you?" she asked. He was anything but warm and friendly. "Haven't had your morning coffee?"

He shot a grin in her direction but kept his focus on the road as he accelerated. "You know me too well already."

For Elisa's sake, she would remind him about breakfast.

She opened her mouth to speak, shutting it as he pulled into a restaurant parking lot just outside of town. "Why are you in such a hurry to get out of town?"

They strolled into the small coffee house. "Would you believe me if I told you I miss Ground Zero?"

She laughed at his unexpected comment. "Nope."

They ordered coffee and pancakes. Vance rubbed his temples and stared out the big windows. Andi wanted to ask him what was going on but figured he would have volunteered the information if he felt like sharing. So, she and Elisa talked about Todd, engaging Vance once in a while. His mind was clearly far from them as he took a long gulp of his black coffee.

*Black coffee?*

"You didn't sleep last night, did you?" she pressed.

He set his mug down and leaned against folded arms. "I worked most of the night, not so unusual really. But I'm exhausted today. Sorry, I'm not in a great mood."

"But we sure had fun yesterday, didn't we?" Elisa offered.

Vance grinned. "Sure."

Andi relaxed against her seat, confused.

He finished his coffee, then asked for a double shot.

"Doesn't so much caffeine give you palpitations?"

"Maybe. Right now I need to be alert." Something in his expression softened. He reached across the booth and took her hand. "I need to deliver the two of you safely home."

Andi enjoyed the effect his touch had on her. Her thoughts from the previous night's girl talk crept into her mind—

*When you had the feeling, it was like a drug and you couldn't get enough. No one could tell you that you weren't in love.*

A girl could be smart, be strong. But when it came to matters of the heart... Even though she knew better than to allow her guard down, she had no control over the way he made her feel. And now, she wished he'd stare out the window again, think about something else rather than give her the look he was giving her.

She slipped her hand from his.

He looked out the window again. Good. Things were better this way. Weren't they?

⁂

Vance concentrated on driving and kept watch in the rearview mirror, wishing he could explain to Andi all that he was going through. But he couldn't even explain it to himself. At the moment he had too much on his mind to carry on a meaningful conversation. And women liked meaningful conversations, sensitive men. In that regard, he was sure he was blowing it with her. She tried to present herself as tough with a hard exterior, but he'd seen her soft side. She wanted what every woman wanted.

The problem was, Vance wasn't sure he could give that to her.

But maybe she wasn't part of God's plan for him. How could she be? He wasn't even sure she was a Christian. Every time he brought up God she couldn't get away fast enough. Then why did thoughts of a life without her sit wrong with him?

He risked a glimpse her way, noticing her dull expression—so different from her glowing demeanor yesterday. Without giving himself too much credit, he believed he was the cause of it.

He looked in the rearview mirror again.

That car. Unless he was being paranoid, he'd seen that car in town near the hotel, near their breakfast stop, too. Elisa needed a rest stop, so he pulled in at the next one, all the while cautious of the suspicious car. Probably nothing. The ladies returned from the restroom, and Vance drove back onto the highway, never seeing the car pass them. Where had it gone?

After ten minutes or so, he noticed the car in his rearview mirror again, though far enough behind that he could be imagining things. He'd made a huge mistake going into ANND Systems. The more he thought about it, the more he suspected that Peter knew Vance never went to Cancun, after all. Had the whole problem with the data been a ruse to bring him in? And, if so, why? If Peter had wanted to know where he was, all he had to do was ask, unless he was up to no good.

What sort of man was Vance to bring Andi and Elisa into possible danger?

Vance finally exited the highway for Herndon. He drove the long way around town to Andi's house, making sure he didn't see the suspicious car. After several stops and a wrong turn, Vance believed it was safe.

"Did you forget how to get to my house?" Andi asked, her voice sweet, yet laced with concern.

He shook his head. "No, I could never forget that." Grinning, he wanted to reassure her, especially after the way he'd acted this morning.

"Then what are you doing?"

"Just hate that our time together is ending." *She's going to think I'm an idiot, if she didn't already.*

A breathy laugh escaped Andi. "You're funny." But Vance saw her cheeks redden before she turned her face away.

Vance looked in the mirror again.

Blowing out a breath, he wasn't sure they'd even been followed. He rubbed his hand over his face, too exhausted to tell if he was only being paranoid.

Finally, he turned into Andi's driveway. While tugging their luggage from the trunk, he watched for the suspicious car. But it never showed. Relieved, he toted the luggage into the house and set it in the living room.

"Would you like something to drink? You're probably thirsty." Elisa offered him a cola.

"Sure, thanks." He took it and popped the top.

Andi came out from the hallway and smiled, looking nervous.

Vance toasted her with his soda. "Well, I'd better get going. See you on Monday?"

"Yeah, of course. But. . .can we talk?" She motioned for him to step outside onto the porch. Elisa smiled and disappeared down the hallway.

Vance took a sip. "What's up?"

"I just wanted to thank you. This meant so much to Elisa, to me. She really needed to get away. We had a good long sisterly talk. It seems like years since we've done that." Andi looked up into his face.

Her crystal blue eyes sparkled like a not-too-distant glittering star, and though her guarded wariness remained, something else took prominence in her gaze. Something big. Huge. Six hundred fifty times the size of the sun.

Searching the depths of her eyes—what he saw in them. . . Admiration. Longing.

He almost took a step back.

Was he. . . ? No, it couldn't happen. He was a geek. She was a non-geek. Never the two shall meet.

But was he finally. . .disarming Andi?

Had it been a game to him all along because he never believed it would really happen? "I. . .uh." Vance shook his head, snapping himself out of the daze.

Andi giggled and gave him a strange look. "Say, Elisa brought up having a picnic tomorrow. Want to come?"

"How about church first? I've tried the one just on the edge of town. Community Fellowship something. Ten o'clock. You want me to pick you up?"

Andi hesitated, her warm smile fading a little. Vance's heart thudded, expecting to be disappointed and hoping he wouldn't be. But he couldn't go further, shouldn't have gone this far, without knowing where she stood with God.

"Sure. Elisa said something about Todd inviting us as well. Who knows, maybe he goes to the same church. It's a small town, after all."

She lingered, and he couldn't help himself. Wanting to see and feel her response again, he traced a finger gently down her soft cheek, then cupped her chin and. . .she closed her eyes, leaning into it.

Her lips parted gently and Vance was there to meet their soft sweetness. He started to wrap his arms around her, bring her against him nice and tight.

*Oh man. Wait!* They were standing on her porch in broad daylight with Elisa probably peeking through the living room curtains. Slow down. Way down.

He gently pulled away and opened his eyes to meet hers. Again, he saw more emotion there than he should ever deserve. Girls didn't fall for him. Not like this. And they were lying if they said so. He knew that from experience.

Apprehension engulfed him. He sucked in a breath. Andi noticed him tense, then hurt flashed across her face.

"Come here." He grabbed her hand and tugged her to him in a hug. No way would he let her throw up the blast door to her heart again. He kissed the top of her head, smelling the scent of sweet watermelon in her hair.

*Lord, I could stay here forever.*

*I think. . .I think I love her. Help me.*

# Chapter 16

After grabbing a few groceries at the local store, Vance drove out of town on the lonely road to Ground Zero, oblivious to his surroundings, not caring about the car that had supposedly followed them. Somehow, he'd dug himself into a lot of trouble the last few weeks. And not just with his company. ANND Systems was about to blow up.

Not even a bomb shelter could protect him.

The scent of Andi's hair, the feel of her lips, had an intoxicating effect on him, making focusing on his company problems almost impossible. A myriad of confusing thoughts and emotions battled to overwhelm him.

What was he thinking? Why had he let things go this far? Andi was a vibrant and beautiful woman. The last thing she needed in her life was a computer geek, especially one that had no intentions of staying in Fargo or at Ground Zero or in North Dakota where the winters were as frigid as absolute zero.

He'd been through enough rejection himself. Usually things never got this far and he hadn't worried that they would. Had he simply answered the challenge she presented with her hard shell? He hated thinking he could do such a thing, but there it was. Or was it because he'd seen her every day before he'd even arrived at Ground Zero by means of the photograph on his desk?

Maybe love was a black hole. You couldn't keep from getting sucked into the vortex of its gravitational field no matter how hard you tried—nothing, not even light could resist a black hole. The only problem was—it was a one-way trip. Once you fell in, there was no way out.

*Stellarific.* Despite the heaviness in his heart, he laughed. He was probably the only guy in the universe to compare love to a black hole. But it was somehow comforting. And, if it were true, then he could stop blaming himself for letting it happen.

Her smile, though guarded, had been the gravity that tugged him ever closer and even now he was falling deeper and deeper.

He'd never had a chance.

Turning onto the main drive that would lead him to the launch facility, the heaviness lifted a little. He wouldn't blame himself for falling for Andi, but there was still a problem—what did he do now?

Two explosive situations waited for him to act, but he had no idea how to proceed. After climbing out of the car he walked to the entrance, his legs dragging. He'd planned to use his vacation time to pray and contemplate his future. Because of distractions, he'd done little of either since coming here. But now, circumstances forced him into having that serious talk with God.

Before entering the underground quarters, he glanced up at the sun high in the sky. It would be hours before he could look at the stars—when he seemed to hear God the best. He grinned. Tomorrow he'd pick up Andi and Elisa for church. A small prick in his heart told him there was hope in that—a small thing really—but huge in God's kingdom. Vance held on to that as he descended into his temporary home nestled deep underground.

✣

It had been so long since Andi had attended church, she wasn't sure what to wear. Elisa, who went to worship services with friends on occasion, assured her that nice slacks were acceptable. Andi was glad because she didn't own a decent dress and couldn't find one pair of pantyhose in her drawer.

Nervous didn't describe how she felt this morning. She'd come very near to calling Vance and canceling. Turned out that Community Christian Fellowship was the same church Todd and his family attended. Andi would attend for Elisa. A Christian family in Elisa's life was a good thing. Never mind that Andi had her own reservations about God.

After dressing she looked in the mirror, then began brushing her hair back into a ponytail.

"Uh uh." Elisa stood in the doorway. "Wear it down again."

Andi sighed. Her sister was right. Vance hadn't been able to take his eyes off her, at least before he'd gone into work on Friday night. She put her fingers to her lips and closed her eyes, remembering his kiss.

"It was nice, huh?"

Andi's eyes flew open. "What do you mean?"

Elisa giggled. "I knew he would kiss you."

"You spied on us?"

Elisa shrugged. "Just wanted to make sure it happened. If you had pushed him away, I would have given you a lecture. I want to see things work out between the two of you."

It felt nice having more sisterly talk.

A knock at the door drew her up tall. She sucked in a gasp. "He's here already?"

While Elisa went to answer the door, Andi opened the bottom drawer of her dresser and pulled out her grandmother's Bible. At least she'd kept it.

In the car on the way to church, Vance and Andi settled into their comfortable banter. When she placed the Bible on the seat between them, she rested her hand on it. Vance covered her hand with his.

Warmth flooded her. She smiled but then looked out the passenger seat window. What was she going to do? She cared deeply for him, maybe even loved him. Couldn't resist his charms, either way.

They drove into the church parking lot and headed for the front doors of the small church. Vance opened the door for Elisa and Andi. She tried to hide her dread.

He lifted her hand to his lips. "Relax. There's nothing to be afraid of."

Though his words comforted her, panic continued to fill her. As they marched up the steps she saw Gladys from the florist shop, who then introduced her family. There was Paul the concrete sub. His wife and boys welcomed her. Cordial, they made her feel comfortable, like she belonged.

There were many more people that she knew, growing up in the small town, and some she was more than surprised to see at church, knowing a bit of their background. A couple walked in ahead of her and Vance. Shame washed over her when she remembered being envious of them—how they'd said God had blessed them. The thought brought back her initial resentment toward Vance and the fact he'd been given the launch facility though he'd not been aware it even existed.

Why had God forgotten her? A knot formed in her throat. This wasn't the way she wanted to start her morning at church—filled with anger and resentment.

As they took a seat on the third pew from the back next to Todd and his family, the trepidation returned. Andi stared at her hands as though to still their shaking with a look. The service began with an opening prayer, announcements, and then music, the first song about God's love. A wave of emotion rolled over Andi. Tears threatened.

*No, not here. Please.* She quieted her emotions, hardening her heart. It had been far too long since she'd been in church, felt God's presence. It surprised her that she could even sense Him today. The congregation sang through more hymns and newer songs she'd not heard before. She decided she liked them.

Apparently more than familiar with the music, Vance sang along without missing a note, his voice strong and melodic. The praise and worship music moved her in a way she hadn't experienced before, and she wasn't certain what she thought about that. When it came time for Pastor Howel to present his sermon, he stood at the pulpit.

He spoke of being content in all things. "Paul says in Philippians, 'I am not saying this because I am in need, for I have learned to be content whatever the circumstances. I know what it is to be in need, and I know what it is to have plenty. I have learned the secret of being content in any and every situation, whether well fed or hungry, whether living in plenty or in want. I can do all this through him who gives me strength.'"

Andi hung on his every word, sure that the sermon was meant for her alone. She'd been anything but content these last few years, blaming God for all the unfortunate things in her life. All the wrong done to her while He appeared to *bless* others. A drop of moisture touched her hand. Another tear slid down her cheek.

At some point, she'd become disillusioned with God. Yet Paul suffered and he was glad to do it. He was a prisoner of Christ.

It dawned on Andi—God didn't exist to answer her wants.

The pastor went on, " 'Take delight yourself in the Lord, and he will give you the desires of your heart.' "

As she listened, she understood that she'd had it all wrong. All backward. If she delighted herself in Him—His desires would become her desires.

The idea was unsettling.

After the service ended, Vance took Andi and Elisa to their home to change and grab the fried chicken they'd cooked the previous afternoon for the picnic. They were to meet him back at Ground Zero.

Before Vance left, he reached for her hand. "You all right? You seem distant since church."

"I'm fine." Regardless of feeling disturbed at the pastor's words, she smiled, wanting nothing more than to spend a pleasant afternoon with Vance.

"Good." The way he looked at her, she was sure he was thinking about their kiss.

Things had changed between them and there was no going back. At least for her. She wondered how it would feel to work on Ground Zero with him always present. That is, until he left. Would he leave now? He hadn't exactly declared his love.

Once she and Elisa arrived at Vance's place, they pulled the picnic basket from the truck and, along with Vance, walked across the flat plains to the far side of the property—at least twenty-five acres—through the sparse oak trees.

A light breeze and the cool of the shade made for an enjoyable picnic. They ate the fried chicken and potato salad, relaxing in each other's company. Andi leaned against a tree, comfortable enough to take a nap but listening to Vance and Elisa discuss science and the universe. He explained his love of creation science, piquing Elisa's interest in the topic.

What a miracle it was that he'd drawn Elisa from her shell. More than any of her other desires, hadn't Andi wanted the best for Elisa?

She closed her eyes as she listened to them along with the breeze through the trees, no longer wanting to deny that God had, in fact, been working in her life. Why had she denied it for so long? Denied Him?

"It's such a nice day, I want to take a walk," she said. When Vance and Elisa made to stand, she stopped them. "Oh no, I mean alone."

Vance frowned. "You sure?"

She nodded with a smile to ease the worried look on Vance's face. Once she was far enough away, Andi poured her heart out to God, all her hurts, heartaches, unforgiveness, and everything until she was spent.

"Now, Lord, You take it from here. This is all I have to give You. My heart." Andi began a slow stroll back to the copse of trees where she'd left Elisa and Vance, knowing her sister was in good hands. "Thank You for sending him."

Still, fear of being hurt stood in her way. Vance rose when he saw her approach. His gaze searched her face, then her eyes. He must have seen their redness but didn't say anything.

*Sure You sent him, Lord, but did You send him for me? I'm not good enough for him.*

Vance took her hand and pulled her to him like he'd done yesterday on her porch. He whispered into her ear, "Oh Andi, there's so much I want to tell you."

Elisa began packing away the picnic items. Andi moved to help, but Vance wouldn't release her. He tugged her hand, urging her to come with him. Once they'd walked a bit, Vance turned her to face him, then brushed her cheek—his usual way.

He closed the distance between them, kissing her thoroughly. Her knees grew weak. She tugged free from him.

Worry laced his expression. "What's wrong?"

"I. . .I don't know if I'm good enough for you."

He shook his head. "What do you mean? Of course you are."

Well, she'd started it, might as well finish, since she was all about confessions today. "I don't have a college education. You're brilliant. I'm—"

"Stop." He pulled her close to him, her face near his chest where she could hear his heart beating. "You're smart, beautiful, independent, an entrepreneur. Should I keep going?"

Enjoying the comfort of being in his arms, Andi could only reply with an "um-hmm."

"Forget about that idiot you were with before. He doesn't define who you are."

"Hey guys, sorry to interrupt, but I told Todd I'd be home by five. He's supposed to call. Look, I've packed the picnic up. Ready to go?" Elisa shaded her eyes against the late afternoon sun.

*Sweet potato casserole.* Elisa had the worst timing for someone who wanted to see things work out between Andi and Vance.

As they strolled lazily back to the missile base, another kind of guilt began growing inside Andi. With everything going on the last few days, she'd forgotten about her search within the walls of the underground missile site. They'd come so far and things between them were different. How would Vance react to the news? How would he feel about her waiting until now to tell him?

Oh, how she wished she'd just told him at the beginning. Maybe together they could have discovered the hidden treasure.

She licked her lips and slipped her hand from his. He would certainly notice her sweaty palm. "I have something I need—"

"Get down!" Vance's agitated whisper scared her.

They all dropped flat against the grass. "What is it?"

"Shh." He squinted, searching the launch facility, still a few acres away from them.

Andi followed his gaze, seeing another car parked next to theirs.

"Vance, you're scaring me. What's going on?" Fear coursed through Andi at his reaction. And if they were trying to hide, the flat prairie wasn't a good place, though maybe the grass was cover enough.

She angled her head to study him.

What did she really know about him?

*Lord, guard my heart.*

# Chapter 17

Heads down." Vance made sure Andi and Elisa pressed their heads flat against the earth. He watched two men climb into the car—the same car that had followed them from Fargo.

*Idiot.* He never should have gone into Fargo, to ANND Systems. The ruse was up. Peter must have caught Vance's unauthorized upload, seen him log into his account, something. What were the chances?

"Lord in heaven, help me," he whispered, not realizing he'd done so aloud.

"Vance, please. You have to tell me what's going on."

"They're gone." Elisa stood and dusted the dirt and grass away. "What was that about, anyway?"

His plans had backfired. "It's complicated." He stood and helped Andi to her feet.

Vance trotted toward Ground Zero, then realizing he was alone, turned around to see Andi hadn't moved.

"I'm not going anywhere until you tell me who those men were. Why didn't you want them to see you?"

How could he explain? He strode back to Andi and tried to tug her to him, while Elisa walked on ahead, still carrying the picnic basket. "I'll explain things, I promise. But not in front of Elisa. For now, can you trust me?"

Andi searched his eyes, a frown forming. "I don't know, Vance. This is all so...strange." She started after her sister. "Let's be real here. I don't know you that well. I have to think of Elisa right now."

"You're right, you do." Vance kept pace with her, head down, contemplating. He hadn't realized what he was getting into, nor had it occurred to him that he would drag others into the problem. He'd never considered himself in any danger—especially the physical kind.

Until now.

He didn't want Andi and her sister in harm's way. He stopped walking and, thankfully, so did Andi. He took her hands in his again. "Believe me when I say I don't know who those men were."

"How can I believe you? You didn't want them to see you. Clearly, you know them."

"I thought someone was following us from Fargo. That was the car."

Andi stared at him. "What? Why didn't you say anything before? What's going on?"

He wanted to brush his hand down her cheek. Kiss her. Go back to the last few hours. "I don't know enough to explain. There's something very wrong at my company. I think I dug too deep, hit a nerve, and those men have followed me."

Andi's eyes widened. She covered her mouth. "Oh Vance, please be careful."

"I'll do my best. In the meantime, I need to get you and Elisa out of here. Take her home and lock the doors."

Andi tugged her cell phone from her pocket. "Let's call the police."

"And tell them what? For all we know, they could have knocked on the door, gotten no answer, and left. I need to check inside to see if anything was taken."

"Tell them about your company troubles. Tell them what you told me." She pressed the phone out to him.

Vance scanned the flat prairie behind her. "And risk the bad guys getting away? No, I need something solid to give the authorities. I was trying to get more information before I called them. But apparently, I've been found out."

"I see." Andi began punching numbers.

Vance stopped her. "Andi, I'll call them. I promise. This doesn't involve you or Elisa. Go home." The words came out too brusque. But he needed her safe.

Hurt filled her eyes. "You don't want my help? Fine."

She stuck her phone back in her pocket, lifted her chin, and strode away.

"Andi." Vance kept up with her quickened pace to her truck. "You were the one who told me you needed to think of Elisa. I'm asking you to do that. I'm trying to protect both of you."

Once she reached her truck, Andi turned to face him. "Right, and I also said I don't really know you. You could *be* trouble. Those guys could have been government agents for all I know."

*What?* "Well, that's just. . ." Vance threw his hands up and walked away. Women.

If his brusque manner would make her leave, get her to safety, it was for the best. He didn't have time to explain or argue. He'd have to find a way to make it up to her later.

Hopefully, there would be a later.

Pain lashed at Vance's heart as the sound of gravel crackled under Andi's tires, taking her away from Ground Zero. He wasn't sure how he expected her to act. The circumstances were unfamiliar to him as well.

As for the two men, the elevator wouldn't work without the key or communication from underground, allowing them in. As far as he could tell, they hadn't penetrated the facility, nor the stairs.

He descended into Ground Zero with as much caution as he could muster. The closest he'd ever come to acting the part of hero was in video games. He wasn't trained in police work of any sort. Then why was he slinking around in ANND's systems, trying to gather evidence to prove his innocence while proving others guilty?

It had become painfully clear that he'd made a huge mistake. He'd look around the place, then make the call and hope—no, pray—the police would listen to him, hear him out before Peter was brought to the table to distort the facts.

What choice did he have now? He was in over his head.

First Vance looked at his laptop and other electronics—the most likely places they'd search if they'd found a way in. He blew out a breath, satisfied they'd not gained entry. Still, they'd followed him. They'd be back. He checked his e-mail to see if Peter had left him a message.

Nothing.

Making good on his promise to call the authorities was the only logical next step. He had to admit he was scared. What kind of people were these men? He'd never learned whom Peter had gotten involved with—but with big dollars involved and anti-government activity, they had to be dangerous.

Vance dialed information. Call waiting indicated another call coming in. Andi's number. He abandoned his other call to answer.

"Vance. The men—they have us. . ." Andi's voice was breathy and filled with fear. "They've got Elisa. . .and me."

☙

The tough guy grabbed the phone from Andi, tugging some of her hair with it. "Ouch." She glared at him. The larger of the two men, he had red hair and looked like a bodybuilder.

Elisa sat on the sofa, petrified. Andi wanted to comfort her sister. Later she'd scold her for answering the door when she'd warned her not to. But Elisa had insisted it was Todd.

Andi could hear Vance yelling her name over the phone.

She attempted to rush to Elisa. The bodybuilder grabbed her upper arm and squeezed. Hard. Tears rushed to her eyes.

He raised the phone to his face and spoke to Vance. "You have twenty-four hours to reverse what you've done to the Nitro Project."

Vance's voice boomed over the phone. "I need more time."

"If you want to see your friends again, that's all you have." He ended the call, then shoved Andi to the sofa. She righted herself and wrapped her arms around Elisa, who whimpered.

"I'm so, so sorry, sis. I should have listened to you."

"Shh. Everything is going to be fine." *Vance is going to get us out of this.* A knot formed in Andi's throat. She wasn't sure she believed her own words, but she had to remain strong.

But this wasn't a part of her normal life, this. . .was a tragedy. She wished she had called the police herself after all.

"What are you going to do with us?" Elisa asked.

Andi went rigid and squeezed Elisa, hoping her question didn't elicit a violent response. The men ignored her.

"What's to drink around here?" the shorter of the two said. Looking slim and agile, he had dark hair and wore a black suit. He moved out of sight and into the kitchen. Andi heard the refrigerator door open and shut, followed by the sound of a soda top pop and the resulting fizz. He reappeared, drinking the soda and looking around the room.

Andi squirmed with irritation at his audacity. Breaking into her home, kidnapping them, and stealing a cola. Who were these guys? An idea began to form. She might know little about them, but. . .she cocked her head, watching the cola guzzler. . .neither did the men know anything about her.

They didn't know about the sledgehammer leaning against the wall in the corner, or the nail gun on the bookshelf, or any of the other various tools lying around the house that could easily transform into a weapon. Andi's home was a never-ending remodeling project. Potential weapons surrounded them everywhere. If given the opportunity, a good shot of air freshener right in the eyes could give Andi and Elisa the chance they needed to escape.

Andi would wait for the right moment. With her newfound faith and trust in God, she sent up a silent prayer for a chance to get away. A shudder rolled over her body at the thought of using her tools in a violent way.

She chewed on her lip. It might be too risky to try anything. She had to think of Elisa. *Oh Vance. Please give them what they want.*

She'd give anything if she hadn't left him in a huff. It had merely been a ploy to try and make him call the police. The maneuver had bombed.

"I have to go to the bathroom, sis," Elisa whispered. "Will they let us go?"

Andi shrugged. "Let me ask, okay?"

"Say, are we allowed to use the restroom?"

Slim nodded to his partner in crime. "See to it."

After Elisa looked at Andi, then between the two men, she cautiously rose and walked to the restroom, the bodybuilder following. Would he go in with her sister? The best Andi could hope for was they could remain comfortable on the sofa. That this wouldn't be any more difficult for them. And, of course, that they would be released soon, without harm.

*Get real.* They had seen the men's faces. How could they let them go free? No, she couldn't wait for this to play out in her favor. Somehow, they'd have to escape.

*The bathroom window.* Andi perked up and looked in that direction. Maybe Elisa would climb through and get help.

*Lord, please let Elisa—*

Bodybuilder appeared in the hallway, shoving Elisa ahead of him. "She tried to escape through the window."

"All right, that's it." Slim set down his soda. "We tried to be nice, but now we're going to have to tie you up."

"I thought we were taking them to—"

Slim shot him a warning glare.

Andi's spirits sagged even lower. "No, please. She's just a kid. She didn't know any better. It won't happen again. I promise."

"Yeah, well, as far as I know, you put her up to it." Slim looked around the room. "Aha. Just what I needed." He found the duct tape resting on the side table. "You're a regular handywoman, aren't you?"

Andi turned her face away from him, hoping he wouldn't discover her tools, potential weapons, lying around and remove them. Still, she or Elisa wouldn't have a chance to escape if they were tied up. And if the men took them to an unknown location? She'd heard you should never let someone take you away. Fight as hard as you could. But these two guys seemed to fill her living room with their presence. How could she fight them to escape?

The men wrapped Andi and Elisa's ankles, then their wrists behind them with duct tape. To her dismay, they taped their mouths shut.

"Now, back the car into the garage," Slim said to Bodybuilder.

The next few minutes played before Andi like her worst nightmare. She and Elisa were lowered into the deep trunk of a car, sprawled precariously side by side, then Bodybuilder, smirking before he shut the trunk, blanketed them in darkness.

*Do not panic. Elisa is counting on you.* Andi reasoned that the men couldn't take them too far or else she and Elisa would run out of air, though she had no clue how long that would take. It seemed surreal. As soon as she falls for someone and asks God to come into her life, bad guys kidnap them.

She sensed the car traveling at a moderate speed, then stopping frequently. They were driving through downtown, no doubt there. If she concentrated, she might be able to make out where they were being taken. This was her town, after all. She counted at least five stops, then felt a right turn, a few more miles, then a left turn onto a bumpy road. The old, abandoned Garrison warehouse? That would make sense, but it made too much sense. Too predictable. Still, these men were counting on a quick job, which didn't give her much time to come up with a plan if she hoped to save them.

When the trunk opened, Andi and Elisa were tugged out and set on their feet. When her eyes adjusted, she saw the dim lighting of the old warehouse, just as she'd thought. The men had obviously searched for an abandoned location to keep Andi and Elisa while pressuring Vance.

Still wrapped in duct tape, they were made to sit in chairs positioned back-to-back, then secured again with more duct tape.

"Nobody can hear you scream here." With an evil grin, Bodybuilder ripped the tape from Andi's mouth.

Pain seared her lips, but she made no sound, not wanting to give Bodybuilder any satisfaction. From behind, she heard Elisa's yelp as the tape was removed.

For what felt like hours, Andi exhausted herself trying to come up with a possible escape. But she had long since realized that the chance had passed when they were tied up. If they were ever set free, for even a second, it would be better to die trying than to remain here. She leaned her head against the chair back, wondering what Elisa was thinking. She'd heard that people's lives passed before their eyes as they were about to die. Instead she tried hard to avoid thinking through the events of her life.

But it didn't hurt to think about the future, did it? Would she ever discover what her grandfather had hidden? Would she even get another chance to look? And what about a future with Vance? Images of his handsome face paraded through her mind. A door slammed, seeming to shake the entire warehouse. *Good gravy.* That's all they needed was for the old building to come crashing down on them.

"Elisa, what happened?"

"One of the men left."

Facing the wall, Andi couldn't see which one. She lowered her voice. "Who's still here?"

"I don't know his name."

Andi huffed. Frustrated, she tried to kick herself, which only shook both chairs.

"Psst. Andi," Elisa whispered, almost too softly.

"Yeah."

"My hands are free."

Andi let the words soak in. "You. . . What?"

"My nail clippers, I tugged them from my back pocket. Took me a couple of hours, but I cut enough of the duct tape. . ."

"Okay, okay. Shhh. Let me think."

Elisa remained quiet.

"I need to know which one is still here. The big one or the small one?" Andi asked.

"The one who looks like a bodyguard left."

*Good.* They had to act now. "We have to hurry. Clip my wrists, then I'll get my ankles, since he can't see me as well as he can see you."

Andi remained as still as a statue in the chair, patiently waiting while Elisa clipped her wrists free. The trick with duct tape was to avoid the ripping sound it made.

Elisa stiffened, signaling to Andi something was up. Footsteps resounded in the warehouse. A pause, then a door shut, sounding more like a door to a room inside the warehouse. Possibly a bathroom or an office.

"Hurry, Andi."

She clipped and ripped the tape around her ankles with lightning speed and helped Elisa do the same. They ran out the door, hoping they wouldn't run directly into Bodybuilder.

"Quick. Over here." Andi tugged Elisa behind some bushes. Though sunset was upon them, they could still be spotted in the dusk.

"What are we going to do now?" Elisa's voice trembled. "We can't outrun him, can we?"

*Okay, Lord. I really need Your help now like never before.*

The railroad tracks. That was it. "Come on, we'll follow the tracks." Andi began jogging next to them.

"But wait, isn't town that way?" Elisa pointed in the opposite direction.

"Yeah, and that's exactly why we're heading this way." Once Slim discovered their escape, he was sure to look for them running toward town. "Besides, Freya Emerson lives down here. We can call for help and borrow her car."

In the dimming light of day, Andi saw Elisa's smile and something else. *Respect.*

She and Elisa followed the tracks for a half a mile, then jogged down a dirt road for another half a mile to Freya's century-old farmhouse. Out of breath, Andi knocked on the woman's door, knowing they'd wake her. Freya went to bed at six in the evening and got up every morning at four.

Once Freya invited them in, Andi quickly explained their predicament. Freya offered her car and cell phone—a Jitterbug.

"Thank you, Freya. We've got to run now. Please call the police and send them to Mr. Erickson's old missile site." She hugged Freya. "And take care of yourself."

"You're not going to the missile site, are you?" Freya crinkled her brow.

"I've got to warn Vance." Andi feared too much time had passed, her only hope being that Bodybuilder hadn't made it back to the warehouse with the car yet.

"Honey, just call him." Freya indicated her cell phone.

Andi opened the screen door and didn't answer until she was on the other side of it. "I will, don't worry."

Fearing they'd already upset poor Freya's schedule, Andi allowed Elisa to come with her. Andi started the car and screeched from the drive, sending dirt and gravel flying.

"Why don't we go to the police station?"

"We have to make sure Vance is okay, too!" The words came out too loud and forced. "Please, just call him and tell him we're free, to get out of there."

"But. . .but. . ."

"Just do it." Andi took a deep, calming breath. "Look, you get ahold of him, and we won't go to the missile site, okay?"

Andi relayed Mr. E's number as she swerved off the dirt road and onto a busy street.

The way she was driving, she might have a cruiser on her tail any minute, which was good. Wasn't it?

# Chapter 18

*N*itro Project? Deep in his gut, Vance had hoped he'd made a mistake. That his fears he'd stumbled onto something nefarious were unfounded. He cradled his head in his hands. "Lord, forgive me. I made all these decisions without really asking You, waiting on Your answer. Thinking I knew how to fix things. Now I'm in deep. Please protect Andi and Elisa, show me what to do."

He stared at the corrected code he'd written, but it only presented another dilemma. If he delivered as requested, would he see Andi and Elisa safe? He'd need assurance before he uploaded. Despite his eagerness, he needed to pray for direction, for the right words before he made the call to let them know his conditions.

*Lord, help me. Their lives are at stake. What do I say?*

Impatience needled.

Footsteps in the tunnel alerted him to intruders, though how would they have gotten in? Vance bolted from the sofa, adrenaline pumping through him. His heart drummed, his palms grew moist.

Andi appeared in the doorway. *How—*

"Vance!" She ran to him.

He caught her up in his arms, squeezing like he'd never let her go, his face in the crook of her neck, breathing in her scent of watermelon and vowing to keep her with him always.

Vance released Andi and gripped her upper arms. "What happened? Are you all right?"

"I'm fine. We escaped and called the police. Called you, too, but you didn't answer."

"What? You know I'd have answered had it been you or the kidnappers." Vance skimmed the caller ID. "Only a Freya somebody called. I don't have time to talk to someone I don't know."

"That was me. I borrowed her phone."

*Idiot.* "Oh Andi. I'm so sorry."

"It doesn't matter. The police should be here soon."

Elisa dashed through the blast door, panic written across her face. "They're not the only ones. I thought to hit the lockdown button, but it's too late. The elevator's moving."

"A bomb shelter won't be much protection from the kidnappers unless we're locked in." Vance began pacing.

"Maybe it's the police," Andi offered

108

"I'm thinking the police would have hailed us first on the intercom," Vance said. "We can't take the chance. Come on."

He jammed his laptop into its soft case and slung it over his shoulder, then tugged both women behind him to the equipment building. They stepped through the blast door that was propped to remain open.

"Why are you going in here?"

"You got lost in here before. Let's do it again." Vance managed a grin.

"I know where we can hide. First, let's close the blast door. They won't be able to sneak up on us this way." Door secured, she located a place in the wall—a panel she easily removed.

She found a flashlight next to a ladder and signaled for Elisa to climb inside the wall. Though Vance believed it could prevent the bad guys from finding them, he hoped they wouldn't get stuck if things went wrong. Next, Andi squeezed into the small space.

She reached her hand out to Vance. "Come on, hurry."

Vance stepped in, keeping his back to the opening. He took her face in his hands and looked into her eyes. "In case. . .things don't work out. . ."

"Don't." Andi's eyes filled with moisture. "For Elisa," she whispered.

"I want to tell you what an amazing woman you are."

"Vance, what are you doing?"

Though it seemed like the wrong time, if they were discovered, it could very well be his last opportunity. Vance pressed his lips against hers, soaking in her goodness, her beauty, her essence, remembering her. Aware that Elisa was watching, he ended the kiss.

"I never did tell you how impressed I was with all you've done, remodeling this launch facility. It doesn't look anything like the old military site it was—I know, I looked up the original images."

She sucked in a breath. "Thanks. Now will you come inside before they see us?"

He'd done everything he could to share how he felt about her and try to give her confidence in herself and her work. Now he knew what he had to do.

Slowly shaking his head, he said, "I'm not coming in. I know how to end this. You wait here until the police come."

Andi grabbed his arm, pleading in her eyes. "Don't do this. . ."

Vance freed himself from her grip and put the panel back in place, securing it with enough screws to keep it in position. He exited the equipment building, closing the blast door behind him. That should give the women enough warning if someone entered the room.

He'd never been in a position like this—where he was literally trusting God with his life. But regardless of what happened to him, it was important that Andi and Elisa were safe. The police would be here soon. The goons Peter had sent had every reason to get rid of Vance because he could talk. And he would talk if he made it out alive. At this point, only God could save him.

He entered the living room and immediately felt the barrel of a gun against his neck. He lifted his hands in surrender. "Easy. I have the program. If you kill me, I can't give it to you."

A large, bulking man stepped from behind him, still pointing the gun. "Bring it then. We don't have time to wait. The police are probably on their way. You're coming with us."

A shorter man stepped beside him. "You take him. I'll find the women. They're around here somewhere."

"But what about the police?"

"You want those women describing us? They'll be insurance in case the program doesn't work."

Vance's heart sank. So, this was it. . .

🌿

Andi kept strong for Elisa, refusing to give in to fear. In fact, she held on to the anger she felt at Vance for wanting to play hero. He could have stayed hidden with them until the police arrived. She wished she could come up with her own plan. Andi pressed her fists against the walls, frustrated. She had planned to explore this space at the right time, searching for her grandfather's secret. But now, all her thoughts were on Vance. She prayed for him. Hard. Harder than she'd ever prayed for anything in her life.

His life was in danger. Their lives were in danger, too, but he'd gone to face the bad guys alone. To protect them.

She couldn't keep up the anger long though.

He'd said all those things to her in case something went wrong and he would never see her again. The words had been sincere, from the deepest part of his heart. She'd allowed herself to see everything through his eyes, and because of that, she realized, maybe she was good enough, after all.

Good enough for a brilliant man like Vance. Allowing her hands to slide down the wall behind her, she felt a slight variance.

*Gasp.* Could it be? She turned her attention to the place where she'd felt the inconsistency and examined it with the flashlight. A four-way cut had been made in the metal sheeting. There was definitely something different here. Her heart fluttered.

"Elisa," she whispered, "I think this is it. This is where Grandpa hid. . . whatever."

"Why do you care about that now?" Some of Elisa's resentment returned.

"I wasn't looking for it, but I think this is it."

Elisa moved to her side. "Well, aren't you going to open it?"

Andi ran her hand over it. "To think those guys were so bored down here, they'd go to this much trouble."

"Yeah, either that or Grandpa really wanted it hidden."

"He could have dug a hole in a field somewhere."

"But this would have been torture for someone who wanted to find it but couldn't get inside—it being a military launch control center."

Thoughts of Vance accosted Andi. "I can't do it. I can't open this without Vance. He has to be here."

"You love him, don't you?"

Andi gave a slight nod. "Yeah, I think I do."

"Have you even told him about the letter?"

"What's he going to think when I do?" What was taking the police so long? "You have to stay here, Elisa. I'm going to find out what's happening?"

"No, don't leave me. Vance told you to stay here."

"And I'm telling you to stay. Something could have happened to Vance. Maybe the police are here but don't know where we are." She hated saying the words but had to admit them. Why else hadn't anyone come to let them out?

*Oh Vance.* Except for Elisa, Andi had lost everyone dear to her. She wouldn't lose Vance, too.

Vance had loosely secured the screws into the panel—enough to keep it in place, but not tight. Andi easily popped them out from her side, climbed out, then secured the panel back to hide Elisa. Noticing the same mallet she'd once used to threaten Vance resting against the wall, she grabbed it to use as a weapon. As quietly as possible, she opened the blast door, all the while believing this was probably a mistake. But she couldn't wait any longer. What if Vance needed her help?

Things couldn't end this way. She wouldn't let them.

She crept through the tunnel connectors and past the elevator and stairwell. Before entering the tunnel she listened for voices. Footsteps. Anything. She heard. . .

*Breathing.*

She screamed. A hand clamped over her mouth, stifling it.

## Chapter 19

Don't be afraid. I'm working undercover," the man whispered, then released her. "Where's your sister. Is she all right?"

Andi turned to face the slimmer of the two kidnappers. She held the mallet high. "You!" She eyed him, still suspicious and unwilling to give away Elisa's hiding place. "How do I know you're telling the truth?"

He raised his hands as though she were holding a gun rather than a mallet. "If you don't believe me, let's go above ground where they're apprehending the assailant as we speak."

"What about Vance?"

"Your boyfriend is safe."

Andi's hand began to shake. She needed to see for herself. In the meantime, Elisa would remain hidden. "Let's go, then."

Once Andi exited the elevator into the night, she witnessed flashing lights, cars, and suited men along with police everywhere. The lights blinded her as she searched through the commotion for Vance. Looking behind as she moved forward, she stumbled into someone.

"Andi!" Vance embraced her with his strength, comforting her. All the words he'd said before he left to find the bad guys came gushing back to her. Though she thought he'd been sincere, doubt crept in. Were the words only prompted by the distress of their dangerous predicament?

A man spoke to Vance. "Mr. Young, we've confiscated your computer and will need you to come with us to give us a statement."

Andi pulled from his arms to listen.

Vance nodded, his expression grim. "Right now?"

"I'm afraid so."

"Give me a sec, okay?"

The man looked from Vance to Andi. "Sure thing." He left them alone.

"What's going on? What was this all about? Are you in trouble?"

"Hold off on the hundred questions." Vance kissed her forehead. "It's complicated. I can't tell you the details, Andi. It's all. . ."

"Classified?" She searched his face.

"Something like that." He grinned.

She loved his grin and wasn't sure what she was going to do when he left. Elisa either. She gasped. "Elisa!"

Vance's eyes grew wide. "Is she okay?"

"Yeah, probably still hiding. I need to go find her."

Vance grabbed her hand. "And I have to go give them a statement."

She frowned, unsure what to say.

"Don't worry, I'm not a criminal."

"So, you won't be here when I get back with Elisa?" She could only manage a small smile.

"I don't know. They'll question you, too, I'm sure."

Andi sighed, for some reason afraid she wouldn't see Vance again.

He brought his face near and kissed her, allowing his lips to linger. All too soon he released her.

"Go get Elisa. She has to be worried," he said, a huskiness in his voice. "I'll call you when I'm done."

✒

Late that night, Vance climbed into bed, exhausted from the day's ordeal. He'd phoned Andi to let her know he was home. *Home.* When had he started thinking of this place as his home? She'd listened as he'd droned on about feeling betrayed, at being used by Peter, someone he thought he could trust—the whole thing gut-wrenching.

He'd come here with only one decision to make—now, one decision had multiplied exponentially into many.

Peter had been trying to double his money—a 1.5 million-dollar contract with the government—but deliver a substandard product for a limited time, all funded by a counter-intelligence ring, with Vance set up to take the fall if the high-tech crime was discovered. Though Peter claimed he didn't know the identity of the buyer, he'd accepted funds to produce software that would give false negatives—hence, slowing the entire process.

Tom, an FBI agent, had worked undercover as a security guard for the company, planting the disk with Vance, hoping to produce a series of events that would expose the crime ring. Then Vance reacted to what he saw on the disk and uploaded a counterprogram. Peter saw the program and called Vance in to fix a bogus problem, knowing full well he wasn't in Cancun, so that Vance could be followed. The girls were in the wrong place at the wrong time—Peter used that to his advantage, calling the shots to force Vance to restore the Nitro Project, but what he didn't know was one of the kidnappers was an undercover agent.

Vance lay in stunned silence, considering the events of the previous few weeks, disheartened that Peter was in trouble and would be for a very long time.

With Peter out of the picture, Vance considered what would happen to ANND Systems. If Vance were vice president of something—once everything was sorted out—could he run the company his own way? Not like this, not in the wake of his long-time friend's ruin.

Vance rolled over, stuffing the pillow over his head.

"Why'd you do it, Peter?" Bad enough he'd engaged in criminal activity, but to drag Vance into it, putting him in place to take the fall if they were caught? He thought he'd known Peter much better. It hurt, but along with that came anger.

How could a person trust anyone? Vance flipped on his side. He was so tired.

Then there was the missile base. He'd never intended to stay, but he'd grown comfortable here. His apartment back in Fargo felt lonely and stale without Andi, a key ingredient to his happiness.

*Andi.*

What was he going to do?

# Chapter 20

Andi parked her car next to Lars's and Karl's trucks. She grabbed the letter from the passenger seat and stared at it, wishing that she'd already told Vance everything.

After listening to him share how Peter had betrayed him, and all the anger and pain in his voice... Andi released a sob.

They'd come so far, and she believed he cared for her. It was a big risk on her part, trusting him after all she'd gone through with Jorgen. Still, she was willing to take a chance. Vance was different.

But she'd kept a big secret from him. Granted, she'd not done anything criminal like his friend and partner, but the timing couldn't be worse for this news to come on the heels of Peter's treachery. Holding the letter in her hand made her feel like she was about to drop a bomb. Another bomb—like the one she'd dropped on Jorgen when she explained she had to quit school and move back home. That situation was entirely different, she admitted, because she had no control over her grandmother's death and the resulting need to care for Elisa.

But this... She'd known all along there was something hidden on the property and she'd kept it from Vance, even after they'd grown close, though that development was fairly new.

Andi leaned her forehead against the steering wheel, wishing she could put it off for another day. But that thinking was what got her into this trouble to begin with.

At least she had the Lord. He would never leave her nor forsake her. No matter Vance's reaction. Squeezing her eyes, she sent up a silent prayer. *Lord, help me explain this. Help him to understand and to forgive me.*

Andi stepped from her truck and headed into the dungeon, as Vance called it. Did he still feel that way?

More importantly, would he stay or would he go? All she wanted was to see him grin, languish in his arms, and relish his kiss. *Wow, could he kiss.*

Yet, how could that happen with what she had to tell him? Gloomy thoughts encircled her. As soon as Andi stepped through the blast door, Vance stood in her path, grinning.

Why'd he have to be so cute?

His grin quickly turned to a frown as he took one step forward. "What's wrong?"

Andi bit her lip, trudged to the sofa, and sank. "There's something you need to see." No matter how hard she tried, she couldn't bring herself to smile.

Not even for him.

He moved to sit next to her, his brows knitted. "Hey, whatever it is, I'm sure it can't be that bad."

Maybe in light of what he'd just been through, no. She smiled a little, soaking in his encouragement. But he had no idea what he was saying. Taking a deep breath, she handed over the wrinkled, coffee-stained letter she'd found after her grandmother died.

He looked at the letter, then into her eyes. "What's this?"

"Just read it. Then I'll explain."

*

Vance stared at the letter. Andi acted strangely, worrying him. Holding the letter, he read the contents.

> *My dearest Lenora,*
>
> *I'm sure you've known my feelings for you for a very long time. Before you and Harold married, I dreamed of the same happening for you and me. I won't pretend that it didn't hurt when Harold took you from me, but I'm happy you had a long and good life together. He treated you well. I was sorry to hear of his passing.*
>
> *I'm writing to let you know that I've purchased property near town. Harold hid something that belonged to you on the missile site. I hope one day soon to give it to you, and that you'll allow me to call on you when I move back to town. For old time's sake.*
>
> *Love,*
> *Vance Erickson*

Vance tugged off his glasses and pinched the bridge of his nose, thinking. What did this mean? He looked at Andi, who had her head down. "I'm guessing Lenora is your grandmother?"

She allowed her eyes to drift to his, a flicker of pain there. "Yes. Your uncle had a thing for my grandmother. I told you that already."

Vance dropped the letter to the coffee table and stood. "You said you'd explain once I finished the letter."

"Yeah, well." She cleared her throat. "I found the letter in my grandmother's things after she died. Honestly, after your uncle died, too. It says there's something hidden here. I decided that maybe that's the whole reason he hired me. I started a business because I was desperate, then your uncle came to the rescue."

Vance put up his hand. "Wait a minute. You're telling me you think he hired you to find this. . .whatever it is?"

Andi nodded.

Vance plodded to the kitchen and grabbed an energy drink. He was going to need some brainpower this morning—something he'd completely exhausted over the last few weeks. He rubbed the cool can against his temple.

"Vance?" Andi's voice was soft and nervous.

"Give me a minute." He hoped he didn't sound harsh, he didn't mean it that way, but he had to think. Peter had lied to him, hidden things, too. What was it with people?

He downed the drink, swishing some of it around in his mouth, and stared at his reflection in the microwave. He was a geek. Why shouldn't Andi use him? Just like Janice.

"Vance, I should have told you sooner. I'm so sorry."

He'd had his suspicions recently, that she was keeping something from him, though he didn't know what. He laughed and shook his head.

At himself, at his company, at Peter, then finally at the situation. After everything he'd gone through, culminating yesterday, this was by far the hardest.

*Lord, give me the faith to believe, to trust again.* Vance took a deep breath and turned to face Andi, hoping to find the answer to his prayer in her eyes, and in them he saw sorrow and regret. Raw anguish took the place of Andi's usual superficial, impossible-to-crack veneer.

Janice had never been sorry. Nor had he seen love in her eyes like he saw in Andi's. The kind of love every guy dreamed of seeing in a girl's eyes. He released a breath, overpowered by the emotions streaming through him. Andi had finally let down her guard, and for that Vance was thankful.

It was all worth it. He slid around the island, enjoying the questioning look on her face, and took her hand in his. It felt good. Right.

*Thank You, Lord.*

Andi stared at his hand and then up into his face, taken aback.

"I know it took a lot for you to tell me this. So, did you find it?"

Her mouth dropped open. Vance grinned, wishing she would close it so he could plant a fat kiss on her lips.

"I. . .uh, no. Yeah, I mean. I think I found where it might be hidden while we were hiding in the equipment building. I wanted to wait for you."

"You *waited* for me?"

Nodding, she smiled for the first time since she'd arrived.

"Okay, before we go on this treasure hunt, there is something I want to make clear. My uncle was eccentric, yes, but he was a good businessman, and he had the money to show for it. I think he hired you because he believed in you, Andi. Believed you could create this." Vance motioned to indicate the entire room.

Andi cracked a half-grin. "Maybe."

It might take some time to convince her. "One more thing. . . Whatever we find, it's yours. My uncle wanted your grandmother to have it. Don't think I want it just because it's on my property, okay?"

Her face brightened. "You've been good enough about this whole thing,

I. . .I want you to keep it."

"Nope, I insist. It's yours."

They laughed together and then made their way to the equipment building where they found Karl and Lars replacing the entire section of the wall.

Andi gasped. "Oh no. Guys, wait."

They both looked up at the same time.

"Can you take a break? There's something behind that wall I need to look at."

Karl shrugged and Lars followed him over to their ice chest where they grabbed some water.

Andi found the place and began removing the wall.

"What do you think is hidden there?"

Without stopping her work, she replied, "For some reason, I always thought—no, hoped—that it would be something of value. Maybe even money. But now"—she looked at him—"I think I was completely wrong. What do you think?"

Vance watched her closely. She probably needed the money and wanted it to be money so badly—she put her hope in it. "I couldn't say. After reading the letter, I didn't picture money."

A section of the wall removed, Vance peered into the hole with Andi.

# Chapter 21

A ndi held her breath as they slid a small box from the space between the walls. "Definitely not money."

Though she smiled up at Vance, she knew he could see her disappointment. She was an idiot to believe it might be something to help her and Elisa. In a moment that should have been exciting, she sagged, her spirits deflated.

Andi held the box out to Vance. "Will you do the honors?"

"I told you it was yours. You open it."

She opened the box to see a folded missive. "It's a letter."

"There's more." Vance lifted a smaller box and handed it to Andi.

It looked an awful lot like. . . "A ring box," she whispered. Andi opened the top to see a diamond ring and gasped. "It's beautiful."

"Are you going to read the letter?" Vance held the folded paper out to her. "Or do you want me to?"

Andi frowned. "I have a feeling I'm not going to like what it says."

Vance chuckled. "Ah Andi, where's your sense of adventure? All this ancient history between two lovers—your grandmother, my great-uncle. It's fascinating."

"Adventurous, yes, fascinating, no." Andi slipped the ring from the box and onto the third finger on her left hand—it fit perfectly—admiring it and considering what it would feel like to be a married woman. To wear such a huge rock on her hand.

Before she realized what she'd done, she caught Vance staring at her, smiling. Her heart thudded. She quickly tugged it off and slipped it back in the box.

Vance cleared his throat as if to signal he wanted her attention off the ring and on the letter. "Looks like it's a confession from your grandfather, Harold. He stole the ring from my uncle Vance and hid it on the missile site when he discovered Vance was about to propose to Lenora. In the meantime, he proposed to her himself, beating my uncle to the proverbial punch—your grandmother."

Andi nearly dropped the box. "Oh Vance. I don't know what to say, I'm so sorry!"

"Why are you apologizing? All the involved parties have now passed to the afterlife. But. . .your grandmother loved two people?"

Andi shook her head, confused. "I don't know. There has to be something more, some other reason she would have married my grandfather if she loved your uncle. Unless your uncle was mistaken about her feelings."

"Could be many reasons. Maybe she didn't know of my uncle's love, or didn't think he was the right man, or her parents didn't approve. Who knows? But sounds like your grandfather felt guilty and wrote this confession to go with the ring. Must have been a serious rivalry between the two of them to win her hand."

"I wonder if he secretly hoped the ring would be discovered one day."

"And I wonder when and how my uncle learned it was hidden here."

"I'm guessing my grandfather told him he'd hidden it here, knowing there wasn't a thing Mr. E could do with it secreted away in the nerve center of a launch control facility, until, of course, he purchased it once it was decommissioned."

Andi sighed as thoughts of all the times these last few years—before Mr. E or her grandmother had died—they'd spent together. They'd seemed to enjoy each other's company, and near the end, she'd seen Mr. E kissing her grandmother. Just as things had begun to warm up, her grandmother had died.

"I still can't believe my grandfather would do such a thing." He stole the ring from Mr. E, effectively stealing the woman he loved. *And I was about to do the same—steal the hidden treasure from his nephew.* Though only a ring, Andi had hoped and believed it was much more.

The disappointment was a direct hit to her heart, and she'd done it to herself. "Look, I know what you said, but I can't keep this." She handed the ring to Vance. "It was your uncle's, stolen by my grandfather. My grandmother didn't deserve to have it, or a second chance with your uncle."

Andi rushed from Vance toward the blast door exit.

"Andi, wait!"

Tears blurring her vision, she turned to face him, walking backward and shaking her head. "Later, Vance. . .just, later."

✒❤

The microwave dinged, signaling Vance that his lunch was ready.

Another day, another burrito. Man, he used to love these things, but now as he stared at it, he realized even a burrito couldn't restore his appetite. He set the plate on the kitchen island. Thanks to Andi, he wasn't hungry. That wasn't fair. He couldn't blame her. She had nothing to do with the problems at his company or with Peter. Vance assumed she needed some time to sort things out. He'd give her that.

The Lord knew they both needed it.

Adding to Vance's stack of decisions to make, a man had left a message sometime in the middle of the chaos regarding purchasing the missile site. He'd heard Vance wanted to sell. Vance hadn't made that a secret.

If he left now, he'd leave Andi. He needed more time to get to know her, to find out how she felt about him, if they were right for each other, to know what to do.

But staying had never been part of his plan. His intention had been to think about whether to stay or leave ANND Systems, but in his heart he'd decided a long time ago he was leaving. His family wanted him back in Texas. He was happier there. His dad's words came back to him. *"Sometimes a person thought he knew what he wanted and when he got it, he discovered how wrong he was."*

The box with the ring rested inches from his plate, the lid open, revealing the diamond shimmering like a distant quasar through the lens of the Hubble space telescope. Either that or, if you looked at it just right, an entire galaxy.

Vance's appetite suddenly returned, so he sat at the counter, eating and thinking. It was all unreal—his uncle bought the missile site to search for a ring a man had stolen from him decades before, hiding it away so he could propose to the woman he loved, stealing her, too. Then his uncle hired Andi, the granddaughter of the guy who stole and hid the ring, to renovate the place and gave the property to his nephew when he died—a nephew who fell in love with the granddaughter while she was renovating. Uncle Vance couldn't possibly have known.

*Real life is stranger than fiction.* He'd heard that old saying plenty of times. There wasn't any denying its truth. But Vance believed the Creator of the universe held all things together and worked all things for good for those who love Him.

Vance dropped his fork. He knew what to do.

# Chapter 22

Elisa walked through the front door after school. "So glad this is the last week of summer school." She looked at Andi. "Sis, is everything okay? Why aren't you at work?"

Andi had told Elisa she could stay home today to rest from yesterday's drama, but she'd wanted to go to school. Probably to see Todd. "I gave myself the day off."

"But I thought you were going to work after you dropped me off?"

"I did."

Elisa threw her backpack on the chair and sat next to Andi. "Did you tell him?"

"Yeah, and we found a box and opened it."

Elisa's eyes widened. "You did? What was in it?" Her excitement dampened. "Oh wait, I guess it wasn't that great or you wouldn't be sitting here depressed."

"I'm not depressed."

"Are we sisters? You always want me to talk to you. The same goes for me."

Andi took a sip of her coffee. "I placed so much importance on finding what was hidden, even believing it would be something to help us financially, that I hid the fact that I was searching for something from Vance."

"How did he react when you told him?"

"You know, I think he was upset at first, but that didn't last long. He helped me open the box. It was a ring." Andi explained about the letter and that she'd followed in her grandfather's footsteps.

"You did no such thing. You told Vance. You gave him the ring."

"It's not only that." Andi's eyes teared up. She groaned and shoved herself from the couch, hating that she'd let down her guard. None of this would have happened, she wouldn't be feeling this way if she'd guarded her heart.

"Well?"

"Someone contacted me, asking about the missile site property. They want to buy. I gave him Vance's number."

"That would mean we get our money, wouldn't it? Isn't Vance going to share some of those profits with you for the work?"

"Technically, we're not finished." Andi set her coffee cup on the kitchen table.

"Oh, I get it. If Vance sells, then he's. . ."

"Gone." That old familiar pang hit her in the chest. When would she ever learn?

"Andi, you can't know that."

"Can't I? He's always made it clear he was leaving. There isn't anything for him here."

For the rest of the day, Andi sat on the sofa, watching mindless television shows—something she usually had no time for. But it was therapy of a sort, giving her a rest from the burdens of her heart and mind.

Close to bedtime, someone rang the doorbell. Andi knew she looked horrid but didn't care. "You get it," she whispered to Elisa. "Probably Todd."

Elisa peeked out the curtains. "Nope, it's Vance. You get it." She ran to her bedroom.

Andi sighed, not ready for this conversation or confrontation. She wasn't sure which. She finger-combed her hair to make sure her ponytail was in place and took a deep breath to quiet her heart. *More like harden.*

The doorbell sounded again. Andi opened it to see a nervous smile spread across Vance's face. As always, he looked adorable with his crooked grin.

"I was beginning to think you weren't going to open the door."

Andi didn't know how to feel, her heart pounding loudly in her ears. "Are you going to sell the site to that guy?"

"Wha— Can I come in first?"

"Oh, sure." Andi stood aside, allowing him into the living room.

They stood there, quiet and awkward. If Andi weren't so down, she would have laughed.

Another nervous chuckle escaped Vance. What was going through his mind?

"This isn't going like I imagined."

Andi angled her head. "What isn't going?"

"Can we go outside?"

"What for?"

Vance must have known that taking her hand gently in his held magical powers over her because he did just that.

"Trust me. This will go much better outside."

Andi couldn't help but smile and follow him.

"Let's take a walk." He held her hand.

Feeling more relaxed than she had all afternoon, Andi tried to enjoy the time with Vance, knowing she might not have much left.

They continued walking until they were in the field near her neighborhood. "Here. This will work. I can see the stars and still see your face."

"Vance, what's going on?"

"My uncle meant for you to have this ring, Andi." He opened the box, revealing the diamond ring.

Andi gasped, uncertain she ever wanted to see the ring again. "I thought we'd already been over this. It belongs to you."

"And I'm giving it to you."

Andi shook her head and pulled away, but Vance tugged her close and kissed her lightly. Keeping his face near hers, he said, "Once you let your guard down and let me in, I realized you're all I ever wanted. Andi Nielsen, will you marry me?"

Stunned with his proposal, her knees wobbled. She nodded.

He grinned. "Is that a yes?"

"Yes." She swallowed, barely able to speak the word. "Yes!" Louder now.

"You've just made me the happiest man in the universe."

Vance smiled, brighter than she'd ever seen—his smile shining like two colliding galaxies.

# *Epilogue*

*An unusual wedding, indeed,* Andi thought.

Under the night sky—the stars glittering like diamonds and the heavens a clear reminder that God held the universe together, even as He held their hearts together—Andi said her wedding vows. Vance at her side, she never dreamed she could be this happy and content. God had remodeled her heart even as she had remodeled the missile site.

"I now pronounce you man and wife. You may kiss the bride."

Andi closed her eyes and accepted her husband's kiss. *Her husband.* The words made her feel like she was floating.

When they finished, they turned to face the small crowd—including Vance's family members from Texas who were willing to brave the mosquitoes on a cool North Dakota summer evening so Andi and Vance could have their wedding under the stars.

"Introducing Mr. and Mrs. Vance Young."

Andi and her new husband hurried down the aisle between the folding chairs, arms linked.

They rushed back to their home across the field at the missile site, where they would host a reception for their guests. They'd agreed to live there for a year, while Vance worked as a contract programmer and prayed about starting his own company. Elisa would stay with Freya Emerson for a couple of weeks to give the newlyweds time alone, then she'd move into her new room at Ground Zero.

He lifted Andi in his arms, swept her into the elevator, and continued to hold her until they'd crossed over the blast door threshold. He set her gently on her feet, then pulled a gift—wrapped in white with a silver bow—from the side table and handed his present to her.

She giggled as she took it. "What's this?"

"I wanted to give you something special." He winked.

If there was one thing she loved, it was a man who could make her weak in the knees with a simple wink. Oh, how she loved him. She carefully ripped open the paper to reveal a certificate and gasped. "You. . .named a star after me?"

"And why not? You're my shining star." He tugged her to him and kissed her on the top of the head. "You should know it's only a novelty gesture. The only thing I could officially name after you through the International Astronomical Union was an asteroid. I didn't think a mere asteroid was a good fit for my beautiful Andi."

"You are amazing. I love that you'd want to name a star after me, and I love you." She stared up into his eyes expectantly.

"You know, the wedding under the stars was memorable, exceptional even. I'm glad we did it." He nuzzled her neck. "But now I'm hoping the guests won't stay too long."

Andi smiled her agreement.

# EXPOSING
# AMBER

# Dedication

This novel is dedicated to my loving family. Thank you for your tireless encouragement and support. My deep appreciation goes to critique partners, Deborah Vogts, Lynette Sowell, Ronie Kendig, Lisa Harris, and Shannon McNear for your commitment. Thanks to the staff of Douglass County Museum of Natural and Cultural History who shared invaluable information, giving me a behind-the-scenes tour and answering my questions. Special thanks go to paleontologist Walter Stein of PaleoAdventures for providing details of the fossil dig experience that I needed to write this story. The views expressed in this novel are not necessarily his, and any mistakes are mine alone.

# Chapter 1

This was supposed to be a rare opportunity, or so Amber McKinsey had been assured.

After the man in front of her finished his purchase, Amber stepped up to the counter. "Where can I find the museum director, Brandon Selman?"

The museum store cashier, an older woman who could easily have been Amber's grandmother, smiled and adjusted her glasses to study Amber. "I'm not sure if *Dr.* Selman is available. May I ask your business?"

Amber didn't miss the woman's emphasis on the title *Dr.* and felt like an idiot. Noting her name badge, she said, "Gladys, Dr. Selman accepted me as a volunteer. You see, I'm an undergraduate student. . . ." She trailed off when she noticed Gladys organizing her work center.

Uncertain if Gladys was still listening or simply multitasking, Amber pushed the coffee-stained acceptance letter forward on the counter. That would explain everything.

Gladys lifted it and read through the bottom half of her bifocals. "Amber McKinsey. Why didn't you say so?"

Amber nearly sagged under the weight of relief. "I'm sorry. I should have told you my name." And she would have except she hadn't thought a store clerk would be the one reviewing her internship acceptance letter.

"That's all right. I should have realized who you were. I've been expecting you." Gladys came from behind the register. "I'm desperate for some help in the museum store. We've wanted someone who has an interest in the past, rather than someone who doesn't know and doesn't care."

Amber frowned. "What. . .what did you say? The museum *store*? I think there's been a mistake." The letter accepting her as a volunteer to intern at the Harrington Natural and Cultural Museum was from the museum director. She grabbed the paper from the counter where Gladys had put it and handed it back to her.

Gladys read the letter again. "It says you've been accepted for a volunteer position at the museum." Gladys held out the letter and shrugged. "I was told you would be helping me in the store."

Gently, Amber tugged it from the older woman's fingers and stared at it again. "I. . .I don't understand."

Gladys placed a hand on Amber's shoulder. "Didn't you request a volunteer position at the museum?"

Amber nodded.

"The museum store is a part of the museum, don't you know?"

Amber pulled her stunned thoughts away from the acceptance letter to look at Gladys who scrunched her face. Slowly, her expression softened.

"I suppose so," Amber said. Gladys hadn't made a great first impression, but Amber could see she meant well.

"Let's get you settled, then. You can explore the grounds today, then tomorrow see me back here at eight o'clock sharp." Gladys handed her a map then opened a small cabinet on the wall. "You're in cabin B-3. Here's the key."

Amber took the key from her and smiled, attempting to mask her frustration. Though Amber wanted to further discuss what she believed was a mix-up, a line of people waiting to make their purchases had formed behind her. Not the best time.

Adjusting her glasses again, Gladys winked. "Don't worry. It'll work out. You'll see."

Only able to offer the smallest of smiles, Amber left Gladys to attend to her customers.

Ignoring the offerings of replicas, toys, and games, Amber pushed past a family with rambunctious children who waited in line behind her to purchase robotic dinosaurs and imitation Native American pottery. Exiting the store, Amber entered the museum lobby and drew in a ragged breath.

She always loved the peculiar smell in museums—a blend of fresh paint, commercial-grade carpet, and musty oldness. But. . .what had just happened in there? She was to present the letter when she arrived, validating her acceptance to work under museum director and notable paleontologist, Brandon Selman. Dr. Young, her professor at the University of North Dakota, had advised her that by working under a professional with a broad field of expertise, Amber could better evaluate her goals. And they had her working in the museum store?

Amber pushed through the double glass-paned doors of the main entrance. When the door swooshed closed behind her, a gust quickly whipped strands of hair into her face. The reflective glass confirmed her long, black tresses were in a mess. Another blast of air ripped the letter from her fingers, sending her chasing it across the grass and sidewalk.

Red hair whipping around her face, Cams leaned against her silver Prius, laughing. "You'd better catch that before it escapes into the North Dakota Badlands."

Finally snatching the errant slip of paper, Amber made her way to Cams, her roommate at UND for the last two years. Somehow, over that course of time, Amber had given Carmen Milewski the nickname. But Cams didn't seem to mind.

Amber held up the key to the cabin. "You ready?"

Cams smiled and nodded as she made her way around to the driver's side. She would take Amber and all her junk over to the cabin. Amber's car simply wasn't long-haul worthy, so she'd left it parked at a friend's house in Grand

Forks. Cams had brought her across the state, loaded down with her bicycle and enough personal belongings to last for the summer.

Thankfully, Amber had gotten permission to bring Josh, her ruby-eyed white Netherland dwarf rabbit, as long as he was in an appropriate cage.

"Okay, so where is this cabin?" Cams asked as she drove to the nearest parking lot exit.

Amber pulled the map out and directed Cams. The museum offered cabins free of charge to college volunteers and interns on a first-come-first-serve basis. As the Prius bumped slowly down the one-lane gravel road, Amber spotted a trail. Perfect. She could take a jog later.

"That building didn't look big enough, on the outside at least, to be a museum," Cams said.

"You should have come in with me so you could see for yourself."

"I didn't want to cramp your style or anything."

Amber chuckled. If Cams only knew—her "style" had been cramped anyway. At the moment, Amber felt like the size of a tiny unimportant fossil. "There's a few thousand feet of floor space, though even that is considered small for a museum. And though I didn't get a chance to browse, I've heard the exhibits feature fossils and dinosaur replicas, period displays, and dioramas of local history themes, including Western and American Indians."

"Sounds. . .uh. . .interesting."

Amber laughed again, knowing full well Cams had no interest in history.

"Here we are." Cams stopped the car in front of a genuine log cabin, nestled behind a copse of trees.

Amber carried her luggage to the door and unlocked it. Unsure if her cabin mate had arrived yet or not, she strolled in cautiously.

"Hello?" Other than furniture, the place looked empty, devoid of life.

Breathing hard, Cams rushed in behind Amber, loaded down with a couple more bags. "I'm glad you're not into fashion." She dropped the luggage on the old wood floors. A large colorful rug rested in the center of the room. Cams looked around. "Nice."

Amber plopped onto one of the burnt orange sofas. "Not too bad. It's even cushy."

Cams smirked a little. "Probably got these at the Salvation Army or something."

"Who cares." Amber rose from the sofa. "I've got to find my room and a place for Josh."

"Okay, I'll get your bike off my car."

Amber found a room she claimed for her own in the two-bedroom, one-bath dwelling. After she finished unloading everything and getting Josh settled in his cage, she spotted Cams opening a kitchen cabinet.

"Good. You've got a few dishes, too." Cams pulled out a glass and filled it with tap water.

"I can't tell you how much I appreciate you driving me here." Amber spread her hands over the small island counter, feeling the smooth, white Formica. At least it was clean.

"Hey, I was going in the same direction."

"Not hardly," Amber said. Cams had gone out of her way to drop off Amber at the museum before heading home to Watford City. "When are your parents expecting you?"

Cams glanced at her watch. "Not for a couple of hours. Listen, it was really no trouble to bring you here. If you change your mind, call me. I'll come pick you up."

"And then what? I can stay at your parents' with you until you go back to Grand Forks?"

A laugh escaped Cams. "Who knows, maybe I'll have changed my mind, too, and we can go back together."

"You're terrible."

"But you still love me. Besides, I'll only be there a couple of weeks."

"I know, I know. You have to get back to that part-time job," Amber said. Cams held on to a hopeless dream that her boss would ask her out. Amber would never let herself fall for a guy she worked with. That could get messy.

"You know me." Cams smiled. "Got to go. Call me if you need a ride."

"Okay." Amber waved at Cams, who climbed into her car and backed from the small driveway, if you could call it that.

Amber sighed and sank into the sofa. Maybe she should have told Cams what happened, that she wouldn't be working in the museum like she thought. But with Cams's generosity, Amber couldn't bear to tell her she'd brought her all this way for nothing.

How could this happen? She'd come to a crossroads regarding courses for her undergraduate degree at UND. Though she'd taken classes in geology and biology, as she progressed, she became less certain about a future in paleontology. Dr. Young had strongly recommended she get hands-on experience this summer. He'd even written a recommendation for her to include in her application for an intern position at the Harrington Natural and Cultural Museum.

She'd been accepted. But with news she'd be working in the museum store?—there went her rare opportunity to intern under Dr. Selman.

⚜

Brandon rushed down the corridors of the museum offices, barely aware that someone called his name in the distance. He tuned out the annoyance while he finished reading through the numbers. Though the museum was a nonprofit organization, it still had to make ends meet.

The bottom line? He needed more donors. And to get more donors he had to socialize and dine and come up with more brilliant ideas, projects, and initiatives, all within their conflict-of-interest guidelines, of course.

He entered his office and sat in his office chair, then looked up from the report to see his desk piled high with catalogs, requisitions for display materials, and the information he'd requested from a talented replica artist who'd come highly recommended. Though it was Harrington Museum's policy to avoid displaying inauthentic artifacts, at times the measure was deemed necessary. When replicas were exhibited, the authentic artifact would be kept safely in the museum's vault.

He loved his job, but at times like these he'd give anything to go back to his old love and dig in the dirt. Feel the exhilaration of discovering a fossil. Other than that, he'd often considered teaching. He'd even put an application in at UND. Then if the museum endeavor didn't fly this time, he'd have something he enjoyed to fall back on.

But right now the museum teetered on the verge of soaring, and Brandon needed to clear everything off his plate to make sure that happened. For the last three years, he'd worked toward gaining accreditation for Harrington in the American Association of Museums.

Once the museum had passed its three-year mark, they'd worked to accession, or formally acquire, the rest of their permanent collection. He sucked in a sharp breath. All that was left now before the formal application was to assemble the needed documentation.

*Soon,* he told himself.

After losing his good standing in the professional community, he needed this museum to gain recognition and credibility. Without validation, he had no value to anyone. *Not even God.*

His cell rang. Brandon read the caller ID and answered.

"Dad, thanks for returning my call." Not the best timing, but his parents often went to bed before Brandon even got home from work, preferring to rise very early. It was now or never.

"Your mom and I were grocery shopping. Sorry we missed your call. What's up?" Despite the fact his father was well into his eighties, his voice remained bold and strong.

"I like to check on you every once in a while, that okay?"

"You called to say you won't be coming this weekend. Am I right?"

Was he that predictable? Brandon sighed into the phone, instantly regretting it. His parents only lived an hour away. "Sorry to skip out on you again. I have too much on my plate this week. I'll have to work through the weekend."

"Son, your mother and I were talking about this today. We're more than proud of your accomplishments. But when are you going to settle down?"

Brandon squashed his sigh this time. He was thirty-nine, and he'd heard the same lecture the last fifteen years at least. "Dad, we've been through this."

"Find yourself a wife before it's too late. Your mom wants grandkids before she dies. We need someone to carry on the family name and legacy."

*Legacy?* Brandon wasn't sure he had much to offer in terms of legacy given his failures. His dad, the great Chappell Selman, had been head curator of a large nationally recognized museum. Attempting to follow in his footsteps had been a daunting task. In fact, Brandon was still trying.

"Okay, Dad. I'll consider your advice. On another topic, how are you doing?"

"I'm as healthy as a horse, or so the doctor said. I know you're busy. Come see us when you can. I'm starting to think that God will have to throw a good woman in your path and make you trip over her."

They said their good-byes, and Brandon stared at his cell, wishing he had time to get away and see his parents. A stack of applications at the corner of Brandon's desk caught his attention. He slid the papers toward him.

"You're going to thank me for this." Jim Russel stood in the doorway.

In his midforties, thin and athletic, Jim had premature silver hair. Even though Brandon was younger by six years, Jim could squash him on the tennis court on Brandon's best day.

"Thank you for what?"

"I accessioned the Hamlin Exhibit. It's on loan from the Prehistoric Museum in Utah." Jim sounded energized.

Brandon squinted, trying to comprehend what Jim had said. He didn't want to get his hopes up if he'd misunderstood. "Say again?"

Jim came fully into his office and pulled out the chair across from Brandon, a victorious smile on his face. "I think you heard me. The Hamlin Exhibit. It's on its way here."

"You're talking prehistoric developmental pottery discovered in Utah, right? That's out of the provenance of our collections, don't you think?" He wasn't sure what Jim was thinking on this one. Their collections, both natural and cultural, were limited to southwest North Dakota. But maybe. . .

Jim sent him a pointed stare. "I think it's an opportunity."

Brandon leaned back as far as the chair would allow and stared at the ceiling. News of the display could certainly give him the edge he needed to solicit more donors.

"Brandon? What do you think?" Jim asked, the ring of impatience in his voice.

Probably because Brandon hadn't given him the slap on the back he was looking for. Jim was an experienced curator with a master's degree in history and archaeology. Brandon figured the man was simply doing his job. And, having worked with Brandon for years now, Jim knew better than to expect kudos.

Brandon rolled forward and sat tall, fixing Jim with a look. "We'll have to rush order the appropriate display enclosures, organize the exhibit."

Jim snorted. "Well, that goes without saying, doesn't it? I thought you'd be ecstatic."

"Oh, but I am. Can't you see the wheels in my head are already turning?"

"Sure. I hoped you'd turn a few cartwheels, too."

Brandon laughed, already visualizing the exhibit. "We'll need to create marketing materials, get the word out. I like for the displays to be as kid friendly as possible. Not sure that's going to work on this. How long do we have the collection?"

"Six months."

"What is the total value of the artifacts?" Brandon asked.

"You know that's relative, depending on who is buying." He grinned. "The museum has the exhibit insured for 150,000 dollars."

*A quarter of our operating budget.* Brandon whistled. That number made him slightly nervous. "Not sure how you managed this."

"Connections are everything, as you know."

Brandon nodded, frowning. He assumed Jim referred to how Brandon had secured his current position as museum director. He didn't enjoy the reminder that his reputation alone couldn't have landed him this job.

The replica artist's materials and business card stared back at him from his desk. The way the artist's references sounded, even a museum expert would have difficulty telling the difference. Given the news Jim had shared, now would be a great time to test the artist's abilities. He grinned at the thought. At the same time, he could test Jim's ability to discern a replica from an authentic artifact, have a little fun with him. Brandon shuffled papers on his desk to hide the information packet. And. . .the way Jim acted lately, the man could probably use getting knocked down a few notches.

"I'd say things are beginning to look up." But he must maintain the foothold he had at the museum while gaining momentum. This could be exactly what he needed to accomplish that. It would mean more hours of work and even fewer free weekends.

*Sorry, Dad.* With the thought, the workload on his desk began pressing on him. "Was there anything else?"

"We'll need more volunteers and interns to make this run smoothly," Jim added.

At that, Brandon leaned back again and folded his arms over his chest. He gave a slight shake of his head. "I'm thinking not."

"What?" Surprised eyes stared back.

"Volunteers, yes. Interns, no. I don't have time to take anyone under my wing right now. I need to focus on making this museum a success. In fact, I've been thinking about this for a long time. Should have done this sooner."

"And what's *this*?" Jim sounded cautious.

"No more protégés." After what someone had pulled five years ago, practically destroying his career, he wasn't sure he ever wanted to be in that position again.

Jim laughed. "Come on. You don't have to mentor anyone just because we bring them on as interns. Besides, they make better workers than volunteers who have no expertise or any interest in furthering their future."

Brandon nodded. "That's what you said last year, and I still ended up with someone expecting my time and energy." He closed his eyes, hating how the words sounded because he truly wanted to give back to others, help them if he could. He loved teaching. But not at the expense of the museum, or his time and energy.

Jim sighed.

"Just. . .not right now. I'm still in disaster-recovery mode." He'd only been museum director of the new museum for three years now. There was plenty of time in the future to mentor interns. "Right now, I have to make sure this museum gains respect and credibility." *That I have a solid future.*

Brandon avoided Jim's eyes, knowing full well the man thought Brandon should let go of the past. But Jim hadn't gone through the scrutiny that Brandon had.

At that moment, he took a closer look at the applications resting on his desk. *Intern apps.* "Therefore, we can toss these in the trash." Brandon did exactly that.

Jim jumped up. "Wait. You can't just throw them out. You have to respond to each one of them. Give them a nice rejection letter."

"Considering I didn't request them, maybe you should send out the letters."

Yanking the stash from the small garbage can, Jim rifled through them. "Do you realize how long these have been sitting on your desk?"

"No, but I'm wondering why they ended up there in the first place." Brandon chuckled, hoping to diffuse the tension and stood, moving to the credenza where he always kept a carafe of coffee.

"No idea."

He poured himself a cup. "Coffee?"

"No thanks. I'm glad we didn't have this conversation until now because we need the additional help. Our summer months are the busiest. We already have a few extra volunteers and interns on the way."

Brandon stopped with the cup halfway to his lips. "What?"

# Chapter 2

Amber stood in the museum lobby. Nausea stirred in her stomach. Why did she have to follow so closely in her brother's career path when it served as a constant reminder of him? She'd spent her childhood idolizing him, following in his footsteps—but he'd destroyed everything.

The museum directory stared back at her, the exhibit listings soothing her thoughts. Maybe all things ancient was simply in the family blood.

Amber ran a finger over the directory's smooth Plexiglas surface, glad for time to peruse the museum. The directory included a floor plan, revealing the location of various exhibits.

She loved that the museum included local cultural history as well as the natural history of the region, boasting a full triceratops skull, duck-billed dinosaurs, and a full-sized model of a *Tyrannosaurus rex*—all dinosaurs that had been discovered in the nearby Hell Creek Formation. Her momentary disappointment deterred, Amber looked forward to exploring the museum.

"Excuse me." A slender college-aged girl touched Amber's shoulder. "You must be Amber McKinsey."

Amber tried not to stare at the pink stripe down the right side of the girl's black hair. "Yes, that's right. How did you know?"

"The lady in the store pointed you out. I'm Muriel Willbanks." She thrust out her hand. "We're going to be roommates." Her smile broadened. "Isn't this exciting?"

Working at the museum store exciting? But then Muriel probably wouldn't be a volunteer in the store. Amber returned the smile.

"I'm heading to the cabin now to unpack."

"Do you need any help?" Amber asked, mostly to be polite. She really wanted to explore the museum now.

"Oh, that would be great. My car is in the parking lot."

Masking her disappointment, Amber followed Muriel out to her dusty, old Honda Accord. The girl seemed nice enough, dispersing any reservations Amber had about rooming with someone she didn't know or like. At least she had wheels.

"So, what's your assignment?" Amber asked.

Muriel fairly squealed. "I'm interning under Dr. Laudan. I'll get to accompany her to the digs. Can you imagine finding a real dinosaur fossil?"

❧

When Amber woke up from a nap, her roommate was gone. Muriel's news had stung Amber in a big way, especially on the heels of discovering she'd be working in the store instead of assisting with real science or museum work.

Amber had been too deflated to go back to the museum after helping Muriel unpack. And now, it was too late. Figuring she had an hour before dark, Amber pulled on her sneakers.

Running had always given her an extra energy boost and lifted her spirits. Things often looked clear where they'd been muddy. These days, with so much weighing on her, she wasn't sure she could survive without the exhilarating exercise. An ache sliced through her heart. She used to pray when she ran. Since the accident that had killed her mother and sister, she'd hardened her heart. She knew it, but what to do about it?

From his cage, Josh stared at her and wriggled his little nose. She opened the top and gently tugged him out, sending a puff of white fur everywhere. Holding the small white bundle close, she rubbed him behind the ears. Mom had always kept rabbits.

*You'd really love this one, Mom.* Amber held Josh up to look him in the eyes then placed him back in his cage.

Stumbling out the door, she stood on the porch. Rocky Mountain junipers and red cedars surrounded the small cabin. She took a deep breath of their strong evergreen scent, then jogged down the gravel drive lined with poplars, easily spotting the trailhead. The sign said the trail was five and a half miles and showed a diagram of a loop connecting with other trails, some nearing the Little Missouri River.

Now that was something Amber desperately wanted to see. Scientists said a glacier had forced the river into a short steep route, which created the Badlands formations. If nothing else, this summer diversion should allow her to explore the region—a huge attraction to geologists and paleontologists around the world.

Amber ran along the trail, enjoying the fresh air. With the sun quickly setting, she quickened her five-mile pace on the loop. Ahead of her, the trail narrowed between two large cedars, and another runner approached from the opposite direction. She made a longer stride between the trees and stepped on a huge rock, seemingly out of place in her path, careful to avoid stepping at the wrong angle since her injury last year.

Pushing from the rock, she propelled around another tree and collided with someone—the other runner? White and blue flashed in her eyes. She stumbled, a familiar pain ripping through her right ankle. Her balance lost, she fell forward, hands and knees catching the brunt of her fall.

Pebbles and rocks pierced her palms. She rolled onto her backside then sprawled flat on her back to stare at the canopy above. "Well, this is just a great addition to an already perfect day."

She wondered if the other person had fallen, too. "You all right over there?"

A handsome face framed with black hair hovered above her. Dark olive eyes stared down at her in concern. He offered his hand. "I'm fine. You're the one who took a fall."

"It's my family heirloom. Clumsiness." Though she wasn't sure how much value she could put on it. Amber accepted his help and stood. She dusted off her shorts. "Are you sure you're not hurt?"

The man scrutinized himself, looking over his smudged white T-shirt and dark blue running shorts. "No, I think I'm good, except that I received an elbow to the ribs." His frown spread into a V-shaped wide grin, producing large dimples. He held his side. "You pack a great punch when you're falling."

Amber stared, unsure if he was teasing. "I'm so sorry."

"Don't be. I'm not the one having a bad day."

Puzzled, it took her a few seconds to form words. "And how would you know that?"

"What? That I'm not the one having a bad day?"

"Okay, you're teasing, aren't you?"

That smile again. "Only partially. When you fell, you said something about this being a great addition to your perfect day. I assumed that was an attempt at sarcasm."

Amber's cheeks warmed. "I didn't realize I'd said that out loud."

"You want to tell me about it? We can run together."

"No, I've got an old war injury I think I just triggered when I ran into you. I should walk for a bit until it feels better."

"Okay, let's walk the trail then."

Amber considered the stranger's invitation, and feeling comfortable with him, she said, "Sure, you can walk with me. I'm heading back though. Want to clean up these scrapes."

He reached down to grab a stainless steel water bottle with the Nike label. Uncapping the bottle, he held it out to her. "Thirsty?"

"No, I'm good."

"So, tell me about your bad day before the fall." He walked next to her when the trail would allow.

Amber readjusted her scrunchie. Did she really want to go into all that? "Oh it's nothing, really. I came here to do a certain job, only to find out I'm doing something else. Something. . .less. And the man I was planning to work under, well, I guess I'm not important enough to warrant his attention." She made it sound like she was actually employed somewhere. But how could she explain all that to a stranger?

She stopped. Through the trees she saw what looked like the breaks—the descent into the Badlands terrain of ridges, bluffs, and buttes. As Amber gazed into the distance, the man came to a stop next to her.

She took a step from the trail, thinking to head for the break in the trees and look at the terrain. "Is that—"

The man gently laid his hand on her arm. "You don't want to do that."

Warmth raced over her skin. Startled, she looked at him. "Why not?"

"It'll be dark soon. It's not called the Badlands for nothing. One misstep could land you at the bottom of a pinnacle. The Sioux Indians called it a word that meant 'land bad' and the French translated that into 'a bad land to cross.'"

Disappointed, Amber frowned. "I'm sure you're right. What was I thinking?"

"You were thinking you wanted to see something magnificent. And especially in the moonlight it truly is. Some of the structures look like ruins from an ancient city."

"Wow, really?" Amber sighed, thinking how beautiful that would be. Then she peeked at the man standing next to her. He wouldn't look a day over thirty if it weren't for the slightly graying hair at his temples, making him appear famous and distinguished.

Standing next to him, she sensed something different about him. Part of her wished there was a way she could see him again. But how?

After a thoughtful moment, the man pulled his gaze from the trees and back to Amber, returning her intense stare.

Brandon held his breath, struggling to remember his father's words. Something about God making him trip over a good woman.

He eyed the young woman with raven hair—shiny and black like that of a thoroughbred—and eyes an unusual shade. Liquid gold with flecks of brown, though it was hard to be sure in the dimming light.

*Striking.*

An uneven rhythm thudded in his chest. *That* was new.

He'd not seen her jogging on the trails before today. Maybe Dad was right. She was beautiful, obviously loved to run, and. . .he didn't work with her.

Feeling tongue-tied as a schoolboy, he wasn't sure where to go from here.

Suddenly, he was hit with the strangest desire—he wished. . .he wished he could share the beauty of the eroded pinnacles that only appeared to look like ancient ruins in the moonlight. Asking her—a woman he'd only just met—if he could show her the sight was completely out of the question. And yet?

No—they were complete strangers. What could he say to her?

She appeared uncomfortable under his scrutiny. *Uh-oh.* He'd better say something and quick.

"I understand about disappointments and failures in the workplace, so I can certainly relate to how you're feeling."

She tilted her head just so. Cute. "You can?"

"Sure." Now what did he say? He was quickly losing his ability to communicate. But how could he tell her the rest? His job had been his life and when he'd lost it because of a vindictive young protégé. . . Brandon took a step back, feeling like he was finally coming to his senses.

"It's getting dark. I should probably go," she said.

Curious, he cocked his head. "So, where do you work? If you don't mind my asking."

She kicked the dirt around, then looked up at him as though bashful. "I shouldn't have said anything about my troubles. Really. I start at the museum store tomorrow. You should stop by some time." She smiled then took off running. "My ankle's feeling better," she called, with a quick glance back at him.

A smoldering sensation filled his gut. She must be one of the new interns Jim had mentioned. Heaving long and hard, he started running again, but in the opposite direction. He'd catch the connecting loop to burn off his frustration.

Jim insisted they needed help, and though he was right, Brandon needed to focus on the mounting work ahead of him. It was an odd twist, bringing in help, only to have to divert energy into these individuals, guiding them in the disciplines, directing their futures. In Brandon's mind, a volunteer intern was almost a contradiction.

He'd just as soon do the work himself at this point. But why had they put this young woman in the museum store? She'd been seriously disappointed.

Years ago he'd been a research paleontologist for a museum. But with a museum director father, collections had always held a draw for him, causing him to harbor the desire to follow his father. He'd forged a friendship with the director in the museum where he worked, who mentored him. Eventually, Brandon learned the process well enough to manage a small museum. When presented with the opportunity, he'd taken it. But then. . .disaster struck.

If it hadn't been for the aid of a well-respected friend, Brandon wouldn't have found his life again in the newly created Harrington Museum. Even though several years had passed, he wasn't ready to open himself up again to risk or criticism.

*No more protégés. . .*

The words he'd spoken to Jim came back to him. He'd stand by them. Even if she was beautiful beyond words, and he'd come within a breath of asking her on a date. Lungs burning, Brandon slowed his run as the museum complex came into view. Only two cars remained—his black Jeep and Jim's silver Lexus. He let himself in through the back, feeling the pain in his joints from the long run. After a quick stop in the men's room to wash the sweat from his face and neck, he continued on to Jim's office. Talking on the phone, Jim turned his back to Brandon, finishing the call.

Finally, Jim faced Brandon and flipped his phone shut. "Have a good run?"

"Not entirely. I ran into one of your new interns. Literally."

Jim quirked a half grin then shuffled some papers. "Sounds like Providence."

*Dad would agree.* "Did you personally interview them?"

"I reviewed applications and took the ones with recommendations from professors. The usual. Why? Is there a problem?"

Brandon rubbed his chin to cover his misgivings. Why was he so upset? "No, I just wished you would have talked to me before bringing on interns."

"Haven't we already been through this? What's done is done. Besides, it's a menial task you relegated to me last year, remember?" A subtle smirk slid into Jim's lips. "Though you didn't accept them, your name is on the letter. You're the director."

Brandon heaved a sigh. He was making too much out of this.

"If it makes you feel any better, I'll make sure you never see a volunteer or intern again this summer, all right?"

"An impossible promise, Jim." Scratching the back of his neck, Brandon sagged, blowing out the last of his frustration.

"So what is it about this intern you ran into that has you upset?"

How could he tell Jim he'd wanted to see this woman again only to discover she was one of the museum's interns?—a dangerous activity in which he refused to engage. "Just ignore me."

Brandon left Jim's office, kicking himself for the knee-jerk reaction.

Guilt chiseled through him. If it weren't for people willing to invest in him during his formative years as a young college student, where would he be today? He was more than obligated to pass on their generosity, despite his personal issues.

He grabbed his keys and exited the museum. Walking backward, he gazed up at the large letters. THE HARRINGTON NATURAL AND CULTURAL MUSEUM.

Everything was riding on his making this museum work. Everything. He'd been given a chance to prove himself.

An image of the young intern with dark hair flashed before his eyes, replacing that of the museum. He turned toward the Jeep and heard the telltale chirp of the lock's disengagement. She was a striking beauty, really. Good thing he wasn't one to easily fall for beautiful women.

The last thing he needed was an ever-present reminder of his past failures, lingering around the museum every day.

# Chapter 3

Standing on the ladder, Amber had a great view of the museum store. To add to the arrangement she was working on, she pulled another bobblehead tyrannosaurus from the box resting on the shelf below. A quick glance behind her told her Gladys had finished with her customer and would soon want to inspect Amber's merchandising skills, which were—in a word—none.

She'd spent the morning learning to operate their computerized register system as well as walking the entire floor to locate and identify each and every item. As far as she was concerned, she should be getting paid for this rather than working as a volunteer. But this was only her first day on the job.

Stocking the shelf with green felt-covered bobblehead dinosaurs was a far cry from digging in the dirt to excavate the real thing or learning the work behind accessions or collections.

Despite her disappointment, she smiled at the display and dusted off her hands. Gladys stood at the bottom of the ladder, looking up. The way Gladys smiled, Amber decided she'd convinced the older woman she had accepted her assignment without further complaint.

Gladys adjusted her glasses. "I thought you weren't sure what to do. Looks like you have a knack for display. I think you might be a keeper." She winked then turned her back to Amber, heading back to the register.

*I'm a keeper?* "Wait, Gladys."

A teenager stood at the register, looking around expectantly. Gladys either didn't hear or ignored Amber and hurried to assist the customer.

Amber didn't want to be a keeper. At least not in the museum store. She began descending the ladder then remembered the box on the second shelf and climbed back up two rungs. As she gripped the ladder to grab the box, her hand swiped one of the bobbleheads. It tumbled over, knocking the other toy dinosaurs over like dominoes, the clattering amplified by the store acoustics.

With an hour until closing time still left, Amber huffed, wishing the day were over already. She wasn't sure she could stick it out. And if she left, she'd have to wait until Cams could return to pick her up. She began restoring the dinosaur arrangement, wondering if the top shelf was really the best place for the display. But Gladys had insisted that children were tempted to play with the dinosaurs, leaving the toys too damaged to sell.

"The top shelf, it is," she mumbled to herself, hoping for a readjustment in her attitude.

"Hi, there." A smooth voice spoke from behind.

Where had she heard it before?

Amber turned around to see the guy she'd run into yesterday on the trail. "Oh, hi. You decided to stop by the museum store. That's nice of you." Why was she being so flirty with him? He was much older. Had to be married. But something about the way he looked up at her sent a warm, giddy feeling over her.

*Please, don't let him be married.* She'd hate to think a married man would look at someone besides his wife like that. A glimpse at his left hand revealed no ring. But that didn't necessarily mean anything. She made her way down the ladder without repairing the damage she'd done, stopping two rungs from the bottom. The bobbleheads weren't going anywhere.

"Looks like you're doing a great job for someone who didn't want to work here." He grinned.

Lifting the cardboard box that she'd tossed onto the shelf earlier, she blew out an exaggerated breath. "Not hardly. I've knocked these things over twice today. I'm so clumsy."

"I know. Your family heirloom."

"My family—" Amber looked at him. He remembered that?

"Starting tomorrow, you don't have to worry about arranging the dinosaur toys. You officially begin your training as an intern assigned to the digs."

She stepped down another rung, lingering on the last one, confusion whirling with panic inside. "How. . .how would you know that?"

The stranger stuck out his hand, waiting for hers. "I'm the museum director, Brandon Selman."

Stunned beyond comprehension, Amber nearly stumbled off the ladder. Embarrassment flooded her thoughts and face.

"You mean, *you're Dr.* Selman?" she asked, recalling Gladys's adamant words.

He chuckled and dropped his hand. She'd never taken it.

"I may have a PhD but there's no need for formalities. Mr. Selman will do in most cases."

As she recalled, Gladys was pretty emphatic about the doctor part. Amber wouldn't take any chances. "I was. . .expecting someone much older."

The warmth in his expression faded somewhat.

"No, I didn't mean it that way. What I meant is that you look so young. You'd think hours in the sun, digging for fossils would age a person faster, making him look older."

He cocked a brow, waiting for her to shut up, she was certain. Probably thought she was as clumsy with her words as she was on her feet.

Uncertain whether to remain embarrassed, be angry or forever grateful, she fumbled over her words. "I'm. . .I feel like such an idiot. Everything I said yesterday. Why didn't you tell me who you were?"

"Miss McKinsey, I honestly didn't know you were an intern here until you invited me to stop by the museum store just as you ran off."

"Oh please, call me Amber." She examined her shoes while she allowed excitement to bubble inside. Had there been a mistake, or had her chance encounter with him on the trail brought her dilemma to his attention?

She smiled at him, feeling shy. Hadn't she just been flirting with the man? Hopefully, he hadn't noticed.

"I don't know what to say. Thank you." She felt humbled to think that this man with a doctorate and who knew how many other degrees, who ran a reputable museum, would have heard the cry of her heart. It seemed like even God hadn't done that. Dr. Selman had listened, and he'd done something about it.

"You're welcome. I'm sorry for the confusion about your volunteer position. As it turns out, someone who works in the digs broke her leg this morning. We've had to juggle people. So, now you get to do what you came here for."

So much for him hearing the cry of her heart. Figured. If even God didn't listen, who would?

Then it hit her. "Oh no. I hope it wasn't Muriel who was hurt. She's one of the new interns and my cabinmate."

"Tori Gillispie was one of our returning interns working under Dr. Laudan, our research paleontologist."

Amber studied his eyes, searching for the right words. "How did it happen?"

He stared down at her, suddenly turning serious. "Remember what I told you last night about the Badlands being dangerous?"

Amber nodded, thinking about that moment. It was then that he'd talked about ancient ruins in the moonlight. At the time, it had felt almost magical.

He cleared his throat, apparently aware her thoughts were elsewhere. "The dig is along the side of a rocky outcropping. There are deep slopes and cliffs. Though it's mostly safe, especially in the amateur digs where the tourists are allowed, there are some risks involved. Tori misstepped and fell."

"I'm thinking it could have been much worse."

He studied her closely. "Are you sure you want to do this?"

"You're referring to my family heirloom."

"I won't stand in your way."

"I'd love the experience. More than you know." A thrill rushed through her. Though this wouldn't be her first time at a fossil dig, it would be her first time as an intern instead of a tourist. She smiled up at the handsome museum director.

Dr. Selman gave her a funny look. "I want your time here to be a valuable learning experience."

She thought again of the girl who'd been hurt. "I'm sure accidents are rare, aren't they?"

He nodded as he subtly glanced at the mess she'd made of the toy dinosaurs, then back to her. "Have you ever been in the field before?"

"Sure I have." Amber swallowed under his scrutiny. Michael had gone with her on amateur digs several times, but she didn't want to bring up her brother now, if ever. *Please, don't let him ask where, when, or how.*

She'd just have to keep her distance, not get too close to anyone. The last thing she wanted was for anyone to know about him. If they did, then. . .he really would have succeeded in destroying her life.

*≈♥*

"Good. Then you have some experience. And you're right. Accidents are rare."

*Except in my world. . .*

Brandon couldn't believe what he was doing. After a night of tossing and turning, feeling guilty over his attitude, he'd made up his mind to find the young intern he'd met on the trail last night. His previous ordeal was a once in a lifetime regret. At least he hoped.

Jim wouldn't be happy. But Brandon couldn't stand the thought of her being stuck there. Early that morning, he'd found her file on Jim's desk and read her request to work under Brandon directly. He knew that was in part thanks to his friend, Phil Young at UND. He almost laughed at the way things turned out—Jim had ended up giving in to Gladys's requests for help. Poor girl.

With the news of Tori's accident, Brandon was stepping in, if just this once.

"Tomorrow morning, report to the certification room. It's in the basement. Jim can put you through the quick start program to ready you for a new group of tourists coming through next week. You'll be guiding the tours and eventually, maybe even assisting with amateur digs. I can't promise you that. But with Tori's injury, Dr. Laudan might request additional help sooner rather than later."

"Thank you again for this opportunity. I won't let you down." Amber flashed him a beautiful smile, her eyes filled with relief and gratitude. Then her smile faltered a bit. "I'm just sorry about Tori and hope she recovers soon."

Brandon nodded. "The museum sent her flowers, wishing her a speedy recovery." On the selfish side of things, Tori's injury could be a setback for his plans for museum accreditation. He yanked his thoughts back to the present and glanced over at Gladys, who finished up with her last customer. She wouldn't be happy about losing Amber either.

"I should at least complete this display for Gladys." Amber laughed a little nervously. "Clean up my mess."

She climbed up and began setting the dinosaurs right. Brandon picked a few off the floor and handed them to her. Despite his feelings about being obligated to tutor others, Brandon was glad he'd given Amber what she wanted for a far different reason. After only a few minutes in her presence, he sensed her enthusiasm, especially about the new assignment, and it was contagious. She'd sparked something in him he hadn't felt in a long while.

Perhaps that's what Phil had seen in her as well.

She smiled down as she took another bobblehead from him, brushing his fingers. "The basement, huh?"

He angled his head slightly. "Say again?"

"You said the certification room is in the basement."

"Hasn't anyone given you the grand tour yet?"

"Um, of the museum store, yes. Of the museum, no."

"You need a tour, then."

"Sounds like a plan." Once the dinosaurs were perfectly in place, some of the heads bobbling, she began her descent down the ladder.

Brandon's thoughts had already pushed ahead to the backlog of work on his desk. There were others to give her the tour. Like Jim or Gladys. Why hadn't Jim scheduled some sort of orientation for these people? Might as well give Gladys the news.

"Gladys?" he called, as he glanced around the store.

"I'm just locking up. Be right there."

Gladys waltzed around a shelf of dinosaur puzzles toward him and smiled. "Did you need something?"

"Miss McKinsey needs a tour of the museum, including the basement classrooms. The works. Would you. . ."

With a disapproving shake of her head, Gladys gave him her evil eye. But he saw the twinkle behind her glare. "Are you stealing this girl away from me?"

Brandon lifted his hands in surrender. "She comes to us from a colleague of mine. He wouldn't be very happy if I sent her back with only knowledge of how to run a cash register now, would he? Could you—"

"Can't do it. I have to balance and lock up the money. I'm afraid giving the grand tour, showing off your museum is your calling, talent, and gift. And considering you're taking my only help from me, and I just spent all day training her—"

"All right. Fair enough. We'll find you someone, Gladys. Don't worry."

Gladys frowned at Brandon then winked at Amber. "You kids run along. I'll put up the ladder."

"Are you kidding? I'll put it away." Brandon wasn't about to let the older woman struggle with the ladder.

After folding it, he carried it to a closet tucked away in the back of the store. He'd never regretted hiring Gladys. She was a faithful and hard worker. When he returned, Gladys was closing out the register with Amber.

When Amber saw him, she smiled.

Her smile was almost too beautiful. Suddenly, his throat turned dry. He was in unfamiliar territory.

*This is strictly business.* Maybe he should have accepted Jim's offer to keep interns and volunteers out of sight. But he knew that was impossible, and like

Jim had said, an intern did not necessarily a protégé make.

"Ready?"

Amber grabbed her purse and moved from behind the counter. "As I'll ever be."

Brandon led her through the back of the store and down a flight of stairs. He opened the door for her. She gave him a brief glance when she walked by, stepping into the long hallway lined with classrooms.

He led her into the first room on the right. "This is the instruction room—texts, videos, and lectures created to keep the attention of adults and children alike."

They moved to the next room. "This is the lab where the tourists can learn the proper procedure for handling fossils."

She ran her fingers lightly over the counter then looked up at him, eager and full of hope and something akin to awe.

The admiration he saw in her eyes reminded him of another time and place, and someone he desperately wanted to forget. Uncomfortable, he turned away. "Next, I'll show you where we receive the collections we've accessioned."

After showing her the remaining rooms, he began flipping off the lights and making sure the doors were locked for the day. Amber chattered on about UND. How grateful she was to be interning at Harrington. He enjoyed listening to the excitement in her voice. He'd been that enthusiastic once.

"Dr. Young assured me that spending time working with you would help me better assess the direction I should take. While I love geology and have considered paleontology as my field of study. . ." She trailed off, shaking her head.

Brandon understood her very well. "You love the idea of collecting on a far greater scale." He glanced down the hallway, making sure all the lights were off and considered her words about spending time working with him. By engaging in the process, he'd already put one foot into a place he had planned to avoid. How should he handle this?

"Why, yes. . .you read my mind." She stared at him as if she had more to say but hadn't figured out how to say it. "Dr. Selman, how did you decide what to do with your life? There's just so much I want to do and I can't do it all."

As his mind filled with a million answers, he hung his head and chuckled. "You mean, how did I decide what I want to be when I grow up?"

"Yes," she laughed, softly.

There was something in her voice. Something delightful, yet unnerving. He turned his gaze to Amber. In her eyes, he glimpsed something both familiar and unwelcome.

She saw herself as his protégé.

"I didn't."

# Chapter 4

*Finally, some action.*

After she'd spent two days going through the museum's certification program, Amber had spent yesterday taking phone calls to register people for the tours, answering their questions. She was more than ready to make her way to the field. But she'd been assigned to accompany and assist Jason, learning from him before taking her own group out.

Inside the museum reception area, they stood together in a circle, a small gathering of mostly families with children, three single twenty-something guys, and two fiftyish women. While the digs were best suited for kids twelve years or older, children had to be at least eight years old. All had been required to sign liability waivers, including a list of rules and possible risks.

Jason began his spiel. "We're glad you joined us today. I'm personally looking forward to spending a week with you in search of fossils."

He continued on for a few minutes, explaining that the tools supplied—hammers, chisels, brushes, and more—would be available at the dig site. Sunscreen, gloves, and hiking boots or shoes were all the tourists were required to bring with them. Water and lunch, supplied by the museum, was included in the tour fee.

A freckle-faced boy raised his hand. Ignoring him, Jason kept talking. But the boy wasn't giving up. Amber figured questions were welcome at the end of his talk. Had Jason explained that?

Finally, he paused. Amber didn't miss his tight jaw when he smiled. "Yes?"

The boy revealed a toothy grin. "What about the dinosaurs? Are we going to see dinosaur fossils?"

Jason's features relaxed. "What's your name, son?"

"Tim."

"Well, Tim, the Little Missouri River Badlands are sedimentary formations from the Cretaceous period."

The boy angled his head, apparently uncertain what Jason meant.

Jason chuckled. "This period is abundant with dinosaurs, mesosaurs, and plesiosaurs. That said, it's been heavily excavated. But there's plenty left for you to see and explore."

"Cool!" The boy bounced, apparently satisfied.

"But mixed in with the dinosaur fossils are those of other mammals like rabbits, mice, and turtles."

"Ah, who cares about them," Tim said as he appeared to wave off anything but dinosaurs.

The entire group laughed at his comment, as though everyone was there solely to get a hands-on look into a past that included the mysterious giants. Who was she kidding? Amber was there for the same reason, only she had never bought into the old earth theory or—as a Christian—evolution. She chewed the right side of her lip. Another thing she'd have to keep quiet for now, biding her time.

This experience was important to her future and career, whatever that might be. After meeting Dr. Selman, she especially looked forward to working with him. Garnering his respect and attention could benefit her in big ways. Plus, it was uncanny how he seemed to understand her, reading her mind almost like her brother.

Amber rubbed her temples. Why'd her thoughts have to go there? How would she keep her brother and his deeds under wraps? Listening to Jason drone on, she glanced around the museum. When her brother was released, could he ever work in his field again? Or in a museum?

Resentment stirred in her heart. Staring at the floor, she wanted to send up a prayer; but she couldn't get past her anger at God either. She knew she shouldn't be angry, but. . .why had He let things happen the way they had?

Jason cleared his throat. Amber pulled her thoughts together and realized everyone was staring at her.

"You have anything to add?" he asked.

*Oh yeah.* Cheeks burning, she tugged the slip of paper from her pocket. Jason wanted her to become accustomed to giving the spiel. "During the tour, we'll give you time to do some collecting of your own, but remember you may only keep specimens that hold no research value to the museum."

"Hey, that's no fair," Tim piped up again.

Amber glanced at Jason, hoping for some help. He held his tongue, prodding her with his eyes. She figured he wanted her to learn to deal with problems sooner, rather than later.

She smiled at Tim then addressed the entire group. "The tour is for you to get a hands-on look at paleontology. The museum has secured our dig site through a fossil lease and proper permits. We're required to document fossils, and important collections are subject to further scientific study. We'll be digging in what we call a bone bed—parts of dinosaur bones and incomplete fossils that have been washed out by an ancient river. They're no longer in situ, meaning they've been disturbed. These specimens usually don't hold much value. You can add these to your personal collection after we've documented them. Are we clear?"

"Yes." Tim stuck a finger in his nose, it appeared, as a means of disrespect. The other boys laughed.

Boys.

Jason led the group out the door and to the head of the trail. "Ongoing research is currently conducted at several sites in the region, but today we'll find our bone bed near an outcropping not two miles from the museum."

Off to the left, a slightly overweight man frowned. Unhappy about the distance? Even if they drove to one of the dig sites, they'd still have to hike a mile or more over rough terrain where the researchers worked. As they moved out and down the trail, Amber brought up the back of the group.

Finally, they arrived at the end of the trail where they had to climb down a short rope ladder to the dried-up riverbed below. From where she stood, Amber could see for miles over the hills and buttes carved by the river and leaving many layers to be explored.

Her chest filled with the anticipation of being part of the paleontology dig at some point. The family heirloom was ever present in her mind as she cautiously stone-stepped over boulders of various sizes to make her way to the dirt. Though the pain was minimal and would often come and go, her ankle began to ache again, reminding her of her recent fall. She felt a small grin slide onto her lips as she recalled her run-in with Dr. Selman. Even before knowing his identity, she sensed he was someone special.

Once they arrived at the site where the tourists were allowed to dig, Jason explained what they would be looking for.

He held a rock in each hand. "Can you tell which one is bone?"

The group gathered in a tight circle. Most allowed the kids "front-row" access. One of the girls slid her hand across the rock in Jason's right hand. "This one."

"Wrong, this is sandstone. It looks smooth but when you run your hand over it, you can feel the gritty texture."

He tossed it on the ground and held out his other hand. "This is part of a leg bone. Notice the porous texture. Lots of air pockets. Bone that you find as you dig will be a tan or pink color and if you break into the inside you'll see dark brown. Also, a bone will bleach as it lies in the sun, so if you see anything that looks lighter in color than the surrounding rocks, that could be bone. When you're exploring the bone bed, you're looking for something that stands out, that doesn't look like everything else lying around."

Jason then pointed to something in the distance. "See the tarp shading the group over there? Researchers are excavating that quarry. One of our tour groups discovered bones that were weathering out but appeared to go back into the layers in the hills. That indicates the bone was in situ where it was deposited."

Ohs and ahs escaped the group. Amber suspected that, like her, they'd rather be there than here.

"Do they know what it is?" Tim asked.

"Yes, that site has yielded a young *T. rex*."

"Oh! Can we go look?"

Jason shook his head. "For now, the only ones allowed on the dig other than researchers are the museum interns assisting them."

Amber tried to get a glimpse of Muriel. She envied her working under Dr. Laudan on an actual fossil dig. Supposedly Amber was to work directly under Dr. Selman, but maybe it was meant to simply look that way on paper. She'd assumed she'd be working more closely with him so that she could ask questions, pick his brain, and look up to him as her mentor. This was only her first week though, and she knew her internship didn't include giving tours the entire time. Dr. Selman had mentioned she might have the chance to assist Dr. Laudan at some point.

At least she wasn't in the museum store any longer. And she'd had a chance to speak with Dr. Selman personally, get to know him a little. Amber sucked in a breath of dusty air and stood tall. She'd do the best she could, of course, no matter where she was assigned because she really wanted to impress Dr. Selman.

Once the gathering dispersed and began walking around in search of fossils, Amber leaned toward Jason, speaking softly. "Won't we get to show them the *T. rex* find at some point?"

"Dr. Laudan doesn't like to mess with tour groups. But I'll ask Dr. Selman about making an appearance to show our group the discovery before the tour is over."

Amber's heart skipped a beat at the thought of seeing him again.

Hours later, the hot dry air had Amber gasping for breath. The blazing sun burned her skin despite the fact that she'd slathered on a thick layer of sunscreen and worn a hat. As Amber wiped sweat from her forehead, an errant drop burned her eye. Although she loved the digging and the excitement, sitting in a classroom for months hadn't exactly prepared her for the labor part of this field. Nor did she feel ready to conduct a tour of her own, which, according to Jason, was on the schedule for next week. She licked her chapped lips, tasting salt.

Two women found what appeared to be a bone and Amber plopped down next to them, guiding them as best as she could to dig up the fossil. With chisels and an ice pick, they gently removed the dirt from around the fossil, then brushed the soil away to get a better look. Then more digging and more brushing.

Once the women got the hang of it, Amber stood back to observe the others, which was part of her assignment—answering questions and making sure no one took something they weren't supposed to.

Amber noticed the man who'd frowned before they even started, sitting on a large rock, drinking his water. His chubby son appeared excited but tired. Though he wore a cap and she'd seen him put on sunscreen, he was already turning red.

She had her doubts that the man would come back tomorrow. What was the turnover rate on the tour? Even *she* wasn't sure she wanted to come back. Every part of her body ached like she was twenty years older. Still, she knew she'd complete her internship this summer—no matter what that entailed.

Seeing the others relatively occupied with their various finds, and Jason busy talking dinosaurs with the boys, Amber decided to grab a quick look at the surrounding land—the Little Missouri Badlands had captivated her. She'd be back before anyone knew she'd left. To get a good view, she'd need to go higher, and she could still keep an eye on the group. Amber made her way up a rise that hadn't appeared as steep as it now felt. Breathing hard, she wondered if she would actually make it to the top.

Finally, the ground flattened out. She'd made it! Still gasping for breath, she stood tall and took in the scenery. Spotting a rock she sat down while she caught her breath and poured water over her head, not caring that her face was probably now a muddy mess.

Wouldn't it be funny if Dr. Selman could see her now?

She groaned at the wayward thought. Expecting someone old enough to be her father, she'd been surprised at his good looks and that she'd been instantly attracted to him. She'd have to curb that somehow. In a moment of weariness, she let her eyes drift shut. Still the bright sun fought to penetrate her lids.

A shadow gave her a moment's reprieve until she opened her eyes. Her heart raced at the sight of him.

"Dr. Selman?"

⊘

Brandon watched Amber snap to her feet like she was in the marines, and he was her sergeant. He fought the urge to give her an answering salute.

He had the strangest desire to wipe the dust and smudge from her face. Now that would go over well with a board member, donors, researchers, and tourists looking on. Instead he simply smiled and said, "Hi, there."

"What are you doing here? I thought you were busy running the museum." The sun directly in her eyes, she held her hand up to shade them.

Her question prompted him to consider why, exactly, he'd made his way up here. But their paths hadn't crossed in a few days. He was glad they did now.

"Yes, well, part of my job is to accommodate potential donors." He nodded toward the two men and a woman standing in the distance, between the tourists and the active researchers under the tarp.

Amber squinted in the direction of the donors.

"They wanted to know what you were doing sitting by yourself. Is everything all right?"

"Sorry to worry you. I'm fine, just needed a break. I was about to head back down." Amber wiped her face with a small towel she pulled from her pocket. After a glance at it, a look of horror came over her features.

Brandon chuckled. "Didn't anyone ever tell you that digging for fossils is dirty work?"

An answering smile replaced her look of revulsion, and it appeared as though she was about to slap him playfully with her towel but thought better of it. Admittedly, had he not run into her today, he would have found any excuse to see her.

Unfortunately, his rule regarding protégés had everything to do with a previous office romance. Only in his case, the affections had been one sided—the young woman whom he'd mentored had her heart set on him. Focused on his research, he hadn't seen her budding affection and the growing danger.

Wasn't there already a natural law that workplace romances should be avoided?

Regardless, he'd governed himself in this matter, and recently proclaimed the no protégé rule. As he recalled, Jim had laughed. Now he knew why. Brandon was given to helping others, teaching them. It was unlikely he would abide his own rule.

And now as he looked at Amber McKinsey—dusty, sweaty, and still beautiful—the natural law was clamoring to be broken, too.

# Chapter 5

Would you like some help down?" Brandon had always said it was one thing to climb, quite another to come down. He proffered his hand.

Ignoring it, Amber scrutinized the hill below. At what should be her descent, her eyes grew wide.

Had she only now noticed how high she was?

She stared at his hand for a moment then shook her head. "No thanks. I'm good."

As he became increasingly aware of his board member's and prospective donors' stares, his relief that he wouldn't be holding her hand as he assisted her down was almost palpable.

Amber took a timid step toward the other side of the hill where her tour group waited at the bottom. Pebbles shifted under her foot, causing her to slip on her backside. Regardless of how he felt about the onlookers, the last thing he wanted was for Amber to get hurt. Nor did he need another incident, and right in front of them.

Still sitting, she looked up at him a bit sheepishly. He cocked a brow. "You're sure I can't help you?"

Offering his hand again, he wasn't surprised this time when she took it. Soft and small, her hand felt good in his. "I'd like you to join me. I'm taking the donors to see the T. rex. That means we're going in the opposite direction from your group."

"But what about Jason? Doesn't he need my help? I was just about to go back down when you showed up."

"I won't keep you long."

"And the tour group? I'm sure they'd love to see the discovery, too."

He smiled at her enthusiasm. "I'll make arrangements for them on another day. Including them with the donors would make too big a crowd and too many questions. But I appreciate your concern."

Amber nodded, and together, they scrambled down the steep side of the hill, over the ragged layers of sediment.

Once they cleared the hill, Brandon led Amber to the waiting threesome and introduced her to Sheila Longstrom—the only board member to oppose his hiring at Harrington—and the two potential donors, John Starks and Arnold Hammers.

"Nice to meet you, Miss McKinsey." Sheila's smile reflected no warmth. "I'm sure someone has explained to you how important it is for you to stay with the tour group. The museum doesn't need any more mishaps."

Brandon felt his jaw tighten. She referred, of course, to Tori's accident. He had the suspicion that Sheila was waiting for something to go wrong so she could prove to the board that she'd been right all along.

Amber's eyes widened as she glanced his way. "I. . .uh—"

"I'm sure Miss McKinsey, as a new intern, would benefit from viewing the *T. rex* site. So, I've invited her to join us."

Sheila pursed her lips, apparently unwilling to press the matter. As a board member, she should be aware the museum needed more donors, and she hadn't helped that cause today.

Fortunately, as they made their way to the tarp that shaded the research site, she joined him in explaining how the field digs opened to the public encouraged education and were one of the museum's biggest draws.

Brandon stepped under the tarp where three of the volunteers were assisting Dr. Laudan, pulling strips of burlap out of plaster of paris and wrapping a large bone.

Dr. Laudan straightened and stared at Brandon, her hands covered in plaster. Brandon didn't miss her subtle frown.

"Why don't you give us some background?" Brandon asked.

She nodded, well aware that Brandon wanted details to impress his guests. "This is called a plaster jacket. In the case of a large bone, like what you see here, we want to keep it safe as we take it back to the lab, so we encase it in plaster of paris."

Dr. Laudan continued, explaining how they would then pedestal the fossil, leaving it sitting on a large slab of rock to carry it back to the lab.

Brandon couldn't help himself. He watched Amber closely. By now she probably realized that had she asked to intern under Dr. Laudan, she very well could have joined the researchers on the *T. rex* find.

Guilt wound its way through his thoughts. She had to be disappointed in him as a mentor.

Like the donors, Amber appeared fascinated. But there was something else, just under the surface. What was it?

As she tugged on her earlobe—an apparent nervous habit—her eyes drifted slowly to his, then a small smile formed. She had perfect lips.

Next to him, Sheila cleared her throat. One glimpse and he knew she'd witnessed the exchange.

❧

That evening, Amber showered then made herself comfortable in the corner of the sofa. Soft lighting emanated from the lamp next to her. Today had been rough. The eagerness to discover fossils had eventually succumbed to the reality of long and arduous, backbreaking work. Amber felt sure that once her body adjusted, she'd regain her enthusiasm for the task.

Still, she couldn't shake the thought that she probably shouldn't have taken that short break from the tour group. They hadn't been out of sight, and at the time, it hadn't seemed that big a deal. . . . Dr. Selman had spotted her, and she was grateful for his help down.

She cringed as she recalled the scene. He'd appeared enthusiastic about showing her the *T. rex*, but when that woman had questioned her, Amber sensed her disapproval. Could her actions prove a negative mark for him, or lose the two potential donors? She rubbed her eyes and pressed her head against the cushioned sofa back. There was definitely more to a researcher's job than dusting earth off a dinosaur bone. Obtaining the necessary funds for their endeavors required the researchers to impress people. And, if *she* wanted to impress Dr. Selman, she would have to do better. No more taking her eyes from the task, no matter what.

She should pray for Dr. Selman, that her blunder wouldn't cost him. Yet, every time she thought of prayer, something she should do daily as a Christian, her heart ached. A huge, painful knot formed in her throat. She shouldn't blame God, but she couldn't help herself.

He could have prevented the accident that killed her mother and sister. They believed and trusted in Him. They'd prayed for safety for their three-hour drive beforehand. He'd let them down. Amber took a long, deep breath, hoping the tears pressuring the back of her eyes would go away.

She ran her hand over the soft maroon leather of her Bible. If she couldn't pray, at least she could read and then maybe God would answer her biggest question. . . .

*Why?*

Closing her eyes, she considered that she was all alone in the world—well, except for Michael. But she was angry with him, too.

She flipped her Bible open and began reading the first chapter in the book of John—her favorite and always a comfort. It was suppertime and her stomach rumbled as though she needed the reminder, but she was too tired to eat, and since Muriel wasn't there, she saw no reason to cook.

Just then, the girl flew in the front door, threw several sacks on the counter, and rushed to her bedroom, tossing a quick, "Hi, Amber!" as she went.

"Hi, Muriel."

Muriel's energy after a day at the dig astounded Amber. Suddenly, Amber felt even more tired, if that were possible, and curled her legs under her. She wasn't in the mood for lively conversation.

Muriel came out from her room and plopped on the sofa next to Amber. "You're reading the Bible."

"Yes, I am."

Muriel's grin was slightly mocking as she looked from Amber to the pages of John. She and Muriel hadn't discussed matters of faith, though Amber expected it would come up at some point. It hadn't been her intent to hide her beliefs, but she wasn't ready for the great debate at the moment.

"And you want to be a paleontologist?"

Amber opened her mouth to answer, but Muriel's cell phone chirped, distracting her and saving Amber from an explanation. Amber had planned to answer that she hadn't committed to paleontology and was leaning more toward museum work in general; still, that wouldn't have answered the question Muriel was really asking.

Amber wondered how long it would take the news to spread. Paleontology was a study involving evolution, and Amber knew scientists didn't have high opinions of what they referred to as Bible-thumping Christians. Yet, here she was. Oh, how she wanted to pray, needed to pray. Yet she couldn't bring herself to speak to God. He'd failed her. But just one little cry of her heart might work.

*Lord, take this anger from me. . . .*

# Chapter 6

The next week, Amber stood with confidence as she spoke to her tour group at the bone bed where she'd assisted with last week's tour. For this group of amateur fossil hunters, however, this area was a new one to be explored, especially since it had rained over the weekend, washing out new fossils from the loose sediment.

She'd enjoyed last week's hunt. There was always a fossil to be seen, whether of a small invertebrate or a plant, and sometimes the tour group members hit the jackpot with a dinosaur bone. At one point, they'd been allowed to assist and watch the researchers as they worked to unearth the *T. rex*.

Nothing of significance had been discovered the previous week, but that was to be expected on most amateur digs. Amber recalled Jason saying the *T. rex* find had been precipitated by a tour group. She smiled to herself.

No one could see what was hidden beneath the dirt except for God.

For most of the day, Jason had kept his distance, watching her manage this new group. Being a guide wasn't as big a deal as she thought. All she had to do was give the little spiel then lead them down the path. Throughout the day she would answer questions and show them how to gently remove the fossils, which were then packaged in reclosable plastic bags for further study or turned back over to the finder, depending on the value of the fossil.

Spotting a frizzy-haired woman and her teenage daughter excitedly examining something, Amber was about to walk over to them when she saw Jason, heading her way.

When Jason stood next to her, he frowned. "Why don't you help somebody? Start digging or something."

Though startled at his cranky mood, Amber smiled. "Sure thing."

She didn't want negative reports traveling back to Dr. Selman. Leaving Jason's side, she made her way to the woman and her daughter. Amber asked about their find. She hated to be the bearer of bad news, but no, the rock they'd picked up was, in fact, just a rock.

Remembering when Dr. Selman had surprised her last week by turning up at the dig and then showing her the research site, she sighed. Watching the researchers had made her even more eager to be involved in the serious side of the museum. . .to work directly under him.

At the simple thought of him, her heart did the little flip that it did every time she'd seen him. Not a good sign.

Amber spotted what looked suspiciously like part of a bone poking from the ground. She invited the frizzy-haired woman and her daughter over and gathered the tools from the nearby bucket, placing them above hers as she sat down in the dirt. The woman eyed her like she'd planned to dig for fossils without getting dirty.

Hearing a loud yelp, Amber looked up from her digging. The shout was from a particularly rowdy group of boys that'd come with their father. She looked around for Jason, knowing she'd need his help to keep a close eye on them. She spotted him with his cell phone to his ear, approaching her.

"Amber, I think you've got it under control. Something's come up, and I need to head out."

All the confidence she imagined she'd gained bled out her feet. Amber stared. "But—"

Jason tugged her to her feet and aside, then spoke in quiet tones. "You'll be fine. I've been watching you for days now. You know the drill. Take a water break, then in a couple of hours head back to the museum and wish them all a good evening." He didn't wait for a response but patted her back and left.

She was going to ask, "But what about those boys?"

The woman and her daughter stared at her. They placed their trust in her. Amber stood tall, and mentally reassured herself. She wouldn't let them down.

A good fifteen minutes passed before she relaxed. The earth hadn't shattered because Jason left. In a few minutes she'd dole out the water. Everything would be fine.

"Hey! What are those boys doing up there?" A short, stout man from her group yelled from a distance, looking in Amber's direction.

With the shout, Amber glanced up to the very same ridged hill she'd climbed last week. The boys didn't realize the other side was much steeper. And wouldn't you know? They were two of the rowdies she'd been concerned about all day. How had they slipped past her?

Amber searched for their father, who knew the rules and knew he was responsible for his kids. She found him sitting with his back to the boys, drinking water and wiping sweat from his brow.

Amber marched over to him. "Your children aren't following the rules. Can you please call them down? I'm going to have to shut this tour down right now because of them, if you don't."

The man eyed her with disdain then twisted around. "They're boys. They'll be fine."

"Sir, you're not hearing me. Your boys could get hurt. This is against our policy. Please tell them to come down."

"Give me a minute, will you?"

The other tourists had stopped digging, and all eyes were on her, waiting to see what she would do. How she handled this. Why had Jason left?

"Fine, if you won't, then I will." And she had every right.

"Stay here," she called to the group as she trotted to the base of the hill. Once there, she shouted, "Boys, this area is off-limits to tourists. Come down now!"

To her relief, one of them began descending. What had they been thinking?

The other one, however, remained frozen, and whimpered. She barely heard him when he said, "I can't! I'm scared!"

*Oh, great!* Now what should she do? This wasn't supposed to happen. In fact, she hadn't even been told how to handle it in case it did. Feeling the stares of her group on her back, she didn't want to reveal her own fear and lack of confidence. If she blew this, she could be dismissed from her internship or worse. . .the child could get hurt.

"Stay there. I'm coming to get you." And then what? She reminded herself that Dr. Selman had easily helped her down by holding her hand.

But this was different. This was a child.

She began scaling the ribbed and rough terrain. At least it wasn't a straight-up rocky cliff, requiring any sort of equipment, but then again, that would have prevented the boys from climbing it to begin with.

Now would probably be a good time to pray for some help, except, she reminded herself, God had let her sister and mother down. She couldn't count on Him.

*Focus, focus.* She couldn't think about that now. When she finally made her way up, next to the boy, she looked him in the eye. Terror loomed there.

In a reassuring tone, she said, "You're going to be fine. I'll climb down with you. It's only a small distance. Okay?"

Seemingly unable to speak, he nodded, looking as if he wanted with all his might to believe her. *I can't let him down. . . .*

They descended slowly until the angle of the slope eased, though still too steep for comfort. She tugged his sleeve. "Now, turn around, sit on your backside if you have to, and make your way to your dad. The soft pebbles and dirt make this a slippery slope, so watch out." The tour would be over for the boys and their father—they knew the rules, or at least their father had signed a paper stating they did.

She watched the boy do as she said, then she started to do the same.

"Amber!" someone shouted.

*Now what?*

She jerked her head around and caught her foot on a rock. Unable to stop her momentum, she tumbled forward and down the slope, rolling over and over, like a log, faster, it seemed, with every turn. Rocks scraped her, dug into her skin. Someone screamed.

Was that her? Pain seared her body.

*God help me!*

Blackness engulfed her.

$\mathcal{L}$

"Is she dead?" A boy in the crowd asked.

"Of course not, son," a man assured.

"It's your fault," a woman accused. An argument erupted between several in the tour group.

Brandon tuned them all out. He'd already phoned for help. Seeing Amber lying there motionless tore his gut, and he laid it wide open before God.

*Lord, please let her be all right.*

"Miss McKinsey. . .Amber. . ." Brandon cupped her head gently between his hands, speaking softly. She didn't appear to have any broken bones but was still knocked out cold. And God help him, he'd seen her tumble down the slope after Jason shouted her name.

Though this incident threatened to bring back a torrent of memories—the accident he'd been held responsible for—he put the unbidden thoughts aside because he only cared about one thing: that this beautiful young woman with her whole life ahead of her wasn't seriously hurt.

Eyelids fluttering, she groaned, infusing his heart with hope. Noticing her lips moving, he leaned in to listen. Soft murmuring met his ears and, at her words, he drew back in surprise.

"Amber. . ." he whispered. "Wake up. Can you hear me?"

Her eyes opened; then she squinted. Frowning, she touched her head. "Oww. . ."

Brandon didn't doubt her pain. "Amber, it's me, Dr. Selman."

"What happened?" she asked.

Brandon helped her to sit up, noting a purple knot forming on her forehead. "Don't you remember? You took a fall."

Both hands on her head, she groaned again then focused her eyes on him. To his dismay, an apologetic look came across her face. "I'm sorry."

"*You're* sorry. Don't be." Brandon couldn't believe what he heard. "Here, let me help you to your feet, if you're able. We need to get you medical attention. I've already called."

Sirens rang out in the distance. *Finally.*

When Amber took a step, she cried out in pain then favored her left foot. Brandon wasn't about to let her walk on that. Tired of waiting for the ambulance, and knowing it would take the EMTs time to navigate the trail into precarious terrain on foot, he lifted her gently into his arms.

She yelped in surprise. "Dr. Selman, please don't think you have to carry me."

"Don't be ridiculous. You're not walking back." To Jason, he said, "Take the rest of the group to the *T. rex* for now." He'd give the man a dressing-down afterward. Right now, he needed to salvage this situation.

He strode carefully toward the trailhead that led back to the museum parking lot where he hoped the ambulance would be waiting. She was light in his arms, and her warm breath caressed his neck. He refused to look at her face, so near his.

"You all right?" he asked, his words breathy.

"This was my first tour to do alone. I've let everyone down."

"Jason shouldn't have left you. Especially with that group of boys when he could see they might cause trouble." He'd spotted the boys with their father in the museum earlier, attempting to touch an exhibit. Brandon had personally addressed them at the time. On his way to the digs, he'd run into Jason in a rush to leave. Of course, Brandon demanded he return to assist Amber with the tour. Museum policy was clear regarding the tour guide to participant ratio.

Once in the parking lot, the EMTs met him. Though Amber assured them she was all right, they took her to the hospital anyway. While Brandon wanted to go along, it was probably not appropriate.

"Dr. Selman? My name is Muriel. I'm interning under Dr. Laudan, and I'm Amber's cabinmate. I was in the lab, helping to secure a specimen when I heard. I'll go to the hospital and stay by her side. Don't worry. I'll be sure to let you know what the doctor says."

*News travels fast.* "Thank you." He was certain he wouldn't hear the end of this.

She jogged off in the direction of the cabins, presumably to get her car.

Watching the ambulance leave the parking lot, Brandon felt a headache coming on. Clearly, several factors played a role in Amber's fall, not the least of which had to be what she termed her family heirloom.

Though relieved she appeared to be okay, he was still distraught as he continued to pace the parking lot. After a while, he noticed others looking at him, so he headed inside the museum.

In his office, he stared at the phone, hoping to hear from Muriel and wishing he'd given her his cell number. Like a fossil waiting to be unearthed, the truth had been right in front of him and he hadn't seen it. His attachment to this woman clearly exposed—he realized he'd not been able to get his mind off her since their initial collision.

Through all his years of study to achieve academic success, all his years focused on his work, he'd never had a woman distract him so. On the road to recovery from his previous misfortunes, his profession teetered on a precipice. With at least one board member looking over his shoulder, he couldn't afford another incident or even the appearance of a scandal.

What was he going to do about Amber McKinsey?

# Chapter 7

Amber lay on the sofa, nursing a mild concussion. Besides that, she'd miraculously only suffered a few scrapes; and her ankle wasn't even sprained, just a tad swollen. Still, the doctor had given her a painkiller, which she'd gratefully taken—mostly to numb the pain in her heart.

She felt like such a—

Someone knocked on the door. Amber shifted on the sofa to get the door.

"Don't you even think about it." Muriel glared at her and rushed to the door.

She had offered to bring Josh out for Amber, but Amber refused her kindness, instead considering Muriel's allergies. Amber relaxed and closed her eyes, wondering who it could possibly be. No one ever came to the cabin. Whoever it was, Muriel would send them away.

Nestled on the sofa, she could easily drift to sleep.

A familiar voice resounded in the room. *Dr. Selman?* Amber's eyes popped open to see the man himself standing before her. Stunned didn't come close to what she felt. She pushed to sit up straight, sending pain through her head. She grabbed it.

"No, no. Please stay right where you are. I didn't mean to wake you."

Amber swallowed, uncertain why he was there. "I wasn't asleep. Just. . . resting."

"Good. I'm sorry I disturbed you. But I wanted to express my sincere apologies for what happened to you today."

A woozy feeling came over her. *Oh no.* The drugs were starting to kick in. She focused hard on his face and on listening to what he'd come to say. His lips were moving. . .what was he saying? What had the doctor given her again? This felt much too strong.

He pressed his lips tight. Had he done that before? She leaned closer.

Close enough to see his stubble, some graying near his chin. His aftershave smelled great.

Amber glanced over at Muriel who sat in the chair across from the sofa. Dr. Selman sat on the edge of the coffee table and took Amber's hand. She stared at her hand. It looked so small in his. Why was he holding her hand? His touch was warm and reassuring. She put her other hand over his then smiled up at him.

He didn't smile back but frowned instead. "Maybe this wasn't the best time."

"The best thime. . . ?" she heard herself ask, the words sounding funny.

"When you're feeling up to returning to the museum, I don't want you going back to the field. We'll find you something else to do."

Had she misunderstood? "You don't want me in. . . ? Because fell?"

"Miss McKinsey—"

"Mith McKwinsey? My name Amber?" She looked at her hands, trying to recall what happened. "See?" She held the palms of her hands out for Dr. Selman. "Just a fwew scrapes."

Dr. Selman stared at her with an odd look. "I wanted to tell you in person, so you wouldn't take the news the wrong way."

His odd look turned to pity. All the hurt she'd been holding inside seemed to burst from her in a torrent of words. It felt good. Too good, and she couldn't stop them. Didn't want to. "Why?" she asked through racking sobs. "You're overweacting. I feel. . .everything wrong."

Without knowing when or how, she was against his shoulder. "Why can't I do. . .something. . .right?"

The tears continued as Dr. Selman held her. What was happening? Why was she crying on his shoulder? Oh bother. . .

"Shh. . ." Dr. Selman gently patted her back.

Though he seemed stiff, his embrace felt good. The awful tumble down the slope rattled her mind again, yet in his strong arms she felt protected and safe. The tears finally came to an end. She was quiet and felt sleepy. So sleepy. Just let her stay right where she was. . .

When Amber woke up, she was covered with a blanket, the lights were low, and there wasn't any Dr. Selman in the room. Had it all been a dream?

"Good, you're awake now." Muriel said, and handed her a cup of something warm. "Green tea. Drink up."

Feeling better and like the wooziness of the medication had worn off, Amber sat up and took a sip. "Thank you. You don't have to take care of me, you know. But I appreciate it."

Muriel sat across from her and smiled gently. "Funny thing. I want to do it. My mom is a nurse; she's a nurturing person. I got that from her, I guess. I wanted to work at the digs to see what I wanted to do with my life. Become a nurse, or a scientist."

Amber couldn't help but smile. "And now you find yourself taking care of me." God had a sense of humor, no doubt there. She took another sip and watched Muriel over the rim of her cup. Could she share that? How could she, when she was still unsure of her own heart toward God? Better to wait until everything she could say about Him sounded the way it should.

"I've got a late supper cooking. Chicken noodle soup. One of Mom's recipes."

Muriel's talk about her mom reminded Amber of her own mother and loss. Loneliness filled her with a deep cold. She needed to talk about something else. "I had the strangest dream."

"Oh yeah? What was that?"

Amber chuckled into her cup. "You'd laugh."

"Oh come on. Tell me." Muriel handed her a bowl of the soup. "Eat up. And in between spoonfuls, I want to hear your dream."

"I dreamed Dr. Selman was here."

Muriel laughed.

"See, told you."

"I'm only laughing because that wasn't a dream. He *was* here."

"What?" Amber sat up straight and quick, sending an ache through her head. She grabbed it and waited until the pain subsided. "I can't believe it. What did he want?"

"Why don't you tell me what else you think you dreamed, and I'll tell you if it happened."

Amber leaned against the sofa back and sighed. "Must have been the medication. What a time for that to kick in. I dreamed. . .oh how embarrassing. Please don't tell me I cried on his shoulder."

Muriel stood up and took Amber's empty cup. "You did, chickadee." With a grin she headed to the kitchen.

Amber groaned and rested her head against the sofa. "How embarrassing. What am I going to do now? I'm just such a mess—"

"I thought it was cute, actually."

"Cute? I feel like I'm bungling everything. And here I wanted to make a great impression. . .oh wait, did he come to dismiss me?"

Muriel laughed. "Are you serious? Just the opposite. He wants you to work with him in the museum."

Amber felt her jaw drop. He wanted her actually *with* him? This was what she had hoped for. . .but not quite like this. "Did he mention what I would be doing?"

"Something about museum displays. He was impressed with your bobblehead arrangement."

Amber and Muriel both laughed because Amber had shared about the disastrous display.

The soup was good, and Amber allowed the warmth to lull her while she considered what happened.

Muriel broke the silence. "Though I think he's just concerned, wants to make sure you're safe. . .honestly? I think Dr. Selman might have a thing for you."

❧

Later that evening, after the museum had closed, Brandon stood in his office, hitting his head against the filing cabinet.

"Looks serious," Jim said from behind.

Brandon froze. He thought the guy had already left for the day. He gave the filing cabinet a good-fisted thump then composed himself, turning to face Jim. "Can't a guy blow off some steam?"

"Sure he can. Mind telling me what's bothering you?" He cracked a half grin and grabbed a chair, making himself comfortable as if they were the best of buddies.

Brandon was in no mood to talk, even to Jim, whom he'd known for years. Funny thing, that. Jim had jumped at the chance to become curator of the Harrington Museum when Brandon began assembling his team, but they'd never been close. Still, Brandon didn't need to be friends with his employees, he just needed them to do their jobs.

He studied Jim, aware that he was waiting on Brandon to spill. So, why was it that lately Jim was getting on his nerves?

"I'm guessing this has everything to do with the new intern's accident today?" Jim asked, apparently unwilling to wait on Brandon's response.

This was going to be a long night. Brandon sat behind his desk, feeling the weight of exhaustion on his shoulders, and hung his head. "Yep, you guessed it."

"Jason said the errant boys and their father left the tour, but the rest followed him over to view the *T. rex* dig site, and the way he made it sound, they were all so excited about seeing it, they probably forgot about the girl."

"Fire him."

"What?"

"You heard me."

Jim stared, pausing before he replied. "But Jason's been with us—"

"He signed an at-will contract, right? You've already put him on probation for not following the rules, right? On a fossil dig, people get hurt when rules aren't followed. The guy's burned out. He messed up big-time as far as I'm concerned. He shouldn't have left Amber."

"Amber? Oh, you mean Miss McKinsey?"

When Brandon didn't reply, Jim continued. "Jason has accompanied her on the tour now for several days. She should have been fully capable of taking care of the small group. If anyone needs dismissing—"

"Stop."

"We're down too many people already. Miss McKinsey clearly isn't cut out for this. Jason is experienced—"

Brandon had enough and threw up his hand. "Follow the correct procedures, but I want him gone tomorrow. And Amber. . .I've moved her from the field."

Jim's mouth dropped open. "But who's going to take their place?"

"I don't care. Find someone. Combine the groups. Figure it out, or lead the tours yourself." Brandon couldn't stop the harsh rush of words, but Jim had managed to pick the wrong time to question him about the day's events.

Jim stood. "Considering what happened before, I'd think you'd be more sensitive to how things look. And right now, my friend, it looks like your motivation—especially where this girl is concerned—is questionable. Why are you protecting her? If anything, it should be my call. You said you didn't want to be involved with the interns, remember?"

Brandon grabbed his suit coat and swung it over his shoulder then held the door in silent warning. Jim walked through and headed to his office without another word.

Once in his car Brandon sagged against the seat. The day's events had spiraled out of control and they just kept going. No matter what he did, he hadn't been able to rein things in. Then, hoping to make sure things were all right with Amber, and there wouldn't be more problems, he'd stopped by her cabin. Big mistake.

He hadn't intended to ask her to work with him. But with her in his arms today, sobbing—though he assumed it was due to the medication—he'd heard her heart and probably much more than she'd ever intended, or ever would under normal circumstances. Then, something inside him snapped, and he'd forsaken his rule, digging in deep this time.

She most likely wouldn't remember anything, but then her roommate was there, watching him with her eagle eyes. She'd remember. Muriel would probably blather about Amber in his arms, sobbing until he quieted her, soothed her. She'd remained in his arms far too long, seemingly comforted until he finally realized she'd fallen asleep. As she rested there against him, he could feel her softness, smell her hair, but then he felt her roommate's stare.

What was he doing? What must she be thinking?

He'd then gently settled Amber onto the sofa and tucked the blanket around her. Again, under Muriel's watchful eyes. Just as well—he certainly wouldn't want rumors to fly had he been caught alone with Amber. However, they were likely to fly anyway.

He could see the small-town headlines already. HARRINGTON MUSEUM'S DIRECTOR SAID TO COMFORT BEAUTIFUL VOLUNTEERS. Brandon wasn't certain what damage control he could do now, except. . .dismiss her as Jim suggested. To protect the museum, volunteers and interns also signed an at-will contract as though they were museum employees but if someone didn't function well in the environment, he or she was simply asked to leave. He'd certainly not intended for Amber to work directly with him, but neither could he bring himself to dash her hopes and dreams because of his own past and weaknesses or to protect his own skin.

What kind of cad would he be to do such a thing? He pounded the steering wheel, noting Jim's car sitting a few spots away. Jim was wrong. Brandon was making every attempt to be sensitive to his peculiar situation. He'd do everything he could to shove aside his personal feelings for her, act like a professional, and give a budding young museum director or paleontologist the chance she needed. People had taken a chance on him, and more than once.

As he drove from the parking lot, he pondered the news about Amber that Muriel had shared with him.

# Chapter 8

Two days later, Amber rolled out of bed in time to grab breakfast before heading over to the museum. The doctor had suggested she take three days off, but it only took two for her to feel better. Not to mention, she couldn't stand another day of being left alone with her thoughts. No matter how hard she tried, she couldn't forget her humiliation at having cried on Dr. Selman's shoulder—and worse—spewing her deepest insecurities.

Muriel assured her that Dr. Selman understood Amber was "under the influence" as she'd put it. According to Muriel, he admitted he'd chosen the wrong time to talk to Amber. Add to her embarrassment, she'd been waiting for this chance—but not like this. The way things had unfolded, she imagined he wanted to evaluate her rather than expand her experience.

Whenever she managed to put those thoughts from her mind, she came face-to-face with her brother's situation all over again. She'd not spoken to him since the death of their mother and sister a year ago. As Amber nuked a bowl of oatmeal, she remembered it had been about that long since she'd had a heart-to-heart with God. When she removed the bowl from the microwave, it felt heavy. . .like her heart.

Once she finished breakfast, she rushed out the door into the fresh morning air. Sucking in a deep breath, she encouraged herself with positive thoughts—like the Bible said in Philippians—she would "think about such things." This would be a good day.

She still had hope. She still had a chance to prove herself to Dr. Selman.

At the museum, she found the employees-only section and looked for the receiving room. Gladys told her she could find Dr. Selman there.

Inside the room, Amber made her way between tall stacks of boxes. When she saw Dr. Selman, she froze and watched him examine a large crate. As she observed his handsome form, she thought about how much he'd accomplished for someone she guessed to be in his late thirties. Some might call him an overachiever. Was there someone in his life who inspired him to great accomplishments?

At one time, Michael had been that someone for her.

Dr. Selman removed the batten that secured the exterior of the crate then worked to pry the top open. The top gave way, and he tossed it on the concrete floor. Peering inside, he began pulling out the material used to pad and protect the contents.

He stilled. The item inside must have drawn his full attention. To her surprise, he turned his head and looked straight at her. She pressed forward, hoping to hide that she'd been observing him.

"Dr. Selman. I was told I'd find you here. Reporting for duty, sir."

A warm smile spread across his face. "You know, this isn't the military."

She stopped in front of him, standing next to the long crate. "What do you mean?"

"I always feel as if you're going to salute me."

Amber frowned. "Oh, I. . .uh. . ." This wasn't the way she wanted to start off. "I just think of you as a very important person."

"Ha! I'm no more important than anyone else." He quirked a brow and half grinned, exposing his long dimple again.

His smile too cute for comfort, Amber blinked a few times, hoping to lessen its effect on her. "Well, in my world, you're somebody."

"Let's change your worldview, then, by dispensing with Dr. Selman. Just call me Brandon."

Call him by his first name? She tugged her earlobe, thinking. Gladys had seemed adamant about his title. And what would the others think?

"I'm sure I couldn't do that. I'm accustomed to calling my professors Doctor. Since I'm here to learn from you, it's easier for me this way."

His forehead creasing, he studied her. "Well, if you must. But this is a small museum and I'm not about titles."

His attention back on the crate, he gestured for Amber to look inside.

A life-size figure rested in the crate. Amber drew in a short breath. "Sacagawea."

"Good, that's the sort of reaction I like to see."

Uncertain what he meant, Amber considered his comment as she laid her bag against a chair. Then she stood tall, ready to work.

"You're not too disappointed about being pulled from the field?" He began pulling out the straw-like stuffing that protected the figure.

"Oh, no. I love history." Amber didn't add that she feared it was his frustration with her family heirloom that led to his decision. Then again, maybe she'd already explained that when she'd cried on his shoulder. "Um. . .before we get started. There's something I'd like to say."

Brandon dropped a handful of what Amber now saw was finely shredded tissue paper, and waited for her to continue. Wow, she was actually going to work with the man. The only downside? Her infatuation—and oh, she was infatuated with him—might actually turn into a full-blown crush. She swallowed against the tightness in her throat.

"Well?" he asked.

"You're not anything like the professors at UND."

"Is that what you wanted to say?"

"No, actually. I wanted to apologize for the other night."

"There's no need to apologize. Really. Let's just forget everything. That is, whatever you can actually remember." He quirked his crazy grin again.

The problem was that his grin was starting to make *her* crazy.

Packing material hung from the box, giving her a hare-brained idea. She snatched a handful of shredded paper.

Anticipating her next move, Dr. Selman threw up his arms as though to protect himself and smiled. "Hey, wait a minute."

Amber tossed the mass at him, but it wasn't cooperative, acting more like she'd thrown feathers. She laughed but stopped when she realized he wasn't throwing the stuff back. "Sorry, I couldn't help myself."

At least he smiled, but he appeared unsure about what to do next. His reaction reminded her of when she'd met him on the trail. He looked like a man who wanted to say something but had no words. Maybe Dr. Selman didn't know how to lighten up.

Or maybe she needed to get serious.

She cleared her throat. "So, what are we doing? Tell me what exactly you've moved me into, because honestly, I don't remember much of the other night."

"I want you to help me with the artifacts arriving in a few weeks. But in two weeks, we host Living History Week, and we have to set up a diorama. We don't want to disrupt the visitors during the day so we'll set up after. . ." He paused as though considering something. "I hope you don't mind working after hours?"

That would mean a long day.

Seeming to read her mind, he added, "You don't need to come in until after lunch, and we'll work through the afternoon and evening hours. How does that sound?"

Working long hours with handsome Dr. Selman? She'd have to think about it. Putting a finger to her lips, she said, "Okay."

"Oh, except for Wednesday nights. I teach a Bible study."

"I. . .uh. . . You teach a *Bible* study?"

Dr. Selman opened another box. "Why so surprised?"

"I think you know why. You're a paleontologist. You can't be a Christian *and* a paleontologist. And if you are, you can't let anyone know about it."

He stopped what he was doing and placed his elbow on an unopened crate, leaning against it. "And aren't *you* considering paleontology as a career?"

The way that he said it—"How did you know I'm a Christian?"

He approached her and stood near. Too near. What was he doing? "Everyone leaves signs, little clues, of who they really are. You just have to pay attention."

He raised his hand, then touched the small cross on her neck and lifted it, holding it against his fingers. He looked from the cross into her eyes. The olive color of his appeared to ebb and flow with an emotion she couldn't read.

Did he realize how close he was?

"Sign number one."

His nearness. . . She couldn't think straight and averted her gaze. As she took a step back, he released the cross.

"Lots of people wear crosses; it's the style." She tugged on the necklace her sister had given to her.

Folding his arms over his chest, he gave her a pointed look. "After you fell, when you were unconscious, just before you came fully awake, you were praying. Sign number two."

Amber felt her eyes widen. She'd been praying? But how? Why wouldn't she know? She couldn't even pray when she was awake.

"And before you get too upset, I saw the Bible on the table next to the sofa. Your roommate told me you read it every night."

This time when Amber spoke her voice was a whisper. "Sign number three. . ."

*

Brandon heard the distress in her voice. He hadn't meant to send her to that troubled place he'd seen in her eyes before.

"So you see? I'm not the only one who knows. I don't think it's something you can hide, do you? And why would you want to?"

For the last two days, a battle had raged inside of Brandon. Had he done the right thing, inviting her to work with him, considering the rule he'd insisted was necessary? Considering Jim had all but accused him of showing favoritism to Amber? Would he also get flak from Sheila Longstrom?

The questions had simply washed away upon seeing Amber step into the room, looking like the picture of health. Her smile had sent a flood of relief the size of a melting glacier through him.

What a joy it was to have another Christian in the museum to work beside him. She toyed with the small silver cross he'd held moments before. A deep longing gripped his heart, but he quickly buried it. "I know a handful of Christian paleontologists."

"Christian paleontologist seems a bit like an oxymoron, don't you think?" she asked.

"Not when you think about them separately. Paleontology is simply the study of prehistoric plants and animals. Prehistoric means before recorded history. And yes, to be politically correct in today's culture one must agree with the evolutionary model."

She looked confused, disappointed.

He smiled, enjoying the discussion. "I never said I was politically correct."

"Tell me, how does a paleontologist end up as a museum director?"

More precisely, she probably meant to ask how did a *Christian* paleontologist end up as a museum director. "Museum directors come in all sizes and shapes. They have an expertise in one field or another. My father was a museum director of a much larger institution. He felt it would be a conflict of interest to hire me where he worked. So I found a job working in the research department of a small museum. It was there that I became friends with the man who managed it."

As Amber watched him closely, he continued. "He was curator, collection manager, and administrator all wrapped into one. He took me under his wing and trained me. I guess you could say the work of the bigger picture fit my personality better."

"Sounds like he did everything." Amber began tugging the packing material from Sacagawea's crate. "Like you. Don't you do everything here? Well, you and Jim."

"Remember, too, this is a small museum. The bigger the museum, and the more collections, the more complicated. Here we have the fossils, the historic items that have provenance in this region, and the dinosaur dig tours."

"That seems like a lot. How do you do it all?"

"Jim is officially curator of new collections. Between the two of us, we manage collections, conservation, documentation, and administration." Brandon had often wondered why Jim had followed him here.

Suddenly, he understood his arrogance and paused. Ashamed, he peered at Amber. "And of course, let's not forget the volunteers and interns who help make things happen."

Her lips curved into a soft smile. *Pretty.*

His throat constricted. Uncomfortable with the thought, he considered what she might ask next. This line of questioning put Brandon on edge. If Amber asked the wrong one, he'd end up having to either explain or dance around the truth about what happened at the last museum where he worked. Dredging up his past failures would probably knock him down a few notches in her eyes. With that thought he'd reached the heart of the matter—he enjoyed the way she looked up to him far too much.

Disturbing.

He frowned, throwing all his attention into freeing Sacagawea. Once the life-size model was out of the crate and standing, he left Amber to clean it off while he moved to the next crate, which contained Lewis.

"Does Jim know that you're a Christian?"

The crowbar slipped from Brandon's hands. He bent over to pick it up. "Yes. He gave me a hard time at first. But not anymore."

He peered over the top of the crate. Amber gave him a questioning look that told him she was waiting for further explanation.

"Several years ago, after I was already ensconced in my career, something terrible happened. I had nowhere else to turn except to God." *Lord, please don't let her ask what happened. Not yet.*

"And after you became a Christian you changed what you believe about evolution and paleontology?"

"I met another Christian—a creation scientist. He spent hours, weeks, and months helping me through things."

"But you're still directing a museum that's in conflict with your beliefs."

Brandon removed the top off the crate. "I prayed and waited for God to lead me. Then, when I was asked to become the director of this museum, somehow, I knew it was God. He didn't ask me to leave what I do. In fact, I believe just the opposite. God is all about science—He created all the laws. I think more Christians need to enter science and biology fields. To be involved in museums."

"What about a creation science museum? Ever thought about running one of those?"

Brandon stopped working for a moment to look at Amber. "I think a creation museum is a great thing. But usually only Christians visit those. Don't you think the people who would never visit a creation science museum could be impacted by a museum that presented multiple viewpoints? So instead of seeing only facts mixed with evolutionary interpretations, they're also exposed to scientific evidence that fits with creation science, evidence that is often hidden. I'm working on initiatives that could potentially set that in motion for this museum."

"Do you think they'll go for that? I mean, really?" Amber frowned. She tucked Sacagawea's hair behind the model's shoulder and released a weighty breath. "I don't know what the answer is."

Something compelled Brandon to rush to her side, slipping between the crates. He gently lifted her face to meet his gaze. "No matter what direction you choose, you'll always face opposition to your beliefs. Don't ever let anyone take away your love for God. Do you hear me?"

"Yes." Her eyes grew wide with emotion.

Releasing her, he retreated to his work. Why had he done that? He'd seen Christians enter the science field and end up losing their faith. If it was within his power, he wouldn't let that happen to Amber.

He'd caught a glimpse of her passion for science, but it seemed already life and circumstances were threatening to snuff it out. If only he could keep that from happening. But how?

Being with her today. . .it felt like she'd somehow reignited his own enthusiasm for paleontology—the zeal he'd left dormant these years working in the museum.

While he tugged Lewis from his cocoon, Brandon prayed silently. *Lord, guide me where this young woman is concerned. I can't grow too close to her. Don't let me.*

The wrong people could use his relationship with her against him, against the museum, drawing her into a potential scandal. She had no idea what it felt like to see her face and half-truths plastered on the front page of a newspaper.

Growing close to her could end in disaster for them both.

# Chapter 9

They'd worked hard on various dioramas and museum displays for the last couple of weeks, preparing for the flood of visitors during Living History Week, and still Amber had her work cut out for her.

With pride, she surveyed Harrington Museum's newest diorama, featuring Lewis, Clark, and Sacagawea. "Last, but not least," she murmured to herself. They'd only just yesterday received everything needed to finish this particular diorama.

"The store's finally closed now," Gladys said from the doorway. "Had one last customer that didn't want to leave." She smiled as she approached Amber and stood next to her, wrapping her in the scent of tea rose. "This was one of our busier days."

"What do you think?" Amber asked, looking at the display.

Gladys cocked her head. "I think that I don't know what Dr. Selman's going to do without you when you head back to that school of yours."

"Thanks. I think." Though Amber smiled at the compliment, a sense of loss coursed through her. She hadn't considered what it would feel like to leave the museum behind. Or Dr. Selman. "Looks like the museum had success long before I came on board. I'm sure he'll be fine."

"We've got a couple of months before you leave us though, right?" Gladys straightened a photograph of Lewis and Clark on the wall.

"Six weeks, give or take. I won't leave until the end of August."

"Time flies, and I haven't even had you over for dinner. How about the week after next, when Living History Week has run its course?" Gladys winked at her. "I make a mean pot roast. I know how college students can miss home-cooked meals. Miss their families."

At the mention of home and family, Amber pictured her mother and wilted.

"What? Don't tell me you don't like pot roast?"

"It's not that. My mother and sister were killed in a car accident a year ago." She'd said too much. Hoping to avoid further discussion, she stepped onto the dais and began adjusting the display, scrutinizing where best to secure the map of Lewis and Clark's travels.

"Oh, I'm so sorry, hon."

"Not your fault, you didn't know."

"I'd love to remedy that. *Will* you join me for dinner?"

Holding the map, Amber gave a short laugh and turned her head to look at Gladys. "I'd like that very much. Thank you." She'd not wanted to disappoint the woman, but she hoped she'd be able to get out of dinner. She didn't want Gladys dragging family history from her.

Gladys nodded. "I'll leave you to it. Say, where's your sidekick?"

The woman's reference drew a chuckle from Amber. She laid the map to rest and hopped from the dais. "You mean Dr. Selman?"

"That's the one."

Somehow, Gladys had a way of cheering Amber up, reminding Amber of her mother. "I thought you knew everything around here. He's having dinner with a donor. I don't ask for details."

"And he'll be back to help you? I don't want you working here alone."

"That's what he said." Amber adjusted Sacagawea's hand, making her look more involved with the two explorers.

Though Dr. Selman had helped her remove the life-size models from their crates and set them in the area designated for the diorama, he'd spent much of his time in his office on the phone, or working in other areas.

When he first asked her to assist, she'd been under the impression she would be helping him, not designing the exhibit herself. It made her feel safe that he hung around the museum, working, as did she, during the evening hours, but she sensed he wanted to keep his distance.

At seven thirty, Amber wiped her brow. She'd been at it for two hours since Gladys left. Alone in the museum, after all. She secured the copy of the rare map of Lewis and Clark's incredible journey and stood back to study the display, featuring maps, illustrations, letters, and figures representing some of the main characters in the traveling party.

Sacagawea joined their expedition that winter in North Dakota. Amber gripped the shoulders of the brave young Shoshone woman and nudged her slightly to the right. Working on the exhibits wasn't exactly what Amber had in mind when she came to the Harrington Museum. Although, maybe Dr. Selman was right—she had a knack for the displays. She'd finished in the nick of time, too, considering Living History Week began tomorrow.

Whether the subject was dinosaurs or American history, she loved working at the museum and was grateful for this opportunity. Almost finished. As she wondered why Dr. Selman hadn't shown up, she heard keys jangling somewhere in the distance. Footfalls sounded through the museum corridors. She'd recognize that cadence anywhere.

*Dr. Selman.*

Her heart did the little flip again. Amber steadied her hands. It wasn't like she didn't see him every day. She stood back from the diorama to study it from a distance. Despite feeling confident regarding her efforts, especially after Gladys's compliment, Amber wanted to hear words of praise from him. His approval was important to her—and just how much, was a little disconcerting.

Dr. Selman appeared in the doorway on the other side of the exhibits and made his way through the display cases to stand next to her, a concerned expression on his face.

*Oh no.* He didn't like what he saw. "What's wrong?" she asked.

A slight smile lifted his lips. "Nothing. Why?" He looked from her to the display.

The smile spread as he studied the exhibit, walking from one end to the other and stepping onto the dais. "You have a real passion for history."

"And you can tell by looking at that?"

"Yes. I can feel the emotion in this exhibit. Consider when someone plays a musical instrument. Are they playing by rote? Or do they inject feeling into their music, putting their very soul into it?"

Though she understood his musical reference, his comparison to her display confused her. How could he actually *see* emotion in what she'd done? "Remember, you helped with much of it."

"I helped lift the figures and directed you, nothing more." From behind the life-size Lewis, he studied her.

Embarrassed, Amber wasn't sure what she was supposed to say. "Thank you?"

He chuckled, then stepped down from the dais. "Which makes you the perfect candidate."

Uh-oh. Leery, she took a step back. "Perfect candidate for what?"

"Two of the actors for the annual Lewis and Clark reenactment have become ill."

"I'm sorry to hear that. What's the matter with them?"

"Stomach virus. They're not sure if they'll be well by tomorrow."

"And that has what to do with me?"

Brandon smiled. "With your passion, I think you'd make a great Sacagawea."

"What?" Amber backed up farther. "Oh no you don't. I can't act."

"Are you telling me you'd have us canceling after all the work we've done, and with the community's expectations? The museum needs this."

"I'm not saying that at all. I'm saying find someone else."

"There is no one else." He handed a large envelope to Amber. "Here's the script. Why don't you look it over and let me know what you think in the morning. The drama isn't until the afternoon. They have a rehearsal at ten."

Stunned, Amber took the script from him. How could she say no when he'd been so convincing? "All right, I'll do it."

"Good."

Seeing the smile slip back into his eyes, she knew one thing—she couldn't stand to see him disappointed. "Who will play the other part?"

A strange look came over his face. "I'm still looking for someone to play Sacagawea's husband."

*Her husband?* Amber felt the panic squeeze her throat. Would she have to kiss the actor? "Any candidates?"

"Not yet." Brandon jumped onto the dais again and adjusted Clark's position, though in Amber's opinion, he was already perfect.

Watching Dr. Selman, she began to see what he meant about the passion in the display. She saw that same enthusiasm in him, and his words to her came back.

*"Which makes you the perfect candidate."* Should she suggest that Brandon play the part of Sacagawea's husband tomorrow?

Responding to the urgent need to splash water over her face, Amber excused herself and headed to the restroom.

❧

Brandon stood at the back of the stage, behind most of the actors. After a frantic search, the part had ended up falling to him, after all. Dressed in period costumes, the group of actors presented a short drama regarding Lewis and Clark as they wintered in North Dakota. Brandon played Sacagawea's husband, Toussaint Charbonneau. He joined Lewis and Clark's group, the Corps of Discovery, as an interpreter along with Sacagawea, on a journey to find out if the Missouri River met with the Pacific Ocean. Such a finding would have provided a water route from St. Louis to the Pacific.

Fortunately for Brandon, Charbonneau hadn't been a respected or infamous character, and therefore had no lines in this reenactment. Though feeling out of his element on the amphitheater stage, Brandon enjoyed the opportunity to watch Amber in action. She spoke her lines with confidence. Two long braids on each side of her head, Amber wore a brown leather costume like that seen in artists' paintings of Sacagawea.

According to history, Sacagawea gave birth to a baby that winter, which she named Jean-Baptiste. Eyes sparkling, Amber held tightly to the swaddled doll, acting perfectly the part of protective mother. Something inside of Brandon stirred. Her lines complete, she took her place next to Brandon while another actor stepped forward. With a quick glance at Brandon, Amber shot him the hint of a smile.

He returned it with one of his own and an approving nod. Her eyes shone much too brightly. And there it was again. That feeling in the pit of his stomach. He both hated and loved the way she affected him.

The short drama ended and the crowd dispersed.

"Great job, Amber!" Peter, who played the part of Lewis, squeezed her shoulder.

"You really think so?"

"Sure I do. Cindy will probably be back by tomorrow, but maybe we can find a way to fit you into the drama."

Brandon waited nearby, wanting to congratulate her on her efforts as well, but it looked like Lewis had designs on Sacagawea. That stung. But who was Brandon that he should interfere? Needing to head back to the museum, he stepped down the stairs carved from rock.

"Dr. Selman, wait." Amber rushed to his side. "I'm glad you asked me to do this. I enjoyed it. Thanks."

"You're welcome. I knew you'd be perfect." He continued down the steps. Amber followed right behind. "What should I do now?"

"Excuse me?"

"We never got past the drama. What do you want me to do during Living History Week?"

Brandon wanted to smack his forehead. "You're right. I was so caught up in preparation...."

"You two made a great couple up there!" Muriel blocked their path while she snapped digital photos. "Let me get a picture of the happy couple."

Brandon bristled, trying to hide his irritation as he smiled for the camera. Muriel's playful teasing wouldn't have bothered him except the same errant thought had brushed his mind as well.

Once Muriel finished taking a couple of snapshots, Brandon distanced himself from Amber.

"If you'll excuse me, I have to get back to work." He smiled and turned to descend the steps.

"Hey, too bad the play didn't include a kiss between Sacagawea and her husband," Muriel said, softly.

"What are you—in junior high?"

Before Brandon was out of earshot, he'd heard Muriel, and now as he pressed through a group of teens, he could still hear Amber scolding her.

Was she merely shocked as well, or did the idea of kissing him really repulse her?

# Chapter 10

Sacagawea is one of the most honored women in American history. And that, ladies and gentlemen, ends our tour."

When no one in her group appeared to have questions, Amber rushed to the employee break room to grab a soda and a few minutes alone. Living History Week had filled her days with guided tours and answering questions about history. She rarely saw Dr. Selman except in passing, which was probably just as well.

She'd been mortified when Muriel had made her happy couple comments and wondered if Dr. Selman avoided her for that reason. Even if he wasn't avoiding her on purpose, though, the week had been too busy for words.

She put her coins into the vending machine. Nothing happened. Frustrated, she pounded the buttons and tried to shake the machine. It was no use. Too tired to remedy the problem, she slid into a chair.

Gladys entered the break room. "Can't say that I'll be upset when this week is over." She opened the fridge and grabbed a cola she'd brought. Noting Amber's empty hands, she tossed the cola to her. "Catch."

On reflex, Amber caught it. "Thanks. You're a lifesaver." The caffeine would give her a lift, especially with three more hours to go before closing.

"Think we'll make it through this week?" Gladys asked.

Amber swallowed a swig of the cool carbonation. "I hope—"

"Oh, I almost forgot." Gladys tugged a slip of paper from her pocket. "A call came into the museum store for you."

She pushed the paper across the table. Amber slid it the rest of the way and looked at the scribbled name and number.

*Michael?* He'd found her. Her stomach dropped as if she were on an amusement park ride. What did he want? She stared at the number. He wanted her to call him back.

"Are you all right, hon? You don't look well."

For a moment, Amber had forgotten the world around her. "I...uh...I've got to go." She rushed from the table, needing a quick exit.

Before she reached the door, Gladys called out. "Wait, Amber."

Amber leaned her forehead against the door, torn between waiting to hear what Gladys wanted and leaving. She needed to be alone. To think. "I really have to go."

"Hon, I'm worried about you."

Putting her back against the door, she faced Gladys. "I'm fine. Really."

"I've got a pot roast in the slow cooker. Why don't you come on over for dinner tonight. You look like you need a good meal. We don't need to wait until Living History Week is over." Gladys's eyes shone with concern, almost pleading.

Amber forced warmth into her smile. "Sure, that would be nice." She backed through the swinging door, resolving to come up with an excuse later.

She rushed from the museum and out into the open, gulping air filled with the scent of popcorn, cotton candy, and hot dogs. Walking along the edge of the grass, she neared the open field next to the temporary pop-up tents and canopies erected for Living History Week. Marching through the crowd, she crumpled the note with Michael's number.

Great. This was just great. He'd destroyed her life once. Why couldn't he just leave her alone? And if he were finally free, having served his time, would he stay away?

*Please, God, just keep him away from me.* She rubbed her arms, walking through the booths and exhibits, needing composure before returning from her break. A glance at her watch told her she should head back to the museum.

Later that evening, Amber towel-dried her hair after a long, hot shower. Once her shift was over, she'd rushed from the museum, making certain she told Gladys she wasn't feeling well. Covering her face with the damp towel, she groaned.

Gladys was a wonderful, motherly type. Amber didn't want to hurt her. Maybe if Michael hadn't contacted her today, then she'd be able to enjoy dinner with Gladys. In fact, learning more about Gladys and keeping the conversation off Amber might even have been possible.

But Gladys could read Amber's mood, no matter how big the intern smiled. She'd want to know the reason for Amber's distress and the conversation would spiral out of control. No, it was best to call and cancel. Gladys had already put the pot roast on before she'd invited Amber, anyway.

"Amber," Muriel said through the door as she gave a light knock. "Gladys called. She asked how you were, and I told her fine. She gave her address and said to come over when you're finished getting dressed."

"What? You told her I was showering?"

"Uh, yeah? What would you have me tell her?"

That she wasn't feeling well would have been nice. Maybe she wasn't physically ill but she was mentally and emotionally distressed. "I don't know." She finished pulling on her shorts and T-shirt.

"Listen, the address looks pretty far. Do you want me to drop you off so you don't have to ride your bike?"

Amber swung the door open to face Muriel. She worked to keep the frustration from her expression. Muriel was interfering. First with Dr. Selman, embarrassing her at the drama, and now with Gladys. "Honestly, I had decided I wasn't going."

Muriel crossed her arms and slumped against the wall. "Well, that stinks. It's not every day a person gets to eat Gladys's pot roast."

A laugh escaped Amber's smirk as she pushed by Muriel, heading to her room. "What are you talking about?"

Muriel followed. "Nobody has invited *me* to eat pot roast. I can't cook one to save my life. What say, I come with you? Maybe you could say you didn't feel right leaving me behind?"

Amber tossed a pillow at her. "You're crazy, you know that?" She plopped on the bed. "All right, but as long as you promise to make sure the conversation never turns to my life as the main topic." She wasn't in the mood for full disclosure.

Pushing up on her elbows, she eyed Muriel, feeling as if she'd said too much, and given the look in Muriel's gaze? Oh yeah. . .way too much.

Amber tugged Josh from his cage and snuggled him. At least *he* didn't care that her brother was a criminal.

*⌇♥*

Brandon's stomach rumbled as he pulled next to the curb at Gladys's home. He'd been putting off her invitation to dinner for weeks now. Just like he'd put off visiting his parents.

The truth? He was tired and could use a meal that didn't come from the freezer or out of a can. This week had gone smoothly and surpassed his hopes. If anything, he deserved to treat himself.

An image of Amber McKinsey in her Sacagawea garb, holding a baby, flashed before his eyes. Giving himself a moment, he leaned his head against the seat back. He thought about the young man who'd played the part of Lewis, appearing interested in Amber. Brandon had let it bother him too much, especially since he'd resolved Amber was off-limits. That he had to keep reminding himself was more than infuriating.

Opening his car door, Brandon sighed and slid from the seat. Standing on Gladys's porch, he knocked on the door and waited. Laughter drifted from inside the house. Familiar laughter. The door opened, allowing the sumptuous smell of simmering roast and vegetables to envelop him. He smiled.

"Dr. Selman, how good of you to come," Gladys said.

"Thank you for inviting me." He handed over the bottle of sparkling cider he'd brought.

Gladys took it from him. "Oh, you didn't have to."

"It was my pleasure." Brandon listened to the voices emanating from elsewhere in the house.

"Make yourself comfortable. Dinner will be ready in a few."

"Do you have other guests?"

"Yes, I didn't think you'd mind. Two of my guests couldn't make it, but just as well. Amber brought her roommate along."

*Amber.* Gladys disappeared and, uncertain what to do, Brandon sank onto the sofa, growing more uncomfortable with each second. A twenty-four-hour news station played on the television set, though the sound was muted. He watched as he considered his options. Muriel, Amber's roommate, had read far too much into his visit to Amber the day she'd been injured. Then she'd suggested he and Amber made a happy couple at the reenactment. He'd never known such an outspoken person.

Brandon slumped against the sofa. If he were honest with himself—he was more wounded at Amber's horrified reaction than anything else. But these insane thoughts had to stop.

"Dr. Selman." Seemingly out of nowhere, Muriel sat next to him on the sofa. "I'm supposed to ask what you'd like to drink. Sparkling cider or tea, coffee, milk, water—"

"Water will be fine, thank you."

"Good. Why don't you wash your hands and go into the dining room?"

What was he doing here? Gladys had made it sound like days gone by, where on occasion she'd invite him over for a decent, yet private, meal.

Once he'd washed up, he strolled to the dining room, marveling that he had yet to see Amber. Covered with a country-home vinyl tablecloth, the dining table was a lavish display of food, even for Gladys. Brandishing pot holders in each hand, she carried an oval turkey-sized dish laden with the roast, carrots, and potatoes.

On cue, his stomach grumbled. Amber appeared behind Gladys, carrying a large dish in each hand.

Brandon abandoned his position and rushed to her aid. "Here, let me help you." He took the green bean casserole from her, making sure to grip the potholder underneath. In the process, his hand touched hers.

"Why, thank you." She gazed at him—her eyes the very amber of her name.

"Dr. Selman," Gladys said, "you can set those here." She pointed where he could place the green beans.

Realizing he'd acted like a schoolboy, it shamed him to feel himself blushing. Grown men didn't blush.

"My, we're the absentminded professor tonight, aren't we?" Gladys winked.

The ladies took their seats, and Brandon followed, sitting where he was told. This wasn't the evening he wanted. He needed to relax, enjoy the meal, but at least two nosy women sat at the table, and Amber sat across from him.

Gladys asked him to say grace, which he did.

Once plates were loaded with food, everyone seemed too busy eating to talk much. Finally, Brandon broke the silence. "I think this is your best, Gladys." He let his fork rest against his plate for the moment.

"I'm not sure I've eaten anything this wonderful before," Amber said.

"I second that," Muriel said around a mouthful. "No, I mean I want seconds of that."

Laughter surrounded the table.

From the other end, Gladys beamed with pride. "You're all too good to me. You know, you're my family, really. I have my sister who lives up near Devil's Lake. She comes to see me on occasion. But that's it."

Her sentiments warmed Brandon's heart.

"Wait until you see what I made for dessert," she said, eyes teasing.

A cell phone rang. Amber frowned. "Excuse me. . . I thought I turned it off." Snatching the phone from her pocket, she exited the dining room.

Gladys stood. "Dessert, you two?"

"Yes, please." Preoccupied with the frown he'd seen on Amber's face, he wasn't aware Muriel had spoken to him until she cleared her throat.

"Dr. Selman. You haven't heard a word I've said, have you?" She slid a few more carrots onto her plate.

"Forgive me, what did you say?" He stared at her plate, loaded with thirds or was it fourths?

"What? I love food, what can I say?"

"You must have a great metabolism."

Sticking another bite in her mouth, she chewed as she smiled, then swallowed. "What I was saying was, you should go check on Amber."

The idea had occurred to him, but she was Amber's roommate.

Seeming to read his mind, again, with a full mouth, she said, "Hello, I'm eating."

Brandon eyed Muriel. Though he didn't consider himself more important than anyone else, he knew that both Gladys and Jim insisted the volunteers address him with a title to ensure at least a modicum of respect. The corner of his mouth drew up. Muriel wasn't the least bit intimidated by him.

He liked that. "I'm sure she's fine. Probably chatting on her cell."

Muriel frowned and stopped chewing then shook her head as if she knew some dreadful, hidden secret.

Concern flooded him, but then he reasoned if it were true, Muriel would be the first to check on her. He'd pegged her as an overly concerned type the evening he'd spent at the cabin, talking to a medicated Amber. He sighed. What was taking Gladys so long with dessert? Maybe she had discovered what had become of Amber. He needed to excuse himself for the evening.

The front door slammed. Gladys called from the kitchen. "Dr. Selman, can you find out who that was? Someone either came in or left. I'll have your dessert out in a jiff."

"See?" Muriel proceeded to scrape the last of the potatoes onto her plate. With larger than life eyes, she said, "I'm eating. Gladys asked you."

A niggle at the back of his mind suggested that Muriel was in cahoots with Gladys in an attempt to pair him with Amber. But he doubted Amber had left in a dramatic attempt for him to follow.

"If you'll excuse me, then." He left the table and exited the house through the front door. Amber was bent over the white railing that surrounded the small porch, looking like someone about to lose her supper.

Brandon rushed to her side. She was trembling. "Amber? Are you all right?"

She stiffened before turning to him. "Yes, everything is fine. I really have to go." Fleeing the porch, she jogged down the drive and into the street.

"Miss McKinsey, Amber, wait!" It was no use.

Brandon jumped in his car and started the engine, driving slowly on the neighborhood street. Street lamps illuminated her as she ran.

When he approached her, he opened the window. "What do you think you're doing?"

She stopped, catching her breath. "I know I must look like an idiot. I just want to go home."

"Hop in," he offered, though confused by her strange behavior.

She climbed into his car, looking wary.

"I can take you back to get your purse."

"I didn't bring one." She stared straight ahead.

"All right, then." Brandon phoned Gladys and explained that he was taking Amber home. To his surprise, she seemed more pleased than concerned.

He ended the call. "If you were that afraid of Gladys's dessert, all you had to say was, 'No thank you.'"

His comment elicited at least a small laugh, but he noted the girl wasn't going to give up the information he wanted. "You want to talk about it? Who called that upset you?"

"Please, I. . .can't."

"Can't or won't?"

He drove in silence until he arrived at her cabin. Stopping the car, he turned to face her. She'd already opened the car door.

The dome light revealed her red-rimmed eyes. "Thank you for the ride. Look, I appreciate all you've done for me, allowing me the experience of working at your museum. It's important to me that you're pleased with my work. But, I need to keep my personal life. . .well. . .personal."

Brandon nodded. Amber shut the car door and jogged up the path to her dimly lit front door. He waited while she unlocked it and slipped into the cabin. Despite the fact that he'd not expressed an interest in her romantically, the cold stab of rejection threatened. Still, he knew that Amber McKinsey hadn't rejected him personally. Something or someone had upset her.

As he backed from the driveway, he wished that she didn't affect him. Wished that he could bury his concern. She'd drawn a line—one that should have been there to begin with.

# Chapter 11

Amber surveyed the group of fifteen children who participated in the museum's summer camp this week. In addition to the camp, Dr. Selman had worked to make the museum child friendly with interactive and hands-on exhibits. He'd incorporated live animals such as lizards, snakes, and turtles—all in appropriately contained environments in their respective exhibits, of course. The dinosaur exhibit included an area where children could don hard hats and dust sand from dinosaur fossil replicas.

His efforts revealed his obvious soft spot for the very young. The thought sent a tremble through Amber's heart. It also made her wonder if he'd ever married. But she didn't have much time to ponder the question.

Katie, a darling little girl with curly blond hair, held up a large sheet of paper covered in wet paint for Amber's approval.

"Oh, that's wonderful," Amber proclaimed.

Katie stuck her fingers into brown paint, expanding on her impression of a triceratops. So far, they'd spent the week learning about dinosaurs, doing arts and crafts, studying the exhibits. Amber even gave them a tour of the nearby digs—a day they'd enjoyed the most. The museum had created a safe path for young children, or those who simply wanted a glimpse of the prehistoric dig site. No actual digging for them.

She put a finger to her lips and smiled. That day had been her first time anywhere near the digs since Dr. Selman pulled her out. She missed it. In fact, she missed him. His company. She'd spent time working with him on the displays and then briefly participated in the Lewis and Clark drama with him.

Then, there'd been dinner at Gladys's home.

Amber recalled that night. After the crazy way she'd acted, she was surprised Dr. Selman hadn't sent her packing. But the museum had been exceptionally busy the last two weeks. They needed her help.

Hating her thoughts at the moment, she walked around the long table where the children concentrated on their art. When Muriel had made the silly reference to a kiss during the reenactment, though furious, Amber had guiltily imagined sharing a kiss with Dr. Selman. During the busyness of that week, she'd longed to see him and had been delighted when he showed up at Gladys's home. But then. . .she'd ruined everything because of her brother's call. He'd left her a voice mail that he was in town, now that he was out of prison, and he wanted to see her. How was she supposed to react to that news?

When she'd told Dr. Selman she wanted to keep her personal life to herself, her heart had screamed in defiance as she watched the hurt shimmer in his eyes.

And now, she couldn't get that image out of her mind.

*If only there were a way. . .*

"Now what do you think?" Six-year-old Andrew lifted his finger-painted stegosaurus.

"I think you're going to be a famous artist one day." Grateful she had the children's camp as a distraction, she tousled his hair.

He beamed with pride. "Can I take this home to my mom?"

"Of course you can. In fact, make sure you take all your creations home to show your parents what you've been up to this week."

She directed the children to begin cleaning up after themselves—a rule put in place from the beginning, thank goodness.

In her pocket, her cell vibrated, causing her pulse to race. It was sad when every phone call scared her. Tugging it from its snug hiding in her pocket, she looked at the number before answering.

"Cams!"

"Did I call at a bad time? I never know when you're working."

"I've got the museum's summer camp this week. This is the last day and we're cleaning up. I really can't talk now."

"No problem. Just wanted to find out how you're doing?" Cams's tone held subtle concern.

"What's wrong?" Amber tugged on her earlobe while watching the children. *Hurry, Cams.*

Cams sighed on the other end. "Have you heard from. . .Michael?"

The garbage can brimmed with paper and art scraps. Amber pressed the trash deeper, allowing the children to stuff more in. "Oh Cams. How did you know?"

"He left a message here, looking for you. I arrived a few minutes ago and found it."

"Look, I know you never would have given me away, had you been there. Who do you think told him where to find me?"

"Considering you haven't told too many about your aversion to him, almost anyone could have told him where you are. My guess would be Dr. Young."

"I figured. He had no way of knowing." *And I plan to keep it that way.*

"What are you going to do? I'm worried about you."

"Keep ignoring his calls, maybe get a new number." *Hope he goes away.*

"Amber. Look, are you sure you shouldn't just talk to him? I mean, come on. He's your brother."

"That's mine!" Jonathan shouted at Greg.

"No, it's mine."

"Cams, I've really got to go. We'll talk later." She ended the call. "Boys, calm down."

The next morning Amber awoke feeling grateful she had a day off. She stretched and rubbed her eyes then rolled to her side. Another half hour of sleep would be nice, especially if it kept her from thinking about all that had gone wrong. About her brother.

If she got out of bed now, she could go for her morning run, something she hadn't done in a couple of weeks. Funny how painful it could be to run, yet it made her feel great. All that oxygen pumping through her body energized her and lifted her mood. An image of colliding with Dr. Selman on her first run in Harrington came to mind. She groaned. Nope. Running would definitely not clear her mind today.

"Knock, knock," Muriel said, in a singsong voice. "Who's hungry this morning?" She waltzed into Amber's bedroom with a plate of pancakes and orange juice on a tray.

Amber pushed up on her elbows. "What are you doing?"

"I made breakfast. What does it look like?" Muriel set the tray next to Amber on the bed.

The pancakes smelled great. "Don't you have to work today?"

"No. We're off on the same day for once. It occurred to me this morning that we should do something together for fun. You seem like you could use some fun in your life."

"Gee, thanks."

"Don't thank me until you've heard what I have planned."

"Uh-oh. Better tell me now before I'm fully awake."

"Horseback riding."

Amber sat straight up. "What? You're crazy. I can't—"

"In the Badlands, Amber. You'll love it."

"I'm. . .afraid of horses."

"Have you ever ridden one?"

"Nope. And don't plan to."

"These are trained trail horses." Muriel sank to the bed next to the tray, careful not to tip the juice. "Look, Amber. You need to get out more. Please, do this with me?"

Why did Muriel care so much? Truth was, Amber could use a distraction. "Oh, all right." She grabbed the orange juice and jumped from the bed, taking a pancake with her as she headed to the bathroom for a shower.

Muriel laughed, following her down the hall. "We leave in an hour."

"You sure you can handle this?" Jim asked, skimming the list of artifacts due to arrive next week. "I can reschedule my vacation if I need to."

"Come on. I don't need you to reschedule."

"It's not as if you have enough help. I wish we could hire more. At least we could bring in more volunteers."

*Like Amber*. Brandon frowned at the thought of her. He'd not been able to get her off his mind, or rid himself of concern for her, even after she'd drawn the strictest of lines. But she was a volunteer for the museum, a sister in Christ—shouldn't he be concerned? Nevertheless, he'd avoided her, telling the Lord that He'd have to give a sign if He wanted Brandon involved.

"I can handle it, Jim." Brandon toyed with a paperweight on Jim's desk. "Sounds more like you don't trust me to cover for you while you're gone."

"You know that's not true." Jim took the paperweight from Brandon and moved it to the credenza behind him.

Brandon laughed.

"You've been distracted lately. Might I suggest you have Miss McKinsey help you? Working under you is the main reason she signed on for the intern program. You've had her doing grunt work, nothing serious."

Earlier Jim had suggested Brandon dismiss Amber entirely. Brandon cocked his head. Could that be sign number one? No, he'd need more. "She's gaining experience in all aspects of the museum."

"Cataloging relics is part of that as well. I'd planned to have her help with that." Jim eyed him, arching his left brow. "Look, we've known each other a long time. What's really going on here? You kept her on and had me let Jason go instead, and now you don't want to use her where she's needed."

Brandon turned his back and walked to the door, then faced Jim again. "Yes, we *have* known each other for a while. Which is why I don't understand your concern over who assists me, if anyone, in your absence."

With that, Brandon left. He tugged on his shirt collar, feeling a little guilty for his brusque response. Jim was only trying to help and yet Brandon had snapped at him simply because he didn't want to explain the odd rapport he had with Amber.

Today was supposed to be Brandon's day off, but Jim had called him in to discuss the arrival of the artifacts next week. Brandon hadn't exactly said that he *wouldn't* bring Amber in to help him, but after how she acted at dinner last week, Brandon wasn't sure working with her would be the best thing. He kept telling himself his concern was appropriate, but his feelings were anything but brotherly toward her.

Not good. Once in his office, he sank into his chair, put his feet on his desk, and leaned back. At least he admitted he *had* feelings. Still, he wasn't a professional if he denied her the opportunity because of his own weakness. He looked up the number at the cabin. He'd ask if she was willing to work with him on the Hamlin Exhibit, starting Monday.

Let *her* decide. If she didn't want the task, then he could work alone. Jim couldn't accuse him of avoiding Amber. And if she agreed, would that be sign number two? Brandon rubbed his chin. A simple phone call would give him the opportunity to ask her if she was all right. How she was doing. Never mind that he wanted to hear her voice.

He dialed the number. The phone rang twice. "Muriel here."

"This is Dr. Selman."

Quiet lingered on the line, then, "Hi. They need my help in the digs today?"

Now it was his turn to give pause. "Actually, I wonder if I could speak with Amber. . .er. . .Miss McKinsey."

"Amber isn't available."

A bad sign. "Please have her call me when she can."

"Okay. Are you working at the museum today?"

Brandon hadn't thought of that. "As a matter of fact, no. Have her call me on my cell." He relayed his number, cringing at the possible gossip that could arise. "I need to discuss a new assignment I have for her starting Monday."

"Got it. Would you mind if she calls back later today? We're going horseback riding in the Badlands, and we're running late. Hey, if you don't have plans, maybe you could join us. It's called Badland Adventures or something."

Could Muriel's invitation be sign number two?

"Thanks for the invitation, but I can't." Considering Amber wanted her personal and business life separate, he'd need more than Muriel's invitation.

"That's too bad. Because. . . ," Muriel fairly whispered, "I think she could use more friends."

At her words, his pulse pounded in his ears. Still, Brandon sighed at the news. "I'll keep that in mind." He ended the call. Ridiculous. No way would he show up at their outing.

Why had Muriel thrown a rock hammer into his thoughts? What had she meant? Most likely, nothing more than she said. Amber needed more friends. Except at Gladys's house, he'd had the funny idea that Muriel had attempted to pair him with Amber.

He rubbed his temples. He should have invited Amber to Bible study when he had the chance.

He considered himself an intelligent person and had the degrees to prove it. Yet even with all his education, he couldn't seem to figure out the right thing. He was attracted to this woman on many levels, and it was that attraction that kept him from thinking straight.

Her frazzled reaction after that one phone call had worried Brandon. Apparently Muriel was concerned as well. . . .

*Okay, Lord, I'm taking that as the third sign. I need to get involved in her life. Personally.*

"Whether she likes it or not."

# Chapter 12

Amber took a deep breath and smiled up at the clear, blue sky. She loved North Dakota weather in the summer. An hour ride into the Badlands would bring breathless views as well, so the guide had said.

"All right." Tom Snickett pointed at her as he led a large brown beast around. "You can have Blue."

*But the horse is brown.* And it looked to be twice as tall as Amber. "You want me to get on *that?*"

Another man brought a stool over and set it next to Blue while Tom held on to the reins. "Blue is one of our calmest. She won't do you wrong."

After a quick glare at Muriel who already sat astride a white horse called Black, Amber took a step. Despite her shaking knees, she forced herself to walk toward the horse. Tom lifted his hand, signaling Amber to stop.

"Try not to be afraid. Horses can sense fear."

*Fantastic.* If he wanted her to feel confident and douse the fear, he'd said the wrong thing.

"Chin up, chickadee." Muriel waved. "You can do this."

Amber tried to think of something else besides riding, and her thoughts landed smack on Dr. Selman. Not good. Her pulse hit high gear as she thought about his phone call. Muriel had said he wanted to speak to her. On the drive over, she dialed his cell. Getting no answer, she left a message.

Tom still stood waiting, so Amber shifted her focus to the horse.

"Okay." Tom held the reins at Blue's head. "Grab hold of the saddle horn with your left hand."

Amber stood on the stool, grateful she didn't have to figure out a way to haul herself up the side of the living mountain and somehow sling her right leg over the beast's back. She grabbed the saddle horn and stuck her left foot in the stirrup. So far so good.

"Now grab the back of the saddle with your right hand, put your weight on the ball of your left foot, then sling your right leg over the horse."

She could do this. Amber bit her lip. Hands on the saddle. Push on the left foot. Right leg over, swivel.

Once her right foot found the other stirrup, she released a sigh.

Tom lifted his hat and handed her the reins.

"Nothing to it," she said.

"Hold the reins in one hand. When you're going left, pull the reins a little toward the left side of Blue's neck. Going right, pull to the right. Not too hard, though. Blue knows the drill."

"Got it." Piece of cake.

Amber drew a long, shaky breath, keenly aware of every little movement and twitch of the horse beneath her. She wasn't sure how many riders were ahead of her in the line, or behind her for that matter, but she counted seven that she could see before the rest disappeared into the tree-shrouded trail. When the line began moving, her horse fell into step by rote, and Amber rocked with the rhythmic movement that was Blue. After a while, Amber began to relax. This wasn't bad. Not bad at all.

Though she'd mastered her anxiety over the horse, for now at least, her emotions were anything but calm as she considered Dr. Selman. He'd never called her about work before.

Again, her last words to him played over in her mind, torturing her. *"I need to keep my personal life. . .personal."* Oh, how she wished the words weren't true. That she'd never said them. How she wished she didn't have to keep to herself—especially where Dr. Selman was concerned—for fear someone would find out the awful truth.

Muriel rode Black directly in front of her and turned her head to peer at Amber. "How you doing?" she asked, while smacking her lips.

"Hey, no fair, where'd you get the gum?"

"I'd toss you a piece but you might fall off trying to catch it." Muriel's eyes grew wide as she peered past Amber. "Oh, my. . ."

Fear squeezed her chest. She took a glimpse behind her, seeing nothing unusual. "What is it?"

Muriel turned her back to Amber once again, her shoulders bouncing up and down in laughter.

"You'd better tell me right now before I spear this horse forward right next to you."

"You mean spur? Considering you're not wearing spurs, maybe a gentle nudge would be better," Muriel called over her shoulder.

"Whatever. Now, please, what did you see?" The trail began to incline and Amber leaned into Blue in order to keep her balance.

"Remember who called earlier? Did I mention I invited him to go riding today?"

"Uh. . .no." What did that have to do with what Muriel had seen?

Amber gave a quick glance behind her but couldn't see beyond the few riders following her. She had a difficult time believing Dr. Selman would spend his morning on a horseback ride. Then again, *she* was. To Amber, he seemed like the sort of person who had important things to do. Far more important than this.

Muriel's words came back to her. *"I think Dr. Selman might have a thing for you."* Amber's palms grew sweaty. Could it be true? She stroked the horse's mane absently. She couldn't believe he was interested. Not really. Any interest he expressed was purely out of concern for her as an intern at the museum, and she'd already squashed his intervention into her personal life.

No, Dr. Selman wasn't interested in Amber. And even if he were it would all blow away like the dust once he found out about her brother.

*◌*

Somehow while sitting in his office, thinking over his concerns for Amber, Brandon had convinced himself that he needed to butt in to her life. When Muriel mentioned horseback riding, of course Brandon had brushed it off as ridiculous. And now, sitting on the back of a horse, his memory was a bit fuzzy. All his well thought out reasons for being here now seemed contrived.

He'd known Tom Snickett for years, and once Brandon made the decision, the deed was as good as done.

He considered his teaching at the previous Wednesday night's Bible study regarding the apostle Paul. Brandon wished he could teach it again next week, considering he now better understood what the apostle had meant when he said he knew the right thing to do but he did the wrong instead.

Brandon shouldn't be here. Yet here he was.

Why couldn't he have seen this clearly before? He had no right to insert himself into Amber's personal life. Never mind that her roommate had encouraged him. A sour taste formed in his mouth. Even without Muriel's whispered encouragement, Brandon would have found a way to interrupt Amber's day. To make sure she was all right. A week of avoiding her hadn't diminished his concern.

The only good news was that he was at the end of the line. He could turn his horse around and head back without anyone being the wiser. He'd taken Tom's ride before and knew the trail would soon open up to a field where the riders had more freedom. Amber would see him then if she hadn't already— that is, if he didn't turn around now.

He reined the horse out of line but had only ridden a few feet when he heard Tom's familiar voice behind him.

"Where do you think you're going?"

Brandon smiled. "I remembered something I need to do."

Tom caught up with Brandon, and they stopped.

"On a day like this? You don't want to miss the view now, do you?" Tom asked.

How could he get out of this? Gladys was right. He really was an absent-minded professor, or rather, museum director.

At least. . .where Amber McKinsey was concerned.

"I guess what I needed to do can wait." Brandon followed Tom at the end of the line.

The trailhead opened up to a meadow where the riders were allowed to break the line as they headed to the other side. There they would tether the horses and hike a few yards through the trees until they came to a high bluff, offering a scenic viewpoint of the rough terrain of the Little Missouri River Badlands.

"I always get nervous at this part." Brandon drew his horse to a stop.

"Is that so?"

"Seems to me you'd get nervous, too, giving these inexperienced riders this much freedom."

"You worry too much, Doc. These horses are gentle. Besides they all know to follow Kevin's lead."

"If you say so."

Tom grinned, then urged his horse into a lope, leaving Brandon who studied the trail behind him, considering his options.

"Dr. Selman! You decided to come."

At the familiar voice, he turned to see Muriel riding up to him.

"Of course I came. What you said worried me."

Muriel's smile seemed to say she held a big secret. "I'm sure you needed some sunshine, too."

"It's a beautiful day."

"Amber isn't too good on a horse. I probably shouldn't have left her."

In his opinion, the riders should have been kept in a tight single-file line for the entire trail ride. Leave it to Tom to be creative. His trail ride was the most popular.

Brandon followed Muriel up the line and then he spotted Amber as several riders spread out to give her space. Her horse appeared skittish, tossing its head. Amber made matters worse by tugging on the reins and kicking the horse with her heels, sending mixed signals.

Kevin and Tom were ahead, their backs to the group. Talking, they were completely unaware of Amber's predicament. When her horse bolted, Brandon kicked his into a canter, coming alongside Amber. The horse was spooked, but worse, so was Amber. Eyes wide, she clearly didn't know what to do.

Reaching across the distance between them, he grabbed her reins and brought both horses to a halt. He calmed the horse with soothing tones. Trembling and gasping for breath, Amber placed her hand on her chest.

She gazed over at Brandon, looking sheepish. "Thanks. I don't know what happened. The horse just got scared. I didn't know what to—"

"It's okay. Not everyone is experienced with horses." He grinned, hoping to inject humor into his comment. "I have an idea. Why don't we walk?"

"Huh?"

"Tom will have us tether the horses up ahead. Let's walk the rest of the way. I'll lead the horses."

Amber offered a timid smile and nodded her agreement. Brandon hopped off his horse then helped Amber off hers.

Brandon and Amber walked side by side, while Brandon held both horses' reins, leading them through the meadow. Even though they walked in silence, it was a comfortable quiet. Being next to her like this felt natural and—as he watched the soft breeze lift a few strands of her dark hair—it felt right.

"Dr. Selman, I want to apologize for what I said the night you took me home from Gladys's."

"There's no need, really. I understand. You didn't want to tell me what upset you."

She looked down, her hair swinging forward to hide her face. "It seems like every time something bad happens, you're there."

Brandon felt as if she'd struck him. What was she saying? He recalled that he'd knocked her over when they'd first met, colliding on their jog.

Eyes wide, she looked up at him. "No, that didn't come out right. I keep having trouble, and you keep being at the wrong place at the wrong time."

"Or maybe it's the right place at the right time."

She smiled gently. "Don't get me wrong. I'm grateful you've been there. I'm embarrassed, that's all. I wish you could somehow know a different side of me."

*I'd love to.* But he kept the errant thought to himself. "I'm just glad I could be of assistance."

"Is that why you're here today?"

"What? A man can't go horseback riding?"

That elicited a snicker. "Sure he can. I don't mean to suggest that you're here for me. It's just that Muriel told me she invited you."

Now it was Brandon's turn to be embarrassed. "Honestly, I've been concerned about you ever since that night when you were upset. I wanted to make sure you were okay."

They approached the tethering line—a rope tied between two trees. Brandon grinned and offered Blue's reins to Amber.

Looking anything but thrilled, she gave a half laugh then reached for them. Her soft fingers swept over his skin, stirring a longing inside him. He focused on the others who were already hiking the trail to the viewpoint.

"Thank you for your concern. It means a lot to me that you would go out of your way."

How could he tell her that it was no trouble at all? He inhaled the crisp air. "Would you like to come to Bible study this Wednesday?"

"Sure, I'd like that."

Warmth buzzed around in Brandon's chest where it had no right to buzz. She was his sister in Christ and an intern at the museum and. . .his protégé.

"There you are. You guys are going to miss the view if you don't hurry." Muriel walked alongside them, appearing out of nowhere. That seemed to be her modus operandi.

"Did you tell Amber about the new assignment?"

Drawing a blank, Brandon stared at Muriel.

"You know—the reason you called today." Muriel's smile irritated Brandon. She started up the narrow trail, leading the way.

Brandon felt like an idiot. Following behind Amber as they made their way to the viewpoint, he noticed her slight form. He liked her runner's physique.

"What's the new assignment?" she asked.

Ah yes, the phone call that had led to trail riding with Amber. "We've a shipment arriving next week—the Hamlin Exhibit on loan. I'm hoping you'll assist me with receiving the collection and cataloging the artifacts."

She stopped and turned to face him. "Really?" Her smile beamed and her eyes brimmed with joy. "Helping you with artifacts, working alongside you—it's the sort of experience I came here to do. I'd feel like a real professional."

She turned away to continue the hike.

Grand. While she might feel like a professional working beside him, beside her. . .he felt anything but.

# Chapter 13

"Good morning, Gladys." Amber stepped through the doorway of the gift store and smiled at Gladys as the woman prepared to open her register for the day.

"Don't you look happy this morning." She stepped from behind the counter to hug Amber.

Gladys was so good to her. "I feel rested." Amber thought back to the horseback ride. Dr. Selman had come to her rescue. Again.

Did she actually *need* rescuing? She wasn't sure. All she knew was that he'd endeared himself to her, deepening what would otherwise be a strong crush.

Though she'd been timid about sitting on a horse, especially when Blue decided she had a mind of her own, Dr. Selman had been there to calm the beast and more. . .he calmed Amber's racing heart.

Gladys cleared her throat, bringing Amber back from her musings. "Looks like you feel more than rested, hon. You're fairly glowing."

Amber played with the dinosaur paraphernalia on the counter. "I went on a trail ride and saw a spectacular view." Muriel had been right about Amber enjoying the trail ride through the Badlands. But Amber knew the experience was even more memorable because Dr. Selman had shared it with her. He'd sounded eager to convey his knowledge of the Badlands with her. She could still hear the enthusiasm in his voice.

"And where will you work this week?"

"Dr. Selman asked me to assist him with the new artifacts."

Gladys lowered her glasses to peer at Amber. "I see."

The look Gladys gave was disconcerting. Was Amber's admiration for Dr. Selman so obvious? "It's what I'm here to do, don't you know? Not crafts with children or playacting the part of Sacagawea."

"Why so defensive?"

Amber sighed. "I'm sorry."

Gladys returned her attention to opening the register. "I'm the one who's sorry, hon. You were happy when you came through the door, now I've ruined it."

"Oh Gladys, don't let my disposition upset you. I'm just ready to be involved in serious work, that's all. Please, don't get me wrong; I enjoyed working with the children and participating in the drama, too."

The cash register drawer opened. Gladys began counting her bills. "Care to come over for dinner tonight?"

Amber almost laughed. Gladys appeared to be using Amber's guilt against her, coaxing her to dinner. "I'd love to. I didn't get to try your dessert.

Is it as good as your pot roast?" In truth, she'd wanted to make up for skipping out. "Maybe I can even do the dishes for you this time."

"Are you saying Muriel didn't rave about my strawberry-rhubarb pie?" Gladys was now counting her pennies.

"Rave about it? I couldn't get her to shut up." Amber joined in Gladys's laughter, happy she'd turned the tension around.

"Tonight then. I look forward to hearing about your day off." The look in Gladys's eyes said she knew more about Amber's experience than she'd told her.

Uh-oh. "As a matter of fact I'd better get to work, too." She needed to douse her emotions where Dr. Selman was concerned.

She didn't dare ruin this opportunity. Her time here, working under Dr. Selman would be important when listing her experience on her résumé or curriculum vitae. And maybe, just maybe. . .she could get into a good grad school and finally make a break from the past.

Shaking Michael from her thoughts, she focused once again on Dr. Selman. Though she was happy he'd chosen to join her on the trail ride, his appearance more than confused her. Then, he'd invited her to his Bible study. With the way she acted around him, he probably considered her a broken fossil in need of repair. In that case, he'd better have a big bottle of glue.

In the ladies' room, she composed herself, brushing her hair back to make sure it was smooth and shiny. *Stop it.* His concern was that of her mentor and a fellow Christian—they shared that commonality, unusual especially in this field. It was nothing more.

Keeping that in mind, she could stay focused on her work. This was an opportunity to crawl from the deep hole Michael had dug for them both. Chin up, Amber pushed through the glass door into the climate-controlled room where they received collections. Wearing gloves, Dr. Selman looked up from the pottery he studied.

"There you are. You're just in time."

Amber let her backpack slide to the floor next to the wall. "What is it?" She moved next to him.

"You're looking at a Hisatsinom pot, AD 600."

Amber angled her head in question.

"The cliff dwellers of the Southwest. They're also called Anasazi, the ancestors of the Hopi."

"I'm vaguely familiar with them."

"They were basket makers but eventually made pottery. This is an early grayware piece with black on red designs. Later, they used more colors. Their artifacts are the best preserved. The Hamlin Exhibit, particularly valuable."

Dr. Selman's gaze shifted to Amber's face. "They've made a new discovery in the Hell Creek Formation."

"Of pottery?"

He chuckled. "No. What looks to be a complete triceratops."

Amber straightened at the news, wishing she could have been there, wishing her time in the dinosaur digs hadn't been so short. But. . .why was he telling her this? She realized he was studying her. Was he giving her a choice? Waiting on her to make a decision? She had the strong feeling that he wanted to know where her heart truly lay.

If only *she* knew.

His left brow arched. "I'm offering you an opportunity, Amber, if you want it."

Unsure which opportunity he meant, she considered his words. She thought of Muriel, who was sure now she wanted to study paleontology. Still, working at a new dig site would certainly mean Amber wouldn't be with Dr. Selman. "I'm here to learn everything you want to teach me."

He nodded, appearing to approve of her response. "The fossils will be brought here to study, of course. You can see them then."

"I'm looking forward to it."

He smiled. "We'll be examining each of the artifacts for preexisting damage. I'll show you what to look for. Then each item must be cataloged on the computer."

"I'm here to help," she said and studied the pot, though she could feel his gaze on her.

"Wait until you see how painfully time consuming the job can be."

"Hopefully, I won't let you down."

He placed the artifact into a specially designed box lined with Ethafoam. "In a larger museum you wouldn't be doing this without extensive knowledge of this time period. I'm here to assist you with that, considering I've broadened my education to include historical artifacts to accommodate the cultural side of the museum."

This time, Amber met his gaze. "But. . .you still love fossils, right?"

"Always." He slipped into his familiar half grin, producing that long dimple in his right cheek.

She loved his grin. Loved it.

❧

The way she smiled back at him. . .

Brandon chuckled. Was it a nervous reaction or his hopeless attempt to shake the effect her liquid gold eyes had on him? Not only was she strikingly beautiful, she was highly intelligent. And when they'd worked on the dioramas for Living History Week, he'd admired her passion. Though there was no doubt he needed her help, his motivation went far deeper than how much she would ease his workload, cataloging the artifacts.

Working with her like this would be difficult.

Brandon explained that a digital image of each artifact was uploaded to the computer; then all cataloging information was entered, including where the artifact would be stored or exhibited within the museum. "We'll store these artifacts until we're ready to display them. And make certain that you catalog before you store."

Amber's eyes grew wide. "I can see that would be disastrous."

He chuckled. "No kidding. It took us weeks to locate an artifact that had been stored before cataloging. The volunteer stored the item then forgot to enter its location. Catastrophic for a museum."

"I can only imagine if the Smithsonian didn't keep good records—how would they ever find anything?"

At the computer, he stood behind her and peered over her shoulder as he directed her through the various components of the process. "Once you get the hang of it, it's really nothing more than data entry."

"When you put it that way, it's not something that would sound good on a résumé."

"Ah. We'll make certain your experience here shines." He shot her a grin.

Her attention focused on the computer screen, Brandon watched her, wishing he had more control over his mind. An unwelcome thought continued to accost him—he wanted Amber to give him a sign that he meant something more to her.

But Amber was young, vibrant, and beautiful. How could she think of him as anything but her mentor? Yet he'd battled thoughts of her from the moment they'd collided, and clearly, no amount of professionalism on his part would change his growing feelings for her.

Thankfully, Amber was a quick learner, freeing Brandon from hovering over her shoulder, tortured with smelling her floral-scented hair. He moved to a table at the other side of the room where he gently removed artifacts from their protective boxes, examined and cataloged them. A comfortable silence filled the room, and they spoke only when necessary.

Focusing on the computer screen, he decided he was more than pleased with the PastPerfect museum software they'd purchased six months ago. He was searching the exhibit items on loan entered so far when Amber's voice gently broke through his concentration.

"Dr. Selman."

Completing the search, he turned on the stool to face her. "What's up?"

"I'm not sure about this one. Would you mind letting me know what you think?" Brandon walked across the room to where she waited.

Her expression told him she was completely involved in the work, her mind absorbing everything like a sponge. Brandon liked to see that sort of devotion.

"This is the first damaged artifact I've had. See the edge here. How do I know if it was discovered that way, or damaged during the shipment?"

"Let's see." He ran a finger over the jagged edge of the pottery. "This doesn't appear to be new. Describe the damage and, along with the digital image, that should be enough."

Amber finished cataloging the item then placed it gently back into the protective box. She moved from the stool, stirring the scent of her perfume around him.

Near the end of the day, Brandon found himself exhausted from the wearisome tasks of cataloging.

Amber yawned from across the room. "Excuse me."

Brandon laughed. "This is definitely tedious, no question there."

"Honestly, I think I'm a field girl, when all is said and done." She covered her mouth, yawning again.

"Careful now. You know that's contagious." Brandon felt a yawn coming on as well.

"I'm so sorry. Please don't think I'm not happy to do this."

Each item took time to evaluate. However, that wasn't Brandon's problem. Could he work next to Amber for that long and keep his distance?

"You know, it could take us the rest of this week, if not two, to make it through this shipment."

She flashed him a broad smile. A beautiful smile.

"Are you saying you're willing to grin and bear it?"

"You know me too well already." A soft laugh escaped before she returned her attention to the computer screen.

In fact, he knew nothing much about her. And it was best to keep things that way. Her back to him, her shiny black hair hung past her shoulders. Was it possible to get to know her better without compromising all he'd worked for?

By Wednesday, they'd cataloged at least half the first crate he'd opened and placed the items in a climate-controlled storage room. Once they'd secured the artifacts, Brandon was ready to stop for the day; but he remembered the box of special items that had arrived earlier that morning. He mulled over whether he should open it now or wait for tomorrow.

Amber looked tired as she waited for his instructions. Considering it was nearly five o'clock, he should send her home; but he wanted her company if only for a bit longer.

He popped the crate open and dug through the packing. "Aha."

"What is it?" Amber was at his side, looking anxiously into the crate.

He liked that she seemed to always be ready for more. And he liked the feeling of her next to him, working with him.

Gently, he removed the shoe-sized box from the crate. Donning his gloves again, he pulled a beautiful pot from the foam-lined box. "This is one of the most valuable items in this exhibit. Here, you can hold it."

She pulled on her gloves, too, and took it from him, cradling yet another piece of pottery in her hands—but one of great value.

Looking at him, her golden eyes were wide and searching. In them he saw the usual admiration typical of a protégé, but there was something else. What was it?

Before he could react, the artifact slipped from her hands. Falling to the floor, it shattered. Colorful shards of clay pottery lay spread across the floor.

# Chapter 14

Mortified, Amber stood frozen, staring at the floor. Broken pieces of pottery lay at her feet. Shock resounded through her bones. Seconds ticked by as her mind grappled with what happened.

Struggling to breathe, she finally lifted her gaze to meet Dr. Selman's. His expression reflected her own—one of dismay.

"Dr. Selman. . ." Her words came out strained. "I. . .I don't know what to say. I'm so sorry."

Amber turned her back on him and moved to the table where she'd spent most of the day. Knees shaking, she leaned against it for support.

Her eyes burned. Somehow she had to compose herself, be professional. Standing tall, she drew in a breath but it was too late. She couldn't face Dr. Selman. What would she see in his eyes? A stern expression? Would she hear reproof? What if he released her as an intern?

Hands squeezed her arms then gently turned her.

He pulled her to him, tucking her gently against his shoulder. "It was just a silly clay pot."

What? He didn't mean that, did he? What was he doing, holding her like this? It felt. . .nice. Suddenly she remembered crying in his arms the night she'd been hurt, she remembered how she felt then—safe. But this wasn't right. She couldn't—no, shouldn't—get too comfortable.

Finally, he released her and she peered into his eyes, still wary of what she'd find there. Concern flooded his gaze. He squeezed her arms again. "Amber. Are you all right?"

What could she say—that she felt much better after he'd held and comforted her? She frowned. "Of course I'm not. How could I be?"

"Yes. . ." Dr. Selman quirked a brow. Releasing her, he pressed his clasped hands to his mouth as he looked at the scattered pieces on the floor. Dropping his hands to his side, he continued. "These things happen. You're not the first person to drop an artifact."

"I can't tell you how sorry I am."

His attention came back to her. She'd never fallen under such scrutiny before. He opened his mouth to speak, then without saying a word, closed it again as he began pacing, careful to avoid the shattered pot. What was going through that mind of his?

As he paced, she couldn't help but think about the way he'd held her. Strong, yet gentle. She shouldn't feel anything for this man. She hardly knew him. But there it was, she cared deeply for him. And her attraction to him?

She shouldn't even think about it. The way he'd held her—could he possibly feel the same way?

A nervous excitement took hold, causing her jaw to quiver. Her knees trembled and once again, she used the work table for support.

At that moment, Dr. Selman looked directly into her eyes. "Miss McKinsey."

Oh no. He'd used her last name. This was it.

He cleared his throat. "Amber. . .I've been troubled since that night I took you home. I can't help but believe there's something more going on, and that's why you're on edge. Why else would you react the way you did over the shattered artifact?"

"Why wouldn't I be upset? You just explained to me how important it was; then I let it slip from my fingers."

With a slight shake to his head, he averted his gaze.

"You don't believe me."

Pursing his lips, he looked at her. "It's none of my business. Not really."

Amber blew out a breath. Had she allowed her secret to burden her so much, that she'd overreacted? Dr. Selman certainly seemed to think so.

He strolled closer. "Amber, please, I want to help if I can."

"I don't think there's anything you can do. Besides, it's not something I like to share."

"I understand." He nodded and left her for the broom closet. "I'd better clean up this mess."

He returned with the broom but set it aside. "How about I share a secret with *you*?" He winked then crouched to carefully retrieve the larger pieces. "The artifact you dropped was only a replica."

*A replica?* "You mean it wasn't even real? Then why did you let me think it was? And what about the artifacts we cataloged today?"

"It wasn't my intention to deceive you. I simply wanted to find out if, after handling the genuine items today, you could tell the difference. Your reaction was answer enough."

Still, he could have told her afterward.

"Amber."

She tugged her gaze from the pottery on the floor to his regret-filled eyes.

"I had planned to tell you. But for the time being, please keep the existence of the replicas to yourself, all right?"

She nodded, thinking about the secret she kept from him. He'd just shared one with her. Then. . .she would share hers with him. Like he'd used the replica, she would use her news to determine if he was genuine and worth the growing affection for him she harbored.

"I give."

Dr. Selman stopped sweeping and met her gaze. "Okay?"

Once she'd told him her secret, she suspected he would look at her differently. Everyone always did. "It's my brother. He recently got out of prison. He knows where I live and work." *And I don't want to see him again.*

Utterly speechless, Brandon took a step back and absorbed the words slowly. She had a brother who'd spent time in prison? And worse—he'd located Amber, who apparently didn't want contact with him. Brandon had asked, hadn't he? Offered to help if he could. He'd seen enough in his own life that he'd been arrogant in thinking she could throw nothing at him he hadn't experienced himself.

But this? This was something new. He squeezed the broomstick.

Amber appeared stricken. Brandon would have to tread carefully. He didn't want to upset her with his reaction.

To his surprise, she thrust out her chin. "You weren't expecting that, were you?"

"Honestly?" Brandon's breath caught as he searched for the words. "No. But I'm glad you told me. It was your brother who called you that night at Gladys's?"

"Yes." Amber put her hand on the broomstick, covering his hand. "Let me do this."

Her hand lingered over his. He'd wanted to know if his feelings were merely one sided. Was she finally letting him know they weren't? He released the broom to her and moved to stare at his computer, oblivious to the words on the screen. Her comment that he knew where she lived and worked made it sound like she was afraid.

Brandon grimaced. What did this mean for her?

An unwelcome thought accosted him, and he couldn't ignore it. Could such a thing have any impact on the museum? Especially since it was on the verge of applying for full accreditation.

Brandon himself was only beginning to stabilize his career. With the news she'd just shared, even if he hadn't allowed himself to care for her, could he afford to keep Amber McKinsey? Still, she wasn't her brother and, as far as Brandon knew, had committed no crime. Yet more than Brandon's personal feelings for this girl were at stake. There was Jim to consider. He'd been displeased that Brandon had requested Jason's termination and had certainly blamed Amber. Then today she'd broken what, as far as Jim would know, was an actual artifact. And now, she had a brother who had served time in prison. Swiping a hand down his face, Brandon shoved the thoughts aside. He was overanalyzing, overreacting as usual.

While he tried to bury those feelings, he reminded himself that he'd asked her about her troubles. No matter what, Brandon would follow through on his offer to help.

"Amber, is your brother a danger to you? Is that why you don't want to talk to him?"

"No, it's not that."

He touched the sleeve of her soft blue shirt. "I'm concerned for you. Promise me you're telling the truth."

She stopped sweeping and peered at him. After a long pause, she swallowed. "I promise he's—"

Brandon's cell interrupted her. The disruption annoyed him, especially since she was most likely on the verge of telling him everything.

He tossed her an apologetic look. "Give me a sec?"

A glance told him it was one of the museum's potential donors—the call couldn't wait. He had a feeling this could take a while.

To Amber, he said, "I've got to take this. Would you mind locking up when you're finished?"

# Chapter 15

*I* *want to know what happened five years ago."*
The words from the phone call squeezed him like a vise as he drove home. His mind muddled with problems, he drove into the center of an intersection before he realized the light was red.

*Uh-oh.*

Too late to slow down. Brandon stepped on the gas, pushing all the way through the intersection while looking both ways.

*Honk.* Tires squealed. A blue minivan careened toward him. Brandon sped up to clear the path for the van. In his mirror, he watched the vehicle barely miss him as it skidded to a stop midintersection.

He'd already cleared the intersection himself and watched the minivan begin moving then continue through. Accident avoided. No harm done.

"Schew." He sagged in relief. *Thank You, Lord.*

A close call. Hoping to make it home alive tonight, he focused on the road ahead.

Flashing red and blue lights in his rearview mirror drew his attention. "This is just the vanilla ice cream on my blueberry pie," he said, and slowed, pulling to the side of the road.

Minutes later, Brandon sat in his car, waiting for the policewoman to finish writing on her pad.

She handed him the ticket. "Drive carefully."

"Thank you, officer." Brandon smiled and grimly pushed the button to shut his window. What a day.

His thoughts clouded, he'd been focused on anything but the intersection. Skidding breaks and a near miss had scared the living daylights out of him. Heart still racing, Brandon drove home and pulled into his driveway.

He trudged into the house and tossed his keys on the table then pulled out a frozen salmon fillet to thaw. Settling in his favorite chair, he thought about Ray Stockholm's question again. He wanted details about Brandon's previous endeavor with a museum. Brandon agreed to meet him for dinner tomorrow evening.

Would he ever escape all that had gone wrong? All his mistakes? And if that weren't enough, he had the strange feeling he'd walked into a field laden with land mines where Amber McKinsey was concerned. She promised, though, that she was in no danger from her brother.

Everything needed to run smoothly. Over the last several weeks, there had been a few incidents. Jim had pointed out that Amber didn't fit well in the environment, causing more problems than she helped solve as a volunteer. Brandon scratched his jaw. Jim was getting more difficult to read, patient with Jason's blunders—though serious in Brandon's opinion—yet intolerant of Amber.

Had Brandon not decided to mentor her after all, then Amber's fate would rest in Jim's hands alone. Brandon had stood up for her. And despite his rule to steer clear of protégés, he'd acquired one anyway. He believed in her. But he was the museum director, and his decisions had to have merit, avoiding the appearance of misconduct. He sagged at the thought, feeling as though he was already failing miserably.

Again.

Closing his eyes, he imagined her in his arms. It felt like she was meant to be there. But was he blinded by his emotions? Was he weak when it came to Amber?

He rose from the chair and prepared his evening meal.

"Lord, show me what to do."

While his salmon sizzled on the small indoor grill, Brandon checked his e-mail and found a note from his colleague Dr. Young at UND, waiting for him.

*How's my star student, Amber McKinsey? I saw promise in her and she needed a mentor. You have too much to offer and shouldn't keep it to yourself. Still considering teaching?*

Brandon skimmed the note, vaguely aware that his salmon was burning.

Troubled, tonight was the first time he wanted to skip his Wednesday night Bible study. Then he remembered—he'd invited Amber. Would she be there?

*ℒ❦*

Amber rolled over, stunned awake by the alarm clock. Six thirty. She'd taken a short nap after work. Dr. Selman's Bible study started in thirty minutes. She wove her fingers through her hair and tugged. What was she thinking? Did she really want to go?

Part of her didn't feel like facing him at the moment. He'd had to rush away due to his phone call while she'd cleaned and locked up like a good intern.

To think she'd told him everything about her brother—well, almost everything.

She should thank the Lord for that—but she wasn't sure where she stood with Him. He could have kept her brother away—that would have gone a long way in helping her to get on with her life. She sat up. If she were going to Bible study, she should start now. It would take ten minutes to get there on her bike.

Scrambling into the bathroom, she brushed her teeth while examining her bloodshot eyes. Toothbrush still hanging from her mouth, she slumped.

She really shouldn't go anywhere looking this way. People could see she'd been crying. Muriel had some eyedrops somewhere. Amber searched through the medicine cabinet, knocking toiletries everywhere.

Muriel stood behind her. "What are you doing?"

Amber spit toothpaste into the sink and rinsed out her mouth. "I've got to go, and I wanted to borrow your eyedrops."

"All you have to do is say please."

In her most respectful, pleasing voice Amber obliged. "Please?"

Muriel squeezed by to look in the cabinet and drawers. "Oh, good grief. Look at your eyes, chickadee. What have you been crying over today?"

"You make it sound like I cry every day."

Muriel quirked a brow and thrust the eyedrops at Amber. "Keep it."

"Thank you, but I couldn't do that."

"You think I want it back now? Ever heard of germs?" Muriel smiled and left.

*Well, when you put it like that.* Amber finished freshening up. She grabbed her Bible from the side table and jammed it into her backpack then exited the cabin and hopped on her bike. Ten minutes until seven. She'd make it just in time.

The crisp air felt good against her face. Riding her bike had always been therapeutic to her—just like running. Lately though, she'd have to run a marathon a day to get the therapy she needed.

She rode her bike straight through an intersection without having to stop. If she kept this up, she'd be there early. Then she turned right into a neighborhood. Dr. Selman's little church, Harrington Christian Fellowship, was nestled in this subdivision off Cheshire Street; but the Bible study actually took place at someone's home across the street, so he'd said.

Her phone vibrated in her pocket. She hoped it wasn't her brother, but honestly, he was the only one calling her lately. Maybe that's why she'd decided to go to Bible study—she needed God to help her through this even though she blamed Him for it.

"Why, God? Why did You leave me alone in the world with only a criminal brother to care?"

The house across the street from the church was a cute pinkish color with groomed bushes. Several cars lined the driveway and curbside. Parking her bike near the porch, she tugged the cell from her pocket, ignoring her fear that it could be Michael. It might be Cams.

A text message from Michael stared back.

I NEED YOUR FORGIVENESS. PLEASE, CAN WE MEET?

# Chapter 16

Amber's feet were glued to the ground as though she'd stepped in concrete and stayed too long. What was Michael playing at? She wished she hadn't looked at her cell, wished she hadn't even come. Her limbs began to tremble.

No. She was done with crying. Grabbing the handlebars of her bike, she prepared to swing her leg over, leaving before she gave the Bible study a chance. But Michael's text had thrown her off balance.

"Hello, there." Dr. Selman spoke from behind.

Amber winced. Not likely she could get out of Bible study now. Despite the heat in her cheeks, she spun to face him. "For someone teaching a Bible study, you're late, don't you know?"

"You're right. But considering it looks like you were about to leave, maybe my being late is a good thing." He offered his hand. "Come in with me?"

When he said it like that, how could she resist? Caught in his intense gaze, Amber wasn't sure when she'd placed her hand in his. Holding hands, they strolled to the front door, though Amber felt more like she'd been gliding. Before entering, Dr. Selman squeezed her hand and winked then released her.

Not that she believed he would actually walk into the Bible study holding her hand, but when he let go, her momentary contentment fled. He opened the door without knocking and waited for her to go in ahead of him.

Vehemently, she shook her head. "I. . .I can't. I don't know these people. Please, you go first."

"Dr. Selman." A short, stout woman appeared in the foyer, beaming warmth. "I was getting worried."

In the shuffle, Amber found herself standing in the living room. Where were all the people?

"Sorry I'm late, something came up." He grazed Amber with a glance.

The woman smiled at Amber. "I see."

"Oh no, he was late before he saw me." What an idiot she was.

"No matter, dear." She gently touched the back of Amber's arm. "We're congregating in the kitchen. Decided to snack first since our leader wasn't here. I'm Claire, by the way."

Amber introduced herself and followed Claire and Dr. Selman into the kitchen, where the sound of soft conversation and laughter mingled with crunching chips. Come to think of it, she hadn't eaten, having taken a nap after getting home. She took the offer of a soda and began dipping chips into guacamole while she listened to the group, which included Claire and

Donita, both fiftyish women and a thirty-something man who was a police officer, two guys and a girl all in their twenties. An interesting demographic for a Bible study.

Finally, the group ended up in the living room, sitting comfortably on one of two leather burgundy sofas, floral chairs, and a few large pillows. One of the guys dragged a couple of kitchen chairs into the room. A candle burned here and there, giving the room a soft glow and nice vanilla scent.

The scene brought back good memories of life before Amber's mother and sister were killed, of life before Michael had been arrested. How she longed for that time once again.

*I don't know if I can ever forgive you, Michael....*

Everyone sat with their Bibles in their laps, either closed or flipped open. Amber did the same, opening her Bible to a random passage. The group members hadn't gotten serious yet, with several still chatting.

One of the younger guys sat next to Amber on the sofa, a little too close for her comfort.

"So, Amber, how was your day?" he asked.

"Don't I know you?" Great. Now, she was giving him a pickup line, but he looked familiar.

"Don't you remember? I was in the drama."

*Lewis.* "That's right. I didn't recognize you in regular clothes." She giggled. "I never got your *real* name."

"It's Peter."

"You know Dr. Selman through the reenactment, right?"

"Actually, we attend the same church. He recommended me when the reenactors were looking for a new Lewis. I've been part of the reenactment team for three years now."

Amber smiled and nodded.

"Listen, I've been hoping to see you again. Maybe we could get together some time."

Dr. Selman cleared his throat. Amber looked around the room and noticed everyone was staring, waiting on them to get quiet.

Sitting in the large recliner in the corner, he looked different. Still authoritative and commanding like in the museum setting, but—a gentle light emanated from him. The Light was no stranger to her. Amber peered down at her Bible—it had to be the Jesus in him, she knew.

Dr. Selman led them in prayer. Guilt wrestled inside her. Even if she could forgive her brother, and God, how could God forgive her?

Vision blurring, she stared at her Bible. Gradually, the scripture became clear, seeming to jump out at her. Though Dr. Selman continued his prayer, Amber couldn't help but read the verse staring back. Matthew chapter five, verse twenty-four.

"*Leave your gift there in front of the altar. First go and be reconciled to them;*

*then come and offer your gift.'"*

And there was the crux of the matter. Whether she interpreted the verse correctly or not, she believed before she could connect with God, she needed to forgive her brother. Though torn, warmth burned in her heart—it seemed that God was nudging her in that direction. She had forsaken Him—after a fashion—but He'd never left her.

"In Jesus's name." Dr. Selman concluded the prayer. "Continuing our study in Romans. . ."

Sitting in his office an hour before the museum opened, Brandon skimmed through the paperwork he'd need to complete today in addition to cataloging artifacts. Jim would return from his vacation next week. Brandon planned to have every artifact inspected, cataloged, and stored before then. They still waited on the display shelves for the Hamlin collection. Hopefully, they'd arrive soon, considering the museum had advertised the exhibit would be open to the public next month.

Adding to his tight schedule today, he needed to gather his thoughts for dinner this evening. He'd agreed to meet Ray Stockholm—a potential donor—to share his understanding of the events that ended in disaster when he directed the other museum. He'd spent five years attempting to shove what happened from his mind. And yet, he always maintained a ready defense of the facts. Though he rehearsed what he would say a million times, fear gripped him anyway.

Brandon hung his head and laughed. He grew weary of having to defend himself. Would it never end?

To make matters worse, board member Sheila Longstrom had called and asked to join them for dinner. What now?

He planted his face in his hands. Maybe that's why the Lord had him talk about forgiveness last night—he needed to forgive himself. Honestly? He thought he'd never recover from the disaster, but here he was in his own office, directing a new endeavor, a new museum and that?—because people believed in him.

He reflected again on the facts as he saw them, mentally preparing himself to talk his way through the tangled mess—an odd set of circumstances that brought a museum to its knees, and Brandon to dread facing himself in the mirror every day since.

In his first year as director of the Landers Prehistoric Museum, he took on an intern whom he quickly began to mentor. He worked closely with her every day and trusted her with increasingly more responsibility. Focused completely on his work, he never took notice of her affections. Apparently the woman fancied herself in love with him, and one evening she surprised him with a kiss and revealed her feelings.

Taken aback by her declaration, Brandon wasn't sure what to say. But in the most tactful manner he could muster, he turned her affections aside. The moment was awkward, preventing them from returning to their daily work in a professional way.

When a large display somehow toppled, injuring her, Brandon's only thoughts were for her safety, and he blamed himself for the accident. She took his words of self-recrimination and ran with them to the courts, suing the museum for Brandon's supposed negligence. Brandon believed she exacted vengeance on him for spurning her. The museum settled with her out of court, of course, and Brandon was asked to leave. He thought he'd never work in a museum again—either in research as a paleontologist or as a director.

Thankfully, many still believed in him; and through their generous favor and recommendations, he once again directed a museum. But those days still haunted him, causing him to tread cautiously where Amber McKinsey was concerned.

Brandon shoved away from his desk and left his office. If he kept thinking on the past, he'd never move forward. And, he looked forward to seeing Amber this morning.

He'd been both happy and surprised to see her at Bible study. His thoughts went to her soft features in the dimly lit room, her face serious as she listened to the discussion. Unfortunately, he'd found it difficult to focus with her there, watching him. Somehow, he had the feeling the words were for her as well as him. But that was speculation on his part. He certainly didn't know her well enough.

He'd wanted time to speak with Amber after Bible study, but Peter had singled her out with an apparent romantic interest. Just as well. Brandon's thoughts regarding his previous experience lingered in his mind, warning him to keep his distance.

But where Amber was concerned, he was in a battle that had raged between men and women from the beginning of time, and he wasn't at all certain of the outcome in this case.

*Mom and Dad must be praying for grandchildren.*

Brandon sighed heavily as he crossed the hallway to the receiving room. As her mentor—if that's what he truly was—he needed to do a better job of instilling confidence in her. At the door, he unlocked it and entered to find that Amber had swept the floor clean of the pottery remnants just as he'd asked.

He considered whether or not to order a replacement, but he still had the replica for the most valuable piece. From one of the two crates he'd opened yesterday, he pulled out another box. He grinned. This artist was good, making even the packaging appear as if a *real* artifact was contained within. If Brandon didn't know better, even he could have been fooled. What was this?

The seal on the box was broken.

Brandon removed the padding.

*Nothing.*

In addition to sweeping up the broken replica, Amber had obviously continued cataloging more items, though he knew she couldn't have worked too much longer because she'd been at Bible study. But. . .she must have logged the replica as the actual artifact and placed it in storage.

Brandon paused, thinking it through. Since he wanted to test Jim's skills anyway, this could work in his favor.

Brandon spotted Amber on the other side of the glass door, a soft smile playing on her lips.

She pushed all the way through. "Good morning."

"I see you did more cataloging after I left. Thank you."

Amber allowed her backpack to slide to the floor next to the table where she worked. "Wait, what? I swept and straightened up then locked up like you asked."

"Well, you cataloged at least one more artifact—the wedding vase. Yesterday was slightly traumatic, wouldn't you say?" He felt a smile slip into his lips, and not yet wanting to reveal that it had been another replica, he turned his attention to his own workstation. The last thing she needed right now was for him to second-guess her.

"Dr. Selman?"

"You'll find it in the system. I'm glad you're capable of cataloguing on your own now, because I have to spend a good part of the day on other matters." He faced her again. She was too beautiful.

He'd prefer to see a smile in place of the frown though. He'd prefer to kiss her forehead and make his way down to her lips. . . . Instead, he squeezed her arms. "Amber, forget about yesterday. Everything will be all right." His words set off an alarm inside him. While he wanted to encourage her, keep her safe—could he really back up his words?

Something in the look she gave him sent a subtle shiver through him.

# Chapter 17

D r. Selman had excused himself—he had a museum to run. Receiving artifacts, a small part of the work. Still, she missed his company.

Feeling the weight of the last couple of days, Amber sighed. Add to that the strange claim he'd made that she'd cataloged another item last night.

For the life of her, she couldn't remember doing it. But maybe he was right—dropping what she thought had been an artifact, watching it shatter into a hundred pieces had almost given her a heart attack. The day had been exhausting.

And then, she'd told him about Michael. Thankfully, Dr. Selman's only concern had seemed to be for her. But, he didn't know the whole of it.

Amber toyed with the artifact box he'd given her as he left the receiving room. Then she logged into her computer and searched the records. Nothing appeared after what she clearly remembered to be her last entry.

Dr. Selman had obviously found the box empty and assumed Amber had cataloged it and put it in storage.

*Oh no!* Maybe she'd put it in storage without cataloging it. Her heart palpitated. She placed her hand on her chest. To put an item in storage required her to leave the receiving area and tromp down the hallway to the locked artifacts storage room. The smell always bothered her in there. No. She would have remembered. Wouldn't she? She might be clumsy, but she was not forgetful.

As she worked to catalog more artifacts, she racked her brain, hoping to figure out what had happened. She recalled that she'd simply cleaned up the shattered artifact—grateful it had only been a replica—then cleared her desk. And lastly, she'd secured the door.

Clutching another piece of ancient pottery, she focused on maintaining her grip on the item. Her hands trembled, reminding her of the incident yesterday. She'd replayed the scene a thousand times in her mind. How had the pottery slipped from her hands? She shuddered. Would Dr. Selman withhold future references or recommendations for this, despite his warmth at Bible study last night?

She encouraged herself with the fact that he must place at least some confidence in her because he'd left her alone with the artifacts today. Stretching, she stood from the stool and saw him in his office through the windows on the other side of the hall. He could see her as well. On the phone, he stood and turned his back to her.

Tapping the workbench with her pen, she considered the circumstances. What would happen if she didn't find the wedding vase? Sooner or later, if it didn't turn up, she'd have to tell Dr. Selman. She knew nothing at all about it though. He trusted her. What would his reaction be if he knew the whole truth about her brother? Would she lose his trust?

She squeezed her eyes, not wanting to entertain the obvious next thought—if the artifact was truly missing, and not simply misplaced, what were the odds Michael was involved?

He was in town, after all.

Amber leaned her head back and groaned. How was she supposed to work under these conditions?

Somewhere deep inside, despair began to rise. Michael's mistakes continued to negatively affect her life. Yet God asked that she forgive him.

She would need help with that.

*Lord, please, let me find that artifact, safe and sound.* With the small prayer, another place in her hardened heart grew soft.

After Bible study last night, she knew without a doubt the right thing to do was meet Michael, listen to what he had to say. On impulse, she'd texted him to meet her tonight at seven at Carl's Ice Cream Shop downtown. At the time, she'd not known an artifact was missing.

Amber finished out her day without taking any breaks, not even lunch. She wanted to plow through as many artifacts as she could. If Dr. Selman returned to receiving, she would tell him the rest of the story—doubtless, he would find out on his own soon enough.

Back at the cabin that evening, she fed Josh a few carrots to calm her nerves. Muriel rushed in and threw her things in her room. Amber headed to the kitchen where Muriel pulled out her fast-food fare.

"Sorry, I know it's my night to cook. Want some?"

"I'm not hungry, actually."

"You need to go to Gladys's for dinner more often. You're much too thin." Muriel paused and took a longer look at Amber. "What's up with the lopsided grin?"

"Can I ask you to drop me somewhere tonight?" Amber absentmindedly crunched on a carrot.

"I have plans, but I can drop you on the way, depending on what time. Then there's the issue of how you will get home."

"You've got a date?"

Muriel froze. "How did you know?"

"The faraway look in your eyes had something to do with it. Is it with that Carey guy?"

"Yes." Muriel squealed. "He finally asked me out. Sort of. I've got to get ready. When do you need me to drop you off?"

"Will six thirty mess with your plans?"

"Not at all. I'm meeting him at eight for coffee, so it's not like a full-blown date or anything." Muriel finished stuffing her face. "Can I just add

215

that you could use a date, too?"

Amber strolled to the small living area and plopped on the davenport. "No, you cannot add that part. What is the definition of a date anyway?" Another crunch on the carrot, and Amber's appetite was completely gone. She wasn't sure she even wanted to eat ice cream.

"It's when an insanely cute guy asks you to meet him, or he picks you up, either way."

"In that case, I have a date, of sorts."

Muriel gasped. "Don't tell me, is it with Dr. Selman?"

"Nope."

"Ah." Muriel let her shoulders droop. "I'm sorry."

Unwilling to share more details with Muriel, Amber busied herself getting ready for her "date," and as nervous as she was, it might as well have been with an insanely cute guy—or at least one who was interested in her romantically, rather than her brother.

As promised, Muriel dropped Amber off downtown. She strolled down the sidewalk, heading to the ice cream parlor. She planned to hang back, standing in the shadows of a storefront, hoping to spot her brother first. Seeing him now with all the baggage she carried would be a shock to her system.

Palms sweating and heart racing, she wanted to pound her head against the storefront. Then. . .she saw him.

*Michael. . . God, please, help me.*

She watched him enter the small ice cream shop and, through the glass windows, saw him go directly to the counter and order. Apparently, he wasn't willing to wait for her to arrive before getting his ice cream.

A quick glance at her watch and she knew she should walk across the street to meet him. But she was frozen. What did you say to a person whom you loved but believed had let you and your family down? Whom you blamed for the death of your mother and sister?

Amber was on the verge of shoving away from the wall and forcing herself to face her nemesis because the truth was. . .she loved him very much. She knew that now, watching him. She'd always loved him. Somehow, God would help her forgive him. But, to her surprise, Michael exited the ice cream parlor.

No. . .

Where was he going? Carrying two ice cream cones, he walked across the pedestrian crossing at the intersection, directly toward her. As he drew near, his eyes grew bright, and his mouth widened into a huge grin.

"Amber," he said, his voice older than she remembered. He handed her an ice cream cone. "If I remember correctly, you like vanilla with caramel sprinkles."

✍❤

Windshield wipers swept the torrent from the windshield, while Brandon gripped the steering wheel and focused on the road. Figured. A day like this couldn't be complete without a hammering rain. It went right along with his mood.

Great for the digs, though, because it could uncover more fossils. However, too much and they'd have to cancel the tours altogether, which didn't bode well for his confidence level going into this dinner meeting.

Fund-raising was the one thing Brandon didn't enjoy about his job. Large institutions had an entire staff to secure funds. But in smaller museums, many jobs fell to a few people. If only he could hire a fund-raising coordinator, freeing him to do—he laughed—everything else.

He'd hoped that by this phase in his life, he could have been more successful, directing a bigger institution. Be more like his father. But like anything in life, there were pros and cons. The advantage he had now was that he could be involved in the many aspects he loved.

He drove into the parking lot and shut off the engine. Twenty minutes early, he watched patrons rush to and from the restaurant, brandishing umbrellas, paper, or plastic for cover. Some simply waited under the protective covering of the entryway until the burst subsided.

Exhaling slowly, he contemplated what would happen over the course of the next hour or two. The price had been paid for his previous mistakes, so he believed. However, the aftermath was real enough. He'd spent two years without employment until the Harrington Natural and Cultural Museum opportunity came his way.

Most donors were only interested in his management and initiatives for the Harrington Museum. But when making a large contribution, some patrons dug deep. Leaving out the personal aspects of the situation with the woman who had sued, he would explain everything that happened. Hashing through that she'd fallen and been injured due to—as she claimed—the museum's neglect, again, wouldn't be pleasant. And considering everything that had happened at Harrington of late, his confidence was beginning to erode.

Jim had called to say he would be returning early. Brandon spent the better part of today catching up on paperwork and knew they weren't anywhere near finished with cataloging the artifacts. He wished he could have been more help to Amber, and hated every minute of being away from her.

Brandon still wasn't sure what to do with the information Amber had shared about her brother, but one thing was certain—she was skittish. He was concerned for her. She'd never actually said what crime had landed her brother in prison.

Blowing out a breath, he looked at his watch. Fifteen minutes before he was due in the restaurant.

Brandon pressed his head against the headrest and agonized over what he wanted—no, needed—to do. Because of his affection for Amber, what he was about to do riddled him with guilt. He hated to pry.

Opening his smartphone, he Googled Michael McKinsey. Pages of links stared back at him. Brandon's throat grew thick.

# Chapter 18

Because a cloudburst had opened from the heavens, they were forced under the awning of the Christian bookstore.

"Oh Michael. . ." Taking the cone from him, a laugh-cry escaped through her aching throat. She hugged her brother, long and hard. "I've missed you so much."

Once she released him, she looked into his eyes—a dark brown, just like Dad's.

His smile exuded warmth even as he studied her. "I'm not sure about that." He gestured toward the bench and she followed, sitting next to him.

"You're my brother. So of course I've missed you." Now that she was here with him, a wound inside her she hadn't even known about lay gaping wide open. "Although, I know it doesn't seem like it."

"Considering how hard you tried to avoid me." Though the words themselves accused her, his voice remained peaceful.

"I'm so—"

"I don't blame you. Not really," he said.

"I can't begin to imagine what you've been through."

"Only what I've deserved."

Licking her ice cream, she watched the sidewalk begin to fill with people again, as the rain subsided. *But what about me?* Or their mother and sister? Did they deserve to suffer for his actions? If it were possible, she thought she heard a ripping sound inside her heart. She'd missed her brother terribly, true—she knew that now. But Mom and Emily. . .she missed them, too. Life was so unfair.

"We can't go back to the way things were," Amber said.

It was good, sitting here with him, though she wasn't sure why he'd sought her out. Closure perhaps?

"No, we can't. I'm not asking you to."

"Then why did you want to see me?" She wished she hadn't asked the question. But it had nagged her since his first attempt at contact.

Michael's ice cream had melted much of the way down his cone. He'd clearly lost interest in it and tossed it into the garbage can near the bench. "Can't a brother see his sister?" He stared at his empty hands. "Don't answer that."

"I can't help but notice there's something different about you. What happened in prison?"

Michael stared at his hands again, then looked at something in the distance, a smile playing on his lips and a light in his eyes. "I found Christ."

Amber gasped then squeezed him. "I'm happy for you." He'd resolved his issues with the Lord. Now Amber would have to resolve hers.

"I became involved in the prison ministry there."

She'd heard people sometimes made up those stories to position themselves back into someone's life. "I can see in your eyes that it's real."

"And I can see in yours what I'd feared." Michael took her hand. "You blame me for the accident. I've always known. Everything changed because of my choices."

Tears hung in her lashes. "I can't deny it."

"I see in your eyes what I saw in the mirror every single day since making my mistake, since Mom and Emily died. I know what that can do to you. Unforgiveness can keep you from God."

Now, Amber was the one to stare at her hands, the tears slipping hotly down her cheeks.

"Amber, please forgive me."

"Oh Michael."

He hugged her tightly as she released the anguish she'd held on to for so long. She wished their reunion could have taken place in a more private setting than in front of a Christian bookstore. "Of course I forgive you. I have to. I. . .want to." *Lord, please help it be so.*

When her tears were spent, they strolled the sidewalks of downtown, peering into the shops. Few remained open in the evening. Amber detected a lift to her step, as though a weight had been removed.

"You know, I want to make sure that you're not blaming God."

She swallowed. "What makes you say that?"

He jammed his hands into his pocket. "I blamed Him when Dad died. I think that's why I ran so far from Him, that I made those terrible choices. I ended up having to find Him again. . .in prison, no less."

Despite his heavy words, she attempted to inject humor into hers. "Don't worry, brother, I'm not going to commit a crime or go to prison."

His left brow arched. "No, you're not. But we all drift away from God in our own way."

He didn't press her further, and they walked to a coffee kiosk where they ordered something to drink.

"What do you plan to do now that you're out? I mean, where will you go?" The words created an awkward moment. How did someone convicted of a crime find a job?

"A good question." Again, he jammed a hand into his pocket. "I don't suppose there are any openings at that museum where you intern." A nervous chuckled escaped him.

*※*

Comfortable on the sofa, Amber had almost fallen asleep when she heard the door open.

Muriel tossed her bag on the couch, a bleak expression on her face. "Want a smoothie?"

"I'm good, thanks." From where she sat, Amber watched Muriel pull out the blender. "So, how was your date?"

"Please, don't ask."

"I already did. Come on, you know you want to talk about it." Amber tugged herself from where she sat and slogged into the kitchen. Muriel dumped ice cream and chocolate syrup into the milk already in the blender. "I thought you were making a smoothie."

"Shake, whatever."

"Well, in that case, I could use a chocolate shake, too."

"Deal, if you set me up with someone cute. Don't you know anyone?"

Michael immediately came to mind. But no, how could she set anyone up with him? She put her face on the counter. What a mess. "I'm afraid I don't."

"What about your Dr. Selman?"

Taken aback, it was a moment before Amber could respond. Jealousy stirred at Muriel's suggestion. She lifted her face to look at Muriel. "I thought you said he likes *me*. And if he's *my* Dr. Selman as you put it, why would you even ask?"

"Well, you don't seem interested."

Amber scratched her head, feeling like her life had spiraled out of control. The truth was, even with Michael's return in to her life, she could hardly stop thinking about Dr. Selman. She must be crazy.

Or. . .*in love.*

"Look, I was only teasing to see if you'd admit you have a thing for him."

*"A thing for him"?* Oh, Amber had a thing for him all right. In fact, her eyes were beginning to open. She had more than just a *thing* for him. But she wasn't ready to go into that with Muriel.

"I do know someone. I met him at Bible study." Oops. That might not sit too well with Muriel.

"You know, for the right guy, I could get into Jesus."

"Oh, bother." Amber knew she had failed miserably. Her blame game had cost her the ability to talk to Muriel about Jesus. But she had to try. "This is how it works. If you want to know the Truth, all you have to do is ask God. He'll show you."

Muriel chose to hit the BLEND button at the beginning of Amber's spiel and stared at her almost cross-eyed, pretending she couldn't hear a word.

Someone pounded on the door. Amber shared a look with Muriel.

"You expecting someone?" Muriel asked.

Standing there in her sweats? "Do I look like it?" Amber hurried to the door, hoping that her brother hadn't decided to pay her a visit. He'd just dropped her off an hour ago. She needed time to process everything.

Opening the door revealed a handsome and familiar silhouette. Her knees went weak.

"Dr. Selman?"

Hair tousled, Amber stared up at him expectantly. Apparently, he'd disturbed her. In her eyes, he hoped he read that she was glad to see him, despite the late hour.

Brandon opened his mouth to speak but nothing came out. *I'm a first-class idiot.*

"Why don't you come in?" she stood aside, allowing him entry.

"Dr. Selman, what a surprise." Muriel smiled widely at him and held up a tall glass as if to say "cheers." Over the rim of the glass she gave Amber an amused look.

He had the funny feeling that, when it came to Amber, Muriel was the expert and Brandon a fossil laid bare.

"Can I get you something to drink?" Amber led him over to the sofa.

"No thank you." This was more than awkward. "Can we talk?"

She brushed her long hair over her shoulder and glanced toward the kitchen. "Uh..."

Muriel finished her drink then set her glass down. She wiped away a milk mustache. "I hope you don't think I'm rude, but I've got a big day tomorrow. Going to hit the sack." After she leaned in to whisper to Amber, Muriel disappeared down the hall.

Amber faced him, her expression wary. "What's this about?"

Brandon stared at the coffee table. "Forgive my intrusion. I didn't feel I had any choice but to speak to you."

"And you couldn't do this tomorrow at the museum?" Amber rubbed her arms. "Must be serious."

Fortunately, his meeting with the donor went better than expected; even Sheila appeared pleased. But he'd had to shove aside his anxiety over the news he'd discovered mere moments before dinner. Maybe he worried for nothing, but after the dinner meeting, he couldn't bear to spend the rest of the night speculating. He had to see Amber. "Please don't take this the wrong way. But I wanted to confirm that you found the artifact today." Brandon dipped his chin, waiting for her response, and feeling the weight of his question down to his toes. He'd wanted to give her the benefit of a doubt.

Amber pressed her eyes shut. As her lips trembled, Brandon felt a deep ache in his chest.

"No, I didn't catalog it. I don't know where it is," she said, her voice a hoarse whisper.

Brandon closed his eyes, too, cringing inside.

He'd give anything if nothing stood between them. All he wanted to do at that moment was hold her in his arms, but not in the same way he'd done on previous occasions when he'd simply comforted her.

No. . .he wanted to hold her in an entirely different way.

When he opened his eyes, she was staring at him.

"What do you think happened?" he asked.

Amber stood. "Look, you don't have to tiptoe around this. It's about my brother, isn't it? I told you he'd committed a crime. Then an artifact turns up missing." She turned her back on him.

He had the sneaking suspicion she was crying again and with what he was about to ask, he wasn't going to make the tears go away. "Have you told me everything?"

The knot in his throat suddenly grew larger. The last thing he wanted was for her to find out he'd hunted for information about her brother. *Cad.*

She whirled to face him, her eyes surprisingly dry. Brandon felt everything rush out of him. He'd entertained far too much hope for something between them. "I'm not accusing you or your brother of anything."

Wasn't he?

Her expression softened. "I met with him tonight. It was the first time I've seen him in at least a year."

Brandon sucked in a breath. Her brother was in town, then?

"I could see immediately that something had changed. He told me that a prison ministry came to visit every week, and that he'd found Christ. Actually, I should say he recommitted his life to Christ."

Though the news relieved Brandon, the heaviness of the situation pressed against him. He leaned back against the couch, absorbing her words. More than anything, he wanted to believe her. But she wasn't telling him everything.

He licked his lips. "Amber. What was your brother convicted of?"

A deep frown appeared in her lips and brows. "I'm guessing you already know the answer to that."

"I'm sorry." Unable to meet her gaze, he stared down at the rug. "I know that he was caught trafficking artifacts."

Amber turned and, to his alarm, walked out the front door. Right now, he hated himself. But what choice did he have?

Needing a handle on this situation before Jim returned, he had to resolve this tonight, if possible. He followed Amber, and found her standing in the shadows of the porch, looking at the sky. Clouds skirted the moon, drifting away.

Brandon turned her to face him and lifted her chin.

"Do you want me to say I think Michael stole the artifact?" she asked. "Well, I'm not going to."

The turmoil in her face cut him deep. He hated to see her hurting. "Your brother's choices aren't your fault. They're no reflection on you. You don't pay the price for his mistakes."

She searched his eyes. "If that's true, then why are you here?"

She had him there. But her question uncovered the deeper truth of why he'd really come. He wanted to see her, be with her, make sure she was safe. At that moment, looking into her pale eyes, then down to her soft lips, he no longer cared about the artifact, the museum, or her brother's crimes. How many times had he thought about her lips? How many times had he wanted to kiss. . .

Before he knew it, his lips were pressed against hers. He lingered against their softness, while she wrapped her arms around his neck. Heart racing, he drew her closer. Her slight form fit perfectly against his frame.

"Dr. Selman." She whispered against his cheek. The way she'd said his name sent shivers over him.

He kissed her again then whispered in her ear. "Will you finally call me Brandon?"

# Chapter 19

Sitting on the porch swing, Amber nestled against Dr.—oh wait, Brandon's shoulder.

Encircled in his arms, she rocked with him.

"I haven't felt this free in years," she murmured, "because I was holding on to resentment and bitterness. Then to see him tonight? I still can't get over the change."

Brandon kissed the top of her head. "I want to hear all about it."

"His last year in college with a double major of archaeology and museum studies, he needed additional funds. Someone approached him about an artifact. Before he knew it, he was neck deep in moving antiquities and kept at it even after graduating. My understanding is that it started small and mostly stayed that way, but there was one big item—and that's when he got caught. He served three years."

Amber thought of Michael's warning—straying from God only a little could lead her far from Him. But she had a feeling that God had a hold of her and was drawing her back. "I had planned to follow in his footsteps with my studies, then because of what happened, I ended up transferring to the University of North Dakota. I was confused about what to study. I didn't want to be reminded of Michael, but I'm drawn in the same direction he was. I was away at school when Mom and Emily went to see him in prison—that was a year ago. On their way, they were killed in an accident. Under the circumstances, and with police escort, Michael was allowed to attend the funeral. I blamed him."

Brandon squeezed her tighter, and she closed her eyes, feeling safe in his embrace.

"I'm so sorry," he whispered.

Amber sat up to look at him. "I know he's changed."

"I believe you."

Studying his face, she ran her finger over his brow and down his cheek. She knew the museum struggled. Brandon worked hard to secure new donors, kept minimal staff, and utilized volunteers and interns. She recalled Michael's question about employment at the museum. There wasn't any way she'd feel comfortable asking Brandon to hire Michael—even for the lowliest position.

"I'd like you to meet him."

He rubbed his thumb over her lips then kissed her again. Amber melted into him, overwhelmed with the joy inside. She'd only dreamed that he could care for her this way.

When he ended the kiss, he drew back and gazed into her eyes, his expression serious. "As much as I hate to say this, there's something you need to know."

Oh no. Was her world crashing again?

"I want to believe that your brother is innocent. But I have to answer to others. The last thing I want is to bring the police in, especially now when the museum is close to gaining accreditation."

"But?"

"I know from experience that the missing artifact could very well be at the museum but has either been stored already or somehow got mixed up with the remaining artifacts. We have to finish the cataloging tomorrow. If the wedding vase doesn't turn up, then I have no choice but to call the police."

Brandon and Amber worked the next day to process the artifacts, but the job was meticulous and time consuming, and they did not finish. He could tell she was tired and, he admitted, he was starting to see two of everything. They needed to break for the day. Brandon would come back and finish, even if it took him all night. Then if he couldn't find the missing piece, he would double-check everything previously cataloged. Reporting an item stolen when it was simply misplaced would draw unfavorable attention to his fledgling museum. But given the proximity of Michael McKinscy, he had every reason to be concerned and couldn't wait too long.

He sucked in a ragged breath. Whatever he did or didn't discover tonight would be the deciding factor.

But. . .however much he believed he was following the correct procedure, it was difficult to determine if he was being reasonable or not because of his feelings for Amber.

When she'd first arrived that morning, there was an awkward silence; then she appeared to understand the importance of remaining professionally detached. Still, to say it was difficult was an understatement. Every time she smiled at him from across the room, he wanted to cover her lips with his. Every time she sighed, he'd wanted to take her in his arms.

The tragedy was that she'd be leaving in a mere two weeks. How could he stand for her to be away from him? How did she feel about him? Really?

Unfortunately, he'd spent his adult life avoiding relationships to focus on his career. This was new territory for him. When on unfamiliar ground, one needed to tread slowly and carefully. But he was definitely not getting younger. Neither were his elderly parents. If he was going to give them the grandchildren they hoped for, moving slowly was out of the question.

*Children with Amber?* His heart skipped a beat.

Bent over a box, he felt a touch at his temple. Pulled from his thoughts, he stood tall and caught Amber's gentle smile. What would she think had she read his mind just now?

"Sorry. I couldn't help it. It seems like hours since. . ." She trailed off, blushing.

"I know. I'm finding it difficult to work with you, too. I think you should call it a day. It's getting late."

"It's only five." She looked down, her lashes shadowing her beautiful eyes. "I know what you're trying to do. You haven't called the police yet, have you?"

Subtly, he shook his head. "I have to make sure it's not here. I have no reason to think it was stolen other than. . ."

"Other than my brother."

"But after what you've told me about him, I don't believe he's involved. If there's been a crime here, why would the thief steal only one item if he'd found a way into receiving? I don't need another scandal. . . ." For the first time, he realized he'd never told her of his own past.

"Scandal?"

He wanted to kiss the top of her head, smell her hair. Reassure her. "Yes." Skipping the details, he summarized what happened before. "I can't afford any more humiliation—not at this juncture of fund-raising, not at this point in my life."

"I thought you were. . ." She sagged, leaning against the workbench.

Not caring if anyone saw him, Brandon gripped her arms and looked her in the eyes. "You thought right. I want to spare you and your brother any humiliation as well. Amber, I. . ." *love you.*

Finally, his heart had voiced the truth.

"Looks like I made it back just in time." Jim stood inside the door, hands on his hips.

Brandon quickly released Amber and shoved a hand through his hair. "Jim, welcome back."

Jim's cell rang and, to Brandon's relief, the conversation drew him out of receiving. Taking the opportunity, Brandon turned his attention back to Amber. "You've done all you can do today. I don't want Jim questioning you. Why don't you get out of here?"

Amber grabbed his hand, letting his fingers slip through hers. "Thank you for believing me about Michael."

She left him standing there and, as he watched her walk out, a morbid thought slammed him. *Oh Lord, please don't let her be using me, playing me.*

That's exactly what Jim would think, once he found out. And he would. Brandon ground his teeth. He cared way too much about what the man thought about him. But maybe that was Brandon's biggest problem—his validation came from others.

Brandon needed time to pray.

Leaving the museum, he headed home for dinner, wishing he'd thought to invite Amber out to eat, but then again, he needed time to think. After he'd skimmed the snail mail, checked his e-mail, and eaten dinner, Brandon took a short nap so he'd be alert for the work ahead of him. Waking after dark, he wanted nothing more than a good, long run, and changed into his running shoes and clothes. Everything was happening too fast, including his relationship with Amber.

He needed a clear head and, more importantly, a clear heart.

Locking the door behind him, Brandon headed down the street, planning to jog the Little Missouri trail to add a few extra miles. The good thing—he had plenty on his mind to keep his thoughts off the ache in his legs and burn in his lungs.

Five years ago when he'd experienced a meltdown, losing everything he'd worked for, Brandon had turned to God. His mother had raised him in church, but he'd never really believed God was personal. While he might have gained knowledge during the course of his education, he'd lost his belief in God, completely. Or so he'd thought.

Then disaster happened, and he remembered the One who'd created him. Or rather, God remembered *him*. Through his desperation, he'd found a personal relationship with Jesus Christ. Always a stellar student, he'd studied and learned all he could about his Savior through the Word, enough that Pastor John had invited him to teach Bible study.

Why, then, did he feel as if he were going through it all over again—as if his life had spun out of control? God had given him another chance, as it were, and now? Would he lose everything again? He'd somehow gotten into his head, and possibly his heart, that becoming a Christian, trusting in God, meant he wouldn't have to suffer as he had before.

Breathing hard, Brandon savored entering "the zone"—that place where the endorphins kicked in. Running along the tree-lined trail, he came to the same place where he'd collided with Amber the first time they'd met.

He stopped and leaned against his legs, catching his breath. Even though he carried his flashlight, the moon shone bright enough for him to see, except when the clouds interfered.

God had given the moon to light the way for nocturnal creatures. Whether full or hidden, it was always there, watching. A raccoon moseyed past as though it hadn't noticed him, or didn't care. An idea began to form.

*Why didn't I think of it before?*

# Chapter 20

At the cabin, Amber sat across the table from her brother and watched Muriel flirt with him. The girl was relentless. No matter. At least it gave Amber more time to consider things, and kept Michael from noticing her complete anguish.

She'd agonized all night—all day, too, but Brandon had kept her busy searching for the missing artifact. It warmed her heart that he wanted to make certain the mistake hadn't been on their part before calling the police. He'd made every attempt to believe her regarding Michael.

More than anything, she wished she could have basked in his attention. Instead the missing artifact and her brother's proximity to the circumstances, along with his appearance back in her life, eclipsed her relationship with the man she loved.

The man she loved? Despite her gloomy thoughts, she found herself smiling.

Amber suddenly noticed that both Muriel and Michael were staring at her.

"She's a million miles away," Michael said to Muriel.

"I'm sorry. I was thinking." Amber smiled.

Michael laughed and pushed back from the table. "Thanks for dinner, ladies. It's getting late, and I think I might have overstayed my welcome."

Amber stood as well. "Can I talk to you outside for a sec?"

Michael chuckled. "Sure." He said goodnight to Muriel then headed out the door.

Amber tried to follow but Muriel tugged her back. "You were holding out on me."

"What are you talking about?"

"Your brother. He's cute. You could have set me up."

"Not now, Muriel."

Looking miffed, Muriel let Amber go.

Once on the porch, she found Michael waiting for her.

"I could tell you were distracted all evening," he said.

Amber hated the gloomy look on his face. He thought it was about him—that she wasn't happy to be in his company. "Something's come up."

He cocked his brow, waiting. Muriel was right—Michael was a real catch. Except that he'd practically ruined his life. Amber sighed.

"There's no easy way to say this. A relic has gone missing at the museum. We spent all day searching for it."

Michael appeared stricken. Tightening his jaw, he turned away.

Fearing he would leave, she grabbed his arm. "Michael, please, you have to believe me. I'm not accusing you. I want to believe you had nothing to do with it. But..."

He stared at something in the distance, frowning. "I won't ever live down my mistake, will I?"

"I don't know."

"And the director—the one Muriel seems to think has feelings for you—he knows about me, then?" Michael searched her eyes.

The knot in her throat kept her from speaking. She nodded.

Michael released a long, slow breath. "I shouldn't have come within a hundred miles of you."

What was he saying? That he'd been tempted and fallen again? Was it like some sort of addiction?

"Say something, Amber."

Pain squeezed her chest. "I want to believe you're innocent. And so does Bran—Dr. Selman."

"You love him, don't you?"

Amber gave a soft smile. "Yes, I do," she whispered. But would her brother destroy this part of her life, too?

*Lord, I forgive him.* She closed her eyes. *Please, help me.*

"Tell me about the artifact."

Her eyes flew open. "Why do you want to know?"

"Maybe I can help. Find out who would want it."

"But couldn't getting involved implicate you somehow?"

"From the looks of it, I'm *already* implicated."

"All you have to say is that you're not involved. I'll stand by you." Amber held her breath, hoping.

"I promise you, I had nothing to do with it."

She released the pent-up air then told him about the artifact.

Even under the dim porch light, Amber could see Michael's face go pale. *Oh Lord, no...*

❧

Sitting in the small room they'd set aside for security, Brandon logged into the DVR software and selected the date in question and multiple video channels, viewing them simultaneously on the screen. He watched for any anomalies. If it turned out the artifact was in fact stolen, the police would want to view this, he was sure, once he contacted them. If he had looked right away, he could possibly have resolved the biggest question—was the artifact stolen or not?

Rubbing his neck to relieve the stiffness, he reviewed the segment from today when Amber had approached him and taken his hand. He recalled the way her simple touch made him feel. Watching it now, he relived that moment.

Then, of course, during the tender interlude they'd tried to avoid all day, Jim had walked in.

This looked very bad for Brandon. Professionally, he couldn't afford a stolen artifact, or involvement with a woman whose brother was convicted of stealing artifacts.

And personally. . .

Hands over his face, he rested his elbows on the small desk. "Why, God?"

From the beginning, he'd been against having an intern, a protégé. Yet he found himself in a similar situation as before—only this time, roles were reversed.

He'd been the one to fall in love. Thankfully, his affections were returned.

Wanting to review Jim's reaction, he played back the video, but accidentally selected to rewind the recording.

"Stupid." He began searching the video then stopped, freezing the frame.

The time and date stamp display indicated Tuesday night. Hadn't he been working late that night?

As he watched the playback of the entire segment, a sinking feeling hit his stomach. He never appeared in the video—but he'd been in the room that night.

"What the. . . ?"

Someone obviously made adjustments to the video. "Clue number one."

This was bad news for the museum. More scandal. Jim took care of security—would he bear the brunt of it this time?

Brandon attempted to sign in to the system administration in order to view the log, which recorded all system and operator activities, but he was denied access. He didn't usually keep up with password changes. Jim kept it written somewhere. Brandon left the security room to pay Jim's office a visit, uncertain exactly where he might find the password.

After unlocking the door to Jim's office, Brandon stepped inside. On a hunch, he knew it was better to search the man's office than call him for the password. Still, shame engulfed him. His cell buzzed in his pocket. Tugging it free, he found a text message from Amber.

News about the artifact. Meet me at the museum?

"Could she have clue number two?" He texted her back that he was already at the museum and would wait for her.

Standing in the dark, in another man's office, Brandon had the odd sense he was being watched. He felt like a criminal himself and flipped on the light.

A man hovered in the corner. Brandon froze.

"Jason?"

# Chapter 21

Amber clenched the door handle as Michael drove into the museum parking lot. Finally, he slowed to a stop. The parking lot was empty. "That's strange. Why isn't Brandon's Jeep here?"

"You told him it was important, right?" Michael turned off the engine. "And even if you didn't, I can't imagine him not wanting to see you." He flashed a grin and a wink.

"Thanks for dropping me off." Before she opened the door, she gave Michael a side glance.

He gripped her arm. "I'm going with you."

"You can't. We've been over this. I don't want you to put one foot in that museum." Amber's heart thumped louder.

"If Brandon's car were here, sure, yeah, I could drop you off. But not like this. It isn't safe."

"I'll be all right. You don't have to do this."

"What kind of brother would I be to let you go alone, knowing the situation. Besides, I'm innocent, and. . .it's the right thing to do." He slipped from the car.

Amber did the same, and together, she and Michael hurried to the front door, discovering it was locked. Because of her late hours while working on the exhibits, she'd been given keys.

Once inside, she walked through the dimly lit museum, Michael close behind. Amber spotted light at the end of the hallway.

She started that way, but Michael grabbed her arm. "Wait. This wasn't a good idea."

"Brandon is here. He said he would be here."

Michael exhaled. "Just be careful."

They hurried down the quiet hallway. Brandon's office door stood open, but he wasn't inside. "He's got to be here somewhere. Let's split up," she said.

"Not a good idea. This could be dangerous if the wrong people are here. We'll find him together."

"Do you really think the thief is running around in the museum tonight?"

Michael's look sent shudders over her. "I don't want you to get hurt. For too long, I blamed myself for what happened to Mom and Emily. Even though God helped me to forgive myself, I'm not sure what I would do if you were to get hurt because of me."

"Because of you? This has nothing to do with you."

"We're here right now, because of me, and we're wasting time. Let's look around."

"I'll call him on his cell." The cell went straight to voice mail. "Brandon, we're here at the museum. Call me back." She texted him as well, but got no response.

After a thorough search of the museum, including the basement class-rooms, they ended at the hallway emergency exit between the offices and receiving room.

Amber noticed something resting on the floor at the end of the hall. She walked to the exit and Michael followed.

"What's this?" She lifted a stainless steel water bottle with the Nike emblem. An image flashed in her mind. "This is Brandon's. Maybe he jogged here. That could be why his Jeep isn't in the parking lot."

"Who else is here, then?"

"Brandon said he'd meet us here and that he'd found something, too." Amber frowned.

"I don't like this, Amber." Michael began pacing the hallway, peering into offices. He lingered at the receiving room where the artifacts had been then peered into the windows of other offices.

"Why didn't he wait for us?" she asked.

"I think I know the answer to that." Michael motioned for her to join him, looking through the glass window of Jim's office.

Amber tried the door and it easily opened. A chair was knocked over, paperwork scattered across the floor.

Michael picked up a paperweight and turned it over. "Blood."

"I'm calling the police." Amber phoned 911 and explained the situation and that she believed foul play was at work. In her opinion, the dispatcher asked too many questions, keeping her on the phone too long. Amber squeezed the cross on her necklace, and then suddenly, an image of Brandon, holding the cross in his fingers came to mind. He'd referenced looking for little clues.

*You just have to pay attention."*

"I'm sorry, I have to go," she said and hung up.

"What is it?" Michael asked. "Why would you hang up on them?"

"He left the water bottle next to the door. If you go out that exit you con-nect directly with the trail to the digs."

"How do you know he didn't simply drop it?"

"Because I just know, all right? He meant that to direct us."

Amber shoved the door open, remembering the day she'd heard Brandon's words of caution.

*"One misstep could land you at the bottom of a pinnacle."*

☙

*Just keep him talking.*

Walking down the dark trail with a gun to his back, Brandon considered every tactic to escape his predicament. He wasn't going down without a fight, and though he'd tried that in Jim's office—a nasty knot on his head to show for it—Jason had pulled a gun.

Brandon's hesitation to involve the police had been a mistake. But as they said, hindsight was always twenty-twenty. There were many things he'd change now. For one, if he had it to do over again, Brandon would have followed his heart from the beginning where Amber was concerned. But he'd been reserved, too worried about what others thought of him, how things would look to his donors. Too worried about carving out a successful career.

Now he clearly saw that Christ was the only one from whom he needed validation.

A painful jab in his back reminded him to focus on the current state of affairs. Keeping Jason talking could serve as a distraction. "You don't want to do this, Jason."

"Oh. . ." Jason sniggered. "I *want* to do this."

"Come on. You're going to add murder to your crime?"

Another jab and Brandon stifled a moan.

"Nothing would give me greater pleasure than to make you suffer. You humiliated me."

"You're going to kill me because I let you go?" Brandon asked. Did he dare remind the guy that he'd merely used his position as a means to an end?

"Who said I was going to kill you? You're going to kill yourself."

Tension jolted through Brandon's body. Still a mile to hike before they reached the digs, he considered scrambling through the wooded area. But Jason knew the terrain better.

*Making me kill myself is still murder.* Brandon thought he knew what Jason had in mind, and he had no plans to cooperate. If he died, it would be by Jason's hand and not some "accident."

On the chance that he made it out of this alive, Brandon thought to draw as much information as he could from Jason. "Can you at least tell me who you're working with?"

"You're really pathetic, you know that? I'd think that would be obvious by now."

Obvious? Brandon tried to wrap his mind around Jason's words while he stayed aware of his surroundings, hoping for an escape. Hoping that Amber would see the evidence of a scuffle in Jim's office, hoping she would notice the water bottle he'd left behind—*Please, God!*—and call the police. Hope and a prayer was all Brandon had.

The trail ended at the digs. If Jason planned what Brandon thought, they still had a ways to go before reaching the cliff's edge.

Brandon slowed his pace and received another sharp jab in the back. He bent over, gasping for breath. "Can we rest for a minute?"

"You've got three seconds."

*Or what? You're going to shoot me here?* Then it wouldn't look like a suicide, but rather a murder. Brandon wasn't about to press the man on that point. "Back to whom you're involved with. I'm afraid it's not obvious, Jason."

Brandon stood tall, waiting for Jason's answer, hoping he wouldn't hear the name Michael.

In the moonlight, Jason looked incredulous. "Jim. Who else?"

*Jim?* Brandon staggered back a few steps. "I don't believe you."

"Well, it doesn't really matter at this point, does it? Now get walking. I haven't got all night."

Brandon started hiking again, this time much slower. He'd grown numb with the jabs to his back and was in shock over the news about Jim. He had come with Brandon from Landers and had been in charge of accessioning the collections there. He'd known him for years. If what Jason said were true. . .how many dollars and relics had he skimmed from the museum without Brandon even knowing?

What a fool he'd been! Except. . .he was still holding one card.

When should he play it? "I don't get it, who can a person ever trust?"

"That's a good question. I'm afraid if you don't know by now, you're not going to have time to figure that out."

They'd reached the edge of the butte. Brandon refused to step too close. He wondered if he could fall off and somehow survive.

"I know who I can trust," he said.

"I don't think I'm interested. Now, jump."

"I can trust God because no matter where I go, He's there with me."

*Even at the precipice of a cliff.*

" 'Where can I go from your Spirit? Where can I flee from your presence? If I go up to the heavens, you are there; if I make my bed in the depths, you are there. If I rise on the wings of the dawn, if I settle on the far side of the sea, even there your hand will guide me, your right hand will hold me fast. If I say, "Surely the darkness will hide me and the light become night around me," even the darkness will not be dark to you; the night will shine like the day, for darkness is as light to you.' "

Brandon spoke the verses from Psalm 139 as though his life depended on it.

"I'm done listening. If you're not going to jump, then you can just face God now."

Brandon wondered why Jason didn't simply push him, but maybe Jason knew that Brandon would pull him over with him. Not a chance would he go over alone. Unless. . .

*The card! Play the card!*

# Chapter 22

**W**ait. The artifact you have is a fake."

"You're lying."

"I'm not, actually. I commissioned an artist to create replicas of the most expensive pieces. The genuine artifact is in the vault."

"You're trying to trick me. I can tell the real thing from a replica. Now turn around and face your demise."

Fear warred with peace as Brandon did what he was told.

Every muscle in his body tightened when he heard the sound of the gun cock. A shot rang out, echoing through the Little Missouri Badlands.

Brandon jerked with the sound, believing himself shot. How was this supposed to feel? He felt. . .

*Nothing.* What was going on?

Was he too shocked to feel pain? He wavered at the edge of the cliff, losing his balance.

*This is it.*

A million regrets plunged through his soul—slowly, as though he could see each one outside of time. *Amber, I'm so sorry. . . .*

Arms gripped his body, yanking him back from the edge. He slammed into the ground next to someone.

Catching his breath, he rolled over to see the most beautiful face in the world. "Amber?" He slid his hands over his chest and abdomen. "I'm not shot?"

She smiled. "No. But I thought I'd lost you."

"You saved me." Brandon wanted to ask what had taken her so long. Grunts and scuffles drew his attention to the fight. He climbed to his feet, helping Amber to hers.

Jason struggled with another man.

Amber cupped her hands against the sides of her mouth. "Michael, be careful."

Sirens screamed in the distance, drawing closer.

Brandon came fully to his senses. Amber and Michael had come to his rescue. Michael was still fighting with Jason.

*Smack.* Michael landed a good punch into the center of Jason's face. The man fell back but managed to cling to the gun.

Michael stomped on Jason's wrist and kicked the gun out of his reach. Brandon scrambled for it. Jason recovered and shoved Michael to the ground, falling onto him with more punches. Clearly the stronger fighter of the two, Michael freed himself, leaving Jason groaning in the dirt.

Brandon stepped forward and took aim. "Don't move."

At that moment, four police officers surrounded them, breathing heavily, their weapons at the ready. Brandon slowly set the gun on the ground and raised his hands as instructed, as did Michael, Amber, and Jason.

Grand.

"Dr. Selman." Officer O'Riley stepped forward. He attended Brandon's Bible study. "What's going on here? We received an emergency call from the museum and then a second call explaining someone was in danger at the digs."

Amber cleared her throat. "If it weren't for Michael's call, you might not have known we were headed to the digs in time to help us."

While struggling to catch his breath, Brandon explained to his friend that Jason, and allegedly the museum curator, had stolen an artifact. Then Jason had tried to force Brandon from the cliff.

Dismissing Brandon, Amber, and Michael for the time being, the police cuffed Jason and ushered him up the trail.

As Brandon looked on in stunned silence, he tried to process everything that had happened. One second, he was on the verge of losing his life, the next, he was alive, standing next to Amber.

"Come here." He pulled her into his arms and kissed her thoroughly. She meant everything to him. Why did it take a near-death experience to make him see how important she was? There wasn't any need for him to take his time. But did she feel the same?

As he held on to her, cherishing the moment, he realized asking her to marry him would interfere with her plans for her education. How could they make it work?

Though he didn't want to end the embrace, Brandon noticed Michael standing quietly in the dark.

Brandon walked over and offered his hand to Amber's brother. "I want to thank you for what you did."

*⌒♥*

No words could express how Amber felt as she listened to Brandon thank Michael. Watching Jason holding the gun on Brandon, she'd almost crumpled.

But she'd drawn on something deep inside. Or maybe Someone. "You have no idea what a hero Michael is. He tackled a man with a gun."

"So I gathered. And apparently, just in time," Brandon said.

While Michael tackled Jason, she had yanked Brandon from the brink of death.

"No kidding. The bullet missed." *I thought I'd lost you.* Was he hers to lose, despite his kisses?

Brandon took Amber's hand as the three of them began the arduous two-mile hike up the trail to the museum.

"Earlier this evening," Brandon said, "you mentioned you discovered something about the artifact. If not for that discovery and your plans to meet me, I might be dead now. Mind telling me what it was?"

Amber started to answer, but Michael spoke up. She was so proud of him.

"I received a message from an old contact wanting to offload an artifact. He needed to move it quickly."

Brandon stopped on the trail and studied Michael in the moonlight. Amber feared he believed that Michael was involved.

"Go on," he said.

"I was furious that I'd been contacted, that word was out I was out of prison. I want no part of that anymore. I didn't respond. But when Amber told me about the artifact stolen from Harrington, I realized it was the same one."

"You realize the police will need to hear all of this information."

"Of course. I thought there was too much chaos earlier to bring it up." Amber lagged behind the two men as they continued up the trail. The police had caught their guy. At least one of them. Michael hadn't involved himself except to help, yet she feared for her brother.

Finally, the museum parking lot became visible. Lights flashing, a few cruisers had stayed behind.

Brandon turned to Michael. "You risked your life tonight in more ways than one. You might have trouble explaining your way out of this situation, considering your proximity and that you'd been contacted about moving the artifact."

Michael studied the ground, somber. "Like I told Amber, it was the right thing to do."

Brandon nodded, approval in his eyes.

"Well, I see a detective over there. I'm going to tell him the rest of the story."

"Michael, wait." Amber grabbed him and hugged him to her. "I'll pray for you."

Releasing him, she looked into his face.

"Prayer is the most important thing." He cuffed her on the chin then walked away.

A smile crept onto her lips. One day, maybe she could set him up with Muriel. She had a feeling that Muriel was close to meeting Christ.

"Are you all right?" Brandon asked as they watched Michael approach the police.

She gazed up at him. "I don't know."

Pulling her to him, he rested his chin against the top of her head.

She loved how safe he made her feel. "Dad died when I was young. But when Mom and Emily were killed, especially after Michael was taken from us by his own actions and incarcerated, I knew just how fragile life was."

Sensing that Brandon waited for her to say more, she continued. "Tonight, it felt like it was happening all over again. I was so afraid I would lose you and Michael. I'm still scared of losing Michael to this situation." And she still feared losing Brandon. She wanted to tell him she loved him, but that was for him to say first.

Wasn't it?

In two short weeks, she'd leave for Grand Forks—on the other side of North Dakota. If Brandon didn't tell her how he felt by then, she would believe she'd lost him after all.

Although, she never really had him to begin with.

# Chapter 23

Two days before Amber was to travel back to Grand Forks and begin another school year, she stared at the display case containing one of the earliest Hisatsinom artifacts ever discovered—the very piece that Jason had stolen under Jim's instruction—or at least he'd thought he'd stolen. Odd to think that the Anasazi wedding vase, decorated with only a few red and black designs, could create such a stir. Though the police had quickly recovered the replica, they'd sequestered it as evidence to be used in the investigation. Now, the authentic artifact was on display. All that had been disclosed to the public was that someone had attempted to steal the wedding vase.

The investigation had taken up any time she might have had with Brandon at the museum. During the evenings, his time had been consumed with dousing the rumor flames and meeting with board members.

To his credit, he'd done a brilliant job. The incident at the museum had been front and center in local and national newspapers, along with Brandon's picture. The article in the newspaper detailed the previous scandal involving Brandon, yet managed to put a positive spin on the story, making Brandon look like the hero then even though he was terminated. Regarding the Hisatsinom artifact, no one doubted his planning had prevented a great loss to both the museums involved.

Amber cut out the article to save. All the attention had increased the traffic to the museum. She stood aside while a new volunteer guided the next tour, showing the now infamous wedding vase. Though the museum hadn't officially opened the Hamlin Exhibit, board members believed it timely and in the public's interest to display the artifact.

Brandon's museum was a great success.

Michael deserved credit, too. Glad she'd forgiven him and stopped blaming him for Mom's and Emily's death, she squeezed the little cross on her neck, savoring the warmth in her soul.

She'd stopped blaming God as well.

Though she'd feared her brother's coming back into her life would destroy what little she had left, he'd not only assisted in resolving crime, but his presence had brought her closer to Brandon.

The man had actually believed in her, believed in Michael's innocence despite evidence to the contrary.

And Michael? He'd risked everything for her. Who could ask for more? Shaking her head in awe, she whispered to herself, "Thank You, Lord."

Someone touched her shoulder. Gladys stood next to her, watching the group. "There's been so much excitement around here lately that I haven't had a chance to talk to you."

Fortunately, Gladys had been able to hire help in the museum store a few weeks ago.

"It's been a madhouse, hasn't it?" Amber asked.

The older woman ducked her head slightly, staring at Amber. "How are you doing? Really?"

"I think I'm going to live." But if she ended up leaving without getting to see Brandon alone, without hearing how he felt, she wasn't so sure.

"You know, I always thought you were a keeper."

"Thanks, Gladys. That's sweet. But I have to go back to school."

Gladys adjusted her glasses. "Leaving in a couple of days, I hear."

"Yes."

"When I said you were a keeper, I was referring to our Dr. Selman."

Brandon and Amber had been careful to hide their affection for each other. "What do you mean?"

"Hon, Dr. Selman has always had his head in his work. That is, until you came along. Anyone with eyes can see."

What did it matter? She was leaving soon. Painful tears stirred behind her eyes. Thankfully, she kept them at bay. "I don't know, Gladys. I think his head is still in his work."

Gladys tugged her on the sleeve, backing her into a shadowed corner, away from the crowd. "Listen to me. Dr. Selman is a quiet man. He's absent-minded when it comes to women and sadly, even the woman he loves."

"Gladys, you can't know that he loves me."

"Oh, he loves you. But I'm not sure he knows what to do about it. Men like Dr. Selman are thinkers. They have to analyze everything."

"What are you saying I should do?"

"You need to be the one to act."

"You can't be serious."

"I never told you about my Frode."

"Your Frode?"

"My husband of forty years."

Amber cringed. At Gladys's home, she'd seen the photographs, but some-how the conversation never turned to the woman or her life. Gladys was all about other people. A good thing and a trait Amber should consider modeling.

"Go on."

"Frode was like your Dr. Selman. A quiet man, devoted to his work and to God. Hon, I had to go out of my way to get him to notice me. And even then, I had to practically propose to him."

Amber took a step back. "You're kidding. I don't know, Gladys, that's just not me."

"When you want something, you have to work for it. Love isn't easy."

"Thanks for your advice. I'll consider your words."

"That's all I can ask."

Amber wondered if Gladys would give the same lecture to Brandon. That might work better. No way could Amber do what Gladys suggested.

In his office, Brandon sat behind his desk, waiting on Amber's brother, Michael. He rubbed his eyes, hoping he didn't look like he felt after two weeks of navigating the investigation while keeping his and the museum's reputations afloat.

For what he was about to do, he could lose donors. Yet, after everything he'd been through, Brandon had now learned to conduct his life and business to please God rather than be concerned with what others thought.

He recalled what Michael had said the night he'd risked his life. It was the right thing to do.

Brandon wanted to do this for the woman he loved. The problem was—what did he do *about* the woman he loved? She still had to finish school. They would be far apart. What would he accomplish by telling her how he felt?

Michael stood outside Brandon's door and knocked lightly then opened it. "You wanted to see me?"

Brandon smiled. "Yes, come in and have a seat."

Michael sat in the chair across from Brandon's desk, looking nervous.

Brandon stood and moved to the credenza where a carafe waited. "Coffee?"

"No, I'm good. What's this about?"

Brandon refreshed his cup. "I want to make you an offer." He took a sip and waited for Michael's reaction.

Michael threw up his hands. "Listen, I don't speak for Amber. No need to ask me for her hand."

Brandon drew a startled breath while swallowing coffee and began coughing uncontrollably.

"You okay?" Michael moved to stand.

Brandon's eyes watered while he worked to regain his composure. He held up a hand, reassuring Michael. Then he sat down and cleared his throat, tugging his collar.

Michael frowned. "I didn't mean to throw you. I thought. . .sorry, I was way off, wasn't I?"

"Well, I brought you in here for something entirely different."

"Please don't tell Amber what I said."

Brandon stared at the papers on his desk and chuckled. "I won't, don't worry. I wanted to offer you a job."

Michael's mouth dropped open but he quickly recovered. "I. . .wasn't expecting that."

"No, I wouldn't think you were. I need to replace Jim."

"But why would you want to hire me?"

Brandon lifted a brow, wishing the guy wouldn't sell himself short. "I'll tell you why. It's the least I can do for a fellow believer in Christ. You need a fresh start. And from what I saw the other night—the risk you took—I can't think of anyone who deserves it more."

"But what will people say—you hiring me after the crime I committed."

"Michael. . ." Brandon toyed with an amethyst paperweight on his desk. "I know what it's like to make mistakes, believe me. God gave me a second chance, and He expects us to do the same for others. I worked with a man for years who I thought I could trust, but he fooled me. You've served your time then proved yourself trustworthy when tested, so I can't believe you'd make the same mistake again. Besides, we can certainly use your expertise—I don't think anyone is going to be stealing from my museum."

Michael responded with a big grin.

"You need to put the past behind you." Brandon should listen to his own advice.

"I appreciate your offer."

"But?"

"Will you hold it against me if I say I need to think about it? Pray about it?"

"On the contrary. I'd be concerned if you didn't."

"Can I ask you something?"

"Certainly."

"What *are* your plans regarding my sister?" Michael gave him a pointed stare.

Still, he could see the twinkle in his eyes. With a half grin, Brandon averted his gaze. So the guy had some old-fashioned protectiveness in him, after all. But why wouldn't he? He'd risked it all for Amber. Definitely a changed man.

Brandon considered his answer. He had to step carefully.

"She loves you, you know that, right?"

The man was direct. Brandon hadn't been certain of her feelings. "You can understand if I need to consider things, pray about it."

"You need to put the past behind you."

Brandon nodded, recognizing his own words used against him. "Not so easy to do, though, is it?"

Michael chuckled. "Nope."

Brandon hoped Michael would drop the subject there. He had no answers, only questions about the future. With Amber leaving for school in two days. . .

A pang squeezed his chest.

Michael stood. "Well, I think I should leave you to your thoughts. I appreciate your offer and want you to know that I'm very interested."

"Good enough."

Michael stepped out, and while pleased with the possibilities of working with the bright young man despite his past, Brandon had avoided Michael's questions.

The desk phone rang and Brandon answered. He warmed to the sound of an old friend's voice. "Dr. Young. Good to hear from you."

"There are people of influence who are more than impressed with your ability to handle crisis situations."

"Thank you."

"I have a proposition for you."

# Chapter 24

G ot everything packed?" Muriel trotted into the living room from the hallway.

"Almost." Leaving for UND in the morning, Amber knew she'd miss the way Muriel nurtured her like a mother. Muriel still had another week before she headed back to school.

"Don't forget your Bible." Muriel moved her hand from behind her back. "Here you go."

Amber took it from her. "Thanks, I was looking for that."

Muriel smiled. "Thought so." She sat on the sofa across from Amber.

"You know. . .I want you to have it." Amber offered it back.

"Oh no, I couldn't take that from you." An odd expression came over her face as she stared at the book. "But I'll buy one as soon as I can."

"I have several at my apartment in Grand Forks. This is my gift. I'm afraid I've been a failure at sharing my faith with you."

"You're wrong about that. I don't think I could have been so strong if I had to deal with everything you did. Maybe you struggled, maybe you even questioned God, but you never lost hope, never stopped believing, never gave up on your faith." Muriel smiled then took the Bible back. "Thank you for this."

Amber's throat grew tight, Muriel's words touching her deeply. Amber held Josh in her lap, running her fingers through his soft fur. Since it was her last night in the cabin, Muriel agreed she could bring him out. "You've got my number, right?"

Muriel nodded. "I'm going to miss you so much. Maybe I can just transfer to UND." Muriel had been the one to cry today.

Amber laughed. "I already have two roommates."

"At least we'd be at the same school, chickadee." Muriel hopped up from the sofa. "I'm making a shake. Want one?"

"Love one."

In the kitchen, Muriel began assembling the blender and ingredients. "Any news?"

Amber knew Muriel referred to Brandon. Rumors had made their way around the museum. He and Amber were an item now. For all the good that did. Tomorrow, she'd be gone. "No," she said, her voice breaking.

Maybe she should take Gladys's advice and tell him how she felt. Find out where they stood. While Muriel ran the blender, Amber put Josh back in his cage and retrieved her cell. Sitting on her bed, she debated what to say even if she made the call. It was already nine thirty in the evening.

Palms sweaty, she found his number in her cell and pressed SEND. *What am I doing?* Heart racing, she ended the call after only two rings.

Muriel appeared in the doorway, holding her milkshake. "Here you go."

"Thanks."

Her cell rang and startled her. She dropped it.

Muriel picked it up and answered. "Amber's phone." A smile spread over her face. "Dr. Selman. Just a sec." She thrust the phone in Amber's face.

Oh no. . .he'd seen her call. What now? She took a sip of the creamy chocolate shake then traded it for the phone. She'd taken the advice from Gladys. Now, if she could just see things through. Muriel left, giving her privacy.

"Hello?"

"Did you call?"

*I'm an idiot.* If he was available to call her back, why hadn't he called her in the first place? "I—I hope I didn't disturb you."

"No, not at all."

Oh, this was ridiculous. "Listen, I'm leaving tomorrow."

"Yes, I know. I was just about to call you when my cell rang. It was you."

"And?"

"And do you have plans tonight?"

What was he thinking? It was already late. "What have you got in mind?"

"There's something I want to show you."

"Okay." Amber wished there was something he wanted to tell her, or. . . maybe even ask her. That was hoping for too much. She knew that now.

"Can you be ready in thirty seconds?"

"What?" Amber hurried out into the living room to see Brandon standing there.

He smiled, and when he spread his arms wide, she ran to him.

"Oh Amber." He kissed the top of her head. "Something came up, and I couldn't get away. Change into some jeans and grab a jacket."

*✺*

Brandon gripped Amber's hand as he led her along the trail that looped through the woods near the Little Missouri River Badlands. The trail where they'd first met.

"Can you at least tell me why we have to do this at night? It's a little eerie out here in the dark. Aren't there coyotes or wolves?"

Chuckling, he said, "I'm glad you weren't worried about the coyotes and wolves the night you saved me." Shining his flashlight to guide the way, he squeezed her hand and tugged her behind him.

This wasn't going like he planned. He could tell she was irritated. Maybe he'd read her wrong all along. But there was no other way to do this.

He reached the spot he'd been searching for. "Now, follow me closely and watch your step."

"What are we doing?"

"You'll see."

"Okay. I have no choice but to trust you."

He led her through the trees and brush into a clearing. "Okay, stay close to me and watch your step."

"Have you forgotten my family heirloom?"

The playfulness was back in her voice. He loved it. "How could I forget?"

Drawing near the rocky edge, he decided that was close enough. "Okay, this will do."

"What did you want me to see?"

"Remember the first time we met, and I told you about the ancient ruins?"

In the light of the full moon, Brandon could see Amber nod and search the rolling and rocky badland formations. Her eyes slowly grew wide. "Oh Brandon, it's beautiful. Thank you for this. I couldn't have imagined it."

"From the first moment I met you, I've wanted to show you this."

Amber turned her face to him, her eyes glistening in the moonlight. "And now?"

And now, would Brandon experience the rejection he'd doled out years before? A thick knot constricted his throat. Would she or wouldn't she?

"I couldn't think of a better place to propose to you."

She gasped, the liquid gold in her eyes muting to silver in the moonlight.

With his thumb, he lifted her chin, searched her gaze, and saw the answer to his unspoken question waiting there. "Amber McKinsey, you are rare and precious—you stand out from all others. I love you. Though I don't deserve you, would you become my wife?"

"Yes, oh yes." Lips trembling, her whispered answer resounded through the Badlands of North Dakota.

Brandon smiled, consumed with relief and joy. And her trembling lips. . .he'd looked forward to kissing them all day long. He leaned toward her, feeling her warm breath against his face. Gently he pressed his lips against hers. Her hands slid up his chest and around his neck, drawing him closer. Deepening the kiss, he surrendered his heart completely.

Amber was the one to break the moment, pulling away. A slight frown broke into her lips.

Brandon had yet to recover from the kiss, but the look on her face worried him. "What's the matter?"

"But how will we do this? Me off at school and you managing your museum?"

"Not to worry. I plan to accept a teaching position at UND. Dr. Young contacted me."

"But I thought you loved directing the museum."

"I do, but I love mentoring and had put in my application to UND in case I couldn't make the museum successful. The accreditation should be approved within the next few weeks, and once that's done, well then, I've accomplished that goal. A change of scenery is in order."

"But you only just hired Michael," she said, the ring of concern still in her voice.

Brandon pressed his nose against hers. "What's with all the questions? Michael knows what he's doing and what he doesn't know, I'll teach him. All I need to do now is work with the board to find a new director."

Amber sighed, seemingly content with his answers. "Just one more question."

"You'd better hurry. I'm seriously close to kissing you again."

"How did you know I'd marry you?"

He considered her question, slowly. "I didn't, actually. I waited for a sign."

"A sign?"

He tilted her chin slightly. "Sign number one, the way you look at me."

Her eyelashes fluttering, she giggled.

"Sign number two. . ." Brandon leaned in and kissed her again, thoroughly. When he released her, his voice was gruff as he said, "The way you respond to my kisses."

She smiled up at him, her face aglow from the moonlight, or was it his kiss?

"And sign number three?" she asked, her voice a whisper.

"You risked your life for mine."

# *Epilogue*

Standing in the foyer of Harrington Christian Fellowship, Amber prayed she wouldn't cry from the sheer delight of the occasion. Though it took thousands of years to create fossils and only time could produce ancient artifacts, she had found something far more valuable in Brandon, and it had only taken a few short weeks.

In the same time, God had restored her relationship with Him and with her brother. Her joy was profound.

"You're the most beautiful bride in the world, Amber." Michael lifted her hand and kissed it. "I'm more than privileged to walk you down the aisle."

The special moment came and someone opened the double doors, exposing Amber to the small gathering—signaling her to begin the once in a lifetime walk. Familiar faces—Cams, Muriel, and Gladys—smiled from the pews, as well as other friends. Claire from Brandon's Bible study played the wedding march on the organ as Amber took the customary rhythmic steps alongside Michael.

In her wildest dreams, she couldn't have imagined that her summer would end with a proposal. Wearing a tuxedo, Brandon stood at the end of the aisle, looking handsome beyond words.

She'd been packed and ready to leave for the fall semester at UND, but she and Brandon decided they wanted to marry as soon as possible. So, she'd taken the fall semester off to spend time with her new husband. Brandon had been invited to teach at UND in the spring, an offer he accepted once she had accepted his proposal. She recognized it as a sacrifice of sorts that he'd made for her, to be with her. She had a feeling—or maybe she'd seen the signs—that they would both end up back in paleontology, a love they both shared. She liked the idea of digging in the dirt with their children.

Before she realized it, she stood next to Dr. Brandon Selman. In her peripheral vision, she could see his sweet, elderly parents sitting in the first row, smiling, his mother wiping her tears.

They spoke their vows, and finally, Pastor John said, "You may kiss the bride."

Brandon's lips held the promise of his love, and Amber knew that a lifetime together, refined by time and pressure, would produce a marriage beyond price.

# PRAYING
# FOR RAYNE

# Dedication

Thank you to Roger Weinlaeder of the Weinlaeder Seed Company for sharing his expertise in North Dakota farming, and to Deborah Vogts, dear friend and critique partner, for her assistance in making the farm scenes resonate. A very special thanks to another dear friend, Shannon McNear, for her commitment and dedication in helping me to polish and edit my manuscripts and for helping me take the stories deeper. Thanks to friends and writing buddies Lynette Sowell and Lisa Harris for being there with me from the beginning, and to Ellen Tarver for her exceptionally keen eyes.

# Chapter 1

*S*ymmetrical curves and spiraling waves rained over the cornfields and danced across the page. . . .

"Rayne Carolyn Flemming." Hands on hips, Rayne's mother stood in the doorway, matching perfectly the antique fixtures in the old farmhouse. "Just what do you think you're doing?"

Rayne allowed her a slim smile, thinking that her mother appeared much older than her age. At forty-five, she'd never dream of putting color on her hair to hide the gray or dressing in anything that she hadn't kept in her closet for fifteen years. Even when her clothes had been nice and new, they had still looked frumpy.

Hating her negative thoughts, Rayne tugged another drawing from where it was pinned to the yellow-and-blue floral wallpaper—a design from years gone by. She sighed. "You make it sound like I'm ten, Mom."

Her mother strode all the way into her daughter's bedroom and placed a hand on the drawings Rayne held then tugged gently. "Let me have those."

Rayne held on. "I need them."

Her mother gave up in exasperation. "What on earth for?"

"I can use these at work." Rayne thumbed through the various sketches she'd pinned to her bedroom wall over the years. Noticing one of her favorites, she slipped it from the stack to peruse more closely. Spirals and waves stared back at her—maybe nothing special to anyone else, but Rayne saw beauty in the patterns. She saw water designs she could use in her job at FountainTech.

Standing next to her, her mother appeared to study the sketch as well. "I know I don't understand what your pictures mean, but they remind me of you. I want to keep your drawings on the wall."

Her mother made it sound as if Rayne had died and the wall was her memorial. Rayne put the sketches on her bed and opened her briefcase to place them inside. "You don't have to keep this as my room, you know. I'm a big girl now. You might even consider redecorating with something new and fresh, make it into a guest room. Dad could use it for an office."

"Nope, I couldn't do that. Your father would never agree. He hopes. . ."

Rayne heard the trembling in her mother's voice. Would they ever let their only child go? "I know. He hopes I'll come home." She wished she'd received news about the promotion she expected before she'd come home for the Christmas holidays. Her success would go a long way to convince her parents she was serious about her work. And maybe, just maybe, they'd believe in her.

"That, and he hopes you'll reconsider Paul's offer. We're farmers, Rayne. This is the life you know. And your father worries about you all alone in the city."

"Fargo? The city? Get serious, Mom." Ah. Stay a farm girl. Marry the boy next door. Why couldn't she eagerly oblige her parents by fulfilling those simple expectations? Be happy with an otherwise uneventful life, though it was a hard life. Her father worked himself to the marrow, as did her mother. This previous year had been bad for their wheat—too much rain.

Rayne zipped up the soft leather pocket holding her sketches and laptop and tugged the briefcase flap over, effectively closing it. She looked around her room. Two pieces from her Samsonite luggage sat on the floor. Everything was tidy, just as her mother had required of her when she was growing up.

"That should do it." Rayne tugged her briefcase strap over her shoulder and lifted a suitcase with each hand.

"Oh no you don't. Your father can get those if you insist on leaving." Rayne's mother huffed. "I don't see why you have to go just yet. Aunt Margaret will be here this afternoon. I'm sure she made the red velvet cake you like so much. Can't you stay a little longer?"

Rayne descended the staircase, still carrying her luggage, her mother following close behind. Guilt heaped on more guilt. That's what her mother did. "I've been here two weeks already, and I should have driven back yesterday."

"But yesterday was New Year's Eve, and you can't drive on New Year's Day."

By the time Rayne reached the bottom of the stairs, her shoulder had begun to ache along with her nerves. She dropped the luggage and slipped the briefcase from her arm, setting it on the floor. Voices resounded from the kitchen.

". . .if this weather keeps up."

"Yah betcha," her father replied. His voice, bold and strong, was always a comfort to Rayne.

"Oh, that must be Paul." Rayne's mother hurried past and headed to the small country kitchen of the farmhouse.

The familiar voice conversing with her father sent dread through Rayne. Maybe North Dakotan farmers were tenacious by nature, their perseverance having evolved over decades in order to survive. That's why her parents continued to plant seeds in her, hoping for her return. That's why Paul Frasier continued to plant seeds in her, hoping she'd agree to marry him.

She strolled into the kitchen, expecting to hear a discussion about how cold it was outside and what the weather would do over the next several days. In the Flemming home, the conversation never veered much from the weather. The weather could make or break farmers.

Rayne smiled at her father, who was piling bacon high on a platter already filled with eggs. "You know what they say—the cold keeps out the riff-raff."

Paul's eyes brightened when he saw her. "Rayne, I didn't realize you were still here."

*What? You didn't see my car parked outside?* Rayne smiled, playing along. "Yep, still here for five more minutes."

His smile dimmed. "You're heading back to Fargo to work at the water company?"

Paul knew perfectly well. It wasn't like him to make jabs. "It's called FountainTech, remember?"

"Oh, that's right." Paul removed his jacket then took the cup of coffee her mother offered. The man was tall and handsome, with strong, rugged Norwegian ancestry. He owned and ran a successful farm. Why hadn't she been able to bring herself to say yes when he'd finally proposed?

Her father set the platter on the table as he peered at her through sad, disapproving eyes. He'd never been impressed with her career. She wasn't sure he even understood what she did exactly. Something inside her seemed to crack like the smallest of leaks in a water main—at one time she had held her father's appreciative gaze. She longed to see that again. She longed to please him, but at what cost? Giving up her dream? Suddenly, her throat constricted.

Uncomfortable silence filled the kitchen.

"Paul, care to join us for breakfast?" her mother asked to be polite, though to Rayne's ears it sounded more like an attempt to change the subject and keep the peace.

"No, thank you, Carol. I've already eaten. Just wanted to stop by to see how you were doing."

"All right then." Her mother busied herself making toast.

Paul and her father took seats at the small table and started up their conversation again while her father ate. It seemed they had nothing else to say to the traitor. When she'd graduated with an art degree, they hadn't considered it a real education. Why would she expect them to consider her work as a water feature designer to be a real job? Part of her wished she didn't care what her family members thought of her chosen career because she loved it so much. Why couldn't they love it, too, instead of withholding their approval?

She loved designing fountains, choreographing the water into art that was emotionally dramatic. Right now she couldn't wait to get back to her job.

Rayne drew in a breath to soften the tension in her neck and breathed in the aroma of breakfast, mingled with the mustiness of a farmhouse built in 1900.

"I need to head back to Fargo, so I'll say my good-byes now," she said, interrupting their conversation.

Holding a plate of toast, her mother froze midstride as though surprised to hear the news. She set the plate on the table and wiped her hands against her apron, a resigned look on her face. "We'll help you out, Rayne. Won't we, Gary?"

Rayne's father nodded. "I'll get your bags."

Finally, Rayne stood next to her car—a white Volkswagen Passat she'd bought when she landed her job—and hugged her mother and father. Paul wished her well. She looked at the small house behind them, laced with the remnants of yesterday's snow. She committed to memory today's characteristics of the house where she grew up. She'd felt loved, safe, and secure. That's what had made these last few years so difficult.

Once her parents knew of her promotion and saw her success, they'd know she had made the right decision. But doubt—maybe all the seeds planted into the soil of her heart over the last two weeks—had wreaked havoc on her confidence.

*Have I made the right decision?*

Though she'd sought an answer from God, He'd been silent on the matter.

*✍*

Jack Kostner pressed his chest to his leg, feeling the stretch in his hamstring. Wouldn't do to injure himself on his first day of work.

Alone on the racquetball court, he stretched tall. Drawing in a breath, he noted the air was devoid of that stale sock and locker room odor—something he could expect to experience once the health club filled with bodies again.

But not at 5:00 a.m.

Jack began slamming the ball—he didn't need a partner to get his practice in. Considering he was new to Fargo and the health club, he'd cut himself some slack. A partner would turn up soon enough, though sometimes he wasn't sure if he wanted one.

Someone pounded on the Plexiglas wall behind him. Breathing hard, Jack caught the ball and glanced at the lanky man dressed in workout shorts and looking eager. Jack could guess at his reason for disturbing him.

The man opened the door and leaned in. "You expecting someone? Or could you use a challenge?"

Jack laughed. Nobody ever beat him. This guy was in for it. "Sure. But I've only got forty-five minutes to play." After that he'd shower and head to work—the first day on his new job. He'd spent last night setting up his office so he could get down to business today. No slacking for him.

The man raised his eyebrows. "More like fifteen for me."

"That'll do." Without another word, Jack slammed a fast serve, catching the man off guard.

They soon fell into the rhythm of the game, the ball bouncing around the walls. Jack loved the sound of it and the smell of the rubbery sphere as it darted around the cube encasing them.

After half an hour, Jack paused and pressed his hands against his thighs, breathing hard. The guy had beaten him three games already.

"I thought you said you only had fifteen minutes," Jack managed.

His opponent's eyes widened. "Yep. I'd better run." He rushed to the door then turned back to Jack. "Name's Carl."

Still gasping for breath, Jack nodded. "Jack."

Carl smiled and exited the court. Jack knew he'd see the man again. He'd have another chance to play and beat him next time. Chagrined, he headed for the shower.

He wondered at his sour start to the day. Usually nobody beat Jack Kostner. At racquetball or otherwise. Still, playing with someone better was a sharpening of the iron, as the saying went. Even though he hated losing, he enjoyed being challenged and, yes, being honed. He wondered if he would find anyone at FountainTech to challenge him, sharpen his ideas and creations. If it would make him better, he'd welcome the competition.

Once an Imagineer—imagination engineer—at Disney, Jack had no plans to be bested. Only a fool ever quit growing and learning. Jack shoved through the door to the showers. Yep. The only thing he'd ever been a quitter at was love. But that wasn't his fault. His fiancé had skipped out on him two days before their wedding last year.

Two days!

And that's why he found himself in North Dakota, being beaten at racquetball at five in the morning.

After his stint in the special effects department at Disney, his experience and education in engineering and product design had come in handy at Elemental Innovations, Inc., that is, until he'd met and fallen in love with Kiera Stemmons.

And she was still working at Elemental in sunny California while he was shivering in the cold up north. She'd almost destroyed him. He'd had nothing left. Jack showered and dressed, furious with himself for letting his mind go there. Fargo was a new start for him, empty of all reminders of that woman.

But hadn't God seen his pain?

*Stop!*

Fuming, he tugged on his socks. *Get a grip, man.*

Okay, Jack was back. At twenty-seven he'd learned his lessons and was ready to throw all of his energy into this company's water fountain designs.

Once he stepped through the exit doors of the health club and onto the snow-lined pavement, the cold slammed him. He wondered if working out this early and then hitting the frigid air was good for a person—could it constrict his blood vessels and give him a heart attack like his grandfather?

With that thought, his mind drifted to his parents and their tragic death. He stiffened and shoveled the thoughts away like so much snow.

Heading to his car, Jack prodded himself to focus on FountainTech, get on with his new life. Why wouldn't the brooding thoughts leave him alone? Maybe it was the lack of sunshine. He was accustomed to jogging outside in the sunshine every morning. Couldn't the cloudy darkness of winter give a person some sort of depression?

Enough. He wouldn't let buried memories of Kiera or his parents bring him down. Jack started his jet black Pontiac Solstice and, despite the snow and sludge, spun from the parking lot.

# Chapter 2

Hold that door!" Rayne called, catching Heidi's eyes.

Heidi held the elevator door for her with a smile, while others appeared annoyed. Rayne gasped for breath when she stepped into the elevator. She hated being late. Her workday started at eight, and it was five till now. Rayne liked to be at work an hour early to organize her thoughts.

Surrounded by a few of her coworkers, as well as others she didn't know, Rayne felt like a sardine in the elevator.

"How were your holidays, Rayne?" Heidi asked.

Rayne felt drab and mousy next to Heidi, who had green eyes and beautiful, long blond hair. *Gorgeous.* She made Rayne conscious of her dull brown, shoulder-length cut. Maybe she was like her mother after all; she had never considered doing anything to her hair to make it vibrant.

"Good, but I was ready to be home," she replied. The word *home* sounded strange on her tongue when using it to describe her apartment in Fargo.

Kathy, a tall, lanky girl from accounting, laughed as though she understood, also having left Fargo to see family. Did everyone go through the frustration of failing their families, as Rayne did? Or did others live up to the expectations placed on them?

"My parents came to see me." Heidi rubbed her nose. "Can't have Christmas without the grandkids."

For a moment, an image of holding a baby flashed in Rayne's mind. If she'd said yes to Paul and married him months ago, might she be pregnant by now? Of course, as a farmer's wife, a brood of children was expected, and right away. She chuckled inside but sobered as she was reminded once again of why her parents wanted her to marry Paul. As an only child, she was their only hope for grandchildren. A marriage to Paul would guarantee the grandbabies stayed close. Just another reason for her parents to hold on to her so tightly.

The elevator doors finally swooshed open, and the FountainTech employees poured out into a small entrance hall. To the left were glass doors, the main entrance to FountainTech. A door on the right of the hall allowed employees through the back entrance, a quicker path to their offices on that side. Kathy headed right, punching the entry code into the keypad to open the back door.

Rayne, Heidi, and two others strolled through the reception area, still wearing their coats, hats, and gloves. Rayne began shedding her winter gear.

Gail, FountainTech's perky receptionist, smiled as they went past. "Coffee's already made."

"That sounds wonderful. I'm chilled to the bone." Rayne exited the reception area into the main hallway. Her office was two doors down on the right. She opened the door, flipped on the light, and took in a deep breath.

Ah, she loved the smell of her office. And by this afternoon, maybe she could even say that success never smelled so sweet, because by then she might have heard about her promotion. She left the door open to hear the telltale sounds of employees as they arrived. She loved being back at work.

Giddy with excitement for what today—what this week—could bring, Rayne was overwhelmed. Humbled. She never stopped being amazed at the sort of talent walking the halls of FountainTech.

Astounding talent. In comparison, Rayne might consider herself ordinary— if not for her designs. She was on the creative team at FountainTech and had demonstrated a unique ability to pull the team together, guiding its direction. She'd also created the company's latest design, now in production. The vice president, Harold Cullins, had spoken to her about her talent and asked if she was interested in managing the team. She knew the position was open, and he'd assured her she would have it.

But that was weeks ago.

After setting the folder with her old drawings on her desk, she hung her coat and stuffed her gloves and hat in the pockets. A glance out her window gave her a good view of Fargo and a few distant fields, snow clinging to both the city and landscape.

A light knock on her door drew her attention. She hadn't taken a seat yet. She looked up to see Barb standing in the doorway holding out an extra cup of coffee.

"Is that for me?"

Barb smiled. "Of course. I couldn't wait for you to get here. You're running late today."

Rayne savored the warm cup as she wrapped her hands around it. She slurped the hot yumminess before answering. "Had too much snow to shovel off my car this morning. Maybe I can move into an apartment with a garage soon." Yep, right after she heard about her promotion.

Barb's eyes twinkled as if she had a secret.

"What?"

The tall brunette laughed. "Have you seen him?"

Rayne shook her head and took a sip of coffee then pulled out her chair. "Seen who?"

She began pulling her sketches from the folder and spreading them across her desk. Time to get the creative juices flowing. They had a new design contract to fulfill.

"The new guy, who else?" Barb asked.

The designs on Rayne's desk were quickly stealing her attention from Barb. Though crude and rough, the drawings still had merit; even the ones she'd drawn ten years ago had a glimmer of creativity in them.

Barb tugged on her arm. "Come on. You've got to see him."

Rayne stared up at her friend. "You've got to be kidding, right? We're not in high school here."

"Yeah, well, professionals or not, this guy is gorgeous. I don't want you to be shocked and have your mouth hang open the first time you see him like Margie did."

Rayne almost lost her coffee at the comment. "I don't think you have to worry about me doing that."

She was interested in one thing—getting her promotion. Besides, handsome men didn't do a thing for her. If the time came when she thought she was ready to settle down, become a wife and mother, she knew that a good husband could be found only in a man who had a good heart.

Barb looked wounded. "Are you kidding? You don't want to see?"

Rayne shook her head. "I'm sure I'll meet him soon enough. I've got to get my thoughts into my work now."

Her fellow employee stepped into the doorway and peered down the hallway. She looked back at Rayne and frowned. Rayne heard someone she couldn't see whisper to Barb.

Barb glanced back at Rayne. "He's in his office now anyway. Door's closed. Sorry I bothered you."

Rayne felt badly. Barb was a member of the creative team, and Rayne would soon be her boss. "How about lunch?"

Barb's expression softened, and she shrugged. "Lunch sounds good."

Voices continued to resound in the hall as the eighty or so employees of FountainTech entered the workplace. To Rayne's chagrin, she heard more whispers about the new guy—his abilities and talents and good looks. It didn't sound as if anyone knew what he'd been hired to do, but the FountainTech employee roster had grown along with the company's glowing reviews and client list. A new employee wasn't unusual.

Rayne shut her door, silencing the gossip.

❦

With the door to his office closed, Jack perused the files of the creative design team he would be managing.

Of course, the vice president of the company, Harold Cullins, had used the exceptional talent at the company to convince Jack to accept his offer. He wasn't sure he'd believed Harold's claims, but it was a great opportunity to come aboard a growing company near its inception. Never mind that he'd wanted to escape California.

He swiped a hand down his face and stood to stare out his window. It had started snowing again. A little bit of snow in San Diego would shut the place down.

Turning back to his desk, he fingered the files of those people he considered the most gifted—the top three members of his team.

One of them stood out above the rest. He flipped through the hard copy of some of her designs. Impressive.

Sitting again, he studied the 3-D design models of her drawings on his laptop. She might very well be the iron to sharpen iron, the challenge he—

The door flew open, Harold occupying the space. "There you are, champ."

Startled by the intrusion, Jack minimized his screen. Hadn't the man ever heard of knocking? Jack didn't like being called "champ" either. His first day was getting off to a great start already.

Harold was at least six-two and appeared to enjoy that he intimidated people. In his fifties, his hair was completely gray, a statement of experience to back up his imperious attitude. His gaze did a 180 around Jack's office, noting the awards and photographs Jack had put up last night.

Jack liked that Harold appeared momentarily taken aback. Jack slipped his hand over his mouth to hide his smile and leaned back in his chair to watch the vice president.

Harold came fully into the office, closing the door behind him. "You've been busy, I see." He took the seat across from Jack's desk and propped his ankle across his knee.

"I came in last night to get organized. No point in wasting time on that during the day."

"That's what I like about you, Jack. You don't waste any time."

Jack wondered if this conversation would be a waste of time. But he couldn't exactly ask that.

"I came in here to inform you we're meeting at nine."

His thoughts scrambling, Jack nodded.

"I plan to introduce you to the company and specifically to your team. Are you ready?"

"Always."

"Another good trait and one of the reasons I hired you. Plan to keep a low profile until then."

Without another word, Harold rose and left Jack to think.

Did Harold want a PowerPoint presentation for the meeting? Jack wondered if he had been right to think that someone on the creative design team would be his challenger. Maybe Harold would be the one to keep him on his toes.

Jack twisted from his chair and out the door. Harold may not have wanted the news of Jack's position to get out until the meeting, but he needed some caffeine. Surely he could manage to grab some coffee without blowing his cover.

He trotted down the burgundy carpeted hall and past the tall mahogany doors of the offices, making his way to the kitchen. He'd made sure to take a private tour of the place last night.

The company effectively shut down for two weeks over the holidays, giving all its employees that time in addition to vacation. Unfortunately, the impact of such generosity was apparent as employees lingered in the hallway, chatting it up with each other. "Catching up." In Jack's opinion, the company was now two weeks behind on its projects.

A few women huddled together near the doorway of an office and stopped talking as he drew near. Faces flashed with expectant smiles. They were waiting to meet him, of course. But he walked right past and saluted them, amused when he heard their quiet snickers.

Almost to the kitchen, he rounded a corner and. . .*smack.*

A warm female body slammed against him then jerked away and gasped.

Coffee painted the front of her blouse. She stepped further back and stared down, a look of horror on her face. With her hands held out as if still registering what had just happened, her mouth hung open. Jack noted her lipstick smeared over her upper lip. A pretty pinkish color.

"Here, let me help you." Jack hurried into the kitchen. "Let's clean you up." He grabbed some paper towels and started to press them against the front of her shirt then paused, thinking better of it.

He handed the paper towels to her, seeing her blush. "Thank you," she said, softly.

Kind brown eyes flashed up at him then down his neck where they lingered. "Oh. . .I'm afraid you have lipstick on your collar."

Jack quickly lost his smile. "Lipstick?" Another glance at her lips and he knew.

That was one thing he'd failed to do yet. He liked to keep an extra starched white shirt in his office, just in case there was a coffee mishap. He'd seen it happen a gazillion times.

"If you try to rub off the lipstick, you'll only make it worse, I'm afraid. I'd like to pay to have that cleaned for you."

"And I should pay for getting the coffee out of that blouse. How about we call it even?"

Though Jack wouldn't say she was a beauty—in fact, she was unremarkable—there was something behind her eyes that whispered to him. *This one is a deep thinker.*

She smiled with a disappointed shrug. "I have an important meeting in an hour. I can't stand up in front of everyone like this."

"You should keep an extra blouse in your office for this sort of thing." Jack hung his hands in his pocket, wondering about her role in Harold's announcement. "I'm Jack Kostner, by the way." He thrust his hand out.

She met it with hers, her hand soft and warm. "Rayne Flemming."

*I know exactly who you are.* Though he'd not seen her picture, he'd read her file. He'd been right—she was a deep thinker, a creative designer. As far as he could tell, she was the most valuable person on his team.

Jack rocked back and forth on his feet, growing anxious. Normally he'd consider this sort of interaction a waste of time. What was the matter with him?

"You must be the new guy."

"Yep." Jack grinned, but he couldn't say more, Harold's words still fresh in his mind. He focused on getting his coffee, and when he turned around, she was gone.

Jack tugged on his collar. He needed to at least inspect the damage in a mirror. Maybe he could draw his suit jacket tight and look like a nerd but hide the lipstick.

And if not? Harold would introduce Jack, the new employee and manager, and he would stand in front of everyone with lipstick on his shirt.

That would give the women something to talk about.

# Chapter 3

B arb was right. Jack was a looker, with the sort of thick black hair that made a girl want to run her fingers through it, and striking blue eyes that seemed to read her thoughts. He had that strong, rugged jaw and athletic physique she often saw on the cover of magazines while standing in line at the grocery store.

But Rayne wasn't attracted to a man simply for his looks. As for his personality, though, Jack seemed pleasant enough.

Warm and friendly.

Rayne glanced at the clock on the wall. Only ten more minutes until the meeting. She fidgeted with her notes—an acceptance speech with details about preparing the team for its next project—doubt creeping in. Before the holidays, Harold had spoken to her in confidence about managing the team, and she'd accepted his offer, though not in writing. In fact, nothing had been in writing, or even set in stone, now that she recalled their exact conversation.

Rayne stood and took a deep breath. Maybe she worried for nothing. Still, why hadn't he spoken to her more specifically about the position? All she could think was that Harold wasn't the sort of manager who coddled. He liked forward thinkers and people who took initiative, who were willing to take what he offered and do something with it.

Unfortunately, that left Rayne unclear about where she stood. She had no way of knowing if his announcement today was regarding her as the new team manager. But she knew the creative team needed a leader, especially on its newest project. If not today, then soon.

Opening her door, she stepped into the hall, joining other employees headed to the small conference room. Of course, only those whose departments were affected would be there to hear Harold's announcement.

Barb appeared, walking beside her. She glanced at Rayne's blouse but said nothing. Rayne figured Barb didn't want to embarrass Rayne further by talking about it in front of everyone.

"So what do you think Harold's going to say?" Barb asked.

Rayne wanted to be excited and expectant, but for the first time since speaking to Harold on the matter of her managing the team, she pushed down her hopes. "I really have no clue."

Questions lingered behind Barb's eyes. "I wonder why he's so hush-hush about it."

Rayne didn't respond, because they'd reached the glass doors of the conference room, held open by one of their fellow employees, Simon Jeffers.

He smiled. "Hi there, Rayne."

She replied in kind and thanked him for keeping the door for her. Most of the sixteen chairs around the conference table were occupied except for one seat near the front. The rest of the planning division employees, which accounted for half the company, leaned against the walls, and a few limber ones sat on the floor, legs crossed.

Had that seat been saved for her? Preparing to be formally recognized, if that's what Harold had in mind, Rayne took the only seat left. She set her file in front of her on the table, a little miffed she didn't know what was going on. If Harold announced her today, and she hoped he would, he should have given her fair warning. Then again, to his way of thinking, she knew from experience, he probably thought he had.

She wanted to sigh but stifled it, putting on a confident smile. As she glanced around the room, listening to conversations about the holidays and seeing most of her team there, her confidence ignited once again.

Yep. Harold would announce that he'd promoted her to team manager. She'd been one of the first hired on at FountainTech a year ago at the company's inception, selling herself on her designs alone. She had proven her abilities to coordinate the team's efforts on projects thereafter.

Rayne slowly released a breath and relaxed into the burgundy leather chair. Two people standing against the wall behind her whispered about Jack and his good looks. Rayne fought the desire to look at the ceiling. The culture these days was focused on one thing, it seemed. Rayne couldn't afford for her thoughts to go there, because she wasn't one of the beautiful ones. It would be too depressing. Instead, she considered it a blessing that God had given her more important gifts.

The knob on the door at the head of the conference room clicked, and a hush spread through the room. Harold was obviously standing behind the door, intending to walk through, but held back for some reason. Then the door flew open quickly. *Definitely Harold.*

Tall and authoritative, he stepped through, followed by Jack. A few quiet intakes of breath resounded around the room as though everyone held their breath. Rayne's eye flicked to Jack's collar. The lipstick was barely noticeable— how had he gotten it out? With the way he'd suggested she keep an extra shirt in her office, she supposed he'd dealt with similar situations before. Still, the guy exuded efficiency. Probably kept one of those Tide instant spot removers on hand as well.

She figured the stain could only be seen if one knew where to look. As Harold began to talk, she became self-conscious about her own coffee-stained blouse and leaned against the table, positioning her hands to hide the stain. How was she going to hide that when she stood to make her speech? Expectant and filled with enthusiasm, Rayne snapped her attention back to Harold.

But Harold's announcement had nothing to do with her. Rayne's heart pounded in her throat. She feared the pulse in her neck was like a neon sign to everyone in the room. Harold was introducing Jack. That was odd. There was never fanfare over a regular employee.

Only managers.

Harold peered around the room. Always in command of his audience, he apparently liked to make eye contact with everyone if he could.

"Welcome back from the holidays. I hope you're rested and ready to focus your time and energies on creating the best fountain designs in the world." His deep baritone filled the room like surround sound.

Most cheered their agreement. Harold expected no less. The atmosphere seemed to bubble with anticipation.

"I expect you're wondering why I called this meeting. We needed to get this year started on the right foot. I've hired Jack to manage the design team." It appeared to Rayne that Harold's gaze fell everywhere except on her.

Rayne's heart seemed to stop. She smiled and nodded as if she were excited, fitting in with her fellow employees. When her heart began to beat again, long and loud in her ears, it covered all other sounds. She was in a tunnel, and time seemed to slow around her.

*Thump, thump.*

Harold's lips were moving, but she heard only the. . .

*Thump, thump.*

In slow motion, she swiveled her head, scanning the faces around the conference room.

*Thump, thump.*

Her gaze fell on Barb, smiling against the wall in the back of the room, her full attention on Harold.

*Thump, thump.*

Then Rayne's head rotated. She was looking at the front of the room. At Jack.

*Thump, thump. . .thump, thump. . .*

He was staring back at her. Rayne had a terrible thought. Did he know?

᯽

Jack loved moments like these. He soared like an eagle, hearing himself announced as the new manager of the design team. He heard Harold speaking, knew the man was introducing him, but his thoughts had already moved on to what he would say when his turn came.

The only glitch in the moment, in his thoughts, was the look on Rayne Flemming's face when Harold made his announcement. Though smiling, the light in her eyes dimmed. She looked as if. . .well, as if the breath had been knocked out of her. Literally.

"You're up, champ."

"Thanks, Harold." Jack smiled and tried not to grit his teeth at the nickname Harold had branded him with. A splinter in his hand would have been less annoying.

Pouring all his energy into appearing enthusiastic, Jack stepped to the front, and Harold eased back against the wall.

Definitely, Jack was back. Today was the premier of his show. He didn't slow to acknowledge the prick of fear curdling his stomach. Failure wasn't in his plans. Not this time.

"I can't tell you how thrilled I am to be FountainTech's newest member. Even more so because of the talent I'm joining here." He paused, for effect, his momentary silence building expectation in the room.

He clicked his remote wand, and the PowerPoint presentation he'd whipped together within the last hour flashed on to the whiteboard at the front of the room. "Much of this information you already know, but I want to show it to you in a new light, if you will. FountainTech's goal is to be the leading provider of water feature designs around the world."

Jack clicked through the three fountains they'd created in the last year. Two in the United States, one in Egypt. Images of multiple fountains lifting water high into the air, like Old Faithful in Yellowstone National Park, played across the screen in a slide show. Music accompanied each of the images.

"Mm." Jack shook his head and glanced back at his hypnotized group. "No matter how many times I watch that, I'll never stop loving it. It will never cease to mesmerize me or to inspire me.

"These images are part of what drew me to your company. You're probably wondering about my background. I came from a similar design company, Elemental Innovations."

He heard a few whispers in the room. He didn't mention he hadn't worked for EI in over six months. In his opinion, FountainTech was far ahead of his old company, and he was jazzed about this opportunity. "And before that I worked at Disney as an imagination engineer—an Imagineer." He grinned, always loving that title.

"And that's what I want from my team. Anything we can imagine, we can create."

Rayne Flemming unexpectedly came into his mind, and he looked her way, but she had her head down, writing on a notepad. Next, Jack chose a slide with employee names. "If your name is up there, you are a member of the team I'll be managing. Over this next week, I plan to find out your strengths and weaknesses and effectively reorganize things. Expect to meet with me one on one."

Finished with his short presentation, he raised the lighting, noting the hopeful looks and shimmering eyes. Good. Just what he liked to see. "Questions?"

Immediately a hand shot up. A blond at the back of the room. "My name is Heidi. What exactly did you do at the companies where you worked before?"

Oh come on. He'd hoped for something, well, more imaginative. For the next twenty minutes, he answered questions. For some reason, he couldn't get his mind off Rayne. He stood at the end of the table, his pant legs touching the edge. She was seated next to where he stood, looking dazed. Disappointment tried to kill his moment, but it would never beat Jack.

He'd expected much more from Rayne than he'd gotten in her reaction.

When the questions finally ended, Harold moved forward to stand next to Jack.

"Thank you, Jack. I'm sure everyone is as equally impressed as I am, and eager to get to work."

Too soon the meeting was over. Frankly, Jack loved the attention. But Harold was right. Time to get to work. The employees filed from the room, Rayne in their midst. Jack frowned. He'd intended to speak to her before she left, but she'd simply melted out of the room with the others.

"I knew I was right to hire you, Jack. I know you won't let me down." Harold winked then started to leave as well.

"Harold, can I ask you something?"

The man paused, waiting.

"It's about Rayne Fleming."

Harold's eyes brightened. "She'll be the star of your team. Treat her right."

Jack shook his head. "Something's wrong."

Angling his head, Harold studied Jack. "You read people well, Jack. Several weeks ago, I talked to Rayne about managing the team. She would do a good job, no doubt. But I needed someone less creative and craftier for the job." Harold squeezed Jack's shoulder. "You're the man. Good thing for me you came onto the scene when you did."

Harold grinned, making a clucking sound out of the side of his mouth, then left the conference room.

Jack stared after him. Had he meant crafty in a good way? Or crafty as in scheming and conniving? Jack considered himself highly creative as well. He stared at the floor, calming his anger.

Rayne's reaction made perfect sense now. Harold had dangled the carrot in her face then offered it to Jack. She'd had no warning. She'd been blindsided. As he gathered up his notes and the flash drive holding his PowerPoint, Jack became worried. Very worried.

The most valuable person on his team, Rayne Flemming, could very well leave the company over this. Jack rushed out of the conference room, only one thought pressing him.

*I can't afford to lose her. . . .*

# Chapter 4

*The higher your aim, the harder your fall."* Her father's words—spoken in a rare moment when he'd revealed his own life's disappointments—seemed to mock her.

Tears seared the back of Rayne's eyes, where she kept them imprisoned. She needed time to order her thoughts. Lunch couldn't come fast enough, but now she wished she hadn't invited Barb to join her. At the time, she'd wanted to appease Barb, and she admitted to herself, she'd been counting on having something to celebrate. Maybe she could use her coffee-stained shirt as an excuse—she needed to change into a new one.

With the back of her hand, Rayne brushed away the lone tear that had managed to slip past her guard. Tears had no place in the corporate world.

She leaned against the windowsill. From the fifth floor, she could see a good bit of Fargo, though the view was somewhat obstructed by a few other tall buildings that stood near the bank where FountainTech leased offices. Snow clung to the rooftops and edged the streets and sidewalks, and though the white stuff was as familiar to her as her mother's voice, today it chilled her soul.

How had she so grossly misunderstood Harold's intentions toward her career? Or had the fault been his—dangling the promotion, knowing from the beginning how important this goal was to her. Was it simply an oversight, or was it intentional? Regardless, she'd assigned far too much significance to the promotion, thinking of it as a fleece that would let her know that she'd made the right decision when she'd left home and left her parents' expectations unfulfilled.

Would she be like Gideon and continue to question God?

She scoffed out loud. It was ridiculous to have considered Harold's decision a fleece to begin with. Promotion or no promotion, she could no more give up this dream of creating her designs than air or water. She admitted to herself that, although she'd not been indifferent to the prospect of the boost to her career, this promotion had been all about proving herself to her parents. Her current position wasn't enough to earn their approval.

The big question now was, where would she go from here? How should she react? She'd better figure that out and quickly. The questions assailed her like a blizzard in her mind, lashing at all her neatly constructed plans, ideas about who she was and where she wanted to go, blinding her to the future.

In the distance, the sky began to clear, and the snow clouds, having spent their load, were beginning to push out. Focusing on the blue edging the horizon, Rayne drew in a weighty breath.

A whiff of burnt popcorn seeped under her door. She hated that her office was so close to the kitchen—something else she'd thought would change after this morning's meeting. Tugging her chair back from the desk, she sank into it, longing for her earlier enthusiasm. She had a new boss now. Someone else to impress.

A light knock startled her. "Come in."

The door slowly opened, and there stood Jack. Panic whirled inside. She wasn't prepared to face him yet but forced a smile. "Hi there."

He slipped in and gently shut the door behind him. "Can we talk?"

"Of course."

He was handling her with kid gloves. He knew. . . .

Sitting in the chair on the other side of her desk, he raised his face and studied the sketches on her walls while she studied him. His clean-shaven, strong jaw and the sparkle in his blue eyes bore the enthusiasm she lacked. But she wouldn't let him see that.

She examined his collar. "How did you do that?"

He shook his head as if her question had given him a start. "I'm sorry?"

Despite her mood, she laughed easily. Jack Kostner had a way about him. "My lipstick. . .er. . .the lipstick on your collar. It's all but gone." She put a hand to her face, feeling the heat.

Instantly, a grin brought dimples into his cheeks. "I got lucky. I found a bottle of Wite-Out in the back of a drawer."

Rayne pursed her lips into a smile and quirked a brow. "That *is* lucky."

Jack turned his attention back to her drawings and stood, taking a step toward the wall. Looking closely at one of her sketches, he tilted his head. "How long have you been drawing these?"

Was this some sort of trick question? "Oh, those are from years ago. I know they're nothing brilliant. I just like to be reminded, to be inspired."

He jerked his head to her, his gaze intense. "Oh, you're wrong. They *are* brilliant. In our business, this sort of creativity means everything."

Sitting again, he tugged the chair forward so he could lean on her desk. He was much closer now. Too close for comfort. Oddly, his nearness made her heart race.

"Thank you," she said. "What did you want to see me about?"

Jack eased back now, his fingers over his lips in a thoughtful pose. Her impression of him during his presentation was that he was an aggressive over-achiever. By the end of his dynamic and motivating speech, she realized why she hadn't gotten the job. As hard as she tried, that just wasn't her. But now she was seeing a different side to him. A thoughtful side—at least it appeared that way.

"You should already know from my presentation that I planned to meet with each member of the design team individually."

Rayne swallowed and nodded. *Pick up your game, girl. The pacing is faster now.* "Yes, and you planned to reorganize the team based on the members' strengths. What have you decided about me?"

Jack grinned again. She felt a tickle in her stomach—unwelcome and unexpected.

"You're right to the point. I like that. I haven't begun to reorganize yet. I'm simply here, Rayne, to tell you that I had no idea, and that I'm sorry."

Now it was her turn to be startled. She shook her head. "What are you talking about?"

"I know you were expecting the position I now hold. It would have been a promotion for you."

Uneasiness hung in the air of her office. She struggled to think what to say. His apology was completely unexpected. And unusual.

"What you need to know is that you're vital to this company, to this team, and to my vision to make FountainTech the leader in water feature designs."

Jack was pouring it on thick. Rayne's heart pounded in her ears again. The room grew stuffy.

*Just breathe.*

Is this how they extracted performance from their people at Disney? Whatever magic Jack was using, it was working.

Her enthusiasm stirred once again, but she cautioned herself. Was he friend or foe? What reason did she have to trust the man she'd lost her promotion to? And the fact remained she'd lost her chance to gain the praise she wanted from her family. She clung to the uncertainty of her renewed enthusiasm and her wariness as though it were her only lifeline.

"So, Rayne, what do you like to be reminded of?"

Rayne stared.

"You said earlier about your sketches, you put them up because you like to be reminded of. . .something. What was it?"

He dropped his smile, and at once his gaze turned intense. Again. Rayne would need about a gallon of coffee every morning to keep up with him. Still, his energy made her feel alive. She considered his question. Did she want to share so much of herself just yet?

Regretting that she'd made the comment, Rayne focused on tracing a knot in the veneer of the maple desk. Jack leaned forward again. Too close.

"The inspiration for those designs came from the wheat, soybean, corn, and sunflower fields on my parents' farm. When the wind blows, waves ripple across the fields. As a child, that fascinated me. I spent hours drawing what I saw. Then when my dad tried various irrigation systems, I was even more intrigued with the synchronization of the water streams and what happened when the wind disrupted them."

Jack stared at her for what seemed like an eternity. "If there is magic on this planet, it is contained in water," he said, in an almost-whisper.

Rayne laughed softly. "Who said that?"

"I forget exactly. Some scientist at the University of Pennsylvania." Jack wore that thoughtful expression again, as if he had gone to a place so far away that Rayne could never join him there.

*⟡*

The air in Jack's office grew stale. He opened the door, inviting in what he hoped was fresh air from the hallway. It was already six, and most everyone was gone for the day, so he wasn't worried about any unwelcome intrusions. His first day had gone by far too fast, filled with meetings and unintentional conversations not of his making. But, he supposed, it was part of the process of settling into his new position.

Harold had popped in on several occasions, swinging the door open without knocking. That was quickly becoming the man's MO. Jack would have to be much more deliberate in his effort to get work done in the face of interruptions. He'd obviously taken time for granted, believing he had plenty available to accomplish his tasks and achieve his goals. Add to that a special project that filled his evenings, and he certainly couldn't afford to waste his daytime hours.

Pulling together the stack of files on his desk, he hated that he'd only made it through half of them. A water fountain feature danced elegantly across his computer screen. Fluid and comforting, his thoughts went right to the creator. *Rayne.*

She'd turned him down for lunch, saying she had to change into a clean shirt. A valid excuse. He'd have done the same in her shoes. He was fairly sure she wouldn't be leaving the company anytime soon—she seemed obsessed with her creations. Still, he'd keep reminding her of her importance to the team. She was his biggest asset in the company. He should keep her close and bolster her if she became discouraged.

Stuffing the files into a desk drawer, he laughed a little at the thought. She'd be near him regardless, because they needed to work together on the new water fountain designs. Tomorrow he'd talk to her about her thoughts on their next design project.

He began the process of shutting down his laptop then stopped it, the design dancing on the screen, compelling him to watch. Rayne had programmed the features into the computer, and in the lab, the engineers and technicians had built and organized the various water-pumping mechanisms and software-driven nozzles that brought the fountain to life. Rubbing his chin, Jack wondered, *Would a working model of this fountain still be set up in the lab?*

Only one way to find out. Whistling, Jack strode out of his office and down the hallway to the elevators. FountainTech's lab—where they tested their designs before installing them for clients—operated in the basement. As he listened to the elevator music, he chuckled. When he'd first heard that

FountainTech was located in Fargo, he almost lost his coffee. Texas, or maybe Southern California, but Fargo?

After doing a little more research, he'd learned that quite a few high-tech companies made their home in Fargo. The elevator slowed and stopped. After the door slid open, he stepped onto the basement floor. In a small, empty foyer, double doors stared at him. He punched in his PIN and heard the locking mechanism release.

Jack walked slowly down the dimly lit hallway to the room where the technicians did most of their work. His people created the original designs, but there was much more to building the features. Unfortunately, removing limits from creativity often met with resistance among the technical crowd. But that was part of his job—smoothing things over between the creators and the technicians. Since he was working on his own design—a new water pump for which he would apply for a patent—he could better understand the technical mind's frustration with the creators and planners.

When he neared the lab where he hoped to find the fountain still intact, he heard music playing softly down the hall. He hesitated. Someone else was here.

No matter, he decided, and continued on his way. Possibly he could get some questions answered if one of the technicians had stayed late. Peering through the small window of the door, he saw darkness set off by minimal light. He stepped inside, allowing the door to slip shut quietly behind him; then he crept around computers and a small stadium-like structure to see a stunning water feature—or fountain—choreographed to the theme song of *Out of Africa*. The real thing would work on a much larger scale, of course, but multiple fountains sprang to life from pumps, similar to synchronized swimmers.

Once his eyes adjusted to the dark, he noticed someone standing at the far end of the water theater. Rayne.

Jack's first thought was to walk over to her.

But then. . .he couldn't move. He watched her stare as though she were mesmerized by the fountain's performance. The water danced for her alone.

# Chapter 5

Rayne stood in the darkened room, watching the fountain shoot up in synchronized waves—forward, to the right, then to the left. Nozzles on each side sent sprays darting in between the streams as though weaving fluid—all in perfect time to the music chosen by the client.

As she allowed herself to be drawn into the splendor, the moment, peace surrounded her. She let go of her troubles. If she were given freedom to create such a thing of beauty every day of her life, what did she care if friends and family back home couldn't understand? Her spirits lifted higher and higher until she fancied herself floating on waves of joy.

The fountain she'd designed would be twenty times the size of this one, once installed at the front of the client's financial headquarters. And despite its striking beauty, she doubted that people dashing to and fro would take time to stop and watch the water's performance.

Rayne closed her eyes and turned her face toward an imaginary sun, soaking in the spray that misted her skin. She drew in a deep breath, the scent of water calming her.

Suddenly, she sensed someone next to her. Alarm sent chills up her arms, and her heart jumped into her throat. She opened her eyes.

Jack.

A soft smile on his lips, he was staring at her with that deep, introspective look. What was he thinking?

The momentary peace she'd savored slipped away.

His smile coiled into a frown. "I didn't mean to disturb you."

*You didn't?* She fought the rising frustration that even here—in her place of peace and joy—the man who'd stolen from her had invaded her world. "No, it's all right." What else could she say to her new boss? It wasn't his fault. He hadn't intentionally stolen the promotion. Giving the position to Jack had been Harold's decision.

In coming here to watch the fountain, Rayne had attempted to silence the questions. Had she allowed this promotion to be taken? Was there something she could have or should have done differently?

"Please." He touched her arm gently, sending a jolt through her, and gestured to the fountain. "Can we watch together?"

*No.* "Of course."

With Jack standing at her side, Rayne struggled to return to the serenity she'd achieved moments before. Then, slowly, she relaxed. Was there nothing the soothing effect of water couldn't do for her?

In that way, she supposed, the water's comfort reminded her of the Holy Spirit. *"Is there anything too hard for Me?"* the gentle voice seemed to whisper in her heart.

*Am I supposed to be here?* She waited for an answer to her heart's question. Silence.

Unsurprised, Rayne sighed and sneaked a glimpse at Jack. His attention was focused on the fountain now rather than her, and with a relaxed expression, he looked much younger. Boyish even. The fountain apparently had the same effect on him. Somehow this reaction they shared gave Rayne a sense that everything would be all right. Maybe the Lord had answered her after all—in His own way.

Or was she simply too self-absorbed, listening to only the answers she wanted to hear, ignoring the voices of those who'd provided for and raised her? God had given her the parents she had, and they considered her a "flighty child," unwilling to settle down to life on the farm.

It wasn't inside Rayne to rebel as much as to simply follow the dream propelled by her gift.

Jack touched her hand, tugging her from her thoughts. "This is even more impressive than I imagined."

Did he know the part she'd played in its creation? She allowed a smile. "Isn't it?" *And thank you.*

"That is, up close and personal." He stared at her, his eyes brooding.

Was he still referring to the fountain? Jack didn't seem to be the sort of man to get tangled up in sexual harassment.

A knot swelled at the back of her throat. She reminded herself that handsome men did nothing for her. But there was something about Jack. He was. . .like her.

They had a connection, something in common. Rayne shook the thoughts away before they planted seeds. The music, the fountain, and the dim lighting had all worked to bring her emotions to the surface.

"Well, I need to get home." She headed over to the controls to begin switching them off. "The plumbing in this room was quite a feat, as you can imagine."

Jack flipped a switch, flooding the large room with light. Thankfully, the bright lighting changed the unbidden romantic atmosphere.

*◦❧*

Jack squinted at the lights and glanced around the large watertight room. Must have cost some bucks. He'd definitely want to explore, but later. Rayne pulled a lever, and the fountain pumps slowly lost momentum, the water spurting until it stopped.

Her shirt was crisp and white, reminding him of their collision earlier in the day. "I see you had an opportunity to change your shirt." He winced and pushed a hand over his idiotic mouth. *Great conversation, man.*

"I told you I planned to go home and change at lunch," she said with a quick glance and partial grin while she focused on shutting off the rest of the fountain.

"According to your file, you were the chief designer of this water feature. It's amazing."

Though her mouth remained neutral, the smile behind her eyes told him she was pleased at his compliment. "We work as a team around here. I can't take all the credit."

"You're right. But although teamwork is important, there has to be a creative lead. You're it."

When she didn't respond but instead turned her attention to clicking keys on the computer, shutting down the driving software, he chuckled and looked down at the floor, feeling heat in his neck. He wanted to give credit where credit was due, encourage an employee who needed it, but this felt more like. . . *No!*

He was *not* flirting. Jack studied her. Rayne Flemming wasn't a striking beauty. Her nose was too rounded and her cheeks were a little pudgy. Her hair was a drab brown, and she wore it simple and shoulder length, rather than styled in the latest fashion—things he never would have noticed except that he had once been engaged to the queen of fashion.

To Kiera, there was nothing more important than the newest hairstyle or the latest fashion trend. All her energy had been put into her appearance, leaving nothing on the inside. Like an empty box that was beautifully wrapped, once the package was opened you were disappointed. The gift had been a facade. It wasn't real.

Then there was Rayne. She had that farm girl natural look. There was something about her, though, in her eyes that whispered to a place deep inside him, stirring him. Whatever "it" was might as well have been spoken in Ukrainian for all he understood about why it touched him so. But he suspected it had everything to do with what was on the inside of her—something real, something of value.

A treasure beyond price.

*Enough!*

Before he realized it, Rayne was striding past him. "Are you leaving or staying?"

He stared, lost in thought.

"Do you want me to flip the light off now, or are you staying?"

Right. Ukrainian. Finally, he snapped out of it and understood her question. "I'm leaving, too. Uh, wait. No, I'm staying." He scratched his head.

Rayne laughed softly then left his sight. From where he remained, he heard the door swoosh open, then shut, signaling her departure. He exhaled slowly.

There were at least six more members of the design team whose files he had yet to preview. He had a feeling, though, that none of them were in the same league with Rayne Flemming. And the more he thought about it, the more he worried that he wasn't in her league either. She would definitely be one to challenge and sharpen him.

As he strolled around the room and examined the pumping mechanisms and nozzles, comparing them to the design he'd been developing on his own in the evenings, he couldn't shut down the niggling. Could he stay focused on the task and succeed at making his dreams for FountainTech and his life come true while working with Rayne?

Why did she distract him so?

# Chapter 6

That evening Rayne trudged up the steps of her second-floor apartment. For the weeks before the holidays, after Harold had mentioned a promotion to her, Rayne had driven around different neighborhoods, considering what sort of house she might like to buy, eventually. Although first, she just planned to move into a larger apartment with a garage for her car.

But a house did not a home make, or at least that's what her mother always told her. She unlocked the door to her apartment and kicked it shut behind her, then turned on the lights. Looking around her lonely apartment, she agreed that her mother had a point. Shedding her coat, she tugged her cell from the pocket.

Her mother had called earlier in the day, but Rayne hadn't recovered from the blow of not getting the promotion and wasn't in the right frame of mind to return the call. Though her mood hadn't improved, Rayne nevertheless called her mother, knowing she'd have to explain if she didn't. The phone rang several times. As she waited for her mother to answer, she thought of the tinny sound the old rotary-dial phone made when she would call someone from her parents' phone.

"Hello?" her mother answered.

"Mom, hi. Sorry, I didn't have the chance to call you back earlier." Rayne forced enthusiasm into her voice. Maybe the action would bring her heart around.

"You had a busy day, then. That's all I wanted to know. How was your first day back at work?" Pots and pans clanked in the background. Rayne pictured the phone cord stretching all over the kitchen as her mother worked and talked on the phone.

Closing her eyes, Rayne could imagine herself at home. "What are you making?"

"Pork roast. Mashed potatoes, that corn I canned last summer."

Rayne drew in a breath of stale air and tried to imagine the aroma of a home-cooked meal. "Sounds good."

"You could enjoy this if you were here."

*Mom, please don't. Not now.* "The first day back at work after a break is always a hard one. I'm tired. I need to go."

"Hold on."

Rayne could detect the faint sound of water boiling as a lid was lifted.

"I've got to pour the water off the potatoes now. Before you go, I wanted to give you some news."

"What's that?" Rayne opened her refrigerator. Was there anything edible inside?

"Turns out that Paul has some business in Fargo this week."

"Hmm." A tub of burnt orange Tupperware stared back at her. Mom had sent fried chicken with Rayne. She'd forgotten.

"He might stop by to see you."

Rayne pursed her lips, relieved her mother couldn't see, though she wasn't sure why it mattered. "Okay, thanks for telling me." Grabbing the chicken and a Coke, she shut the door with her elbow. "I'll call you this weekend."

"I love you."

"I love you, too."

Before she could take a bite of a drumstick, someone knocked on her door. With a look through the peephole, relief swept over her. She imagined Paul standing outside her door. She opened it with a smile. "Hey Theresa, come in."

Her petite brunette neighbor stepped inside and shut the door, tugging off her red mittens and navy wool coat. "It's cold out there."

"Welcome to North Dakota." Rayne took a bite of her chicken.

Theresa rubbed her hands together. "I wish these apartments had fireplaces."

"You can get one."

"Yeah, for more money." Theresa smiled and sat on the edge of the sofa.

"Well, I do have this." Rayne turned on the television and the DVD player. The cozy image of a fire roaring in a fireplace filled the screen.

Theresa laughed. "Gotta love technology." She turned her attention to Rayne. "So, any news yet?"

Rayne washed down the chicken with her Coke. She shook her head, knowing what Theresa was asking. The girl next door was the only person she'd shared her hopes with.

"They brought in someone outside of the company for that position."

"Oh Rayne. I'm so sorry."

"I think I'm going to live. Want some fried chicken?"

Theresa nodded. "Sounds good."

After offering Theresa the Tupperware filled with chicken, Rayne took another bite of her drumstick, savoring her mother's cooking—something she definitely missed here. Together she and Theresa ate dinner while they watched a game show. But Rayne couldn't push Jack's face from her mind. He'd seemed to touch a chord somewhere inside her.

She didn't dare harbor an emotional connection with her boss. What was the matter with her?

*✲*

Jack shuffled through Simon's conceptual drawings as the guy explained his ideas about the structure and sculpture of water. It had taken Jack more time than he'd expected to meet with his team members individually, getting to know them like he planned, and he hadn't finished yet. Interruptions, phone calls, and meetings made each workday speed by before he could accomplish his goals.

Now, two weeks later, he was finally concluding one of the last of the private conversations. Understanding each person's gifts, goals, and dreams would go a long way in helping him mold his team together. He'd dug deep into their lives, into their creative sides, and after assessing their strengths and weaknesses, he tried to fuel their imaginations. But he could feel the effort draining him.

"What do you think?" Simon asked.

"Now all we have to do is put our brilliant heads together on this next project."

"I mean, what do you really think about my ideas?" Simon gave him a pointed stare.

Meeting the look, Jack smiled inside, recognizing some of himself in Simon. "I think these are excellent."

"But where do I fit in to our team as a whole?"

"What are you asking me?" Simon was fishing. Might as well get to the point.

"I want to be creative lead."

"Ah." Jack leaned back, contemplating. "Let me give it some thought."

Simon frowned and sat forward in his seat. "Look, my stuff is better than Rayne's. Just give me a chance."

Jack hated hearing the pain and desperation in Simon's voice. The guy had a lot to learn. Never appear desperate. Maybe someday he'd give him that tip.

"Look, Simon, everyone's gifts are different. One gift is as important as another's." *And some people's gifts are inspiring beyond words.* "That's why I'm here, so I can fit the talents together—like pieces of a puzzle—to create a beautiful picture, or in this case, fountain."

Simon blew out a breath. "Okay. If you say so."

Jack stood to escort Simon to the door, needing a cup of coffee. He squeezed Simon's shoulder. "Your day will come; don't worry." He winked.

Simon nodded, disappointment on his face as he left Jack's office. Rayne stood in the hall and greeted Simon when he passed. Jack wondered how she would react if she knew Simon had just tried to outmaneuver her. The moves were only good when there was talent to back them up.

Rayne leaned against the wall, waiting. "Are you ready? Or should I come back later?"

He hated that his throat grew taut when she was near. "Have a seat while I grab another cup of coffee. Do you want one?"

"No thank you. I'm good." Entering his office, she strolled past him, leaving a light floral scent in her wake. The room tilted, if only a smidge. She would sink him if he let her.

As he moved down the hall to the kitchen, he considered all the people he'd met with this morning, desperately wishing that someone else could be lead creator, but then again, could he do that to Rayne after already telling her she had the position?

After filling his cup, he headed back to his office. He'd struggled to sleep the last couple of weeks, his mind warning him to steer clear of her. In this morning's meetings, he'd tried hard to inspire the artists he'd met with, pouring his heart and soul into them, but in doing so, he was afraid he left himself open and vulnerable—not a good place to be when Rayne Flemming stepped into his office. At the very least, he should have met with her first, when he was fresh and on top of his game.

That night at the fountain, she'd revived something in him—something he wanted left untouched and undisturbed. And she'd done it on the very first day. In the doorway of his office he paused, shoving a hand through his hair. Fortunately, Barb, whom he'd interviewed earlier in the morning, stood next to Rayne in his office, chatting. Unintentionally, she'd given him a moment to compose himself.

Once Barb spotted him, she smiled brightly and excused herself.

After shutting his door, Jack glided around his desk, set down the mug, and sank into his chair. "Now, where were we?"

"I'm not sure. You've seen my sketches already. Barb said you looked at her designs, asked about her goals for the company."

Jack detected a hint of guarded resistance in Rayne's voice. Probably a good thing, but then, it could impede their creative development. He leaned back, considering her words. "You're right. I have seen your sketches, and you've shared what inspires you. I've already told you that you're creative lead. But you need to understand that others are trying to position themselves."

"Position themselves?"

"When you're the best at something, people are jealous." Even Jack was jealous of her gift. "They want to knock you down, if possible, and take your place." Jack hoped his comments didn't make her think of him taking the position she'd wanted. He needed her to focus on creating the best fountain yet.

Unfortunately, he wasn't sure he could do the same when he was near Rayne.

Rayne's lips parted as she quietly inhaled.

"Simple office politics, Rayne. Don't be surprised at what people will do."

She nodded. "Is there anything else?"

"Yes. Since you're creative lead, you and I will be working closely together. I'll spend more time with you than with the others. At some point, we'll travel to the project site. Do you have a problem with that?" Some part of him hoped she would say she did, in fact, have a problem with it.

Rayne swallowed. "Of course not."

Had she hesitated, or had he imagined it? "Good. Now I need you to dig deep and pull yourself out of this hole."

Eyes wide, her brows knitted. "Excuse me? I don't understand."

"You know what I'm talking about. You wanted this management position. But Harold hired me. You can't lose your creative edge because you didn't make it this time. There will always be other opportunities." Jack winced inside. He was roughing her up a bit. But she needed a good kick. The Rayne he'd collided with on his very first day at work had been enthusiastic and vibrant. That was the day she thought she would be receiving her promotion. He'd not seen that Rayne since he'd become her boss. He knew that the loss of the promotion bothered her. And how could it not? Nor did he blame her. But he had a job to do, part of which was getting the very best out of the vast talent in this group.

He leaned forward against his desk and peered into her stricken gaze. "This company needs you at your best." Then—he couldn't help himself— softer, "*I* need you at your best."

Rayne appeared to contemplate his words and drew her shoulders back. Something behind her eyes shifted. "You're right. I appreciate your honesty, Jack."

*Good girl.* Jack sat back and smiled, until he realized he liked the sound of his name on her lips.

# Chapter 7

A week after her meeting with Jack, Rayne leaned back in her chair and enjoyed the energy in the conference room filled with her creative design team colleagues. Everyone lounged in their chairs, relaxed, as they discussed the conceptual designs for their new project—a financial group headquartered in Dallas.

Jack sat at the head of the table, grinning as he flipped his pencil around. He was undeniably in his element managing this team. Rayne's gaze brushed over his crisp business shirt. Broad shoulders accentuated his lean physique. Warmth simmered against the collar of Rayne's blouse, and she quickly doused the wayward thought.

She could tell that everyone had accepted him. The women definitely loved him, especially Barb, who never missed an opportunity to flirt with him, though Rayne doubted it was intentional on Barb's part. Her friend simply didn't realize how she came across.

Rayne hoped.

At that moment, Barb spoke up. "You mentioned your plan for us to be more personally involved with the clients. That some of us would travel to the site. Will you be going as well?" Barb's eyes twinkled.

Oh brother.

Jack responded with a smile and the hint of something behind his eyes that Rayne couldn't read. "Initially."

More questions erupted about travel arrangements. Everyone seemed to be getting ahead of themselves, focusing on the benefits their new manager brought with him, rather than the purpose of the meeting—to brainstorm. She was interested to see how he would refocus their attention.

One question nagged her all morning during the meeting. How would they have felt toward her if she'd been named their manager? Jack's words about jealousy came to mind. Rayne fought to keep from frowning. He'd encouraged her to move past her regret at losing the promotion. Harold had probably made the right decision by bringing in someone outside of the company. But it certainly gave a person doubts about working her way up within this organization. She might have to go elsewhere in order to move up.

"All right, people. We've spent the morning going over this company and the image we want to portray. Let's not get off track with talk about travel." Jack stood and opened the door. Boxes of pizza floated into the room, the delivery guy hidden behind them. Jack lifted one of the stacks to help. "Or talk about pizza."

His comment elicited laughter.

"Consider this a working lunch. I want to hear your ideas. Let's get them on the table this afternoon without missing a beat."

Barb joined Jack in opening the pizza boxes then spreading them over the credenza behind the conference table, as well as the table itself. The receptionist entered, holding stacks of paper cups and plates.

Gail smiled at the delivery guy then addressed the design team. "Jack had me pick a variety, so I ordered pepperoni, supreme, cheese, Hawaiian, all meat, and vegetarian." She tugged large bottles of soda from a paper sack and set them on the table as well. "Now, if you don't mind, I'll just have a slice."

More chuckles resounded in the room as everyone grabbed paper plates or drinks and selected their slices of pizza.

"All this brain work burns a lot of calories," Simon said around a mouthful of Hawaiian pizza. "I'll have to eat twice as much now."

Rayne sat in her chair, watching. She'd wait until everyone got what they wanted then get her food. On the farm, when the men came in from the fields, they filled their plates first because they worked so hard during harvest and planting; then she and her mother ate what was left. For some reason, today's working lunch reminded her of those times. The habit of waiting had been instilled in her from an early age. She sighed.

Jack approached, carrying two plates filled with pizza. "What'll it be, Rayne? I think I've got one slice of every kind of pizza here."

He made her feel all warm inside. She smiled up at him. "I'll have cheese."

Jack slid into the chair next to her, ignoring the fact that someone else had been sitting there. "Working lunches can be like a shark feeding frenzy. If you don't jump into the fight, you might be left with nothing."

Rayne laughed. Should she share the reason she'd waited? Instead of replying, she took a bite of her pizza. It was hot, burning the top of her mouth, and she blew out a long breath, wishing she'd gotten some water. Jack hopped up and poured soda into a cup then handed it to her.

She took a quick drink. "Thank you." He was being far too attentive. From her peripheral vision, she could see Barb watching. Did Barb have designs on Jack?

While several conversations about the Dallas firm and fountain ideas buzzed around the room, Jack leaned toward Rayne and spoke softly. "You're up first after lunch. That's why I wanted you to eat now."

Rayne stared. "I'm up with what?"

"I want your first impressions, your ideas for the designs. Remember, Rayne, you're lead designer. I can give you the title, but it means nothing if you don't demonstrate your abilities. We need you to jumpstart the inspiration for the project."

Her nerves puddled at her feet. What were her artistic impressions about the project? Her thoughts had been focused on Jack as a manager.

When she didn't reply, Jack spoke again. "I have complete confidence in you."

How did she tell him that this wasn't how she worked? She couldn't think up designs in the middle of a crowded room. Ideas came to her when she was alone in her office, in the quiet of night, or on the farm. . . .

Rayne took another bite. Over time she'd learned to be creative on a consistent basis in order to do her job, not just when the muse decided to visit. Could she learn to become artistic and imaginative while others watched?

Rayne sighed. Jack had given her an opportunity. She swallowed hard. She wouldn't blow it.

Gail appeared in the conference room again, this time holding a huge bouquet of roses. The room erupted.

"Who's the lucky girl?"

"Someone has an admirer."

The receptionist walked along the length of the table and came to stand in front of Rayne. Rayne glanced next to her and across the table. Who could they be for? But no women were sitting near Rayne at the moment.

Leaning forward, Gail carefully placed the roses in front of Rayne.

She gasped. "These can't be for me. There has to be a mistake." She stood, both embarrassed and surprised.

The room grew increasingly hot, and she fought her desire to look at Jack's expression. For a fleeting moment, she'd imagined him sending her roses.

Absurd!

"Well, girl, open the card." Gail took the liberty of snagging the small envelope from the bouquet. She handed it to Rayne.

Rayne glanced around the room. Everyone stared at her, except, well, Jack. He appeared engrossed with something on his laptop.

"I really. . .this is embarrassing. I'll open it in my office." Gripping the small card, Rayne snatched up the roses and rushed them out of the conference room. Once in her office, she slammed the door behind her.

"Oh Paul, these had better not be from you." Paul had invited her to lunch a couple of weeks ago while in town, but she'd had too much work and turned him down.

She struggled to rip the small card open. The harder she tried, the less success she had. Finally, she cut it in half with scissors just as Barb entered her office.

"What are you doing? You'll destroy the card!"

Rayne pieced together the two halves of the card.

*Enjoyed seeing you over the holidays. Can I take you to lunch while I'm in town?*

*Paul*

Rayne blew out a frustrated breath, just short of growling. "Why did you send these?"

"Why did who send them?" Barb asked. "Tell me, Rayne."

Shrugging, Rayne let the card slip from her hand into the wastebasket. "An old friend and would-be suitor back home."

Barb gasped and rifled through the garbage, pulling out the card pieces. "I can't believe you would be so cold. This guy must really be into you. Is he that bad?"

Rayne huffed again and sank to her chair. "No, he's a nice guy. Good-looking, too." She looked up at Barb. "You'd like him."

"I don't understand. What's the problem?"

*He's not Jack.* Rayne felt her eyes grow wide, but at least the errant thought hadn't been spoken aloud. What had gotten into her? "I'm embarrassed that he sent these to me at work. And I just hope he's not harboring hope for something between us."

Apparently, he wasn't one to give up.

Still, she was touched by his gesture, if only slightly.

❧

Jack stood outside Rayne's door, his hand poised to knock. He could hear the women talking inside. Footfalls resounded in the hallway. It would look like he was eavesdropping, but that wasn't his intention.

He didn't want to throw the door open like Harold, asserting himself, especially in this situation. Rayne had just received flowers; he should give her a moment. But he didn't want to lose the momentum of this morning by her disappearance.

He knocked softly on the door.

Barb snatched it open, her face spreading into a giant smile. "Oh, hi. Come in."

Her tone was light and flirtatious. Annoying.

Rayne's hands covered her face. She slowly let them drop in her lap.

Jack's throat grew tight. This was a good thing, really. She had an admirer, a boyfriend. Jack wouldn't have to be afraid of an emotional connection with her. He should rejoice.

The women stared at him. He should say something. He wanted to ask who the roses were from. But it wasn't his business. Completely inappropriate.

"Rayne, when you're ready. We need you back at the meeting." He grinned. "That is, if you can come down from cloud nine for a bit."

Rayne's lips flatlined. She shook her head. "It's not like that."

Jack threw up his hands. "It's not my concern."

He backed from the office, looking into Rayne's eyes. Though he shouldn't attempt to read her reaction to his comment, there it was.

*Disappointment.*

As he made his way to the conference room where the others finished up

284

their lunch, Jack thought about what he'd seen in her eyes.

He had to be wrong, which meant he was losing his touch, unable to read people anymore. Or maybe he simply wasn't able to read Rayne.

*✐*

Later that afternoon, Jack was relieved to be alone in his office. The rest of the meeting did not go as planned, at least for him. Rayne gave her initial impressions of their newest client, as Jack had requested she do. But the energy present during the morning hours had dissipated.

Flowers. How could a bouquet of roses disrupt his thoughts? He could tell that Rayne had become distracted as well.

Hands jammed in his pockets, he tried to peer through the glass, but it had grown too dark outside, and all he could see was his own frayed reflection. He kicked over the wastebasket.

Rayne's familiar laughter in the hallway penetrated his door. Who had given her the roses? Why should he care?

He scraped the paper back into the wastebasket and set it right, then blew out a frustrated breath. Opening his door, he peered down the hall. Rayne leaned against the wall outside her office, chatting with Heidi, one of the techies, if he remembered correctly.

He would have stepped back into his office, but Heidi spotted him.

"Hi, Jack. Are we making too much noise?" she asked with a smile.

"No, not at all. Just wondered who was working late, that's all." Jack meandered toward the women.

Rayne looked away from him.

Jack felt a wry grin slip into his lips. How was it that others in the company offered him warm smiles, but Rayne always seemed detached when he was around? Moments before, he'd heard her laughter. It was nice.

But he was done with love and relationships, so her reaction to him shouldn't bother him in the least. He didn't care about the roses either. Jack was back, all about the job.

Heidi cleared her throat. "I was just about to leave. Rayne is going ice-skating with me. Would you like to go?"

Rayne lifted her eyes to Jack. "Heidi's going with her church group. It's their couple's night. So unless you have a significant other, you might feel uncomfortable."

She studied him, a question in her gaze.

Jack's throat constricted again. Rayne was probably going with her secret admirer.

Heidi squeezed Rayne's arm. "It really makes no difference. Sure, we're getting together, but anyone can come. Rayne's coming, and she's single. How about it, Jack?"

Jack grinned. "I've never been ice-skating." He scratched his chin.

Heidi smiled. "Well, maybe it's time to change that."

# Chapter 8

Rayne skated to the side of the outdoor rink—part of the new park in Fargo—and grabbed the wall, feeling winded. When she was younger, ice-skating had been a favorite pastime. That and snowmobiling.

Heidi skated over to her and put her hand on the rail. "There's a good crowd here tonight."

"Thank goodness. It's easier to skate in a crowd—nobody pays attention to the clumsy skater."

Heidi laughed. "You mean like Jack?" She gestured with her head.

On the other side of the rink, Jack tumbled on the ice.

Heidi laughed. "Poor guy."

"Why on earth did you invite him?"

"Oh come on. I was trying to be friendly. You might try it sometime."

Rayne yanked her gaze from Jack to give Heidi a questioning look.

She lifted her mouth in a huge grin. "You know I'm only kidding. But why don't you go over and give the guy a hand?"

"I still can't figure out why he came." Rayne could hardly stand to watch him struggle. "He's like a little kid out there."

"Adorable."

Rayne wouldn't step up to the bait. "He's not allowed to be adorable. He's my boss."

"So what? Look at Carissa and John. They met at work."

Rayne wasn't going to fall for what appeared to be another matchmaking scheme. Heidi was happily married and had a child. Married women with children wanted everyone else to know what they were missing. Heidi had made an attempt at matchmaking for Rayne a few months ago.

It didn't work then. *And it won't work now.*

Heidi's husband, Jim, skated up and into her. She squealed and they laughed, pushing away from the wall together. "See you later, Rayne."

As Rayne shoved off as well, deciding this would be her last go-around, she discovered she was next to Jack. "You're doing much better," she said.

He cautiously took his eyes from the ice to glance at her. "You think?"

She couldn't help but smile. Heidi was right. He was adorable. And Barb was right; he was beautiful. "I think."

"You should see me on the racquetball court. I'm much better."

"Racquetball, huh? I don't think I've ever played that."

Jack opened his mouth; then. . .he was on his back.

Rayne stopped. "Ow! That had to hurt."

Wincing, he sat on the ice and looked up at her. "I have no idea why I even came."

Rayne pressed her lips together to keep from laughing. She was actually beginning to feel sorry for the guy. "Here, let me help you up." She offered her gloved hand.

He arched his left brow. "Are you sure about that?"

Rayne braced her legs and gripped the ice with her skates. "Of course."

He thrust his hand into hers and tugged.

Rayne's skates slipped as the wall seemed to fly past. Pain met her backside. She looked over at Jack. He smiled.

She erupted in laughter, and then Jack joined her. She smacked him on the arm. "You did that on purpose."

"You think?"

Warmth spread through her despite the cold. "I think."

"I needed your help. I didn't think I could get up one more time."

Skates scraped the ice. Heidi and Jim stood over them. "You two would look cozier if you were sitting in front of a fire."

Rayne glared at Heidi. "Help me up, would you?"

"And end up on the ice with you? No thanks." Heidi and Jim skated away, holding hands.

"Of all the—"

Jack scrambled to his feet, and before Rayne could do the same, he gripped her arms and lifted her up with hardly any effort. The man was strong. He brushed the snow off her shoulders.

A few snowflakes stuck in his dark hair. Rayne wanted to brush them off, as he'd done for her, but she feared she'd end up running her fingers through. Of course, to get the full effect, she'd have to remove her gloves. Her eyes widened. What was she thinking?

Jack stared at her expectantly; then with a half grin, he said, "I think I'm done. Good night, Rayne."

"Good night," she said. As she watched him skate over to the exit door, Rayne didn't want him to leave. Not yet.

She'd just welcomed the fact that he was here. Skating around the rink, she stepped off the ice and saw Jack enter a warming hut. She followed him and, once inside, spotted him tugging off his skates.

"Hi there," she said.

He pulled off a skate and peered up at her.

"Mind if I join you?" she asked.

After tugging off his other skate, he sat tall. "Not at all. I'm about to leave though."

"Why did you come to skate when you don't know how? It must have been torture." *What are you doing, girl?*

"You mean embarrassing." He hung his head then looked up at her.

He had the most amazing eyes. "True." She giggled.

"I don't know. I guess I wanted to get to know a few people. I'm new to Fargo, you know?"

"Heidi attends a great church. You should try it sometime. You'll get to know people there. Make friends."

"Is that where you attend?"

Rayne stared at him. Why did he want to know?

"She's invited me, and I've visited a few times, but I'm just so accustomed to the church I grew up in, it's tough finding someplace new, fitting in."

Jack studied Rayne. She shivered. For a moment, she wished he would tug her to him, warming her.

"Listen, I noticed an ice sculpture on display in the park. Thought I'd go check it out. Want to come with me?" he asked.

Two men came into the warming hut, followed by several kids. "It's getting crowded in here. Sounds like a good idea. I have to get my shoes first."

After putting her shoes on and returning her skates, Rayne found Jack waiting for her next to the ice rink. "There you are," she said.

He pointed to the other side of the rink. "The sculpture is over there."

Rayne tugged her coat tighter. "The snow is beginning to fall heavier now."

As they trudged side by side through the snow, couples and families walked nearby, many heading to their cars, ending their fun evening. For some reason, Rayne felt self-conscious that so many held hands. She almost felt as though she and Jack should hold hands if they wanted to fit in. But how many others were walking in the park with their boss?

Rayne stopped. Heidi and Jim stood next to their car in a romantic hug. Then Heidi tilted her head up, and Jim met her with a kiss.

Shaking off the scene, Rayne continued to walk. She glanced over at Jack. He was watching her. "What's bothering you?"

"Nothing. I'm fine." What could she say? *You're my boss, and I can't hold your hand*?

"Here it is." Jack put his gloved hands under his arms, shivering.

The ice sculpture appeared to be an abstract of a flock of geese.

Rayne sent him a sympathetic smile. "You look so miserable."

"I'm from Florida. But I ended up in Southern Cal when I went to work for Disney. I prefer it hot—what do you expect?"

Rayne nodded her head in an exaggerated manner. "Right."

Jack laughed. "Tell me what you see."

"What? In this sculpture?"

"Yes."

"I think you've got me wrong. I only do fluid water sculptures."

Jack threw his head back and laughed. Rayne thought it was the most delightful thing she'd ever heard.

Rayne was. . .Jack shook his head. There was just something about her. "So, she has a sense of humor, after all."

She grinned—a beautiful grin—and shook her head. "Listen, it's been a long day. I'm tired and cold to the bone. Do I really have to turn on the creativity right now?"

"You don't have to. This isn't work."

Rayne circled the sculpture. "I'm standing next to a water sculpture, ice sculpture, rather, with my boss who wants to know my impression. How is that not work?"

Jack wanted to run his hand down the sculpture, but the sign warned people from touching it. How to answer her question. . . ? He rubbed his gloved fingers over his face. His lips must be blue by now.

"I don't know, Rayne. It doesn't feel like work to me." From across the circle, he stared at her, trying to read her expression. *Maybe because you fascinate me.*

"I'm sorry if I didn't seem focused enough this afternoon during the brainstorming meeting."

"Well, you did just receive a bouquet of roses. I'm sure any woman would be starry-eyed after that. What can a boss expect?" Ugh. Had he actually brought up the roses? He thought he'd convinced himself he didn't care who had sent them.

Rayne reached toward the ice sculpture as if she planned to touch it, then drew back. "The flowers. . .it's not like that. I mean, the guy who sent the roses is someone from back home who can't let go."

At her news, pressure seemed to ease from Jack's chest. Had he really held on to hope that the flowers had meant nothing to her?

He shouldn't even care. His stomach soured when thoughts of his previous broken engagement deposited a snowdrift of unwanted memories in his mind. "Go easy on the guy, okay? I know what it feels like to be hurt in love." Jack shivered. Why had he revealed that to her?

He chuckled, embarrassed. When he glanced up at Rayne again, a soft smile caressed her lips. Maybe she was just too easy to talk to and he'd allowed himself to get too comfortable with her.

"I think the cold is getting to you." Rayne trotted around the sculpture and grabbed Jack's arm. "Come on."

"What are you doing? Where are we going?"

"You like it hot?" She giggled. "Then there's nothing better than hot chocolate on a cold night like this."

Jack snapped out of it. She was right—the cold had numbed his brain. "You should probably get home before the roads get too messy."

"Oh, really? Remember, I have lived in the North my entire life. I know how to drive in this, unlike others who come from the sunny, warm states." Rayne laughed.

Jack grinned, liking that she'd loosened up, cast off that professional veneer for him. It was nice having her not think of him as her boss all the time.

But then, what was he doing?

Concern jabbed him, taunting him. *Are you nuts, man?*

"No, really. You need to get home and warm. Maybe you're not worried about driving in this, but I am."

She slowed and released his arm, turning to face him. Her expression grew sober. Oh how he wished he would have kept his mouth shut.

"You're serious, aren't you?"

"Let me walk you to your car," he said. Rayne acted as if she might resist at first, but she let him hold her gloved hand. In the parking lot, Jack searched the few cars left. "Let me guess."

He glanced at Rayne to see where she was looking, but she stared at the dark sky, smiling. "I'm not going to give you any clues. And you'd better get it right."

"Let's see. Which car would a creative and beautiful woman like Rayne Flemming drive?" Boy, had he dug himself in deep with this one.

Jack tugged Rayne behind him as they walked past cars. A gold Toyota Camry, a black Prius, a red Hyundai Sonata. Jack enjoyed holding her hand and having her near him. He stopped, unwilling to take the test. "I can't. I have no idea."

He turned to see her expression. She smiled a simple, sweet smile; then her lips parted just so, seeming to beg him to kiss them. Her eyes slid shut. At that moment, he almost answered the tug on his heart and pressed his lips against hers.

Her lids fluttered open. "I. . .uh. . .Jack," she whispered his name.

He'd already decided he loved the way she said his name. He leaned in, but wait. . . . *What are you doing, man?*

She backed against the door of a white VW Passat. "This is it, Jack. You found my car."

# *Chapter 9*

Jack shoved the door to his apartment closed behind him and shook his hair over the tiled entryway, dumping snow. He brushed off his shoulders—should have done it outside, but he was too cold to care. He shrugged out of his coat and gloves, thinking he'd need to buy a cap to keep the warmth from seeping out of his head.

Tomorrow he'd be sore, all right, from all the falling. He hurried to the kitchen and turned on the stovetop to warm his hands. Rayne was right—hot chocolate was a great idea.

Part of him wished he would have shared it with her. Thankfully, he'd come to his senses before he'd done something crazy like kiss her. That would have been a quick way out of a job. She'd given him no indication of her interest—at least not in so many words. Feeling the blood flow back in his hands, he poured cocoa mix into a cup of water and stuck it in the microwave.

Then there was the matter of his pact with himself. After what had happened last year, he could never give his heart to someone—the risk was too great.

Too wound up to sleep, he sipped on the hot chocolate while watching a comedy and unpacking a few remaining boxes. Originally he'd planned to leave a few things boxed so that when he finally bought a house, he wouldn't have to repack.

But that side of his life wasn't on his fast-track plan. Might as well get cozy in the apartment for a while. He laughed at a comical scene playing on the TV as he cut open a box and looked inside.

*She* stared at him.

Jack stumbled back. Who had packed that picture of her? He knew he hadn't done it. Jack rubbed his eyes, thinking back to the week he moved. Several of his buddies in San Diego had helped him pack. All of them knew that she was the reason he left the company.

And now it was as though she laughed at him, laughed at his cold misery, and reminded him of why he would never love anyone else. Loving a woman gave her too much power over you.

Jack groused at himself for his melodrama. He tugged the framed photo from the box and considered that he hadn't thought about her much over the last several weeks. No, he'd been thinking about someone else.

The picture was one of Kiera's best. She'd given it to him on his birthday—so sure he'd want to see her every day. Luscious golden hair tumbled over her shoulders. Stunning eyes—made even more striking with mascara and shadow—stared back at him. Perfect lips opened into a sensual smile—just for him.

He closed his eyes, feeling dizzy with anger.

She'd toyed with him. They looked good as a couple, she'd said. But her heart wasn't in it—did she even have a heart?

Jack sank onto the sofa, ignoring the television and the neighbor next door who banged on the wall for him to turn the volume down.

Rayne was the exact opposite of Kiera—Rayne was beautiful where it counted. She was real.

Stumbling from the couch over to the kitchen, he pressed the lever on the garbage can and dropped Kiera's picture into the container, putting her where she belonged.

And as for Rayne? She worked for him. End of story.

He loved what he was doing at FountainTech. Why risk everything again?

He turned his focus to his new invention.

☙

For the next several weeks, Rayne worked with the design team members to translate their designs into the 3-D model on the computer, and from there, once they were satisfied with the results, they entered the creation into the software. Their special software would then control the pumps and nozzles, resulting in a water fountain. Jack told her that the magic all started with her as lead designer, and then continued with her ability to translate all the ideas into something that could be visualized.

She hadn't worked much with Jack at all, which concerned her, considering he'd given her creative lead and made certain she understood they would work closely together. But she'd hardly seen him since the night they'd gone ice-skating.

Rayne stared at the computer screen and then hung her head.

Jack was out of town this week with Barb, visiting the customer site to fine-tune details of the project. As creative lead, Rayne knew she should have gone with him. He hadn't invited her. She sensed he'd built a great divide between them—but perhaps that was her overactive imagination—as if there were, in fact, any reason for him to distance himself from her.

She stood tall and stretched her back, needing some fresh coffee to jolt her out of this melancholy. One of the problems with being an artistic person was the tendency toward extremes. She was either flying high, soaring with the eagles, or her mood was deep in a cave with the bats.

And right now that cave was looming just ahead of her.

Rayne strode down the hall to the kitchen, offering half smiles to coworkers here and there as she passed. Turning the corner that would take her to the kitchen, she bumped into Terry, a man she rarely saw on this floor.

He sloshed coffee all over himself and winced, then glared down at her. "Oh, I'm so sorry. Let me get you a towel."

"No, that's all right. I'll take care of this in the men's room." He trotted off in a huff.

The incident reminded her of the first time she met Jack. Rayne sighed, pouring herself a cup of coffee. They really should have put her office somewhere else to keep her from running into people. She needed to focus when she approached the kitchen.

She laughed to herself, glad she was alone. As she left the kitchen, she decided she missed Barb, and. . .she missed Jack.

Back in her office, she stared out the window, unable to concentrate on the fountain. The snow had finally let up, and the sun beat down on Fargo, though the temperature was still below freezing.

Once Jack returned, he wouldn't be impressed with her anymore.

When he'd chosen Barb to accompany him on the trip, he'd sucked all the creativity out of Rayne. Barb had a thing for Jack. He had to know that, and going on a business trip with her might be dangerous for him, especially with the way Barb flirted with him. That is, if Jack wanted to avoid an office romance, Barb would be hard to resist. She was beautiful—the kind of woman who could easily catch any man's attention. Who was she kidding?

She was jealous of Barb. The woman had a right to like Jack. Who was Rayne to say she didn't?

Rayne plopped in her chair, feeling anything but inspired about this fountain. She was losing her touch.

That night at the ice-skating rink, Rayne had been sure Jack was going to kiss her. She closed her eyes, remembering how she felt, how she longed to feel his arms around her, but they had both snatched themselves from the magic moment. Or could it have all been in her head alone?

That had to be it  Jack had seen that she had feelings for him, knew that's why she had tried to be aloof around him and failed. That's why Jack had appeared reserved around her.

Her emotions and his actions could be a huge detriment to the client. Harold would see that this team wasn't producing as well as it did before Jack came on board.

And that would be all Rayne's fault.

How did one escape romantic tension in the workplace? Maybe this was a sign from God. She couldn't work in this environment.

With Jack.

Her office phone rang.

*Jack!*

Heart pounding, she answered. Gail told Rayne that a Craig Hammerman was on the line. Rayne wasn't familiar with the name, but she took the call anyway, feeling the fool for wishing Jack would call her. She had to nix these fantasies.

"This is Rayne Flemming."

"My name is Craig Hammerman. I'm a headhunter, and I have a company very interested in your talents."

Rayne held her breath, trying to comprehend what she'd just heard. "I'm not interested."

"Miss Flemming. It would be worth your while to hear me out. Get all the facts before you make your decision."

"I. . .I don't know."

"This company is very similar to FountainTech, only working in a different market niche entirely. You would manage a team of designers. I can promise you a better salary than you're making now."

Rayne shook her head. "How did you get my number?"

"You mean, how do I know about you? Let's just say my client is aware of your designs."

"Where is the company located?"

"I can't give you that information just yet. But it's not in North Dakota."

"I'll have to get back to you. Give me your number."

"Miss Flemming, this opportunity is short-lived. There are other designers being considered. Don't think too long."

Rayne wrote down the phone number and said good-bye. She drew in a deep breath then exhaled. Just a few short weeks ago the news that she'd lost the promotion to Jack had almost devastated her. For so long, she'd planned to work her way up and show her family that she was meant for the business world. For so long, she wished she could put aside the hold they held over her—but it wasn't that easy.

To some extent, thanks to Jack, she'd been able to put the loss behind her. In a short period of time, he'd earned her loyalty. Still, didn't she owe it to herself to consider this new opportunity? And she'd already decided Jack's fountain would be better without her, considering her misplaced feelings toward him.

*"When opportunity knocks, and you walk through that door, just remember it comes with a price. Count the cost."* Though she'd left the farm, her father's words of wisdom were never far away.

❧

Jack leaned his head against the seat back, feeling the pressure against his body as the jet took off. He closed his eyes, relieved that this trip would finally end.

Barb sat quietly next to him, flipping through a magazine she'd tugged from the seat back in front of her.

He pinched the bridge of his nose. Rayne should have been the one with him. The client would have been amazed with her perceptiveness and her impressions. Instead, he'd brought a Barbie doll. The woman was talented, too, but it wasn't the same.

And her focus was off. Though she was professional in every way that counted, he could tell that she had romantic notions about him. All he could do was ignore her subtle overtures. The tension brought to light his own emotions where Rayne was concerned.

Was that the reason Rayne had acted standoffish toward him? Had she sensed something from him and consequently felt trapped by her boss? He slid his hand down his face and groaned. Oh, he hoped not.

"What's bothering you, Jack?"

Jack opened his eyes. Barb was still flipping through the magazine. "Oh, I could really use one of those"—she pointed at a massage gizmo—"since I don't have anyone at home to rub my back."

Jack shut his eyes again. Barb was an exotic beauty.

*Like Kiera.*

Any other normal red-blooded man would struggle against the temptation she offered. But Kiera had cured him. Utterly.

Simon would have been a better choice on this trip, but then Jack would have had to listen to him comparing himself to Rayne.

*Rayne...*

"Jack." Someone tugged on his arm.

He opened his eyes and squinted. Where was he? Oh right, the flight back from Dallas to Fargo.

Barb's sensual perfume drew him fully awake.

"Hey there, you're awake now." Barb leaned in close to whisper in his ear. "You said someone's name in your sleep. I promise to keep it just between you and me."

Stunned, he couldn't respond. Had he said Rayne's name? He'd had a dream about her.

He turned his head, despite the danger in Barb's proximity, to read her eyes.

A slight smile quirked the right side of her lovely mouth. She looked pleased with herself.

"Barb," she whispered. "You said my name."

# Chapter 10

O w!" Rayne jerked her hand back from the hot roaster, nearly dropping the pan as she slid it onto the stove. Nudging the oven door shut with her foot, she took one step across the small kitchen to the sink and ran her wrist under cold water, thinking she could just stick it out the window instead.

She laughed at her attempt at humor. She usually spent Friday evenings in a tired daze on the sofa, resting up from the week. Tonight she wished she'd taken Heidi up on her offer to join her at some church event.

Removing the roaster lid, she picked at the meat with a fork to see if it was tender like her mother's.

Tough as leather. Would she ever learn to cook?

She lifted a piece on the fork and blew on it to cool it off, then stuck it in her mouth, prepared to chew the leather, but it was impossible.

Opening the pantry, she grabbed a box of macaroni and cheese. What she needed at the moment was comfort food. Unable to get her mind off her lack of enthusiasm for the fountain she was charged with creating, or the fact that Jack and Barb had been gallivanting around Dallas this week, Rayne had decided to create a home-cooked meal, a reminder of home.

But she'd failed.

As she brought the water to a boil for the macaroni, Rayne decided she was about to fail again. She stared at her cell phone on the counter, dying to call Barb.

Fear stayed her hand. What would Barb say? Would she talk about the client and her experience, or would her conversation be filled with little details about her time with Jack?

Rayne poured the macaroni into the water and watched it boil. A few minutes later her cell rang, just as the water boiled over onto the counter. This wasn't her night to cook.

She flipped open her cell. "This is Rayne."

"Rayne, it's Paul."

"Hi, Paul." Rayne frowned. The day after she'd received the roses, Paul had called to invite her to lunch, but she'd been in a meeting all day again.

"I'm in Fargo this weekend."

"What are you doing in town so often these days?" Rayne wasn't sure she wanted to know but asked before she thought.

"I'd love to tell you all about it. Have breakfast with me?"

Rayne weaved her fingers through her hair. She had no excuse. "Sure. What time?"

"Seven o'clock too early on a Saturday?"

At that, Rayne laughed. Growing up on a farm, she was more than familiar with the fact that things didn't come to a stop for the weekend. "That's fine."

"Great, I'll pick you up at seven."

"Uh, Paul. . .I'll just meet you." Rayne turned the stove off and moved the macaroni aside. It was going to be mushy. She hated mushy macaroni and cheese.

Paul was silent for a moment. "Have any place in mind?"

She'd disappointed him. A sick feeling hit her stomach. "Martha's Waffle House just off Main."

"I'll be there."

"Looking forward to it." Rayne snapped the phone shut and leaned against the counter. She cared for Paul, and, she admitted, there was a small part of her that still found him very attractive. After all, she'd dated him and had come close to marrying him.

She'd never been one to date much in high school or college—only two boyfriends and one other admirer. It was a vicious cycle—liking someone who liked someone else. If the world were perfect, would she be able to return Paul's feelings, loving him with abandon?

In a perfect world, she'd have no feelings for Jack.

*❤*

The next morning, Rayne shoved through the glass doors of Martha's Waffle House and stood in the small foyer, looking around the restaurant for Paul. She'd seen his truck outside.

There. He waved his arm, catching her attention.

She hadn't wanted to meet him this morning, but she didn't seem to have an out. He was a family friend. If nothing else, a neighbor, just taking her to breakfast. Sliding into the booth across from him, she smiled, hating the shy feeling that came over her as though she was his date. She'd spent enough time romantically involved with him that she too easily slipped back into the role.

"I took the liberty of ordering coffee for you." Paul's lips curved into a grin, and he winked. "I know you love your coffee."

"Thanks." Rayne poured some into her cup from the carafe then looked at Paul. He'd always been a considerate man. With his piercing blue eyes and blond Norwegian look, what woman wouldn't fall over herself to go out with him, or. . .marry him?

They ordered breakfast. After the failed attempt at her mother's cooking and the mushy macaroni, Rayne was famished.

"So, what are you doing in Fargo?" she asked.

"I'm selling the farm, Rayne." He studied her.

She sucked in a breath. He'd landed a punch to her stomach. "But. . .why?"

The words fairly croaked from her. She'd had no clue that she could even care so much.

"I want something else for my life. I've been looking for a job here in Fargo."

Confusion flooded Rayne's heart and showed in her expression, she was sure. She welcomed the plate of food—steak and eggs—the waitress placed before her, coupled with a fresh carafe of hot coffee.

Rayne inhaled deeply. "What are you doing, Paul? The farm is who you are."

Paul finished smothering his short stack with butter and syrup. He looked up from his work of art at Rayne, giving her a stare filled with hurt. "Oh, so I'm forever relegated to be a farmer in your eyes?"

Rayne shook her head, chewing her eggs. She swallowed. What was he really trying to say? That he wanted to work in Fargo so that he would be more appealing to her? How could she make him understand?

But maybe he was right. Rayne couldn't see past the farmer in Paul. She took a sip of her coffee and shut her eyes, recalling memories of her time with Paul when they were growing up. An image of him sliding into the mud, unable to stand without slipping once again came to mind.

Rayne grinned. "Do you remember when you were stuck in the mud?"

"And you came to my rescue, only you ended up just as muddy as me?"

While they ate breakfast, Rayne and Paul reminisced about the good times and the bad times they'd had together on neighboring farms. For Rayne it was easier to slip into discussing happy memories, and she sensed the same from Paul. Talking about their past was safer than talking about the future. At times in her life, she considered him her best friend. What had happened? Why had she drifted away?

Why had she wanted more?

The price for pursuing her dream seemed to be leaving behind the people she loved, leaving behind the security of what she knew. Leaving behind so much of herself, of who she was.

Rayne looked from her plate, where her food was quickly disappearing, and into Paul's eyes, feeling herself warmed by his company. She'd forgotten moments like these when she enjoyed being with him. She was glad she came after all.

Paul reached across the table and took her hand, startling her. Her hand was so small in his large, calloused one. Did she feel a spark, or was it simply warm familiarity that she welcomed? Her hand in his seemed to magnify the lonely ache in her heart. From the look in his eyes, she feared they were back to what Paul really wanted to discuss with her.

"Rayne, I've watched you pursue your dream. You seem happy enough. If you can do it, then maybe I need to be bold enough to step away from the farm. You're my inspiration."

She slipped her hand from his. "Oh Paul, I can't say that I'm happy. Right now I'm more confused than anything." With all the stress and pressure at work lately, Rayne longed to be curled in her warm bed at the farmhouse, the smell of bacon and eggs wafting up from the kitchen in the early morning. Though the farming life was marked with long and laborious days, Rayne almost missed it now.

"If I lived here in Fargo, had a job; if I weren't a farmer. . ."

Pain sliced through her. Was he actually considering selling the farm, thinking that it would make a difference? She hoped not—that would be too big a burden for her to carry.

Rayne fell back against the booth, fearing the rest of his question. "But Paul, you *are* a farmer. I can't see you as anything else."

Pain flooded his expression, the creases in his brow and around his mouth making him look much older.

This time Rayne was the one to reach across the table. She placed her hand over his and pressed gently. What Paul did for his livelihood had nothing to do with how she felt. But at the moment, she knew those words would fall cruelly if she said them, crushing him further.

Speaking softly, Rayne said, "I don't think you would be happy doing anything else. That's all I meant."

Finally, they fell to reminiscing again and talked until there was nothing more to say. Paul ushered her out of the restaurant to her car, and she hoped he wouldn't invite her to spend more time with him today. Being with him, all the good memories seemed to surface, making her miserable with the choices she'd made.

He smiled down at her. "Thank you for having breakfast with me today, Rayne. I've missed you."

"I've missed you, too." She smiled, startled by her feelings. Her gut twisted. Though true, she shouldn't have spoken her thoughts.

Before she knew what was happening, Paul leaned down and pressed his lips against hers, lingering. Rayne allowed the kiss, trying to draw something from it. But what—an answer?

When Paul pulled back, he ran the back of his hand down her cheek. "Come home, Rayne."

"Oh Paul. . ." *If only you knew.*

Tears blurred her vision. Rayne's heart was traitorous, betraying him with thoughts of Jack. Betraying Jack with thoughts of Paul.

❧

On Sunday morning, Jack rolled over, flopping his arm across his bed, and groaned. He'd just had a terrible dream in which he'd kissed Barb. A nightmare. With one squinting eye, he peered at the clock on the nightstand. Nine thirty.

What time did Heidi's church start? Jack rubbed his eyes, his face, and his chin then stared at the ceiling. He'd liked the few people he'd met from her church that night he'd joined them at the ice-skating rink. Would Rayne be there?

Jack crawled from bed, yawning, and stumbled to the bathroom where he brushed his teeth in an attempt to remove any remnant of the Barb-kissing dream. Had the woman somehow planted her spores in him? She was like a bad taste in his mouth that he couldn't seem to get out. In fact, he could still smell the scent of her perfume.

Searching his room, he grabbed the clothes he'd thrown over a chair—her perfume still clinging to them because he'd sat next to her on the plane—and threw them into the hamper where they should have gone in the first place.

There was no way—*no way*—he'd said her name while sleeping on the plane. Why would she claim he had?

If anything, he should have said Rayne's name, because he'd thought often of the moment he'd almost kissed her.

Could he actually have said Rayne's name? Not good. The idea that he wasn't in control of any facet of his life, even dreaming, scared him.

Shaking off the thoughts, he made coffee, and while it brewed, he showered and dressed.

Scrambling eggs, he thought about the fountain models he'd seen yesterday. A few days away from the office left him feeling unsure about how the project was progressing. Anxious to see what Rayne had come up with, he'd gone into the office and looked at her computer models of the fountain.

Something was missing from her design. Jack knew it took more than one person to create a water sculpture, but he also knew that Rayne had more to give than she put into the model.

Substandard work wasn't acceptable on Jack's team. Joining FountainTech, he felt like his yacht had finally come in, but right now it was springing a lot of little leaks, one of which was Barb. Why couldn't he take this company where he wanted it go to without people issues?

Jack blew out a breath. As he had told Rayne, there would always be office politics—the human element. He'd been avoiding Rayne because he had to stanch the flow of feelings he had for her, and now he would have to avoid Barb because she apparently liked him. Jack had not prepared for these types of obstacles in his plan for creating the world's best water sculptures. He couldn't very well call Barb on her lack of professionalism, because he had the same problem. At least he was that honest.

Thankfully, his eggs were done. He had twenty minutes to eat and make it to Heidi's church, which started at ten thirty. After finishing his breakfast, he pulled the curtains back and stared out at the snow-laden landscape. Another gray, empty day lay ahead of him.

It reminded him of his life. He chugged the rest of his coffee to warm his insides, but the warmth couldn't penetrate deep enough. At that moment,

Jack recognized that something was missing in his life. He sensed it, just like he'd sensed something amiss in Rayne's design. But what was it?

He tugged on his coat and mentally prepared himself to step into the cold. Then he knew what was missing. . . .

Jack stepped outside into the frigid North Dakota air. The day was gray and cloudy, devoid of light. Just like his soul.

He followed the directions he'd found on the Fargo Community Church website. He couldn't recall the last time he'd been out and about on a Sunday morning. Traffic was minimal, offering a stress-free and peaceful drive. If he wasn't on his way to church, he might enjoy taking in the scenery.

But he was a man on a twofold mission. This morning he was missing two things in his life, though he wasn't completely prepared to admit to either. Feeling as if he had an enormous, dark cavern inside, he recognized that he might need to exercise some spiritual muscle if he wanted to get in shape. After all, he went to the gym and played racquetball to keep himself physically healthy. Any idiot had to know that the same held true for the inside of a person.

He'd been an idiot for too long already.

Jack pressed against the seat back, not certain he was ready for this.

At least he was taking a first step in going to church, right? If he was recalling it correctly, there was a saying that went, "The journey of a thousand miles begins with a single step." He hoped that God could see that he was at least making an effort.

Just outside of Fargo, Jack began scanning the roadside. There. The Fargo Community Church sign seemed to smile at him from the left side of the road. After waiting for a truck to pass, he turned into the parking lot and drove slowly, looking for an empty spot. His palms grew sweaty against the steering wheel, especially when people stared at him as they headed across the parking lot toward the church. They must be curious about the visitor.

Maybe this wasn't such a good idea.

Jack found a parking spot near the exit. Good. He could leave quickly if needed. Swiping his hands down his slacks, he tugged on his gloves for the short jaunt to the church doors. Someone opened one of the double doors for him as he approached, and he rushed through, uttering his thanks through white, cloudy breath.

The gentleman offered him a church bulletin and silently pointed toward the sanctuary. Someone was already speaking to the gathering, so Jack slipped in and, after spotting a vacant place in a pew, crept over to the space. A family with three small children peered at him, the mother smiling as one of her children crawled onto her lap.

A quick scan of the large room told him there were about two hundred people attending. While the man at the pulpit gave the announcements, Jack perused the bulletin, hoping to ignore the inquisitive stares, but he really wanted to look around himself. Was Rayne here?

He should have thought to look for her car.

Guilt slid around his neck, tightening, because he knew that Rayne shouldn't be his reason for going to church. Feeling the heat, Jack realized he'd not removed his coat and attempted to slip out of it without drawing too much attention. While he did, he took the opportunity to gaze around the church, searching.

He caught the back of Heidi's head near the front, he thought. A few other familiar faces from when he'd gone ice-skating were scattered throughout the sanctuary. Recognizing a few of the congregants gave him a measure of peace, and he relaxed against the pew, ready to listen.

Except, where was Rayne?

A lively tune sprang from the band up front; then everyone stood. Jack followed suit, and though he only knew a few of the songs, he did his best to fit in. After what seemed to Jack like an eternity, the worship ended and the gathering took its seats once again.

From the bulletin, Jack learned that Pastor Luke would be preaching today. Jack frowned, remembering that he should have brought a Bible. Fortunately, the church kept a copy of the book in the racks on the pews. He tugged a New American Standard Bible from the back of the pew in front of him and opened it up to 1 Samuel 16.

Jack couldn't seem to wipe the frown from his face. He really missed Rayne, wanted—no, needed—to see her this morning. Could he ignore his disappointment long enough to hear the sermon?

Pastor Luke told the story about how God chose a shepherd boy to rule over Israel while he was yet a small boy. God overlooked his older brothers to choose the youngest and most insignificant of Jesse's gang because God looks at the heart.

The pastor read from 1 Samuel 16:7. " 'But the Lord said to Samuel, "Do not look at his appearance or at the height of his stature, because I have rejected him; for God sees not as man sees, for man looks at the outward appearance, but the Lord looks at the heart." ' "

Jack rubbed his chin, considering the words. What exactly did God see in Jack's heart? He wasn't sure he wanted to know the answer. So far, over the years, ignoring the pain he felt inside had worked for him. That is, until this morning.

As he allowed the words to sink deeper, he thought of Rayne. Again. Whatever attracted him to her, he knew, came from what was inside her. What was in her heart.

The realization made him smile. He was deep in thought when the church service finally ended and he stood, gathering his coat. The couple next to him shook his hand and welcomed him.

"Jack, so good to see you here." Heidi reached across the pew between them to grab his hand. With her other hand, she gripped the smaller fingers of a beautiful little girl with blond curls and Heidi's soft green eyes.

He smiled back at Heidi and the little girl, who he assumed was her daughter. "I'm glad I came," he said, and glanced over Heidi's head, searching the dispersing crowd.

"I'm guessing that you're looking for Rayne." An amused smile played on her lips.

He pinned her with his gaze. "And what makes you say that?"

"Are you denying it?"

Jack laughed. "I guess I can't hide anything from you."

Heidi ran her palm over her daughter's hair, affection in her gaze. "She's not here. Maybe if she knows you're coming, she'll come, too."

"I don't know if that's the right reason for anyone to go to church, is it?" he asked, a frown grazing his lips. Hadn't he come in part to see Rayne?

Heidi sighed. "No, but in Rayne's case, she often drives all the way out to her old church. She has such deep roots there, it's hard for her to let go and find a new church family."

"I see." Jack stuck the Bible into the back of the pew. "It was nice to see you, Heidi."

"You, too, Jack." Heidi's attentions were quickly drawn away by her little girl.

*Sweet.* What would it be like to have a wife and child of his own? If he married Rayne, would their daughter have Rayne's infinitely thoughtful eyes?

A longing gushed through him. Coming to church today hadn't solved anything, but instead seemed to magnify the hole in his life. Now the emptiness had become a gaping abyss.

A sudden thirst gripped Jack, and he headed to the water fountain. He strongly suspected this thirst couldn't be quenched with water.

# Chapter 11

Monday morning, Rayne perused the fountain model she'd developed last week, utterly disappointed in it, though it wasn't near being complete.

She'd arrived at her usual hour earlier than the rest of her coworkers so she could focus and organize her thoughts. The time she'd spent with Paul on Saturday morning was still fresh in her mind, his request that she return home still tugging at her heartstrings.

But no matter how hard she tried, she couldn't seem to push aside her giddiness—Jack would be back in the office today. Yet Jack was her boss. Her excitement over seeing him again was completely inappropriate, but it remained nonetheless.

A frown slipped into the corner of her mouth. What would Jack think of her fountain? His opinion of her and her creations had become too important to her.

"Knock, knock," Heidi said, leaning into her office. "I hope I'm not disturbing you. You looked engrossed."

Turning away from the computer screen, Rayne looked at Heidi and smiled. "No, you're fine. What are you doing here so early?"

"Had some things to catch up on. I thought better earlier than later. You?"

"Oh, this is my usual time. So, what's up?"

"Nothing, really. Just that several people asked about you at church yesterday. Ever think you'll visit again?"

"I will. I promise." Rayne couldn't think of a reason why she hadn't, at the moment.

"I'm not trying to pry." Heidi's smile brightened. "It's great that you can at least show up at some of the functions. Everyone loves you."

"Thanks for letting me know." Rayne smiled.

"Guess who showed up yesterday."

"I really couldn't say." Rayne edged her gaze back to her computer.

Heidi looked down the hall then leaned forward, talking softly. "Jack. Can you believe it?"

"Huh." Rayne tried to look unfazed, like it wasn't any of her business because, of course, it wasn't. She wasn't going to be like Barb, throwing herself at the man.

"He asked about you."

Jack asked about her? What did Heidi mean, specifically? Did she dare ask for details? Rayne considered what to say next.

Heidi made a face. "I'll catch you later." She disappeared before Rayne could respond.

Jack stepped into her office. "You're here. Good." He shut the door behind him and sat in the chair across from her.

"I see you made it back alive." Rayne chuckled then looked at the model on her computer, hoping to muffle her pounding heart.

"And why wouldn't I?" Jack asked, teasing in his voice.

The sound of it sent tendrils of pleasure up Rayne's spine. She wished she could open a window so the rush of cold air could slap sense into her.

"How did your meeting with the client go? I assume you'll be briefing everyone today."

"Not as well as I had hoped."

His blatant honesty surprised her. Usually people liked to brag about their work, make everything they did sound successful. She faced him and locked her gaze on his eyes. His gorgeous eyes. "What do you mean?"

Jack was the first to break away. Averting his gaze, he looked down and studied his hands. "I took the wrong person with me."

Rayne held her breath. She thought that was a given. "I'm sure you don't mean that. Barb is exceptionally—"

"Talented." Jack cleared his throat. "Yes, I know."

Between the lines, what was Jack saying? Had something happened between them? Rayne wanted to scream, because she couldn't possibly voice these questions. It was none of her business. Yet Jack was in her office, saying much more than he should, she suspected.

"What are you telling me, Jack?"

"I think I could have accomplished more for the client if you had been with me." He glanced at her computer screen, which continued to show the model of the fountain. "You see things differently than others. I'm confident that if you'd visited the site, breathed the air, and viewed the skyline, your creative genius would have kicked in."

Rayne raised her chin in a slow nod. "Ah, now I understand. You've seen my model."

"Yes, I've seen it."

Tension spread through her shoulders. She'd let Jack down.

"My comment has nothing to do with your fountain. I knew I made a mistake about the trip to Dallas before I came in on Saturday morning to see your model." He gave her a soft, reassuring smile.

She relaxed against the chair back, feeling some of her composure return. So Jack still believed in her. "You came in on Saturday just to see it?" The news stunned Rayne. While she was breakfasting with Paul, Jack was looking at her design without her. "I wish I had known."

Jack looked at the clock on the wall. "Listen, Rayne. After being gone for a few days, I've got a lot to catch up on."

With a glance down at her blouse, his eyes lingered, making warmth creep into Rayne's cheeks. She hung on to the breath in her lungs.

"And since you don't have coffee on your shirt today, can you join me for lunch?" He gave her a lopsided grin.

Rayne slowly exhaled. He referred, of course, to her rejecting his invitation before because she'd had to change her blouse. His attempt at humor made her nervous. "I can't think of a single excuse today."

"Good." Jack stood up. "There's a lot we need to discuss."

As Rayne stared up at him, he seemed to be referring to so much more than work. But that was just the imaginings of Rayne's errant and traitorous heart. She took in his determined jaw, rugged good looks, and the emotion in his eyes.

What was he really thinking?

She wanted to run her fingers through his dark hair. Ugh.

He opened her door and took a step into the hall, though one foot remained in her office. "See you later, Rayne."

Then he shut her door, disappearing behind it. When Jack smiled, all was well with the world—except Rayne could not work like this. She knew, beyond any doubt, concern over her relationship with Jack, or lack thereof, had shadowed her fountain. If she continued down this path, FountainTech would suffer along with her reputation.

She'd prayed for an answer, a direction, but God always seemed to be silent when it came to her career path. She doubted attending Heidi's church would give her any more clarity, and she certainly wouldn't attend simply because Jack did.

The headhunter's phone number was saved in her cell phone. She'd find a private moment today to call him and schedule a meeting with him.

A muted knock on the door interrupted her thoughts.

Rayne shook her head. "Come in." What was her office this morning? Grand Central Station?

Barb stuck her head in, a mischievous smile on her face. She slipped through the small opening she'd made and shut the door quietly behind her, then sank into the chair. "Hey girl."

Elbow on her desk, Rayne put her fingers to her temple. "So, how did it go?" Rayne hadn't wanted to ask, but she knew Barb was expecting her to.

Barb fairly bounced in the chair, though she appeared a little flushed. "You won't believe how well it went."

"Really?" Rayne asked, fearing what she would hear. Barb had apparently gotten something much different out of the trip to Dallas than Jack had.

*❧*

One last phone call and Jack would head to Rayne's office and take her to lunch. Maybe out of the office he could dig a little deeper, find out what

# PRAYING FOR RAYNE

had been bothering her while she had worked on the design for the fountain model, if anything.

Avoiding her had been a mistake. His entire project could suffer—he wouldn't live up to his reputation, the reason he was hired—if he couldn't control his feelings for Rayne. He would prove to himself today at lunch that he could kill what she stirred in him, that he could work with her and remain oblivious to her charms. He had to. It was his job, and he was a professional.

Jack was back.

He lifted the receiver to return a call when Rayne stepped into his office, looking haggard.

"Jack," she said in a rush of breath, and staggered forward.

"What's wrong?" He sprang from his seat and ushered her into a chair, then closed the door. He kneeled next to her. "Rayne, what's happened?"

She shoved her hands through her hair, pushing it back from her tear-streaked face. "Sorry, just give me a minute. I shouldn't have rushed in here like this."

Jack rose. "Don't tell me. You can't go to lunch."

She stared up at him. "What?"

Seeing the hurt in her eyes killed Jack. "I shouldn't have said that. So, this is serious, isn't it?"

She nodded, sniffling. "It's my father. He's had a heart attack. We think, anyway."

A wall of memories and dark emotions slammed Jack. A house burning with his parents inside. He braced himself against the impact. "I'm so sorry. Is he going to be all right?"

"I don't know. Mom called to tell me. The ambulance is on the way." She peered up at him, a feeble smile slipping onto her lips. "That means I can't have lunch with you."

Jack stuck his hands into his pockets. "Is there anything I can do?"

Rayne nodded. "Forgive me?"

He chuckled, incredulous. "For what?"

"For the fountain. I know it wasn't what you were expecting."

"Rayne, don't worry about that now. Please. Go to your father."

"I might need a few days for this. Just. . . I'll use my vacation time or something."

"I'll take care of it. Don't worry."

She stared out the window as though looking into oblivion, or into the possibility of a morbid future. Funny, Jack only had to look into his past for that.

He held his hand out to her, unsure what he was doing, unsure of her response. She placed her small hand in his, reminding him of the night they'd gone skating and finally held hands, though their gloves were a protective barrier. Her hand was soft and trembling. Using him for support, she stood to her feet.

"Let me walk you to your car," he offered.

She gave him a wary glance. "That's not necessary. I only came to tell you because. . ."

"Because I'm your boss of course. Plus, we had lunch plans, which you obviously can't keep now. And I'm only walking you to your car because, as a coworker, I want to help."

Her right cheek lifted in a partial smile. "Just so we're clear."

Something wonderful coursed through Jack, despite his continued avoidance of feelings for her. Rayne seemed to be playing the same game that he was playing—dodging an office romance. Her eyes and her words convinced him—but how long could they dance around the obvious?

Jack escorted Rayne to her office, feeling the weight of her crushing news along with her. Coworkers walking the halls could see something was amiss and hung back to watch, questions in their eyes. He would explain everything later. In her office, he assisted her in gathering her briefcase and a few other items, and with his hand on her elbow, he gently guided her through the reception area, out the FountainTech doors, and onto the elevator. He rode down with her.

"Rayne, are you sure you're in a state of mind to drive?"

"They're bringing him to Fargo. It's the nearest hospital with decent cardiology facilities."

"I'll drive you over," Jack said, trying once again to assist her.

The elevator opened, and Jack stepped out with Rayne. She turned to face him and gave a pointed look. "Jack, you don't need to drive me."

Jack didn't get it. Why would she refuse his offer? It stung a little. "If not me, then someone else. What about Heidi?"

"There you are, Rayne." A tall, blond man stepped up to Rayne, jangling car keys.

"Paul," she said, choking back tears.

"Your mom said the ambulance had arrived." Paul wrapped his arm around Rayne's shoulders. "Let's go."

Jack stared, watching the lumberjack-looking guy whisk Rayne away. She appeared to melt into him for support, as though comfortable in his arms. Was this the guy from back home who'd sent the roses? Jack squeezed his fists, scolding himself for probing where he shouldn't. For caring about her in a way that he shouldn't.

Still—Jack clenched his teeth, angry at the determined thoughts—if this man was Rayne's type, how did he even have a chance?

# Chapter 12

S itting in the passenger seat of Paul's truck, Rayne stared at the snow melting against the window as he drove her back to her parents' farm.

After two days of tests, her father had been sent home from the hospital to rest. Though his heart attack was mild in relative terms, lifestyle changes were prescribed. Her father wasn't a man who liked changes. Rayne knew her decisions to go to college and then leave the farming community for the city had been hard on him.

"You okay?" Paul asked.

Rayne tugged her attention from the watery formations on the window to look at him. He watched the road, his glances intermittent and concerned.

"I'm fine." Rayne knew her halfhearted answer was less than convincing. She couldn't help but wonder if she'd caused her father stress because of her unwillingness to comply with his wishes. Yet she was a grown woman.

When would they let her go? Her throat felt like a cardboard box was expanding inside. She'd give herself this ride home to shed the tears, then no more—she had to be strong for her father.

Rayne sucked in a shaky breath then flipped open her cell and called the office. Gail answered in her professional receptionist tone.

"Gail, this is Rayne. Can I speak to Jack?"

"Hi, Rayne. He's in a meeting, but I'm sure he'll want to speak to you."

Rayne feared her connection wouldn't last even though she paid for the best plan in North Dakota.

"Rayne?" Jack came on the line.

"Thanks for talking to me. Gail said you were in a meeting."

"No problem. How's your father?"

"They're sending him home. I need the rest of the week off—maybe even two. I know it's not. . .what others do."

"Everyone is different. Don't beat yourself up."

"I'm willing to use my two-week vacation on this if I have to. It's just that, if I come back to work now, I'll just be a basket case, no good to you."

Jack took a long breath, loud enough for Rayne to hear over the phone. "Just promise me something?"

Rayne glanced over at Paul, who seemed intent on listening, though how could he avoid it? "What's that?"

"When you come back, I want you to put your heart into this project. We'll do everything we can do from this end, but Rayne. . ."

"Yes?"

"I need *you* to make this work. Without you, it won't be the same."

Rayne wasn't certain she liked the burden Jack placed on her; still, there was a part of her that warmed to the fact he had so much faith in her.

"I promise I'll do my best."

"Fair enough."

"Thanks for everything, Jack. I'll call you soon."

Jack was silent for a moment, making Rayne wonder if she'd lost her connection.

"Let me know if there's anything else I can do. And Rayne. . .take care of yourself."

"See you soon." Rayne flipped the phone closed, wondering at the call.

"Your boss seems like a nice guy."

"You could hear him?" She stared at Paul.

"Of course. The cab is pretty quiet, and he was talking loud."

"Yes, he's very nice." Rayne leaned back against the headrest and shut her eyes.

"He seems to think a lot of you."

Rayne let the conversation rest there, refusing to answer.

"What do you think of him?"

Apparently, Paul wasn't willing to let it drop. "I think he's a gifted person and will be good for FountainTech."

"He's seems to be interested in you as more than a coworker."

Rayne jerked her eyes around to Paul, who stared straight ahead at the thickening snow. She hoped they wouldn't run into a whiteout. "How could you know that? You've met twice, once at FountainTech and then again at the hospital."

Rayne thought back to that moment when Jack had come into her father's room to check on his status. The gesture had been a soothing balm to her soul.

"Guys just know. He cares about you."

Rayne sighed then rested her head again. "I'm talking to another company, Paul. I'm not sure I'll be at FountainTech much longer." Rayne wasn't sure why she'd shared the information. She wasn't thinking straight. If she'd thought that telling Paul she wouldn't be working with Jack would ease his concern, it probably didn't make him feel better to know she would be working elsewhere—possibly out of state. Far from her parents' home and from Paul. When Paul didn't say anything else, Rayne let her mind drift back to the crisis with her father. The very second she'd learned of his condition, she feared she might lose him.

In that moment, everything looked different. She would have given anything to have been home and spent time with her parents. She would have given anything for her father to think the absolute best of her. They'd always had a good relationship, and he'd always appeared proud of her. That's why her decision to pursue a profession outside of farm life had been the most difficult decision of her life. Her father hadn't approved. If she came back to stay, would she hear the words of praise from his lips that she longed to hear?

Silently, she prayed. *Lord, help me to know what I should do. You know the future. I'm more than willing to do Your will for my life, if only I know what that is.*

"We're here," Paul said.

Rayne opened her eyes to watch Paul maneuver his truck around the circular drive in front of the Flemming farmhouse. He jumped from the cab and jogged around to open the door for Rayne. He held his hand out to her.

She took it, feeling the calluses and reassuring strength in his grip, and stepped down.

"I'm here if you need help. Do you hear me? Don't hesitate to call me."

Looking into his eyes, she could see the love behind them. It took her breath away. "Thanks."

She glanced away so he couldn't see her apprehension—fear that he hoped to endear himself to her. But if the small spark she had for him could be kindled. . .

Should she allow that to happen?

Paul tipped her face back to look at him, keeping his hand under her chin. "While you're here, please think about what I said before. You're focused on your father now—I know that. But give us some thought, too, okay?"

Her vision blurred. She pulled herself from his grip, uncertain if she liked his persistence. She trudged up the drive empty-handed because Paul insisted on carrying the luggage. Paul wanted something from her, and for that matter, so did Jack.

Before pushing through the door, she closed her eyes and sucked in a breath, mentally preparing to face whatever might come over the next few days. Jack's handsome face, that brooding look in his eyes, came to mind.

Could Paul be right about Jack caring for her?

*❧*

Four thirty Friday afternoon, FountainTech offices grew quiet as people left early for the weekend. Jack pulled up the schematics of his invention on his laptop and finished up a few details—a modified pump that he'd labored on for months. He should be ecstatic. And he was, except he hadn't seen Rayne in two weeks. Make that three, because he'd been in Dallas most of the week before her father had his heart attack.

Though she was expected back in the office Monday morning, Jack was beginning to feel uneasy—would she really come back? His team had worked on the fountain in her absence, but her creative touch was the missing ingredient. If Jack could define it, could put a name or label on it, he wouldn't need Rayne—at least for the fountain. . . .

The problem was, Jack should not be feeling this way about the woman—she was off-limits. He'd told himself that a hundred times. But no matter how hard he tried, he hadn't been able to shake her from his thoughts.

Now that he was sure he'd accomplished an engineering feat, was there anyone else he would want to share this news with? Regardless of his feelings, Rayne should be the one to see it first—she would be the person who would see the most potential in it.

Suddenly, Jack couldn't stand it any longer. He flipped open his cell and phoned her.

Getting Rayne's reaction would go a long way in telling him where her thoughts were. If her heart was into coming back to work.

"Hello, Jack?"

Jack closed his eyes, savoring the sound of her voice. *Idiot.* "Hi, Rayne. I hope I didn't interrupt dinner."

She laughed softly. "No, we're just finishing up a card game."

"How's your father?"

"He's much better, though cranky about having to eat low-fat. Bacon and eggs are a staple on the farm, don't you know."

Jack smiled. She sounded good. "And you? How are you holding up?"

"If you're calling to make sure that I'll be at work on Monday, you can count on me to be there."

Monday was three days away. He couldn't wait until then. He really was an idiot. "Actually, Rayne, I have some important news that I need to share with you."

Rayne sucked in a breath. "What is it?"

"Any chance you'll be heading back to Fargo tomorrow?"

Jack heard a man guffawing in the background, and Rayne covered her phone to answer. "I'm sorry, Jack. They were waiting on me. I folded so I could talk to you in private. You're asking if I can come in tomorrow? Has something happened to the fountain?"

Jack hesitated. How did he say this? "Yes and no. I would really rather show you than tell you over the phone."

"And this can't wait? I hadn't planned to come back tomorrow."

Jack cringed and scratched his head as an idea began to form. Could he do that? More importantly, should he?

"I've got it. Why don't I drive out to you? I can show you there." He really was losing it, but the more he thought about it, the more he liked this idea. He wanted to know more about Rayne and her life on a farm. See where she was first inspired to create her designs.

"Are you serious? Jack, I don't think that would be a good idea."

"If I would be intruding, I won't come. But I promise not to take much of your time. Rayne. . .I've been working on this project even before I came to FountainTech." Jack pinched his nose. Should he say it? "I can't think of anyone I would rather share this with than you."

Saying the words left him feeling completely exposed.

"Oh Jack. I didn't mean to sound as though I didn't want you here. That would be rude. I thought you were just making the offer in jest, out of kindness. I would love to see. . ."

"Rayne?"

"I would love to see your project."

Rayne proceeded to give directions, which Jack wrote down. GPS didn't always work accurately in remote places. He recalled the time when GPS directed him to turn right, only there was a two-hundred-foot drop instead of a road. He didn't need to experience that twice to learn his lesson.

When he hung up, Jack stared at the phone. He wanted to crawl through it to be with her right now. Plus, he allowed himself a grin, a change in scenery would do him good. As he headed home to change clothes before driving to see Rayne, he wondered why he was letting this happen all over again.

Was he destined to destroy his career over women? Then again, he was simply showing her his new design—something that would benefit FountainTech. His initial plan when he first started was to keep his most important asset close to him—that's all he was doing.

On his way out of Fargo, Jack navigated a few slippery spots, heading north toward the Flemming family farm. The nearer he drew to his destination, the more he thought this was a bad idea. He had never been more indecisive.

By seven o'clock that evening, he drove around the circular drive to the farmhouse. As he slowed his vehicle to a stop and turned off the ignition, he watched Rayne talking to Paul next to his big dual-wheeled pickup, the door hanging open. Jack figured the Brawny paper towel man was leaving, but instead of stepping into his truck, he moved away from the door and shut it.

Paul started toward Jack's sports car, Rayne following. She smiled at Jack, a tentative look on her face, and gave him a little wave.

Jack opened his car door and stepped out. This was either a huge mistake or. . .

He was just in time.

# Chapter 13

*J*ack *actually came!*

If it weren't for the thrumming in her heart, Rayne would have thought she was seeing things. Apparently, Paul was taken aback as well—he suddenly decided to stay for dinner. Her mother had insisted on having dinner ready for Jack when he arrived, though Rayne explained that Jack would likely eat before he got there.

Paul's long legs carried him too fast, closing the distance between him and Jack. Rayne had to run to pass Paul, making it to Jack first. As she darted in front of Paul, she imagined herself as a barrier between the two, diffusing the tension in the air. Or so she hoped. But she wondered who she was protecting from whom.

She smiled at Jack, oh so glad to see him. "You're just in time for dinner. Have you eaten?"

"Oh, I couldn't intrude like that. I just wanted to get your input on something." He avoided looking at her—*really* looking at her—and glanced at Paul who stood behind her.

Paul thrust out his big hand. "Good to see you again, Jack. If you can't stay, we understand."

Jack shook his hand, a funny look on his face.

Rayne wanted to jab Paul with a stare.

"Dinner's waiting. It would be rude to refuse," she said with a teasing smile, while her heart seemed to stutter at the thought that he might leave so soon.

"Since you put it like that, I'd love to stay," he said, and flashed his dimpled grin.

Then, as if the Jack she knew had suddenly returned, he stared into her eyes, searching.

With Paul standing right behind her—hovering as if he owned her—the moment was awkward, but in a comical sort of way, like in a funny movie. A blizzard snowing them all in for the weekend would keep things right on track.

Looking down, she dug her foot into the snow and chuckled. "Well, since that's settled, let's go eat."

Rayne struck out toward the farmhouse, confident the two men were close behind.

"What brings you all this way out on a Friday evening?" Paul asked.

"It's regarding a project that Rayne and I are working on. I didn't feel I could wait until she returned." Jack's voice sounded confident, and she sensed that whatever he had created had exhilarated him.

She opened the door, laughing a little inside that neither of the men had thought to open the door for her, proving to the other he was the better gentleman.

"Rayne, can you help me in here?" her mother called from the kitchen. "You two make yourselves comfortable. Dinner will be ready soon."

Whenever Paul stayed for dinner, which had been a lot lately, he usually helped set the table. This evening he gestured for Jack to join him in the den. Rayne left the two alone and headed toward the kitchen.

After setting the table and putting out the fried chicken, mashed potatoes, and home-grown corn and green beans, Rayne strolled to the den to call the men.

Arms crossed, she hung in the doorway and watched Paul showing Jack one of her father's rifles. "Okay, boys, the fun is over. Let's eat."

Paul snapped the barrel of the rifle shut, and Jack looked up at her, relief spreading over his face.

"I hope you like fried chicken," she said.

Jack's grin was impish, making him look like a little boy. "Love it."

Rayne guided him to the dining room where they usually ate their evening meal. Her father stood at the head of the table for the first time since his heart attack.

"Dad." She rushed over to him. "You sure you feel up to this?"

Though a little pale, he'd been steadily improving. He squinted an eye at her then looked at Jack and Paul. "Your mother told me I had better come down because you had two suitors here for dinner. Looks like she was right."

Fire spread over her cheeks. She helped her father into his chair. "Jack isn't a suitor, Dad. He's my boss. Do you remember meeting him in the hospital?"

Rayne looked over at Jack. He and Paul remained standing. She assumed they were waiting on her father to be seated. Paul had a triumphant grin on his face. Jack was unreadable.

*❧*

Jack sank into the sturdy oak chair at the table across from Rayne, who sat waiting. She smiled at him. She had more color in her face than he'd seen before. He looked down at his empty plate. Being at the farm was good for her.

Paul slid into the seat next to her, only increasing Jack's unease. Eating with the family hadn't been part of his plan. The decision to drive out to the farm had cost him—he'd quickly lost control and now found himself being washed out to sea by a strong current called Rayne. He smiled to himself. With that analogy, Paul was a barracuda.

Suddenly, everyone bowed their heads, and Jack followed suit. Rayne's father said a quick blessing, thanking the Lord for their food and for their guests.

When he finished, Jack slowly lifted his head to the immediate clinking of utensils and dishes being passed around the table. Rayne's father seemed disconnected from the activity as he eyed Jack from the far end of the table.

Rayne's mother dished food onto her husband's plate—a heaping spoonful of mashed potatoes—while he squinted an eye at Jack, studying him. "The potatoes have got no fat. But you can't have the fried chicken." She handed him a plate of baked chicken. "Here you go." With a fork, she encouraged a chicken breast onto his place.

"Why'd you make fried chicken, woman? You know it's my favorite."

"For our guests. Rayne said we'd be having company." She looked up from preparing his plate and winked at Jack.

"I didn't say for dinner, Mom." Rayne appeared embarrassed. "But I'm glad you were thinking ahead."

Rayne's father grunted his disapproval, keeping his eyes on Jack. "Rayne tells me you're from Florida."

Jack liked that Rayne had been talking about him. "Yes." But he felt, as had already been suggested, like a suitor on trial. The room tilted a little at the idea.

Paul passed the mashed potatoes to Jack. "What part?"

"The sunny part." Jack dropped a large spoonful of the potatoes on his plate and laughed at his own joke, then looked up to a table of stares.

Rayne was the only other person who chuckled. "I'm sure it's hard for Jack, coming from a warmer state to North Dakota."

As soon as Jack finished eating, he'd have to find a way to show Rayne the reason he came then escape. Fortunately, the rest of dinner wasn't focused too much on him. Paul and Rayne's father hogged the conversation, engrossed in a farm-related discussion.

Make that weather-related.

Corn, soybeans, wheat, winter wheat, dry beans, barley, durum, potatoes, sugar beets, sunflowers, canola, oats. Then there was the soil temperature, and was it too wet or too dry? And the weather—was it too hot, too cold, or too windy? Would it be early planting or late planting this year? The worst cases, of course, were the extremes of flooding or drought.

Fascinated by it all, Jack smiled to himself. Both men were thoughtful and intelligent. Jack quickly recognized how important farming was to them—it was their whole life, consuming most of their time and obviously their thoughts. If he were in their position, how could he blame them? Now that he considered it, most of his thoughts and time were consumed with his career, his evenings spent on related engineering projects.

"They say we can expect a drought this year." Paul slid his plate forward a half inch and leaned against the chair back.

"Don't remind me. Say, did you hear that Tom Bly broke his leg?"

"Yep, that's too bad."

"As soon as I'm feeling myself again, I need to get up the road and pay him a visit."

"That'll be soon enough, Gary." Rayne's mother rose to gather up the dishes.

Rayne stood, too. "I'll do the dishes, Mom, since you did most of the cooking."

"Nonsense. You've got guests."

"I'll help her, Mrs. Flemming," Paul said, throwing a quick glance at Jack. *Of all the. . .*

Apparently, Paul was attempting to earn points. Jack wasn't sure he was entered in the contest for Rayne, even if he wanted to be.

When Rayne leaned over him to take his plate, she smiled down. "We usually wait for an hour after dinner for dessert. Would you like yours now?"

"No, thank you, on dessert. I need to get back."

"Just give me a few minutes to finish the dishes. Then you can show me the reason for your trip."

Paul hung around the table, grabbing up the remaining utensils. Jack stood. He could do something at least. He picked up the larger platters that held the remaining food.

Rayne's father rose from his place at the table. "It was good to see you again, Jack."

Jack paused, holding a plate with two pieces of fried chicken left. "I'm glad you're doing better."

"Not at the moment. I need to lay down now." He walked slowly from the dining room, Rayne's mother hovering near his elbow, then turned back. "Take good care of my little girl at that company of yours if you want to keep her."

"Of course I will, sir." Jack nodded with an easy smile.

"Just remember, we could use her here, too."

With that, Rayne's father began climbing the stairs. Her father had just confirmed Jack's fears—making Jack glad he'd come for the first time since he'd arrived. He finished helping clear the table, but with Paul lingering near Rayne in the kitchen, and her mother, having returned from helping Mr. Flemming, chattering away, it was too crowded for Jack.

He made his way to the den to wait for Rayne. He'd been there less than two minutes when she appeared and grabbed his arm. "Come on." She looked back through the wide doorway. "Hurry."

Jack stood. "Where are we going?"

"Shh." She crept through the front door, and Jack gently closed it behind them. "Follow me."

Jack hurried behind her through the snow. It was beginning to come down hard and thick, and the chill seeped through his sweater. "Rayne, what are you doing?"

"Hiding." Rayne trotted ahead to the barn about forty yards from the house. She tugged Jack inside.

"What's going on? Why are we in the barn?" Jack rubbed his shoulders. "Shouldn't we have at least put on our coats?"

Rayne giggled. "I don't think Paul is ever going to leave as long as you're here. This was the only way for us to speak privately."

Couldn't she just ask Paul to leave? Jack looked at her, noticing that the dim light in the barn created a halo around Rayne's face. Her expression, her features, appeared soft and. . .beautiful.

"Now, what was so important that you drove out here?" She folded her arms, teasing in her eyes.

She had beautiful eyes, too. They were deep and penetrating tonight.

Suddenly, Jack's mind went completely blank. Why had he come to the farm? He shook his head, searching for the words. The pump. . .

"I designed a new fountain pump. It's more efficient, using less horsepower and yet streaming higher than any other."

Her eyes brightened. "Are you kidding me? I'm thrilled for you, Jack."

Jack sagged, uncertain if he witnessed all the enthusiasm in her eyes he'd hoped for. He was an idiot. "The schematic is in my car."

She took a step toward him. "You drove all this way to show it to me?"

"I. . .uh. . .well, yes." The huge barn felt like it was closing in on him. He stared at the ground and tugged at his shirt collar sticking out of his sweater, then looked back at Rayne. "I'm sorry. I just thought you would understand."

"I do understand. I'm already thinking of a fountain design. I'm just flattered that you wanted to share it with me."

"Who else?" The cold, the smell of the barn, the pump design, all disappeared from his world because his focus was now on Rayne's face alone. When had she come so near to him?

She tipped her head just so, the way she'd done the night they'd gone ice-skating. He'd wanted to kiss her then but hadn't. He'd thought about kissing her ever since that moment.

Jack relinquished the last of his control and gave in to his natural impulse, leaning toward Rayne, meeting her. At that moment, she was all that mattered to him.

He pressed his lips against her perfectly shaped ones and melted into their softness.

*☙*

Delight spread over Rayne, rippling from the top of her head, then down her body, all the way to her toes. Contentment enveloped her, and yet she wanted more. . . .

So much more.

As if in answer to her heart's longing, Jack wrapped his arms around her, drawing her closer. Of their own accord, her arms slid up and over his shoulders then around his neck. She weaved her fingers through his hair, his wonderful hair. How she'd longed to do just that.

She melted into him, balancing between the dizzy heat of his kiss and the reality of the cold barn enclosing them. With all her heart, she wanted his kiss to intensify, but a noise tugged her back from the edge, the world around her entering into her awareness.

Gently, she unwrapped herself from this man who'd captivated her heart. "Oh Jack," she whispered, pressing her head against his broad chest. There she felt content, safe. Like she belonged.

She breathed in the scent of his cologne, making her light-headed. Finally, she eased away from him and gazed into his eyes, a dreamy, faraway look in them.

She adored the lazy grin on his face.

Someone cleared his throat. Rayne stiffened. Paul stepped from the shadows.

At seeing him, her heart raced. She dreaded reading his expression. Had he witnessed the kiss she'd shared with Jack? Their tender moment?

"Sorry to interrupt your discussion," he said, tension twisting his voice.

"No problem." Rayne and Jack answered simultaneously, both appearing eager to hide their indiscretion.

Rayne grimaced. Indiscretion? Had she been reckless in kissing Jack?

Appearing hesitant, Paul looked from Jack to Rayne, an awkward silence filling the barn.

"Your mother was looking for you," he finally said.

"I need to head home anyway." Jack jammed his hands into his pocket and blew out a breath. He gave a nervous chuckle. "Besides, it's getting late."

Jack headed for the barn door, as did Rayne. She gave Paul a soft smile in an attempt to hide her annoyance as well as reassure him, though she wasn't sure why. She didn't owe Paul an explanation. Did she?

Outside, Rayne wrapped her arms around herself as the threesome hurried to the farmhouse. The weather had taken a turn for the worse. Once inside, Rayne stomped her shoes on the rug.

Jack did the same then reached for his coat on the coat rack. "Thanks for dinner, Rayne. I hope I wasn't too much trouble tonight." He subtly glanced at Paul, who remained in the foyer with them.

Paul thrust his hand out to Jack. "It was good to see you, Jack."

Ready to explode, Rayne pursed her lips instead.

"And where do you think you're going, mister?" Rayne's mother appeared in the foyer, hands on hips.

Before Jack could answer, her mother closed the distance between them and tugged on his coat. "You can't go out in this weather. There's a serious storm brewing out there."

"I don't remember hearing anything about a storm."

"Wasn't supposed to be here until Sunday. We've got plenty of room, and another day at the farm won't kill you. But driving a lone North Dakota road as far as you have to go just might."

Rayne stared at the floor, laughing inside. This was one time she more than appreciated her mother's gift for persuasion.

# Chapter 14

Yawning, Rayne rubbed her eyes. She felt oddly at peace with the world. Happy. She knew there was some reason for this feeling inside. But what was it? Still groggy, she searched her thoughts.

Then she remembered. Jack was here at the farm.

And in the barn last night. . .

She shut her eyes and allowed her mind to linger on Jack's kiss. With her finger, she traced her mouth, recalling his lips against hers, and drew in a long breath.

Suddenly, Paul's kiss came to mind. Though at the time, she had felt the tiniest rekindling of any feelings she might have harbored for Paul, his kiss had not stirred things in her like Jack's—his kiss potent, making her heady with emotions she'd never experienced before.

She allowed the rush of excitement to swirl once again.

A big smile spread across her face. She'd have to tone that down, she knew. It wouldn't do to have people asking questions. How would she explain?

Filling her room was a calm that she easily recognized as the muted quiet of a snow-covered landscape. The blue-and-yellow wallpaper reflected a shimmer from a break in the curtains hanging against the window. A white radiance only created by snow. Or did everything just look brighter today?

A million questions bombarded her thoughts—what did this mean? Did Jack feel the same way she did this morning? How would they work together now?

With a single kiss, her relationship with Jack had altered into something much more than coworkers. Something much more than friends. Oh how this changed everything.

But for better or worse? Rayne wasn't sure she wanted to know.

And what would he think if she told him she had been talking to another company?

On the side table, her cell chirped, letting her know she had a text message. She reached over and lifted the phone.

From Jack. He'd left the text message in the middle of the night? She'd slept hard, then, because she hadn't heard the message come through.

Rayne rose up on her elbows to read the words, *Forgive for my actions. Leaving first thing in the morning.*

What? Pain stabbed her heart. Was he sorry for kissing her? Or was he afraid of Rayne's reaction? What might have happened, what might he have said, had Paul not interrupted them in the barn?

Though her mother had convinced Jack to stay the night to be safe, they'd not had another moment alone. And now it didn't look like she'd get one.

Rayne wasn't so sure it would be safe for him to drive back this morning either. Worry for his safety tore through her. Apprehension over his apparent regret of kissing her sank heavily in the pit of her stomach.

Rayne rose from her bed and thrust open the curtains. It was snowing so hard she couldn't see the barn from her window. She pulled on her jeans and a sweatshirt and opened the door. The aroma of bacon and eggs met her as she bounced down the stairs, hoping.

When Rayne turned the corner into the kitchen, her heart leaped.

Jack sat at the kitchen table, her mother's best breakfast spread before him. He was buttering toast and, though he smiled, uncertainty lingered in his eyes.

She couldn't help the big smile she launched at him.

Her father busied himself, scooping fat-free margarine from a tub, frowning. Her mother turned from the hefty pan of bacon she was frying and glanced at Rayne. "Good morning, sugar pie."

Rayne hoped her father wasn't eating the bacon. "Good morning." She tugged out a chair and sat at the table, tossing a questioning look at Jack. "You're not going to drive in this, are you?"

Her mother leaned over the table, setting a plate of eggs in the middle. "Of course not. He's agreed to stay for at least another day." Her mother winked. "Isn't that right, Jack?"

His dimples deepened with his smile, along with the color in his face. "Looks like a blizzard out there."

Rayne hung her head, allowing a soft laugh. Her mother appeared to have a way with Jack. A way that she didn't have with Rayne ever since she'd taken the job in Fargo.

Rayne's father chuckled. He looked like the image of vigor this morning. Jack was good for him. Apparently, he was good for them all.

Had they given up on Paul, then? At the thought, Rayne was surprised he hadn't made his way over this morning, especially after walking in on her and Jack in the barn. He'd been right about Jack caring about her. She saw that now. Would Paul continue to pursue her, or would he step out of the picture?

Rayne grabbed a slice of bacon and crunched on it while her mother poured her a glass of orange juice. Jack and her father discussed weather. Good. Jack was fitting in.

Rayne focused on eating breakfast and pondered what this day would bring, snowed in with her family and a man she couldn't stop thinking about.

✍

Jack smiled for Rayne's family, but he was suffocating inside, feeling like a first-class moron. He'd wanted—no, needed—to see her. He'd needed to show her his design, so he'd driven to her family's farm. Who does something like that?

A moron, that's who. A moron on the fast track to losing his focus and, worse, his job, if he kept this up.

And then what did he go and do? He'd kissed her. Listening to her father tell him an account in which he'd almost lost the farm that had been in the family for years, Jack nodded but was only half listening as he glanced over at Rayne. He looked down at his plate, shuffled his eggs around, and day-dreamed about kissing her again.

Rayne possessed something that Jack found irresistible. He couldn't have imagined something so powerful could emanate from her. She seemed like such a quiet, creative soul. But maybe that's where the secret lay, and he was drawn to her in a way that he was never drawn to Kiera, Rayne's exact opposite.

Jack took a bite of the eggs. This was all so. . .unexpected. It wasn't part of his plan.

"Never, ever take your eyes of the mark, off the goal," her father said, and continued with his farm tale.

The words seemed to stab at Jack's heart, at his mistake this weekend. He'd prided himself in being a focused man, shooting for the goal. But now his focus was a jumbled mess.

Rayne's father had a penchant for tossing out proverbial words of wisdom. Most were true and well placed, of course, but over time a person might think he sounded a bit condescending. Still, Jack liked him. He was a good man. And clearly, Rayne loved her father, her family, deeply.

He sensed she struggled with being away from them.

"Well, I'm going to rest. Thank you for breakfast, Mamma." Rayne's father scooted from the table and took his plate to the sink where Mrs. Flemming was already doing the dishes. He leaned over and kissed her on the cheek.

Jack felt a little guilty for catching them in a personal moment. Rayne was lucky to have her parents, a family to go home to for a visit. Something Jack had lost long ago. Memories Jack had worked hard to shove from his mind began to seep back in. What was he going to do all day to keep his mind from them?

Rayne's father shuffled from the kitchen, Rayne at his side. Jack stood and moved next to her mother at the sink.

"Is there something I can do?" he asked. "Since I'm here until the storm lets up a little, maybe I can help."

She stuck a dish into the dishwasher and chuckled. "Well, when Paul finishes up at his own place, he's heading over here. As soon as the weather lets up a bit"—she peered out the kitchen window at the clouds—"and it looks like that'll be soon, maybe you can help break the ice on the ponds for the cattle."

"Uh, sure, I can do that." He didn't have a clue how. "As long as you don't think I would be more of a hindrance to Paul than a help."

A warm hand slid over his shoulder. Rayne was at his side. "I'll help. Jack isn't accustomed to farm work, Mom."

Jack bristled but then saw the teasing in Rayne's eyes. What was he getting into? "I can work."

"Are you sure about that?" Rayne squeezed his bicep and smiled, color creeping into her cheeks.

Good thing he worked out.

Rayne's mother laughed. "I know what you're thinking. The snow is too deep for the truck, even if it's a four-wheel drive."

"That's what I'm thinking, all right." Rayne smiled, a twinkle in her eyes.

Her mother thrust her hands into the steaming dishwater, apparently washing the dishes before sticking them in the dishwasher. "A few years ago, Rayne talked her daddy into using snowmobiles to feed the cattle during the winter. She could talk her daddy into just about anything."

Rayne had turned a farm chore into something she considered fun. He smiled down at her. Right there, in the kitchen, with her mother standing next to them, Jack wanted to kiss her again. He looked at the smile on her soft lips, recalling how it had felt to kiss her, how his soul had stirred. His gaze traveled back up to her eyes.

Had she been thinking of that as well?

"Before you head out, can you stoke the fire for me?" her mother asked.

"I'll show Jack what to do and then be back to help you finish up here."

Jack followed Rayne out the kitchen door to the back porch where she loaded his arms with logs for the fire. In the distance, Jack spotted a familiar truck lumbering down the road.

Rayne carried a few logs as well, and Jack followed her into the living room where they stacked the wood against the wall a short distance from the large wood-burning stove.

"Mom and Dad use this to help heat the house." She stood straight and gestured to the stove. "Just stick a few logs in while I go help Mom finish up in the kitchen. Then we'll head out."

Jack snickered. He had the feeling Rayne was enjoying bossing him around for a change. Peering inside the stove, he carefully placed a couple of logs inside. Boots stomped near the front door; then it swung open.

Jack turned to see Paul standing in the small foyer, tugging off his gloves and glancing around the house. "Anyone home? I came to help with the chores."

His gaze landed on Jack, and Paul frowned.

# Chapter 15

Sitting on her snowmobile, Rayne looked up at the sky and saw a small break in the clouds as the heavier snow moved to the east of them. She watched Jack shove the last of the hay from the small trailer attached to the snowmobile. Fortunately, they didn't keep many cattle, or using the snowmobiles would have taken them too long.

She smiled to herself, thinking about the day she'd talked her father into them. She'd wanted a snowmobile for fun, of course, but on a farm, pretty much every purchase has to be work-related. Of course, her father didn't use them, preferring the truck, and Rayne had been gone the last few years at school and then to work.

For the first time, she considered that her father might have purchased the snowmobiles as a way to keep her on the farm, entice her to stay. Regret seeped into her thoughts.

"Hey, what's wrong?" Jack stomped over to her.

Had she allowed her momentary doubts to show? She took stock of Jack, who wore her father's too-big extra work boots, farm clothes, and coat. She liked the look on him. "You know, you make a better farmer than I thought you would."

Jack fired off his big-dimpled grin again. It warmed her cold bones all the way to the marrow.

"You're enjoying this, aren't you?" He kept smiling as he waited for her answer.

She couldn't help the laugh that escaped. "Yes."

He closed the distance between them and snatched the cap from her head. Laughing, she didn't have the strength to grab it back as they wrestled.

Rayne shoved Jack a little too hard, and he toppled, pulling her with him. The snow hit her face, sobering her, and she looked at Jack's face, so near hers. "Are you up for a little fun?" She pushed to her feet and dusted off the remaining snow.

Still on the ground, Jack studied her, taking his time to answer. "Sure."

"Let's unhitch these trailers then. We can grab them on the way back."

After freeing the snowmobiles from the trailers, she hopped on and sped away, listening for Jack to do the same. Quickly enough, she heard the whir of his snowmobile behind her.

The sky was beginning to clear, turning the day beautiful. Rayne enjoyed the freedom of speeding across the snow, and the wind, though cold, gusting against her cheeks, and best of all, Jack enjoying the day with her.

Snowmobiling was one of her favorite things. What could be better than doing this with someone she. . . What exactly did she feel for Jack?

Rayne shoved the serious thoughts to the back of her mind so she could enjoy this moment. It might never come again. She sped up and glanced back. Jack wasn't far behind, and his snowmobile jerked forward as he squeezed the throttle, giving it more gas.

His bright smile flashed, and Rayne turned her back to him, intending to race far ahead. Laughing, she whirred over a rift and felt the jar, even though she'd plummeted into soft snow. The family farm was a little over a thousand acres. Soon she'd reach the place she wanted to show Jack.

As she drew near the copse of trees, Rayne slowed the snowmobile to a stop. Jack joined her, grinning from ear to ear.

She tugged off her helmet. "So, what did you think?"

"I think there's more to farming than meets the eye."

Rayne laughed and slid from the recreational vehicle's seat. "We won't hear the end of this, just so you know. Work before play."

"Are you saying we weren't finished with the chores?" Jack hopped off his snowmobile.

"Are you kidding?" Rayne began trudging toward the trees and motioned for Jack to follow. "Come on."

Rayne made her way through the trees, stepping in thick snow. Soon her breathing was becoming harder.

Jack sidled next to her. "Where are you taking me?"

"You'll see. Say, why aren't you breathing hard? You can't be in that great of shape."

"This isn't exactly exerting to me. But I admit, the morning chores made me a little tired." He grinned.

As Rayne neared the edge of the grove that opened up to a small bluff, she snuck another peek at Jack. This was her secret place, yet she'd brought him here.

When they broke through the trees, Rayne stopped. "This is it. It's not much, but this bluff gives me a good view of the surrounding area."

"It's beautiful, Rayne."

"I come here to think and pray." Why was she sharing this with him? She angled her head at him to gauge his reaction.

"Is this where you came to watch the fields, where you were inspired to create your designs?"

Rayne huffed a laugh. He'd brought the fact that they work together back into the mix. Funny how she'd tried to forget that part of their relationship.

"Rayne, I'm sorry if I offended you last night. . . . I shouldn't have—"

"Oh Jack. I wasn't offended. I kissed you back. Couldn't you tell?" Despite her willing them away, tears welled in her eyes.

She turned to face him, and suddenly he was there, sweeping her up in his arms yet again. His lips pressed hard against hers this time, and she slid her arms over his chest, her hands around his neck, drawing him downward, closer.

☙

Rayne was in his arms. What more could he want? He savored the moment, feeling her small form against his, her tender lips responding to his. . . .

*No, no, no, man. What are you doing?* Jack gently untangled himself from Rayne, and with both hands, held her at arm's length. "Rayne. . ."

Rayne frowned, and tears flooded her eyes. "Jack?"

"What are we doing?" He released her and, shaking his head, turned his back on her to stare out over the snow-covered landscape. "I'm an idiot."

"What are you trying to say, Jack?"

What happened to the guard he'd erected around his heart? He shoved a hand through his hair. "I should never have come to the farm to see you."

Jack could hear the strain in Rayne's responding sigh.

"I admit, I find you irresistible. That makes me vulnerable, and I can't work like this. We can't work like this."

"What if. . .what if I work somewhere else?"

Incredulous, Jack chuckled and stared down at the ground. Suddenly the cold was beginning to creep through all the layers he wore. "Not a good idea either. You see, FountainTech won't work without you. I can't make it the premier water feature design company. You're the key. . ." *To my heart.*

Jack shrugged off the errant thought. Getting romantically involved with Rayne hadn't been part of his plan.

When she didn't answer, Jack realized how that must have sounded. Like he was putting the company before any feelings he had for her. His shoulders tensed. Wasn't that exactly what he was doing? But his reasons involved so much more than the company.

"Rayne, please accept my apology."

She was staring at her feet. He lifted her chin and slid his thumb down her cheek. "I care for you. I think you know that."

"Why? Because you come out to my farm, stay with my family, kiss me, and now. . ."

"That's exactly why I'm putting a stop to my actions now. I never should have come here. I made a mistake."

"Well, that's just great, Jack. Thank you for sharing." Rayne began stomping back through the trees.

Jack followed, feeling as if he'd made a monumental blunder. But he wasn't sure which mistake was worse—coming to the farm and allowing the kiss with Rayne or now rejecting her.

What a jerk he was.

He trudged behind her, hoping to make her understand. "You should know I'm damaged goods. I'm no good for you as anything other than your boss."

"I'm not sure you'll have to worry about that much longer."

Jack hoped Rayne didn't mean that. "What? You're not going to quit, are you? Look, I apologized, didn't I?"

"You said it yourself—we can't work together."

Jack snatched her around to face him.

Seeing her so visibly shaken pierced his heart to the core. How could he hurt her like this? "All right."

She frowned, confused. "All right, what?"

Jack gently tugged her toward him. She resisted at first then willingly came into his arms. He pressed his face into the crook of her neck. "Let's try to make this work. I can't stand to hurt you."

She drew away from him. "So you want to try this, whatever it is between us, because you feel sorry for me?"

"No, that's not what I mean. I feel sorry for myself. I would be a mess without you. But we have to be careful. We have to take this slow. It wouldn't do for anyone at work to know. Not yet. We need to keep this personal and private."

"I think Barb is the only one who would care."

"Don't kid yourself. There are plenty who are jealous of you. They would think I'm showing you favoritism. Harold would certainly care."

"You're right, then. We should take this much slower." Rayne reached for the handlebars of the snowmobile, preparing to throw her leg over.

This weekend Jack had seen a different side to Rayne. He'd watched her maneuver a snowmobile like a pro, watched her break ice on a pond and feed cattle, watched her interact with her family.

Grief squeezed his chest. "You know, seeing you with your family reminds me of. . ."

Emotions lodged in his throat, creating an ache.

Rayne released the handlebars and slid her hand over his shoulder to rest on his arm. "Of what?"

"My own family. They're gone now though."

"What happened?"

"They died in a fire."

"Oh Jack," she whispered, her eyes watering. "I'm so sorry."

"Reminds me of all I've lost." He'd closed this off for years, kept it buried, and now he wasn't sure he wanted to experience the pain again.

She stared up at him, more than concern emanating from her face.

At the moment, Rayne was all Jack wanted. But why did caring for her have to be so complicated? Why did being with her invoke painful memories?

Growing close to Rayne would cost him.

# Chapter 16

Jack ballooned his cheeks, capturing air in his mouth before releasing it in a sigh. Staring at his computer screen, he saw nothing but the mess he'd made of everything. When he'd first accepted the position with FountainTech and moved to North Dakota, he'd had big plans for himself and for the company.

First, he'd planned on getting his personal life back on track. Kiera was out of his life for good. He wouldn't have to see her every day at work, or happen upon her anywhere in the state of California. Second, he wanted a new start professionally—this time *he* was heading up a division and calling the shots.

Jack's desk phone rang, but he was too busy looking at everything that had not been accomplished in the last few weeks. Nothing appeared to be going as planned or on schedule. And the fountain design itself—Rayne had not been involved in the process enough to touch it with her magic. Granted, she'd taken time to be with her father as he recovered.

This week she was back in the office, focusing on tweaking the fountain design the rest of his team had labored on in her absence. Passing her office to get his morning coffee, Jack couldn't decide whether to stop and say hello. They'd agreed to slow down their rapidly accelerating relationship. Fortunately, someone had been in Rayne's office, effectively making the decision for him.

Once in his own office again, Jack leaned back in his chair and clasped his hands behind his head. He almost regretted that he'd been right about how much he needed her to make his plans for FountainTech work. Depending that much on one person was never a good idea.

He thought about how that wisdom applied to matters of the heart as well. How had he become this attached to Rayne so quickly? Though his painful and embarrassing breakup with Kiera two days before their wedding had happened months ago, that wasn't enough time, was it?

The phone rang again. Jack ignored it. Calls always came through the receptionist unless he'd given out his direct number, which he hadn't. *Take a message, Gail.*

So much for his "Jack is back" motto. His vow to avoid love had crumbled the second he'd looked into the deep pool of Rayne's eyes. They'd brimmed with emotion, seemingly giving a meaning to his life he didn't realize he needed.

And then going to the farm had dragged out memories he'd kept buried for years. They'd tortured him since leaving Rayne's farm two days ago. But now that he was back in the real world, he saw things clearly—caring for her the way he did wasn't good for either of them, and apparently it wasn't good for FountainTech either.

He was off his game.

A soft knock on the door jolted him back to his surroundings. "Come in."

Gail stuck her head in. "Uh, Jack. I've been trying to reach you."

He leaned forward to lift a pen on his desk and shuffle through a stack of paperwork. "I know. I'm busy. Didn't you take a message or send it to voice mail?"

She frowned. "Harold wants you in his office five minutes ago."

Jack stilled. "I'm on my way."

He snatched up his laptop, dreading Harold's untimely request. Had he heard something about Jack and Rayne? Pasting a confident smile on his face, he strode down the hall to Harold's office. If he smiled big enough, he just might convince himself that he was on top of things before he got there.

With his knuckles, he gave a knock on the opened door and grinned. "You wanted to see me?"

Frowning, Harold focused on the papers strewn over his desk. "Come in and shut the door," he said without looking up at Jack.

*Not good.* Jack did as he was told and tried to ignore the shrinking feeling he always had around Harold. But that was the man's intention—he loved to intimidate.

While Jack waited for Harold to acknowledge him, he opened his laptop. Harold wasn't the only one who was busy. Jack could give as good as he got.

Harold cleared his throat. Jack pulled his gaze from the laptop screen and shut it, smiling.

"How's the creative design team doing?" Harold rocked back in his leather executive chair.

Jack guessed that Harold had heard something, or else he wouldn't be asking the question in this manner. They had meetings for this sort of thing, where Jack would present a PowerPoint that he'd prepared ahead of time.

Maintaining his confident veneer, Jack tugged his laptop open and waited for the screen to load the image of the water sculpture the team had been working on. He placed the laptop on the desk, allowing Harold to see, and smiled like he was a proud new father. Harold might not notice anything missing.

As Jack expected, Harold simply nodded, unaffected by what would normally mesmerize anyone else.

"The client wants to move the project up by two months," Harold said.

Jack stared. *Two months?* And he was already behind.

"Don't let me down, champ. I'm counting on you."

How could Harold have agreed to that? It was lunacy. At the moment,

Jack was too stunned to think of an adequate response, but he had to recover, give Harold something—anything—so he could remain his "champ," even though he hated the reference.

"I've got something you should see," Jack said. Sooner or later he planned to share the news with Harold anyway, though before he did that, he'd prefer to be certain it would perform the way he hoped.

"What's that?"

On his computer, Jack pulled up the schematics for his new pump.

Harold leaned forward, appearing a little curious, momentarily taken aback.

*Good.* Jack had made the right decision. His confidence began to soar for real now.

Harold put on his black-framed reading glasses to study the schematic more closely. "Anyone else know about this?"

※

Rayne rubbed her eyes then squinted at the design team as she explained again the nuances that she'd added to the fountain—what Jack had defined as Rayne's magic. She hoped he was right, because she was certainly not feeling the magic today.

Instead, she was beginning to feel the sleep deprivation of the last couple of weeks as the team had labored hard to make the new deadline. Add to that, they were in the middle of a bid for another large-scale water sculpture and would need to start on that one immediately. All of the busyness had trumped any expectations she had of having time with Jack.

She caught a glimpse of him in her peripheral vision, leaning against the back wall as though standing out of her way. His lean physique distracted her. As the team members, including Simon and Barb, discussed the fountain, Rayne couldn't focus on their words. The kisses she had shared with Jack seemed like a lifetime ago. The pressure they had been under to complete this fountain was probably a good thing—keeping them both busy. Keeping her from having time to think about Jack. Or his kiss.

Still, she felt that something between them had changed. Yes, she and Jack had decided to slow things down, but she sensed a distancing in him. And she'd noticed he'd been purposefully avoiding her—his creative lead.

The way things were working out, Rayne was almost thankful that her mind had been consumed with work. Even though the team's ramped-up schedule had forced her to reschedule her lunch interview to this evening.

*Oh Jack, I hope you understand. . . .* She drew in a ragged breath, hoping that entertaining thoughts of a new opportunity at another company wasn't a mistake. Working somewhere else could give her and Jack freedom to explore whatever was between them. Maybe even give her a chance for the promotion she'd lost at FountainTech.

Except there was one small detail that needed to be worked out. The man she would be interviewing with tonight, Carvis Clark, had lured her with the possibility she could work from Fargo and not have to leave North Dakota. That incentive persuaded her to at least listen to him.

Suddenly, she realized that everyone was staring at her. "I. . .uh, I'm sorry. Did I miss something?"

"I'm still not seeing it, Rayne." Simon smirked. "What exactly makes this fountain better than what we did before you worked your *magic*?"

Rayne frowned, never having heard Simon speak to her this way. Jack was right—Simon was jealous.

"All right, let's break for lunch." Jack stepped into the fray, standing next to the computer screen. "You've all been working very hard to meet the new deadline. I'm proud of you. We'll meet again tomorrow—plan for a working lunch."

A few sighs and groans escaped the group, and Jack frowned. Rayne knew they all probably blamed him for accepting the new deadline. She grabbed her notepad to leave, a small part of her wishing that Jack would tug on her sleeve, ask her to stay behind while he discussed some attribute of the fountain he wanted added.

That would have been a normal thing to do. It would even have been expected. Instead, as she swung open the door, she glanced behind her to see Barb sliding herself to sit exotically on the conference table.

"Jack? I've got some ideas I'd like to share with you." She crossed her slender legs, easily showing them off with the short skirt she wore.

For a moment, Rayne hung back, waiting—no, hoping—that Jack would shove Barb away, or at least flash Rayne an apologetic I'm-sorry-I-have-to-endure-this look. But no, he simply smiled at Barb.

Burning with rage, Rayne shoved the rest of the way through the door and marched down the hall to her office, the surroundings a blur. She slammed her office door behind her, quickly regretting it. Someone would certainly question her actions, and then what was she supposed to say? That she didn't appreciate Jack smiling at Barb, responding to her flirtation?

Rayne covered her face with her hands, hating the tears that came. *Lord, I can't do this. I can't keep this up.*

❧

Jack smiled down at Barb, careful to keep his gaze on her face and not on the bait she dangled.

"It's difficult to find time to talk to you with this new schedule. How about dinner tonight? I could share some of my ideas then, away from the pressure of the office." She toyed with the solitaire diamond hanging against the bare skin at the edge of her low-cut blouse just above. . .

Jack jerked his gaze back up to her eyes. In them he witnessed a look of victory, as though she'd seen his eyes traveling where they ought not to go. "I'm sorry, Barb, but I have a project that I'm working on at home, too, and I have to complete that soon. Maybe you could come in, say, about seven in the morning. We could meet before things heat up around here."

Inside, he cringed at his word choice. He suspected Barb wanted things to heat up.

She smiled, a slight quiver on her shiny, glossed lips. "Seven it is. Before things heat up." She slid from the conference table, and Jack couldn't help himself; he watched as her willowy legs carried her to the conference room door. She tugged the door open with a slight twist and sassy glance back in his direction, catching his look once again.

Jack flamed inside, angry that any woman would use her attributes like that. He raged that he'd been watching her without even realizing it, before he could stop himself.

He had no feelings toward her whatsoever, not even lust. Rubbing his temples, he closed his eyes. He had so much work to do in addition to completing his pump. He wanted to test that soon. But all he could think about was Rayne. She must be terribly hurt.

Maybe. . .could that be for the best?

# Chapter 17

My contract included a noncompete clause. What about that?" Rayne toyed with the chicken breast on her plate and glanced up at Mr. Clark. She refused to eat the broccoli that came with her dish for fear it would end up in her teeth.

In his midthirties, Carvis Clark wore expensive-looking tan slacks and a cream-colored polo shirt with a tweed sports jacket. He looked—and she hated herself for this—very good. Since when did she make a habit of noticing handsome men?

*Since. . .Jack?* Rayne hated the fact that Jack was so handsome, because she wasn't the only one who'd noticed him. An image of Barb sitting on the conference table, crossing her legs in a short skirt, while Jack stood there, burned in her thoughts. Bile seared the back of her throat.

Mr. Clark cleared his throat, tugging her focus back to the interview. She took a sip of water, hoping it would hide the heat she felt in her face.

He'd invited her to meet him at Giovanni's, a pricey Italian restaurant in West Fargo. Initially, he'd wanted to fly her out to Southern California for the interview, but with FountainTech's schedule, and the fact that Rayne had recently taken off to be with her father, she couldn't afford the time to get away. So, here she was, sitting across from Mr. Carvis Clark, vice president of Elemental Innovations, Inc.

He flashed his perfect, white smile—the guy was as slick as they came, Rayne thought.

"California doesn't recognize noncompete clauses, even one signed in another state, and regardless, you might find that yours has expired by now. And if it makes you feel better, we've made plans to move into some new market niches, which I can't share with you just yet, but we've no plans to compete with FountainTech directly."

Rayne offered a flat smile. He had a point there. She'd worried needlessly, and yet she'd agreed to meet him in spite of her concerns.

Mr. Clark laid his silverware on the side of his plate and his napkin on the table, indicating he'd finished.

Rayne was relieved and hoped he wouldn't expect her to stay for dessert. She'd barely touched the food on her plate as it was. She glanced at her watch. Nine thirty already?

"It's getting late. I should probably go. You've given me enough to consider for right now."

Mr. Clark flashed his credit card, and the waiter appeared quickly, taking it from him. "We don't have a lot of time here, Rayne. What do you think?"

"I think I'm going to need at least a couple of days before I can decide."

He inhaled deeply, giving Rayne the sense he was disappointed.

"I'm afraid I can only give you one. You see, we've waited a few weeks for you as it is, and we have a big project that needs to move forward. With or without you." With his chin ducked, he studied her from beneath thick brows. "I'll be waiting for your answer tomorrow evening."

*❧*

Rayne felt as if she practically stumbled out of the elevator as it opened onto the FountainTech floor. She'd forgotten her laptop, leaving it in her office in her rush to escape her frustration with Jack, with the difficult schedule, yet again with Harold for not promoting her, and finally with Barb. Didn't the woman have any sense of self-respect?

At least it was ten at night, and she didn't have to worry about running into another employee. Everyone was burned out and ready to leave as soon as they could these last couple of weeks. She fumbled with her office door and, finally entering, flipped on the lights and flopped into her chair.

One day. She had one day to decide. Jack would be furious with her.

An image of Jack smiling down at Barb, who had effectively situated herself to reveal her ample bosom, flashed in Rayne's mind.

"Ugh!" Rayne threw a file at the wall. It slid down, spilling papers across the floor.

She sagged in the chair. Since when had she become a violent person? What was happening to her? This thing with Jack was turning her into a monster. A monster who couldn't work. Who couldn't produce the magic fountains that everyone expected.

Even Simon had noticed. She'd stood in the conference room this afternoon, pointing at all the little touches she'd added to make the fountain sing, but did it? She claimed it had, but it was as if she were in a poorly remade rendition of *The Emperor's New Clothes*.

There were no clothes, and only one person was brave enough to stand up to the truth. In this case, Simon had been all too happy to point out that nothing Rayne had added to the water sculpture had made it special.

Jack hadn't said a word. He believed in her. And since he believed in her—maybe even loved her—could she in good conscience desert him in the middle of this project?

Desert him when he claimed he needed her to make FountainTech the best it could be?

A little voice whispered that he said those same things to Barb. Rayne stared at the ceiling, unwilling to listen. She didn't believe that for a minute. Or at least, she didn't want to believe it.

Rayne and Jack—they had something special; they'd connected in a way that couples rarely found. Or was she fooling herself? Was it all part of her overactive imagination?

Her father would certainly say so. What words of wisdom would he give her for this moment? For a minute, she wished she were sitting at the kitchen table at her parents' farmhouse, listening to her father complain about the weather or lecture her about the best method to harvest wheat.

She could hear him now, giving her the advice she longed to hear.

*Don't count your chickens*—no, that seemed too cliché even for her father. Rayne exhaled loudly, wondering why his proverbs couldn't come to her when she actually *needed* them.

Something was amiss on her desk and drew her attention from her thoughts. Her laptop wasn't in her office. Could she actually have been that stupid? That distracted?

"Oh come on," she said, frustrated for leaving her laptop in the conference room. Hopefully, it was still there.

The halls remained lit during all hours, and Rayne was thankful for that as she made her way to the conference room. Through the glass doors, Rayne could see her laptop still resting on the table. She wished someone had thought to bring it to her office. Everyone was probably too beat to notice or care, the same as Rayne.

She shoved through the doors, relieved they weren't locked, and grabbed the laptop, then left. Harold spoke in hushed but agitated tones from his office, and she found herself involuntarily creeping past, as though she had something to hide.

Did she? She'd just finished dining with Carvis Clark, of a somewhat competitive company, though he'd claimed they weren't in direct competition.

*Oh Jack. . .what should I do?* She knew exactly what Jack would say, should she bring it up. But wasn't he only thinking of himself and his career? Why shouldn't she do the same?

How was she to make a decision when she felt so torn? *Lord, could You please, this one time, show me what to do?* She squeezed her eyes shut, marveling that she'd gone from wondering if she should have taken this job or stayed on the farm where she belonged, according to her father, to wondering if she should keep this job or move on to the next.

When she opened her eyes, she glanced over her shoulder and saw Harold peering at her from the doorway of his office.

His eyes narrowed.

*⁊*

Jack stared at the water pump resting on his dining table. Pulling resources from the local hardware store and a few items special ordered on eBay, he'd been able to jury-rig the basic concept behind his pump design—a powerful but streamlined pumping system.

He wanted to enjoy this moment and reflected that Harold had seemed intrigued with his schematics. After quitting EI to free himself from seeing Kiera every day, Jack had worked to come up with a new idea for the next six months, and had even considered starting his own company. That's when he'd gotten the call that FountainTech wanted to talk to him.

Jack only had to couple Rayne's creativity with the latest in technology, and companies would stand in line to acquire a unique water sculpture design created by the exclusive FountainTech, Incorporated.

Harold mentioned using the new design in their bid for the next contract, but Jack was anxious to test it first. The only problem was—Jack slid a chair back from the table and slumped onto it—he'd hurt Rayne. No matter how he'd tried to convince himself that it was for the best, he couldn't get the look on her face out of his mind.

He'd caught her dismay when she'd rushed from the conference room this afternoon. An ache pumped against his ribs—how had he allowed her to leave, allowed his attention to be pulled away by the likes of Barb? In his own defense, he reminded himself that Barb worked under him, too, that she had wanted to share her ideas with him, and he was obligated to listen.

Yeah, right.

Jack kicked the leg of the table, regretting he'd ever allowed himself to grow close enough to Rayne to kiss her. She didn't deserve to be hurt by a cad like him. His stupidity could cost the company as well.

He tapped his cell phone against the edge of the table. Should he call her? Or should he not? For too long already he'd deluded himself into thinking that he could have it both ways—he could pursue Rayne romantically and continue to work with her while she injected the creative spark into the fountains.

Together, Jack and Rayne would create the most spectacular designs the world had ever seen while they explored their feelings for each other. In the meantime, they would ignore the conflict in the workplace their office romance would inevitably cause. All the sticky situations, the jealousy and favoritism that others would point out.

Uh-huh. They'd only attempted to make this work for a short two weeks, and already things had failed miserably. He pictured a fountain when the power had been cut, gurgling and sputtering until it died.

The only way they could be together, really, was if Jack gave up his dreams for FountainTech, for his life, to make something of himself this time.

If he could be sure where things would lead, if he could be sure that Rayne would end up loving him—would he be willing to give it all up for her? Wasn't she worth that?

He smiled to himself a little, remembering how it felt to kiss her. Bolting from the chair, he headed for the fridge to get a soda to wet his dry mouth.

But things were too new, too fresh, for him to know that yet. Weren't they? Jack dialed Rayne's number. He needed to hear her voice. When the call went through to her voice mail, Jack scrambled to think of something coherent to say.

What would he say? After ignoring you at work today, I miss you? The voice mail signaled for him to leave a message. Jack hung up.

*✍♥*

Jack woke the next morning, groggy and running late. Not the way he liked to begin his day. He called Carl to let him know how sorry he was that he'd missed their racquetball date. Lately, he thought the game was all that was keeping him sane. It didn't require conversation or too much thought. Instead, it was about reflexes and raw power, slamming the ball as hard and fast as he could, and an opponent who could give as good as he got.

After a quick shower, Jack dressed, tucked his pump securely in the trunk of his car so he could test it in the lab this evening, and headed to FountainTech. He phoned Gail on his way to ask her to order pizza again for a working lunch and let his team know to assemble in the conference room again.

"I've got to put you on hold for a minute," Gail said, and then the expected elevator music resounded through the Bluetooth in his car.

He clenched his teeth. He didn't have time for this.

While he waited for Gail to return, a knot thickened in his throat. Was he focused on work, or was this just his way of seeing Rayne, but in a crowd and from a distance? She would have known he'd called last night, regardless of the fact he'd not left a message.

Why hadn't she called him back?

He supposed he was destined to remain a moron forever. As he raced around the corner to FountainTech, he spotted a large cross on the church located a few blocks down. Sure, he knew it was there and had seen it a hundred times since moving to Fargo, but for some reason, today, he *really* noticed it.

Why now, he wondered? He'd attended Heidi's church a few times, but that was mostly to make friends, and if he was honest, to see Rayne, though she'd never shown up.

Because God had ignored Jack's pain, was Jack ignoring God? Hardening his heart?

He frowned at the idea as he whizzed into the parking garage.

"Okay, Jack, sorry about that." Gail came back on the line. "Something's up."

"What are you talking about?"

"Well, there's some buzz around the office already," she said then lowered her voice so that he could barely understand her. "You need to head straight to Harold's office when you get here. Not sure you want me to assemble your team in the conference room. That's all I'm saying. Oops, gotta go."

She hung up.

Jack clenched his jaw as he rolled into his parking spot. Grabbing his cell, briefcase, and coat, he jumped from the car, carrying his coat over his arm. The days were getting warmer, and he'd just have to tug it off again anyway.

Finally, he stepped from the elevator onto FountainTech's floor and rushed through the glass double doors into the reception area. Gail was on the phone, and with wide eyes, she shrugged at him as he passed, as if to assure him she didn't know what was going on.

Jack hated being in the dark and had the fleeting thought that he should have called Barb to find out what she knew, but of course, that would be a mistake.

*Barb!*

He was supposed to meet with her this morning at seven. His chant, "Jack is back," slapped him in the face. He practically trotted down the hallway, dashing past a few members of his team who looked at him warily.

What was going on? He shoved through the door of his office and found Barb sitting there, waiting. She appeared flustered. Unusual for her.

Jack threw his coat over his chair. "I'm terribly sorry that I'm late. I'm afraid I can't meet with you this morning. Something's come up."

"Oh? What is it?" she asked.

He didn't dare look at her but unfolded his laptop on his desk and drew in a calming breath. *I don't know, and if I did, I wouldn't share it with you.* But then again, Barb probably already knew. Jack resisted the temptation to ask if she did.

When he looked through his schedule for the day, ignoring her, she finally broke the silence.

"Well, let me know when you're ready to hear my ideas. I'll be waiting."

Without looking up from his computer, Jack called after her, "Okay, will do."

"Jack." Gail stuck her head in the doorway that Barb had left open.

He glanced up to see her expression. With her head, she gestured toward Harold's office. "Uh, yeah, I'm on my way," Jack said.

Jack swiped his sweaty palms against his slacks. When had he ever been this nervous? And he didn't even know why he was supposed to rush to see Harold. It was probably nothing. Maybe even good news.

As Jack strode the hallways, he injected positive thoughts into his mind. Harold had good news for him. All Gail had said was that something was up. Could be something good, right?

He tapped on the door and stepped inside, shutting the door behind him without being asked.

"Jack, glad you could make it."

Jack gave a half grin at Harold's sarcasm. "Sorry I'm late. What's up?" Why did he have to be late today, when Harold of all people would notice? And Jack was *never* late.

"We have a situation with one of our employees."

"Yeah?" Okay, so this wasn't good news after all. Was Harold referring to Jack's dreaming of a relationship with Rayne that he hoped no one knew about yet? "What kind of situation?"

"I'm afraid our star creator, Rayne Flemming, is fraternizing with the competition. You'll need to terminate her immediately."

Stunned, Jack stared at Harold. *Oh Rayne, you didn't.* "So, what company? You can't blame Rayne if someone is trying to recruit her. That doesn't mean she's accepting a position with them. Let me talk to her. We'll convince her to stay with us." Why would Harold want to fire her over that? After all, Jack came from a competitive company himself, though he'd quit because of a romance gone bad long before hiring on at FountainTech. But still. . .

Harold raised his hand to silence Jack. "It's much more serious than that, son."

*Son?* So Harold was calling him "son" now? Jack drew in a breath and shrugged. "What then?"

"She's selling company secrets."

Harold had to be mistaken. The ache behind Jack's rib cage suddenly ramped up like it was fueled by a jet engine. He had to throw Rayne a lifeline somehow. What could he say in her defense? "What secrets?"

Because, really, how secret were their secrets once the fountains were out there for anyone to look at?

"Namely, your new pump design. The schematic you left with me was stolen from my office. Then someone saw Rayne with Carvis Clark last night."

# Chapter 18

J ack stared out the window of his office, hardly recalling how he made it from Harold's office to his own.

He'd worried, needlessly, about hurting Rayne.

However, he'd been correct to worry about getting hurt himself. He'd been right to decide he never wanted to love again. Why hadn't he abided by that rule?

Jack thought he'd successfully hardened his heart against the pain, but Rayne had managed to inflict a new kind of pain on him—betrayal. With it came the realization of just how much he cared for her.

He thought he could avoid feeling the pain of loss again, having successfully shoved away the memories of his parents dying in the house fire and recently shoving aside what he thought was love for Kiera.

Falling for Rayne—and he realized now, that he had fallen hard—opened his eyes to the fact that what he had with Kiera wasn't love at all. How could it be love when he hadn't known the real Kiera? But clearly, Rayne wasn't who Jack had imagined her to be either, and she hadn't cared about him. Just like Kiera hadn't cared about him.

He'd prided himself in being able to read people. Was he doomed to lose when it came to love?

The sting of Rayne's duplicity overwhelmed him, drowning him in misery.

Both his office phone and his cell continued to ring, and although someone knocked on his door, he'd locked it and remained unresponsive.

Maybe that's why he'd noticed that cross this morning. God was mocking him, knowing full well what news waited for him. Until this moment, Jack hadn't fully understood what was required to protect his heart. If he'd done a good job, he wouldn't feel this gut-wrenching pain inside. And now he'd do what was needed to freeze his heart. Everything inside him would need to congeal, and soon. Harold expected Jack to fire Rayne.

He closed his eyes and drew on the anger that lingered in the shadows of his heart, anger created from a hundred frustrations—Kiera for starters, and then there was God, who allowed his parents to die. And finally, yes, that was it. . . Jack drew in a breath and fanned to life his fury at Rayne for what she'd done to him.

That was the only way he would survive this moment.

She'd duped him. Finally, when he thought he would explode with rage, Jack composed himself and lifted the phone, dialing Gail.

"Yes, Jack?"

In a calm, flat voice, he said, "Send Rayne to my office, please."

He hung up the phone and stared at the door, remembering he needed to unlock it. In a few short moments, a woman he had been ready to give up his career and dreams for, a woman who had used and duped him, who had sold his design to the highest bidder—might as well have been his soul—would walk through the door of his office.

Jack noticed that he was squeezing the arms of his chair, his knuckles white, so he relaxed his hands, only to see they were trembling. Perhaps if Harold had known how Jack felt about Rayne, he wouldn't have assigned him this task. Then again, had Harold known, Jack could be implicated as well.

A new concern flooded his thoughts. If someone found out about him and Rayne, might he be accused? Though it was Jack's design, Harold could possibly terminate Jack, too, and try to keep the design. Contracts always included the clause that anything the employee created relating to the company while in its employ belonged to the company. Fortunately, because Jack had been working on a design beforehand, he'd negotiated on that point with Harold before joining FountainTech.

Someone tapped on the door, and Rayne stuck her head in. "You wanted to see me?"

"Please, have a seat."

He watched her shut the door and drop into the chair across from him. There were shadows under her eyes, and she looked more fatigued than he'd ever seen her. She must be all too aware that her game was up.

Emotion flooded her expression, filled her eyes. "What's wrong, Jack?"

For an instant, he thought she might reach across the desk, closing the distance between them. Jack imagined quitting FountainTech and leaving with Rayne. They could be together.

A vise gripped his chest and squeezed his throat. That's all he wanted—for them to be together. Finally, he shut his eyes.

But, no, Rayne had used him.

❧

Rayne held her breath. She had never seen this look of complete desperation on Jack's face. And she thought *she'd* had a tough time making a decision—torn about taking an opportunity with another company that would allow her and Jack to be open about their relationship. She'd prayed all night long for a sign from God. Surely He would frown on a relationship that she had to hide. But to go to another company? It reeked of disloyalty.

If she'd learned anything from her father, it was to remain loyal, no matter the cost. And that's why it was so difficult to seemingly turn her back on her parents as she pursued her career and dreams.

She'd call Mr. Clark this morning and given him her answer—she wouldn't be leaving Jack or FountainTech.

As she looked at Jack, the room felt like all the oxygen had been sucked out. Jack's face was lined and pale. His rigid frown deepened, and there was a sadness in his eyes that she'd never seen before. In anyone.

Suddenly, all of those emotions vanished, and his face grew stern, his eyes freezing over. She sucked in a breath. "Jack, please, you have to tell me what's wrong. What's happened?"

Did Jack have family somewhere who had been in an accident, or worse—died?

Jack drew his gaze from hers, and for that instant, his eyes seemed to reflect the tears of a thousand fountains. He toyed with his smartphone, tapping it against the desk.

Clearly, he was searching for the right words.

Whatever it was obviously involved her. An image flashed in her mind, and the room began to spin. "Oh no, Jack. Has something happened to my father?"

His stern expression infused with concern. "What? Of course not," he snapped, his words harsher than she'd ever heard. Softer, this time, he said, "No, Rayne, no."

"Then what?"

"How could you do it?"

Rayne's jaw dropped open, as she tried to form words. "Oh. . ."

"Oh? That's all you have to say?"

Obviously, someone had seen her meeting with Carvis Clark. "Listen, it's not what it looks like."

"You steal the schematics for my pump and sell them to another company. Tell me how that's a misunderstanding."

The walls tilted again as the blast of his words exploded through her, piercing her like shrapnel. "Wha—?"

"As of this moment, you're terminated." A deep frown lined Jack's forehead, and he rocked his chair around to face the back of the office.

How could he believe she'd do a thing like that? Stunned, Rayne could barely stand, much less voice, the thoughts igniting in her mind in her own defense. Of all the reasons she'd imagined he wanted to see her this morning, something like this hadn't occurred to her.

Regardless that she was being terminated under false pretenses—well, partially false, because FountainTech wouldn't want an employee who was fraternizing with its competition for any reason—she could no longer work with Jack. Not after this. Not after he had believed a complete lie about her and, and. . .

*Fired* her!

As tears blurred her vision, Rayne knew one thing. God had answered last night's prayers for direction quickly this time.

# Chapter 19

Jack stared out his window, willing himself to remain composed and in control of the situation, willing Rayne to just. . .leave. He watched the clouds gather.

The tension in his office felt statically charged, one wrong move from either of them and the room might explode in white light.

Rayne sniffled behind him. "How could you believe such a thing, Jack?" she asked, her voice barely audible.

Her words sliced him open, severing the last of his control. How was he supposed to endure this anguish? He squeezed his eyes shut, *God, help me. . . .*

Jack whirled his chair around to face Rayne, but she'd left without another word. His office door stood open. He grabbed his coat and rushed out and through the reception area. He had to get out of there, get some air.

"I'll be back after lunch," he said, answering Gail's questioning gaze as he shoved through the glass doors.

In his car, Jack pulled out of the parking garage and into traffic. How he wished he could just drive until all his frustrations were spent. Once out of Fargo, he found himself on a lone stretch of highway, and then he passed the little country church where Heidi attended, Rayne supposedly attended, and he'd visited a few times. Fargo Community Church. He recalled his earlier thoughts this morning when he'd noticed the cross on the church he passed on his way into work.

Pain throbbed in his chest, an emotional pain so powerful it had become physical—something Jack had never experienced before. And it scared him. After looking both ways, he made a U-turn and zipped back toward the church, then drove into the parking lot, stopping the car in a marked space farthest from the front door.

Leaving the engine running, Jack pressed his forehead against the steering wheel. What was going on? *Lord, what am I doing here?*

Maybe it was a last desperate attempt to get God's attention because God had ignored Jack and his anguish for far too long. He considered that he should go inside the church and sit in a pew or maybe kneel at the altar if they had one—was there an altar inside the church? Jack couldn't remember. All he knew was that the grief had paralyzed him. He flat out could not move, and if he could, he was sure he would collapse to his knees.

*Thump, thump, thump.* Jack startled at the sound, bolting upright to see Pastor Luke standing next to his car, knocking on the window.

"Are you okay?" Pastor Luke said despite the fact Jack hadn't lowered the window.

Jack did just that and forced a smile. "Sure, I'm fine."

"I'm not convinced." Pastor Luke lifted a brow. "Why don't you come in, and we'll talk."

Jack shook his head. "No, I couldn't bother you."

"Come on, son. You and I both know that you're here for a reason. Could it be that God brought you here?"

Jack pressed his back against the seat and exhaled slowly. Maybe, finally, God had seen the agony Jack carried. Maybe now God was ready to talk. "All right. You win. I've got a few minutes to spare."

Jack cringed, his last words hitting him squarely in the gut. Could it be all this time that God had been there, waiting on him? Could it be that Jack was the one ignoring God, only giving Him "a few minutes to spare," which rarely happened, if ever?

"Don't worry. You might not have much time, but God has all the time in the world for the perfecting of the saints."

Jack climbed from the car and slammed the door behind him. Pastor Luke squeezed his shoulder and led him into the little church. Jack took in the pulpit and the stained glass windows, but they did nothing to ease his soul. Pastor Luke then entered his office, Jack on his heels.

"Now, tell me what's bothering you."

Sitting in the chair across from Pastor Luke's desk, Jack stared down at his hands. "I don't have a clue where to start."

How did one go about sharing things like this with a complete stranger, though he was a pastor, a shepherd to the members of this church?

"I should have suggested we pray first, I'm sorry," Pastor Luke said. He bowed his head and began thanking the Lord for all His blessings. Then he moved into praying earnestly for Jack, that God knew his heart and was even now working in Jack's life.

The words disturbed Jack, but probably because they were closer to the truth than he wanted the pastor to know. He hated the moisture surfacing in his eyes, but with it came the lifting of a weight, a washing away of his burdens.

Jack opened up then to Pastor Luke, and to God, as he'd never done before. All of the hurts and frustrations that had occurred in his life, the pain that had left him scarred, seemed to gush out of a deep well. It surprised Jack that he had so much pent up inside him. At times his words sounded harsh and cutting, even to his own ears.

To his credit, Pastor Luke just listened with a concerned but caring look. Jack could see nothing judgmental in the man's expression. When Jack finished, Pastor Luke asked if they could pray again.

"Son, only God can heal these wounds. He's more than willing, but you have to let go of them and give them to Him. I believe you've done that today here with me and with our heavenly Father listening. He's right here, too.

Pray again with me, and let's give Him these burdens. They're too much for you to carry."

So Jack prayed with Pastor Luke, and for the first time in years, he forgave and was forgiven. He hadn't realized the weight he'd carried in his heart. Now he almost felt as if he was floating—spiritually speaking, of course.

"Because God has given us free will, much of the turmoil in our lives is caused by our own decisions and, unfortunately, the decisions of others around us. You can't blame God for your hurts, but you can thank Him now for using this situation to bring you to your knees." Pastor Luke chuckled. "Pun intended. God is in the business of making beauty from ashes."

Feeling like a man newly freed from prison, Jack wished Pastor Luke well and assured him he would call in a couple of days. Walking to his car, Jack noticed he had a bounce in his step that hadn't been there in a while.

The sun broke through the clouds and shined on his car, and at that moment, Jack wondered why he'd so easily believed the news Harold had shared with him about Rayne. He hadn't even questioned the accusations.

❧

Taking a deep breath, Rayne opened the front door. "Hello, Mom, Dad. Anybody here?"

In the middle of the day, her father was probably in the fields, planting his crop. Rayne headed to the kitchen and almost collided with her mother.

Her mother gripped her arms. "Rayne! What a surprise."

Rayne smiled, still wearing her sunglasses to hide her eyes. "Hi, Mom. Sorry I startled you."

"I was just about to throw together a casserole for this evening. What brings you here in the middle of the week?" She tugged on an apron.

Rayne found a glass in the cabinet and poured lemonade from a pitcher on the counter. "I have some time off and wanted to check on Dad."

Her mother gave a wave of her hand then dragged a casserole dish from under the counter. "You know your father—he's back to work like nothing happened. We've got a farm to run, Rayne. Don't forget that."

Relaxing a little because her mother wasn't scrutinizing her, Rayne shoved the sunglasses onto her head. She took a few swallows of the lemonade then set down the glass. This was it, then. God had finally answered her prayer for direction, and now she'd be moving back to the farm. Her family needed her, and evidently FountainTech did not.

But it wasn't by her choice, and she felt like a failure. Worst of all—

Rayne leaned against the counter for support as she pushed an image of Jack's face from her mind.

How had she even made it all the way out to the farm?

"Honey, are you all right?" Her mother wrapped an arm around her waist. "You sit down here."

Rayne felt herself being guided to the kitchen table and into a chair.

This wasn't how she wanted to look in front of her mother. The last thing she needed right now was to have to answer questions. How could she tell her mother that she'd been fired, and that Jack had believed the worst and been the one to do the deed?

"Are you feeling ill? Is that why you came home?" Her mother held her palm against Rayne's forehead.

Rayne leaned her head out of her mother's reach. "I've already told you I came home to see how Daddy was doing." Nausea began to spin in her stomach, and she pressed her hand against her waist. "But you're right. Must be something I ate."

"Well, let's see." Her mother put one hand on her hip and a finger to her mouth. "I've got some Pepto-Bismol in the bathroom upstairs."

"You finish your casserole. I'll lie down for a little while." Rayne forced a smile, though weak, hoping to reassure her mother.

At the bottom of the stairs, Rayne's gaze followed the steps up to the door to her room. Why had she come back? She'd not even stopped at her apartment to pack, and she'd asked Gail to pack her office things up and ship them to her at the farm. She never wanted to step foot in FountainTech again.

Rayne trembled. No. She couldn't go to her room, because right now she could hardly think straight. She knew that it would only make her feel as if she'd been imprisoned. She thought of all she'd had to overcome to leave this place. Even though she loved the farm, loved her parents, she'd wanted more, and now she was thrown back into the middle of it.

What she needed most was to find solace in the same place she'd always found inspiration. The problem was that place only served to remind her of Jack now.

The front door swooshed open, and Paul rushed in without knocking, just like he owned the place.

*Something must have happened. Dad!*

"Is it my father? What's wrong?"

His eyes grew wide as he drew in a breath. "No, Rayne, it's you. Are you all right?"

Confused, she shrugged. "Of course, why would you think—"

"Because. . ." Paul glanced around the house. "Let's talk in private."

Rayne wanted to tell Paul no, but how could she? He didn't deserve to be treated poorly. No matter that her life had been shattered today.

"What is it?" she asked.

He tugged her out the door, and she willed herself to follow him over to his truck.

He touched her shoulder. "Rayne, I sent you flowers at your work today."

Rayne didn't think she had any blood left in her face. Her knees went weak, but she clung to the truck door with all her might, still unwilling to admit anything to Paul.

The Adam's apple in his throat bobbed up and down. "Is it true, Rayne? Have you come back to us? They told me you no longer worked at FountainTech."

"They *told* you that?"

"The flower people called me to say they tried to deliver the flowers. When you didn't answer your cell, I called the company directly. The woman there wanted the address to the farm. Said you wanted your stuff sent there."

This day could not get any worse. Rayne rubbed her hands down her face. "Okay, Paul. You cannot tell a soul. I'm not ready to tell anyone. I don't know what I'm doing yet either."

Paul looked hurt, confused. "What do you mean?"

It was ironic. Her parents hadn't believed in her when she wanted to pursue this career. And now Jack didn't believe in her. But Paul. . .

"You've never stopped believing in me, have you?"

A slow smile eased onto his lips. "Or that you'd come back."

Rayne thought he might squeeze her, swing her around in a circle, and then kiss her. That's what made the moment all the more awkward. "Paul, there's something I have to tell you."

# Chapter 20

He should have relied on his instinct about Rayne instead of taking Harold at his word.

*Lord, this is a new thing for me, asking You for help. But, please, show me what to do.*

Using the Bluetooth in his car, he called the office. Gail answered, "FountainTech. How may I direct your call?"

"Gail, it's Jack. I need to speak with Harold."

"Harold's in a meeting. He's not taking any calls."

Jack pressed the gas pedal, accelerating. What could be more important than what Jack had to talk to him about? "Can you tell him that it's me? I'm sure he'll want to talk to me."

"Okay, Jack. Give me a sec."

Fields zoomed past, littered with huge commercial farm tractors, as Jack raced down the lone North Dakota road, waiting for Harold to come on the line.

"I'm sorry, Jack," Gail said. "He's not responding. I'll let him know as soon as I can that you need to speak to him. Is everything okay?"

"Everything is fine, why?" Jack wanted to know what she'd heard about this morning's incident.

"When Rayne left this morning, she asked that I pack her office up and send her things to her family's farm." Her voice trembled.

Jack blew out a long breath he was certain Gail didn't miss. What could he say? At least now he knew his suspicions had been right. When Rayne hadn't been at her apartment, Jack headed toward the farm.

"There's something else. It's probably not important. I just. . ." Gail definitely sounded like she was going to cry. "I had to reject a beautiful bouquet of roses this morning. They were for Rayne."

*Oh boy.* That *Paul* again.

And Jack? He was nothing but a cad. While Paul was sending her flowers, Jack was firing her.

Though Jack certainly didn't blame him, and it only fueled Jack to keep trying himself.

"Thanks for letting me know. I have an appointment and will be out of the office."

And he did have an appointment. With Rayne.

*I hope.* He also hoped that before seeing Rayne he would be able to solve the mystery of who passed on a company secret—Jack's new design.

Unfortunately, he knew exactly who to call next.

A woman who doubled as a shark and knew industry secrets that slipped past others.

A woman he once thought he'd loved.

He laid off the accelerator. What was worse, her cell number was still in his phone, that is, if she hadn't changed it. Using voice commands, he called Kiera, though he seriously doubted she would answer. But he had to try.

She answered after the second ring. "Jack? This can't be you," she said, in a mocking tone.

He grinned. She'd answered, after all.

"Kiera." It felt funny, saying her name out loud again. At one time he loved the sound of her name. Not any longer.

"I never thought I'd hear from you again."

And Jack was certain she never wanted to either, but that was beside the point. "How are things?"

Her laugh was incredulous. "I'm engaged, now. I suppose I shouldn't even have answered."

"Whoever he is, he's a lucky guy. Congratulations." Surprisingly, the news didn't sting. In fact, it might make this conversation easier. Jack needed to quickly steer this discussion away from their personal lives, though, or things would take a dive—as though they could go any lower. "Listen, I didn't call to talk about our personal lives. Let's talk shop."

"Oh, I get it. Your new job not working out?"

"As a matter of fact, I might be looking." Jack cringed, but truthfully, wasn't everyone always looking for a better opportunity? And right now, yes, he was definitely digging.

"Ah, and you think they might want you back here. Well, I for one will not put in a good word for you if that's what you're asking."

Oh man. This wasn't going as he wanted it to. No wonder he wasn't a lawyer. He couldn't play good cop–bad cop either. Jack did not want to do this, but he was going to have to beg. *Okay, here goes.* "Kiera, I'm sorry that everything between us went sour."

He drew in a breath. *I could use a little help here, Lord.* "And I apologize for every nasty thing I ever did or said to you." There. Actually, that did feel better. "I wish. . .and I wish. . ."

What? Memories of the good times, though few, he'd shared with Kiera drifted over his heart. No. He couldn't possibly wish that he and Kiera were back together because. . .because. . .

He was in love with Rayne.

There, he'd admitted it. And it felt wonderful.

Yes! He pumped his fist.

Except—Jack exhaled long and hard, feeling a deep ache creep back in— he'd just fired the woman he loved.

"Oh. . .Jack." Kiera sounded softer now, oozing femininity. "I've waited so long to hear you say that. I made a mistake."

Say what? Oh no, what had he said? "Kiera, wait. What I mean to say is that though things didn't work out for us, you've obviously moved on, and there's someone in my life who is special, too."

There. He hoped she felt like she had the upper hand again, though he'd almost just blown it.

She sighed.

He knew that sound. Jack cut her off before she could turn nasty. "I want us to be friends, Kiera. Good friends. We don't have to be angry with each other, do we? Especially since you've found someone better than me."

And oh, he'd found someone so much better for him than Kiera. *Please, God, let me win Rayne back.*

"Oh all right, Jack. Truce. Let's be friends. So, why did you really call?"

"Carvis is trying to steal one of my employees."

"Jack, you know I can't say anything about that. I don't think she took the job anyway."

Really? Jack wasn't sure if that was a good thing or not—because Rayne had reasoned they could be more romantically engaged if she were to work elsewhere—but that was beside the point. Where did he go from here?

"I'm not sure he needed her anyway. He got his hands on something else."

*Bingo.* Jack froze. "What did you say? Who did he get the drawing from?"

"I don't think I said the word *drawing*. Come on, I've said enough already."

"Look, Kiera, I don't care about the design. I need to know who he got the design from."

"I can't believe I'm talking to you about this. But I don't know anything anyway."

"Can you do this one thing for me? Find out who passed on the design?"

"You could always make me talk, you know that? And now, what are you doing? Trying to get me fired so you can take my job?"

"For old time's sake and because we're friends now."

"How important is it?" her voice grew stern and demanding.

Dread coursed through him. She could very well use this to stab him in the back. But he had no choice. "There's nothing more important to me."

"Really."

He had never liked the Kiera he was hearing now. He bit his tongue, holding off his own sarcastic reply. *Lord, help me. Give me grace here.*

A memory from a Sunday school class he'd attended as a child slipped to the forefront of his thoughts—his Sunday school teacher speaking softly. " '*A gentle answer turns away wrath, but a harsh word stirs up anger.*' " Although he couldn't remember the scripture reference for the verse, it had to be from Proverbs. That much he knew.

Jack slowly released a breath, feeling any remnants of pent-up anger toward this woman seep away with it.

"I hope this new guy knows how to treat you. I hope he knows what a real gem he has—you're one of the most beautiful women I've ever seen." And he meant that.

"I'm onto you, you know that? But I guess if you're willing to grovel like that, it must be pretty important. I'll see what I can find out then call you back."

Jack released the breath he'd held and grinned. "That's all I can ask, Kiera."

"Yeah, well, that's asking a lot, Jack. You owe me."

"Fair enough."

Jack ended the call and tried to think positive thoughts. While he now believed in Rayne, believed she wouldn't have sold him out, there was still a reason to be uneasy. Kiera could come back with Rayne's name. Still, even if Kiera did, there might be some mistake or someone might be trying to place the blame where it didn't belong.

🖙

A cool breeze swept against Rayne's face as she stood at the ledge that allowed her to look over her father's fields—her secret place, as she'd told Jack.

This year had been too wet to plant wheat, so her father was going with corn. But he had to get the soil prepared and the crop planted before mid- to late April or else he'd plant barley or soybeans. The farming thoughts settled her heart. In the distance, she spotted several tractors hauling corn planters behind them. In just over a week, she would be able to see the slender blades emerging from the soil, creating row after row of corn.

Her father was one of the few in North Dakota to use a watering system, but he only used it on corn or potatoes because their revenue was much higher than other crops. If she stuck around, she'd be able to watch the water again. Her spirits sagged at the reminder of FountainTech.

When she was a child, this was not only her secret place, but to her child's heart, it was *sacred*. Here she'd talked to God. Here she'd been inspired to create her drawings that depicted wind flowing over wheat. Here she'd watched her father's water sprinkling system irrigate the cornfields, and she'd fallen in love with the fluidity of water.

What had she been thinking, to bring Jack here of all places?

When she thought about it, the hours she'd spent here, after chores of course, had led her to her job at FountainTech. And now she was back.

She rubbed her sleeve against her eyes and cheeks, wiping away the last of the tears—evidence that she'd failed. Her father had been right—it had been a pipe dream at best.

All his proverbs, all his wisdom, and still he was blind to life outside of his farm. Rayne chided herself for thinking about her father in a negative light. But she couldn't help it. At least she wasn't blind to the fact that pride was eating her up inside—she dreaded, with everything in her, the moment when she would tell her father what happened.

That she was back at the farm after all.

Her parents wouldn't gloat that things had worked out according to their plan and not hers. Nor would they care that she was in her twenties and an independent woman, capable of taking care of herself. An incredulous chuckle escaped. They would, however, expect her to marry Paul when all was said and done. He was one of their kind, and surely Rayne could find it in her heart to love him.

If only that were true. But she'd lost more than her job. She'd lost her heart and had nothing left to give to Paul.

She hoped she had put an end to that line of thinking by telling Paul the truth. She loved someone else. Rayne pressed her hands against her chest and squeezed her eyes against the pain balling once again around her heart, constricting her throat.

Crunching footfalls resounded in the copse of trees behind her. She steeled herself, hoping it wasn't Paul. Her heart grew sad at the thought—he was persistent as a mule, considerate and forgiving to a fault. But she would not, could not, love him. Not like she loved Jack—though she'd been woefully mistaken where Jack was concerned. She couldn't marry someone she didn't love, not after tasting something as powerful as what she felt for Jack.

But that was over now. Drawing in a breath, she prepared to face Paul, or whoever had come to seek her out. She whirled around.

*Jack?*

And took a step back into air. . .

"Watch out." He reached out and gripped her arm, tugging her away from the ledge.

Rayne was stunned to see him, and she looked down to where his hands still held on to her. Slowly, he released her.

Words and thoughts of anger, hurt, and love were jumbled in her head. She couldn't speak.

"Rayne," he said, in a hoarse whisper.

"How. . .how did you find me?" Her throat hurt, but finally she found her voice. The terrain had been snow-covered when she'd brought him here before.

"Paul brought me."

Paul? Why would he do that? Rayne didn't believe Jack. Feeling more confident, she asked, "Why are you here?"

Jack had the strangest expression on his face—a mixture of hope and fear. "Can you ever forgive me, Rayne? I'm so sorry about what happened. I need a chance to explain. Will you give me that?"

He searched her gaze, his eyes roaming down her face and then back to her eyes as if he hadn't seen her in years. Like a man who. . .

No, he couldn't have any feelings for her. "You fired me, Jack. You believed. . ." *A lie.* She allowed the anger and hurt to harden her, protect her.

He didn't deserve to know the truth if, after all they'd shared, he couldn't believe in her, couldn't defend her, and was more concerned about keeping his precious job. Making a future for himself. "You've got some nerve. All you care about is yourself."

Rayne had never heard herself speak in such a hateful tone. It hurt and yet felt good at the same time. *God, please help me. You brought me to this point. Now show me what to believe.*

Jack's face contorted, apprehension flooding his eyes. "I've been trying to figure out how to tell you everything."

Now she turned her back on him again, afraid to let him see how much he'd hurt her. Never again. "There's nothing more to say. Go back to FountainTech."

"I need a second chance. Please hear me out. After what happened, I went to church and met with Pastor Luke."

Rayne frowned at his words, now compelled to listen. She said nothing, though, and waited for him to continue as she watched the tractors planting corn.

"He helped me work through all the hurt and frustrations I've held on to all these years so I could finally resolve that I blamed God for everything bad that ever happened to me."

Rayne looked at the ground to her right, glimpsing Jack in her peripheral vision. "Go on." She still wasn't sure what this had to do with him firing her.

"This was all part of God's plan, leading me to that church today, Rayne. And now I'm free from a lot of pain I've carried."

Finally, Rayne turned to face him. She shrugged. "So, firing me was all part of God's plan to get you to church?" Rayne gave him an incredulous laugh. "I'm glad you've reestablished your relationship with the Lord, Jack. But what does that have to do with me?" She hated the bite that still lingered in her voice.

"Don't you see, Rayne? I've been avoiding a real relationship with anyone, not just God, for a long time, because I was afraid of being hurt, of being betrayed. When Harold said that you had given the design for my new pump to a competitor, all I could see was betrayal. It wasn't within my DNA, within my power, to think anything else, though I wanted to. With everything in me, I struggled to believe that you could ever do such a thing."

"And yet you did believe that."

"It wasn't until getting right with God that the skies cleared for me, so to speak. I saw with clarity that you couldn't be the culprit. I tried to speak with Harold, but he was in a meeting. I drove directly here."

Rayne wanted to believe Jack, but he'd made that very difficult. "Okay, so you found out who stole your design, and it turned out to be someone else. I'm still not coming back to work." She turned her back to him again.

He only believed in her after he'd learned the truth. Where she came from, that didn't count as trust.

# Chapter 21

Moron. Jack was fumbling and badly. Rayne wasn't buying.

He fought to retain his composure, though everything in him wanted to melt into the ground like the spring snow.

*Lord, give me the words. . . .*

"No. That's not it. I haven't found out who sold the fountain pump design."

Rayne's shoulders stiffened. Maybe she would listen now.

"I just know, with everything in my heart, that it wasn't you, because. . ."

Jack couldn't believe it, but Rayne slowly turned to face him, tears brimming in her eyes. Her lips trembled.

"You believe that?" she asked.

*Now's the moment to be bold.* Jack nodded and took a step closer to her, sliding his hand against her neck, cupping her cheek. "How could I believe the woman I love could do such a thing?"

Her eyes grew wide before she squeezed them shut. "Oh Jack. To believe in me, to trust me like that, despite what it looks like. Well, it means everything."

"Rayne, I love you." Jack studied her face, watching her reaction.

She opened her eyes, and in them he saw the depth of her love in return. He saw what he'd hoped and prayed to see. "Will you forgive me?" he asked.

"Oh Jack, I love you, too. There's nothing to forgive. Now, will you kiss me?"

Jack felt his grin nearly split his face. "Will *I* kiss you?" He covered her lips with his, pouring all the pent-up emotions into it, feeling her heart mingling with his. The world seemed a million miles away.

Then Jack's cell phone chirped in his pocket. Rayne tried to tug free.

"Ignore it," Jack murmured against her lips. He loved the feel of her arms around his neck, especially when she pulled him closer.

What he had with Kiera was nothing compared to this.

Oh. . .*Kiera.*

Jack gently ended the kiss then hugged Rayne to him, whispering in her ear, "I need to see who called."

He tugged the phone from his pocket. "It's Kiera. The call I was expecting."

Rayne had a dreamy smile on her face. "Who's Kiera?"

Jack considered what to say to Rayne. Bringing up that he was trying to find out who had passed on his design was bad enough, given that he'd just shared that he believed in her, regardless. But add to the mix that he'd contacted his ex-fiancé to do it probably wouldn't go over well.

"I'm trying to get to the bottom of things." He winked as he waited for his call to connect, thankful and surprised that he had two reception bars out here.

Kiera answered quickly. "Jack, I have only a second."

"What did you find out?"

"Oh, I'm fine, and how are you?"

Jack surmised that someone was near Kiera that she didn't want listening in. "It's great to hear your voice, Kiera."

"I can barely hear yours. Where are you, anyway?"

"You said you didn't have much time, now give."

"Okay, here's what I've learned." Kiera spoke softly.

Jack had to strain to hear and even stuck his finger in his other ear.

"Carvis just sent an offer letter to a guy named Simon Jeffers. My understanding is that Simon is bringing a design with him. Carvis wanted another creator but went with this Simon guy instead, for obvious reasons."

Jack wanted to curse. He'd only recently started the laborious task of patenting his design, but would that matter if someone were bent on stealing it anyway? All Simon would have to do was change the wording on even a small element of Jack's design to create his own patent. "Thanks for the information, Kiera. It means a lot to me. But Carvis is going to have to face the music. Simon, too."

Harold had already contacted the company's attorney. Jack was beyond relieved that Rayne wasn't involved.

Kiera sighed. "I'm sorry. I know this is a blow to you. This business can be so cutthroat."

Jack certainly didn't need to hear that from Kiera, but he shoved his previous summation of her aside.

Harold had pinned the whole thing on Rayne just because another employee saw her talking to Carvis Clark. She was close enough to Jack and knew about the design. He wondered how Simon found out and if someone else was involved. Barb flitted to his mind—she and Simon were pretty close. But let the lawyers figure that one out.

Jack looked at Rayne and gave her a reassuring smile.

"You asked where Carvis got the design, and I've found that for you. I have to go now, Jack. Don't be a stranger."

And just like that, Kiera ended the call.

Jack sighed, feeling as if a weight had been placed across his shoulders again. He tried to tug Rayne to him, but she refused to budge.

"What's going on, Jack?"

He scratched his head. Where did he begin? "Why would Harold think that you sold my design to the competition just because you were seen talking to Carvis? But then again. . ."

Rayne frowned and looked out over the fields. "Apparently he wanted me gone. But why?"

"You're the company's top creative genius. That wouldn't make sense," he offered. Jack tried again to hold her, and this time she stepped back into his arms. "Simon is going to work for Elemental Innovations. Carvis hired him because he's bringing a new design with him. He obviously hasn't given his resignation letter to Harold yet, because Harold didn't accuse him. I wonder if Simon will even come back to work. Probably too scared." In spite of the situation, Jack allowed a chuckle. "Simon was jealous of you though. And now he positioned himself to take a job offer meant for you. Now *that* makes sense."

"I don't want to think about it anymore," she said and lifted her chin.

Jack answered her pleading lips, shoving thoughts of FountainTech far away.

With a cry, Rayne tore her lips from his. "I know why. The night I met with Carvis. . ." Rayne offered him a sheepish grin then continued. "I went to the FountainTech offices late to get my laptop, which I'd left in the conference room. Harold was there talking to someone on his phone. He must have thought I overheard something, because he looked like he wanted to skewer me alive. But honestly, since I hadn't heard what he was saying, I didn't think another thing about it."

"Until you kissed me," Jack said and grinned. Then he injected a serious tone into his voice. "That might explain things. He discovered the schematics stolen, saw you in the office late, heard about your meeting with Carvis."

A knot grew firmly in Jack's throat. Where did that leave him then? How could he work for FountainTech now, considering that Harold—though he'd misconstrued the circumstances—had asked Jack to fire Rayne? Considering that Jack had gone through with it?

Footfalls pounded and crunched through the trees until Paul appeared, breathless. "Fire. . .there's a fire at the barn!"

※

Rayne sat in the center seat of the truck's cab, squished between Paul and Jack, as Paul steered his truck over the unpaved and bumpy road. Her head struck the top of the cab at one point.

But she didn't care. Fear coursed through her at the thought of the house burning. Too many things were crashing down on her at once. As Paul swerved the truck around a bend and onto a better road where he accelerated, Rayne wanted to ask him why he'd brought Jack to see her.

But her thoughts were smothered when she finally saw for herself the plumes of smoke spiraling into the sky. Rayne clasped her hand to her throat. "Lord, please keep my family safe."

At her words, she recalled that Jack had lost his family in a house fire. A quick glance at his face showed her the deep lines there. She reached down and squeezed his hand. He'd called 911 for them because Paul couldn't find his cell phone, and she wondered if it had brought back memories.

He squeezed back and then wrapped his arm around her, pressing her head against his shoulder. "Everything is going to be all right."

"I'm not so sure. We live so far out. I don't even hear the sirens yet." Rayne untangled herself from Jack and gripped the dashboard as Paul yanked the truck into the circular drive behind Jack's sports car.

Flames licked out the top and sides of the barn. "At least it's not the house," Rayne heard herself saying.

Paul, Rayne, and Jack were out of the truck in no time, running to assist her father, who had hooked up a water hose and sprayed the barn. He must have seen the smoke from the fields and come in.

This couldn't be good for him. Rayne's mother just stood there, sobbing, which surprised Rayne. She'd always seen her mother as a strong person. But then again her mother had carried a heavy burden since her father's heart attack. He'd just recently begun working the farm in full force again. Rayne's heart ached to see her mother like this.

Paul stepped forward. "Let me do that, Mr. Flemming."

Rayne's father fought him off. "I can do this."

"Of course you can. I'm just giving you a break."

"Please, Daddy," Rayne offered with a soft smile. Finally, her father relinquished the hose to Paul and stumbled back. Rayne hugged him. "Fire trucks are on their way."

"They won't make it, Rayne."

"We have to think positive; we have to pray."

"Our only hope now is that flames or sparks don't reach the house. I guess we could pray for rain."

Rayne couldn't stand to hear the sound of defeat in her father's voice, but his comment reminded her of when her mother told her about her name. She'd been born during a severe drought, and they'd been praying for rain every day. The day she came into the world, it finally rained. Her mother said she'd been an answer to prayer, so they named her Rayne.

Her mother had then paraphrased a Bible verse from Acts. "He has shown kindness by giving us rain from heaven and crops in their seasons; he provides us with plenty of food and fills our hearts with joy. You are my rain from heaven, child."

Rayne couldn't help but weep at the thought. *Lord, can You send Your rain now? Save my parents' farm? I'm sorry for wanting more when You've already given me so much.*

"Oh honey." Her mother handed her one of the ever-present tissues from her pocket and squeezed her. "Don't cry."

Rayne smiled at her mother, who'd apparently composed herself. This was the strong woman Rayne knew as her mother. *"A strong man is a man who gets back up after he falls."* Her father's words comforted her. Maybe her mother had recalled something that brought her strength as well.

While looking at her mother, understanding washed over Rayne: Despite her mother's plain appearance, through the years it had been her mother's inner strength that had supported them all.

She was the glue that held them together.

"It's going to be all right," her mother said.

"That's just what Jack told me." At the thought, Rayne looked around. "Say, where'd he go?"

Jack wasn't anywhere to be seen. Rayne began to worry. "Jack!"

Though Paul was doing everything humanly possible, the water coming from the hose wasn't nearly enough to dampen the flames. "Paul, have you seen Jack?"

He shook his head, concentrating on focusing the water on the fire. "No! I could use his help, too. We need to spray water over the house, keep it wet in case some embers hit the roof."

"I'll help you with that." Rayne looked at her mother. "Where are the fire trucks?"

Rayne's mother pulled her red-eyed gaze from her husband, her expression somber. Rayne's father looked pale and stricken. "You take care of Daddy. I'll see to everything else."

Her mother nodded her agreement and walked over to Rayne's father. She ushered him toward the house. He looked crushed. How could he give up so easily? Rayne knew that her mother was far more concerned about her father's health than she was about the farm.

Her mother escorted her father through the front door. The fact that he would go so willingly surprised Rayne and could only mean that he wasn't feeling well. *Lord, please let the emergency crews get here quickly.* She didn't even hear any sirens.

Then, to her horror. . .

The wind kicked up, and she watched as an ember from the barn floated across the distance and landed on the roof of the house.

"No! Paul, the house!" Rayne yelled. "Focus on the house."

Where did her father keep another water hose?

Suddenly, it was as if the heavens opened up and dumped rain on all of them. Only it wasn't coming from the sky. Water soared to an incredible height then came tumbling down onto the house, effectively stamping out the ember that had landed on the roof. As the water continued, Rayne felt confident the house would be too wet to catch fire. As the sirens finally sounded in the distance, she wasn't sure the firefighters could top what she was seeing.

But where was the water coming from? She dashed around to the back of the house and found Jack standing next to a pump. He'd apparently tapped into the well pump, going directly to the source for the water, and plugged his pump into the house. Scattered around him were the junk parts from an old wheel line irrigation system her father had attempted to fix.

He grinned at her. "Well, what do you think?"

Relief washed over her. Love for this man flooded her heart. "I think you just saved the day in more ways than one."

$\mathcal{L}_\blacktriangledown$

That evening, after all the fire crews had left the Flemming home, the scent of smoke and wet ashes lingered in the air.

Crickets chirped, and stars shone brightly in the night sky as though nothing out of the ordinary had happened. As though the barn hadn't burned, or Rayne hadn't lost her job, or Jack hadn't fired her. None of those things seemed to matter now.

Jack smiled at the peace that flooded his thoughts, and continued to rock the swing where he and Rayne nestled on the Flemming porch. He knew she remained overwhelmed with the events of the day, but all he cared about was that she was in his arms.

At last.

They were together. Jack vowed to allow nothing to keep them apart again. Not FountainTech or any other company for that matter, not a farm or parents who wanted her to marry a farmer. Nor would Jack allow his career plans to stand in the way of their happiness.

He chuckled to himself, remembering Paul's lecture as the guy drove him to Rayne's secret place. She'd only imagined it was secret.

"What's so funny?" Rayne asked, her head against his shoulder.

"Would you believe Paul?"

Rayne pulled away from Jack and sat forward, twisting to stare back at him. "How is Paul funny?"

Her hair was crumpled against the side of her head. Jack reached out to run his fingers through it. He could tell she was beyond tired and probably needed rest. But he couldn't bear to let her out of his sight. At least not yet.

"When Paul drove me to find you at your secret place, he gave me a lecture on treating you right, what sort of woman you are, your likes and dislikes. Rayne, the guy loves you."

Rayne sighed, clearly not pleased. "I talked to Paul already about how I feel."

"I know, Rayne. Don't get upset. Paul loves you enough to give you up and even make sure that the man who won your heart won't hurt you. I don't think I could have done the same."

Rayne smiled softly. "You're saying Paul knew that he was bringing you to see me because you love me?"

"Yep."

Rayne frowned. "He'll make some woman a wonderful husband some day."

"Well, since you brought it up. . ." Jack's heart drummed like he was in a rock band. He cleared his throat.

She looked at him, studying his gaze, a question in her eyes. Did she realize he had a question for her? "With everything that's happened today, I haven't found the right time to talk to you."

*Come on, man, do this right.* Jack feared the timing was all wrong, but he wouldn't leave anything else to chance. Wouldn't let her slip away again. He pushed himself out of the swing then bent down on one knee.

Rayne leaned forward, her hair hanging over her face, but he could see the shy smile on her lips and the reflection of moisture in her eyes. It was all the fuel he needed to proceed.

He placed a hand over his heart. "Rayne Flemming, my soul was dry and cracked until you came into my life and gently watered it, nurturing me back to life. Will you marry me?"

She threw her head back and laughed then gave him a teasing punch. "Some people might think that was corny, but"—she drew near and pressed her forehead to his—"not me. I loved it." Emotion was thick in her throat as she continued. "You know, my family didn't want me to take the job, to pursue my dreams, believing it would tear our family apart. My parents and their parents before them were all farmers. This farm belonged to them. If I left, who would continue on in the same house that has been in the family for generations? Who would farm the land? But in following my dreams, I found you, and you filled a need they could never have anticipated. You saved their home. You saved the farmhouse, Jack."

His knee aching now, he climbed up to sit next to Rayne on the bench, keeping his face near hers. "So, is that a yes?"

Rayne smiled softly and wrapped her arms around his neck, just the way he'd grown to love, tugged him forward and kissed him, long and thoroughly.

He had his answer.

Rayne pressed her head against Jack's chest, cherishing the warmth and love she felt there, floating on the dreamy high produced by his proposal as he brushed his fingers through her hair.

The screen door creaked. "Oh Rayne. I'm sorry to interrupt," her mother said.

Pulled from the moment, Rayne disentangled herself from Jack. "Is everything all right?"

"Yes, it's just that. . .your dad wanted a few words with you."

Rayne stood and looked down at Jack. "You coming?"

He smiled up at her. "I'll wait. You probably need some time alone with you family to deal with the loss of the barn."

"I'll just be a minute." Rayne followed her mother into the den. Surprisingly, her mother had a peaceful expression on her face.

Her father sat forward, his hands clasped between his knees as though he was preparing words for Rayne. She swallowed. She had some news for her parents, too.

How would they take it?

Rayne dropped into the chair next to the sofa where her father waited.

Though circles rimmed his eyes, his face was a mixture of pain and joy.

"What's wrong, Dad?"

"Nothing and everything." He slid over to the corner of the sofa and took Rayne's hands in his. "There's something I need to tell you."

"What's wrong?"

He stuck his hand up. "Don't imagine the worst now; just let me say what I have to say."

"Okay." Rayne couldn't remember her father ever speaking to her in this manner. It scared her.

"When I had the heart attack, my mind filled with all manner of thoughts. What would your mother do without me? How would she work the farm? Who would look after you since you're not married?"

Rayne opened her mouth to object, but her father thrust his hand up again. She kept her words to herself.

He seemed to relax a bit, having eased into his spiel, and slid to sit against the sofa back. "When a man has a close call, when he almost dies, he thinks crazy thoughts. I even thought that maybe God would use my heart attack to bring you home to us."

His audacious words astounded Rayne, but she held her tongue, knowing he had more to say.

A moist sheen filled his eyes, and he pursed his lips, waiting until he could speak. Rayne's eyes watered as well, unable to watch her father so near tears.

"Oh Rayne. I've been so arrogant."

Her mother stepped into the room at that moment with a carafe Rayne assumed was coffee. She'd apparently already set a tray of cups and condiments on the coffee table. Rayne hadn't even noticed until that moment. Her mother gave her a soft smile, and Rayne once again focused on her father.

"When the barn caught on fire and I feared we'd lose the house, too, I realized that as important as these things are—they've been in our family for generations—they mean nothing to me compared to you."

"Oh Daddy," Rayne said, her voice trembling through the rush of tears.

"Baby, I've been selfish, refusing to see that God had other plans for you. He gave you this incredible artistic gift, and now I realize He wants you to use it for something special. You've been doing the right thing all along." Her father looked down at his hands as though he feared her reaction.

"What your father is trying to say"—her mother, who'd been leaning against the doorway, now dropped onto the sofa next to Rayne's father and took his hand—"is that with all that's happened, God opened our eyes."

Her father smiled. "And when I saw that water spraying from your boss's pump, saving the house from the embers that traveled from the barn, I saw how special your work is. And it takes strength and character to follow your dreams. You've done that. I couldn't be more proud of you, Rayne."

He stood and tugged Rayne to her feet and into a hug. Unable to help herself, she sobbed, releasing all the pent-up anguish she'd held inside because she wanted—no, needed—her parents' approval.

When her father let her go, he gripped her shoulders and looked gently into her eyes. In his, she saw the approving look she'd been missing for several years now. It felt good and nurtured her thirsty soul.

She swiped at her cheeks. "You have no idea how much it means to me to hear you say this. No idea how important this was to me." And Rayne had no idea until that moment how crushed she'd been, living without their approval.

Her mother hugged her as well.

Rayne stood back and eyed them both. "I've got some news for you, too."

"This wouldn't have anything to do with Jack, would it?" Her father grinned.

# *Chapter 22*

The corn stood tall in the fields of the Flemming farm by the time Rayne waited in the foyer of the small church where she would marry Jack.

Only a few minutes and a short bridal march down the aisle separated Rayne from her future husband—a man with a good heart. The sort of heart she'd been waiting for. So what if it happened to be packaged inside an incredibly handsome man? She hadn't been looking for him, but then, she'd heard that was sometimes how a person found his or her spouse.

Heidi had agreed to be Rayne's matron of honor and stepped out of the little room where she'd dressed, revealing her beautiful mauve silk and taffeta dress. When she saw Rayne, she gasped. "You look gorgeous. As in every man's dream gorgeous. Jack is a lucky guy."

Rayne's father lifted her hand to his lips and kissed it. "My little girl getting married. Never thought I'd see the day."

"Oh, of course you did, Daddy." Smiling, she stifled any words regarding her father's previous expectations that she'd marry Paul.

Fortunately, Paul had already found a lovely young woman from a neighboring farm to lavish his attentions on. Rayne had never doubted he would make a wonderful husband but just not for her.

She was more than grateful she hadn't succumbed to the pressure to stay at the farm and marry Paul.

*Thank You, Lord.*

Moisture brimmed in her father's eyes, surprising Rayne. He squeezed her hand. "I know I've already told you this, Rayne, but I love you, and I've always prayed for you. For God to give you direction. You looked so lost to me, not seeing where you needed to go. Now I realize it was me all along. I didn't see where you needed to go. Praying for *you* changed *my* heart."

"Oh Daddy." Rayne dabbed at the corner of her wet eyes. "You're going to mess up my makeup."

He grinned. "I want you to know that I couldn't be more proud of you."

Rayne thought she would lose it right there and then as her father pulled her into a gentle hug.

God was so good. Though she'd thought He wasn't answering her prayers for direction, He knew exactly what He was doing—everything worked out in His timing the way that it should.

In a way, Rayne would be returning to the farm. She and Jack had started their own company called Dream Fountains. Though they planned to focus on creating water feature designs, they also agreed to develop water sprinkling systems for farmers that would deliver water more efficiently and be more cost-effective.

Rayne struggled to believe how everything had worked out—for her good and for Jack's. The scripture in Romans gently floated into her heart. *"We know that God causes all things to work together for good to those who love God, to those who are called according to His purpose."*

Suddenly, with the scripture spoken to her heart, Rayne recognized the Holy Spirit's gentle voice—all this time she'd wanted to hear something from the Lord, to know if she was going in the right direction. Now finally she saw that God had been directing her all along. He'd never left her side. Each step she'd taken had been part of the process, and Rayne was called according to His purpose.

Eyes tearing up again, Rayne looked anywhere but at her father. Out the window, autumn leaves had already begun to fall. As the seconds ticked by, Rayne skimmed the small foyer, taking in the plush carpet and the gorgeous flowers in mauve and off-white—her wedding colors—sitting on ornate pedestals. Fargo Community Church had been the place where Jack had found the Truth. God had been ready to listen, and Jack had given Him his pain. Then Jack had believed in Rayne. Rayne had since agreed to join Jack at the small church, attending weekly. She quickly wondered what had taken her so long to join. In addition to enjoying time seeing Heidi and the others, she'd made new friends. They'd all been such a blessing to her. Made her feel welcome and at home at her new church.

Suddenly the sound of the "Wedding March" began, and the double doors gently opened. Rayne stood in the center of the doorway, her heart in her throat as the small gathering stood and turned to face her. Gripping her father's arm, she took the measured steps forward, feeling self-conscious that all eyes were on her.

But when she drew close enough to see into Jack's eyes, the world around her faded. All her thoughts, hopes, and dreams stood before her, wrapped inside a gorgeous, honorable man with a good heart. He was deep-thinking and understood her thoughts before she even spoke.

Together they were like the magic in the water features they created. Before she knew it, she stood across from him, only the splash of wedding colors in her bouquet between them. Looking into Jack's eyes, she repeated the vows, as did he, but she was too nervous to comprehend it all.

Then he was slipping the wedding band onto her finger where it fit snugly in place next to her solitaire diamond engagement ring. Heidi held the bouquet for her.

"I now pronounce you husband and wife. You may kiss the bride," Pastor Luke said, joy in his voice.

Jack took her hands in his and bent, pressing his lips against hers. His kiss was soft and gentle yet held all the power and promise of a glorious future together. Still holding hands, they turned to face the crowd as they were instructed during the rehearsal.

"I'm pleased to present to you, Mr. and Mrs. Jack Kostner."

Jack and Rayne hurried down the steps and across the aisle between the pews to the doorway. Before they could leave for their honeymoon, they planned to remain in the church fellowship hall for a short reception.

Rayne could hardly believe it—she was a married woman. Her father was right when he said, "The higher your aim, the harder your fall."

She'd aimed awfully high when she set her hopes on Jack, deciding that she loved him. In that moment, Jack glanced over at her, his unspoken love apparent in his eyes.

Rayne had fallen very hard, indeed.

✍

Rayne squinted in the sunshine as she and Jack emerged from a side exit of their elegant hotel in Maui—the perfect place to honeymoon.

Palm trees waved in the salty ocean breeze, and the scent of exotic flowers enveloped Rayne, intoxicating her. The long flight over the Pacific Ocean to Hawaii had left her with jet lag the first couple of days. But now on her third day here, she was feeling like herself again—although newly married, she might never feel like the old Rayne again. But why would she want to?

Jack's love was taking her to places she'd never been before, and she never wanted the adventure to end. He angled his head toward the sun. The sunglasses he wore seemed to enhance his handsome appearance. How she'd ever ended up with such a gorgeous man, Rayne would never know. Still, all good gifts came from the Father above. She grinned.

Her new husband flashed a brilliant smile then bent down, fitting his mouth against hers. She succumbed to a rush of emotions then fought them. "No, no. I want to see Hawaii before we leave. Is that all right with you?"

Jack laughed. She'd never grow tired of hearing that sound.

"There's something else I want you to see," he said. Walking arm in arm, they meandered along the sidewalk, passing families and other couples who looked like they were also in love, until they came to the front of the luxurious hotel and stopped.

She gasped and watched as a choreographed fountain danced to theme of the movie *Australia*. Powerful emotions kept her riveted, for how long, she wasn't sure. It was all she could do to finally speak.

"Oh Jack. It's beautiful." Tears of joy slid down her sun-warmed cheeks.

Seeing a fountain like this, performing full-featured and live, rather than on her laptop or in the mini-lab, stole her breath. She pressed her hand against her heart. While she'd worried over the details of their wedding, Jack had planned their honeymoon, and now she understood why he'd wanted to.

Though difficult, she tugged her gaze from the fluid motion of the water and studied her handsome new husband. In response, he turned his head to her and smiled. He looked like a man without a care in the world. Like a man in love.

Rayne's head swam with the dizzy thoughts of his love.

"Is it your design?" she asked.

"Yes, I created it while at EI."

"Seeing the actual fountain like this, the real thing, I can't find the words."

Jack watched the fountain in silence then faced her again. "Nothing I've ever done can compare with your talent." Jack drew near and whispered against her lips, "Or with you. Rayne, *you* are the real thing for me."

# ABOUT THE AUTHOR

ELIZABETH GODDARD is the award-winning author of over a dozen romance novels, including a romantic mystery, *The Camera Never Lies*—a 2011 Carol Award winner. Elizabeth graduated with a B.S. degree in computer science and worked in high-level software sales for several years before retiring to home-school her children and fulfill her dream of becoming an author. Though she has deep roots in Texas, she makes her home in central Louisiana with her husband and four children.